THE
DOLL
BROKERS

THE DOLL BROKERS

A NOVEL

HAL ROSS

Any permissions if necessary.
Library of Congress Cataloging-in-Publication Data

Ross, Hal, 1941-
    The doll brokers : a novel / by Hal Ross. -- First edition.
      pages ; cm
    ISBN 978-0-9911938-4-4 (pbk. : alk. paper)
1. Toy industry--Fiction. 2. Women executives--Fiction. I. Title.
    PR9199.3.R598D65 2014
    813'.54--dc23

                              2014009557

For information, or to order additional copies, please contact:
TitleTown Publishing, LLC
P.O. Box 12093, Green Bay, WI 54307-12093
920.737.8051 | titletownpublishing.com

Distributed by Midpoint Trade Books
www.midpointtrade.com

Printed in the United States of America
Cover by Michael Short
Interior Design by Pre-Press Solutions

FOR

FRANCINE

ACKNOWLEDGEMENTS

Special thanks to Beverly Bird, May Wuthrich and Liz Trupin-Pulli, without whom this book would not have been possible.

First readers Carol Diggs, Linda Fox and Kathy Lyons.

In memory of Mac Irwin.

And praise for those few men and women who—despite all odds—help make the toy industry a unique environment in which to work.

PROLOGUE

When the diagnosis was first pronounced, she'd taken the news stoically, with a sense of déjà vu. However, battling breast cancer for the third time was not the way she had envisioned spending her declining years. Wasn't seventy supposed to be the new sixty?

Just home from the hospital after yet another round of chemotherapy, she rested quietly on the deep velvet chaise in her luxurious living room. Seeking diversion from the nausea that washed over her, she forced her mind to focus. Here, in the beautiful Central Park West apartment she had proudly acquired through perseverance and hard work, she contemplated the successful business she had created in one of the fiercest competitive arenas—the toy industry.

When her husband died of heart disease, she had become a widow at the age of fifty. As a woman alone, the odds were stacked against her. But in a business where trends changed with the wind, and risk often overshadowed reward, she had allowed her good instincts to guide her. Valuable alliances were formed by knowing whom to trust. Her company's volume grew, as did its profit.

Until the accident she was riding a high that she didn't think would end. So the news almost derailed her. Having a son killed in such a tragic fashion would most likely have brought anyone of lesser will to her knees. If the truth were known, it very nearly did her in.

Her poor, sweet boy. Gone now for almost fifteen years.

She was still haunted by questions about the accident, questions she was determined to have answered before she went to her grave. It would require some cunning but she would get to the truth, no matter how painful it might prove to be.

The woman's eyes had been closed; she opened them now.

Today, this very afternoon, her company was embarking on something new. God willing, the deal would be signed before she went to bed.

And what a deal it was.

The highest risk of her long career. An investment of millions. All for the sake of one particular product.

She knew that much of her success was a result of her ability to discern between the winners and the losers, and her willingness to gamble. Here was a product that would either secure the company's future or bring it down.

Shivering a little, the woman shut her eyes again.

Her thoughts turned to her remaining sons. She was unashamed to admit that the youngest was her favorite, and that she had always hoped he would succeed her in the business. But he had been insistent on pursuing the life of an artist. And she had encouraged him, not once anticipating that she would later come to regret it.

Her attempts to mentor his older brother had been a mistake from the beginning. The man's talent—if he possessed any—lay elsewhere. He wasn't incompetent as much as lazy. His drinking and philandering had become much more than an embarrassment; they'd become liabilities.

Luckily, she had found a protégé. A stroke of fate had brought her and the girl together. She had taken her under her wing when she was still in her mid-teens. A temporary living arrangement became a permanent one, and she soon became a member of the family. It had paid off—through nurturing and formal schooling, the girl had blossomed. But her eldest son's petty jealousy had become another terrible hindrance. She could not allow it to continue. One way or another, their differences would have to be resolved.

Obviously, she had much to do in the weeks and months ahead. Her strength would be put to the test like never before. Only time would reveal the outcome of her efforts … although this was a commodity that was clearly running out.

CHAPTER 1

I t was a sweltering August day in New York City, the kind of day where you could see the heat shimmering off the sidewalk. At the corner of 45th and Broadway, Ann Lesage crossed the street with the light, then glanced quickly over her shoulder and scanned the crowd.

Nothing untoward caught her eye. Unable to shake the unsettling feeling that she was being followed, she deliberately turned her thoughts to the Marriott Marquis Hotel, imagining herself walking through its doors and feeling the cool air on her skin.

Arriving at the hotel, she took the elevator to the eighth floor and strode through the open-ended bar of the lobby. This was Ann's bar of choice, where numerous business deals had been consummated. Chosen not for comfort but its layout and bright lights, it was the kind of place that helped keep everyone on point, which was exactly how she liked it.

Making her way through the room, past tables filled predominately with men, Ann felt hungry eyes follow her. It was her all-American looks that attracted attention. The blonde hair, the long legs, and of course the breasts—nothing about her was particularly petite. But even after so many years, this awareness of the stir she created bothered her. To compensate, she made a habit of keeping herself as hidden as possible. The sleek off-white Ann Klein pants-suit she wore, with its tailored jacket that zipped to the neck, did the trick nicely.

The men who awaited her couldn't entirely disguise their anxiety. The moment they caught sight of her, something small and electric seemed to prod their spines. They snapped to attention and sprang to their feet.

They had secured a corner table, one far enough away to give them some semblance of privacy. Each was nursing a glass of water. They had probably been there since before five o'clock, Ann thought, going over final calculations, solidifying their strategy to get her signature on the dotted line. She took a deep breath and paused.

Her nerves were raw but she wouldn't let it show. Much was riding on this meeting. She needed no reminder of the huge risk her company, Hart Toy, was undertaking.

"Gentlemen," she said more easily than she felt.

The shorter man—Japanese and diminutive, well into his sixties by now—clasped her outstretched hand. Koji Sashika, the man who had been their business partner in Eastern Asia for twenty-some-odd years, had eyes that Ann had always liked. "Ann. Good to see you," he said.

"You, too." She extricated her hand gently when he seemed disinclined to release it. She turned to the other man. "And Edmund. It's been a while."

"Too long," Edmund Chow agreed. "And you grow more beautiful with every moment I stay away."

"You flatter me, or perhaps it's just your eyesight," she said, with a twinkle. He laughed—a startled squawk—and frowned. He had never known quite how to read her, Ann thought.

Chow was an independent contractor based in Hong Kong who, among other things, had spent the past ten years managing Hart Toy's manufacturing and product development.

There was no time left for pleasantries. Ann knew exactly how she wanted this meeting to proceed. She either accomplished what she had come here to do, or Edmund Chow would go elsewhere. And neither she nor Koji Sashika would be able to stop him.

Before taking her seat, she once again felt eyes boring into the small of her back. The last thing she needed was to appear paranoid, but she took a quick look around anyway, then sat, crossing her legs neatly and placed her laptop on the table in front of her. Koji and Chow followed her cue and took back their seats.

"You saw her?" Chow asked. "The doll?"

"Last week, as a matter of fact. Felicia showed me the sample you sent."

"And?"

It was one of the most extraordinary new inventions Ann had seen, but she wasn't about to admit it. "Felicia likes her," she said casually.

Koji threw back his head and laughed. His gaze went in Chow's direction. "You'll get no more from her, my friend. Not until this deal is nailed down."

Ann patted Chow's hand. "Don't worry. I'm just a tough sell."

She reached to the floor for the briefcase she had placed beside her chair. When a waitress appeared, she ordered a Perrier without glancing up. She smoothed the contract Edmund had sent her on the table beside her laptop, then regarded both men.

"You know, Felicia thinks this doll has some potential but, personally, I think she could bankrupt us." Ann paused and looked at them. "Since the buck stops with me, I need to be convinced."

Edmund cleared his throat. "These terms are absolutely in line with what is common in the industry. How would it bankrupt you?"

The waitress brought her drink. Ann squeezed the lemon into it. "I've got concerns. You're acting on our behalf as well as the other party's, this … this … what's his name?" She broke off and flipped through pages, looking for the designer's name. She already knew he was couched as an entity, a limited partnership.

"He's a friend of mine," Chow said. "A local Chinese designer. He was gong to go to Mattel but I stepped in."

"Why?"

"*Why?*" Chow looked stymied.

"If you're his friend, why would you do that?" Ann knew of the convoluted approach to business in China, how honor was often confused with dollars and cents, causing it to be interpreted in many different ways. "Mattel would be a sure, solid bet. They might even pay these extravagant terms you're asking me for."

"But my loyalty is obviously with you."

She still didn't quite trust what he was saying, but she went past it. Ann began scrolling through screens on her laptop. Her raw cost to manufacture the doll was eight dollars and fifty cents. Once she factored in freight, overhead, royalty and advertising, she was left with a total price of over twenty dollars.

Ann turned her computer screen to show Edmund. "See what this amount says?" she asked.

He shrugged. "This doll can handle it. She converses. Her heart beats. She reacts to stimuli."

"She does all that," Ann agreed. "But what happens if we only sell half a million dolls instead of a million—which would, in effect, double our advertising costs?"

"Then you would cut back on the advertising," Edmund suggested.

Ann drank her Perrier, met his eyes. "We're being asked to commit earlier and earlier every year. Come January, our plans must be in place for Christmas. Otherwise, the big boys will grab the best TV times and we'll be shut out." She paused, then turned her attention to the other man, as if seeking him out as an ally. "Koji, you know this. We're David. They're Goliath." Ann turned back to Edmund. "I won't let Felicia become the stone in the slingshot."

Chow looked boggled. "You want me to go to Mattel?"

God save me, Ann thought. "No. I want you to work with me here. Felicia wants this doll. But we're small. I want you to remember that." Ann knew where she stood. She was protecting a legacy.

Felicia had been dirt poor in the Canadian province of Ontario when she'd started her small toy business. Her own rags-to-riches story was part of the reason she had extended a hand to Ann, had given a hungry, runaway teenager a chance she could have never dreamed of. Ann would not let the woman's trust be misplaced.

"It all boils down to this," she said. And she explained how her published selling price of twenty-six seventy-five would be reduced to twenty-four dollars and eight cents, once the discounts that the major retailers expected for advertising, freight and warehouse allowances were deducted. "Do you see my problem here?" she asked.

"Problem?" Edmund choked on his water. "You'll still end up with over three and a half million dollars in profit."

"Are *you* willing to guarantee it?" she shot back.

"*She* will." Chow was equally as vehement. "The baby doll."

Ann didn't roll her eyes, but she came close. "And I am the Virgin Mary."

Edmund reached for his glass again.

Ann steeled herself for what was to come. Both humbled and emboldened by the negotiating process, she hoped she wasn't overplaying her strategy. She leaned back in her chair and closed her laptop. "I'm sorry, times have changed. These days, we're at the mercy of most buyers. It's their way or the proverbial highway. I don't relish being in this position but we have to face reality. Now, when we sit with a major retailer and get a number for a TV-advertised product, it's only a number, not an order. Then we wait. October Toy Fair followed by the fair in February, where the number gets adjusted—up or down. By March or April, we might get official confirmation for ten percent of the original quantity we were promised. The balance goes into limbo until they see if the doll starts to sell."

"It will," Edmund said earnestly.

"Unless someone comes up with something better," she pointed out.

"There's no better doll—"

"Maybe not, but there are always new innovations, some new toy that could come along. It only takes one to cause a craze, and then this little doll would get bypassed and pressed into cold storage. At your terms, Hart Toy would go broke."

Edmund reached for his napkin and dabbed at his mouth. "We might be able to compromise," he said. "As I mentioned, the designer is my friend."

"Friend-*schmend*." Ann drank from her glass and wished fervently for a Scotch. Later, she thought. It would be her reward once the deal had closed.

She sat up straighter and forced herself to focus. She could not allow that unsophisticated Newark girl to show herself. She re-crossed her legs and sat back. Chow took a pen and pad from the inside pocket of his suit jacket and turned Ann's laptop toward him to use the calculator. "We can reduce the royalty to twelve percent."

"No dice."

"What do you want then?" he asked, exasperated.

"Seven percent. Two-year contract. Advance against royalties of one million the first year, half a million for the second. I also want the rights to the rest of the world at one-third of the U.S. advance."

Chow and Koji stared at each other

"I can go for ten percent on the royalty," Chow said. "Not a penny lower."

"Nine," Ann said automatically.

He shook his head.

It was like pulling teeth without an anesthetic. As each part of the agreement was resolved, Ann felt her nerve slipping. The risk was explicit. Felicia may have wanted this doll, but Ann was the newly appointed president of Hart Toy, and the doll's success would ultimately be her responsibility.

Percentages washed through her head as the haggling continued. They were too far along in the process to call a timeout. Within a half-hour, they had reached an agreement. Her palms had become damp, she could sense the slight sheen on her forehead, but it was done.

Less than ten minutes later, Ann watched Koji and Chow exit the lobby bar. She collected her laptop and briefcase, then stood, her legs not quite as steady as she would have liked. She headed towards the part of the bar she preferred—the one with the windows facing Broadway, and a panoramic view of neon. The atmosphere was more congenial here, a place to socialize rather than conduct business. The men no longer outnumbered the women, and some of the women were dressed for a night on the town, formal dresses and the odd gown, costume jewelry and just as many diamonds.

She eased up to the bar and let her business paraphernalia take her place on the stool. She stood there for a moment, then reached into her hair and pulled out the clip that held it in a respectable twist. It fell to her shoulders, sleek and straight and yellow-blond. Pulling at it slightly, she felt a release of tension in her scalp. She flashed a smile at the bartender. "Glenlivet. Two fingers. Rocks on the side," she said.

She turned again, digging into her briefcase for her cell phone, and tapped in Felicia's number. When the woman answered, she let out a short laugh. "Damn, I'm good."

"I know that, dear." There was a pause. "So tell me your news. Did you get me that beautiful doll?"

"I did. And with any luck, she won't send us to the poor house."

"Thank you."

The simple words made Ann's stomach lurch. "Felicia, please, you know I hate it when you say that. You never, *ever* have to thank me. For anything."

Felicia didn't rise to the argument. It was an old one. "Bring me the contract in the morning."

"I plan to do just that."

"And enjoy your Scotch."

Felicia knew her so well. Ann brought the glass to her lips and sipped. "I will." She paused. "I love you."

"I know that, too. Good night."

The line disconnected. Ann dropped the cell back into her briefcase. *Please, God, please, let this deal work.* She took another swallow of Glenlivet. She closed her eyes briefly and repeated her silent prayer. When she opened them, the Scotch almost came back up her throat.

She had been right, after all, she thought. Someone *had* been following her. Standing behind her, watching her in the mirror, dark eyes smoldering, was the one man she knew would never share Felicia's opinion of her, the one person who didn't think she was good at all.

CHAPTER 2

Jonathan Morhardt dropped a hip onto the stool beside her. "I'll have a Sierra Nevada," he said to the bartender. "The Pale. And refresh whatever the lady is having. It's on my tab."

"Thanks for the offer, but this lady is leaving." Ann took her credit card from her wallet and snapped it against the bar.

"Don't let me run you off." His brows climbed in a challenge, dark brown hair topping a face that was a little too chiseled to be called handsome. But at thirty-five he had hazel poet's eyes that were mesmerizing, and the hint of a smile that was both mischievous and intriguing.

Ann hated surprises. Seeing him here unexpectedly took the wind out of her. She looked sideways at him, trying to assess the situation, and felt for an instant his hatred of her. Or was it merely hostile indifference? It had been seventeen years since she'd come to live with Jonathan and his family. A lost sixteen year-old. In all that time she had yet to get a handle on his true feelings towards her. The acrimony that had always seemed to exist between them was intensified by her own suppressed desire, the need to know him better that had always been denied.

She touched a manicured fingernail to the edge of her credit card and slid it back toward herself. "On second thought, I don't want to deny you the chance to spend money on me." She looked over her glass at him and took a sip of her drink. Their bickering was safe, secure, familiar ground. It was eminently more comfortable than negotiating the biggest deal of her career.

"Good," he replied.

"Aren't you out of your element?" she asked, knowing he gravitated towards darker, moodier places.

"A sacrifice worthy of the cause," he said. "I'm here to keep an eye on you."

Consternation turned her muscles to wood. She hadn't noticed him in the other room when she scanned the place. That in itself bothered her, but not half so much as his stated purpose and apparent lack of trust in her. Had he come here on his own volition, or had he been sent by Felicia or Patrick?

Ann had never hurt Jonathan, had never infringed on his territory. They were removed from each other because of his lack of interest in Hart Toy. Patrick, of course, was a different story. Of Felicia's two remaining sons, Patrick had reason to despise her. She'd stolen his thunder, but Patrick did not have the capability or talent to grow the company or even run it. She would not feel guilty over that. But Jonathan was quite a bit different. He had the smarts to run the family business but wanted no part of it.

Ann had always been aware that it would take her forever to convince Jonathan that she'd never asked for the things Felicia had given her. Years ago, she had relinquished that battle. He had always questioned her motives and no matter what she said it seemed he couldn't, or wouldn't, believe her.

Jonathan Morhardt was his father's son. Frederick had kept a step clear of Hart Toy, too, at least as much of it as he had lived to witness. He was a dreamer, and profit margins were alien to them both.

"Your brother sent you," Ann said now, forcing a tone of bored acceptance.

"I haven't spoken to him in weeks," Jonathan offered.

"Then what interest could *you* possibly have in my meeting?"

"As I said, I'm keeping an eye on things. I refuse to let you destroy everything my mother has built."

"Oh? You think I'd act on my own?"

"I don't know what to think. And that's the problem. So, tell me—how much of Felicia's money *did* you spend?"

"Seventy-five percent of what she authorized. Your inheritance is safe."

"I don't care about the money; Felicia is my concern."

Ann reached for her drink, just to prove to herself, to him, that her stomach was fine. She had been living with the Morhardts—with Felicia and Patrick, Jonathan and Matthew—for all of four months when Jonathan first discovered her weakness. She wasn't comfortable in their well-to-do home with its lush carpets and big rooms filled with beautiful things. She knew who she was—the abandoned daughter of a drug addict. Homeless with nowhere to turn, she'd spent those first four months in a type of dreamlike limbo, waiting for Felicia to turn on her, kick her out, become a person who would break her.

Instead, Felicia had showed her nothing but gentle kindness. And in their home, on the eve of a party celebrating Felicia's fifty-fifth birthday, she'd brought Ann a dress, a sleek, shimmering azure sheath that still hung in her closet. It had caught the blue of her eyes, had sculpted her skinny frame into something that was somehow voluptuous and provocative. Ann allowed herself to fall in love with Felicia the moment she slipped that dress over her head and gazed into the mirror. It was as if the actress had found the perfect costume. The dress transformed her instantly. And suddenly she saw herself as the person she could be. From that moment on she had strained and strived, and applied herself in every way to become a woman worthy of wearing that dress and to earn Felicia's respect. It had been grueling work, and to all outside appearances it had paid off. Yet, too often, Ann would awaken in the middle of the night with a question rolling around in her mind—was she merely an actress performing a role or had all that effort and Felicia's steady hand actually resulted in a true transformation?

How had Felicia understood that Ann was no longer a child, that she had ceased being a child when the unimaginable had happened, forcing her to flee Newark? Instead of dressing her in flounces and pink, Felicia had nudged her into becoming a woman to be reckoned with. But that night, the night of the party, even Felicia had been powerless to curb Patrick's jealous tongue.

"Look, it's Lady Ann," he'd hissed in her ear when she'd arrived at the bottom of the stairs. "Come to steal the silver."

The look on Patrick's face, the smell of his sour breath, had been so ugly, that after a few minutes of forced gaiety, with face flushed, stomach churning, she had literally run up the stairs to be sick. No one could have possibly suspected the reason behind her retreat. But just as she arrived at the bathroom door, Jonathan stepped out. Ann had practically crashed into him in her frenzied rush to get inside. He hadn't moved fast enough and, face to face, she had spewed all over him.

Ann jerked herself back to the present. She wasn't sixteen anymore. She was thirty-three.

"I don't like the name," she said flatly and suddenly. "Felicia wants to call her Baby Talk N Glow. It sounds seventies to me. Too pedestrian. But I guess we'll just have to hope that she's unique enough to overcome the shaky moniker."

Jonathan's eyes narrowed as he realized that she was talking about the doll. "Go on."

"I've run the numbers in every imaginable way, starting with sales of a million pieces and regressing down to five hundred thousand." Her breath felt short. She didn't want to believe it could come to that. "I think I've accounted for every possible contingency."

"To protect your own salary, I'm sure."

She felt it as a slap in the face but chose to ignore the comment.

Her stomach twisted and she raised the glass of Scotch to her lips, then continued. "On the one hand, dolls are comparatively safe. They account for volume of over two billion dollars in the United States alone. On the other hand, we could still end up in trouble because of the enormous risk. One glitch with this product, one misstep with the marketing plan…"

"Then take a pass."

His comment hardened her spine. "No. Felicia wants her. And there are eight or ten other companies who will snatch her up if we don't."

He leaned back on his stool. "What's in it for you?"

Ann fought to breathe. She reached for her briefcase. "Your time's up, Jonathan. I've got better things to do with mine."

"Just know, I'll be watching."

"Spare yourself the trouble," she said as she stepped down from the bar, lost her footing, and practically fell into his arms.

He went to steady her.

She pulled herself upright, turned abruptly and walked away. "Good night, Jonathan," she called over her shoulder.

He watched her leave, thinking that she didn't move so much as cleave through space.

She'd played her own part in his younger brother's death, Jonathan thought. He would not let Ann hurt Felicia again. He couldn't explain the bad feeling he had about this doll, but Ann's influence over his mother in her weakened state could not be overlooked. And neither could the possibility that the cancer had impaired Felicia's judgment. Jonathan had a fierce need to protect his mother. No matter what the personal cost, he would put his own life on hold and watch Ann like a hawk. He'd stick to her until he finally understood everything. And when he got to that place, perhaps then this absurd fascination with her that had plagued him for years, would finally disappear.

CHAPTER 3

Ann dropped the knocker against Felicia's apartment door and it swung inward, giving way to an imperial foyer lined with large oil paintings of country landscapes. Beyond was a spacious parlor, now bustling with visitors.

Patrick Morhardt greeted her. Once, long ago, he had been an attractive man. As blond as his brother was dark, as suave as Jonathan was brooding, over the years his physique hadn't so much softened as it had relaxed. Today, at thirty-nine, gravity tugged gently at his skin. Time—and probably more alcohol than Ann could even begin to imagine—had leeched much of the life from his brown eyes.

"Hail the conquering hero." He swept a hand out exaggeratedly and ushered her inside, where she joined a crowd of people summoned by Felicia to celebrate the acquisition of the doll.

She dipped one shoulder and let her cashmere shawl slide down her arm. She caught it on the tips of her fingers and offered it to Patrick, an obvious insult. Color crept slowly up his neck, but he took the wrap. Ann crossed to Felicia, seated in a chair in front of a window that afforded a spectacular view of Central Park from thirty-seven floors up.

"You're the real heroine here," Ann whispered as she leaned in to kiss her cheek.

Felicia smiled, and Ann thought she could hear her facial skin moving with the effort, almost like paper rustling. "I'll let you think so, dear."

"Where is she?" Ann said, straightening. "I know you. She must be on display around here somewhere."

"In the dining room."

Felicia's living room and dining room had once been housed in separate apartments, combined when the wall between them was removed. The décor had a distinctly Far Eastern flavor: proud marble figurines from China on multi-colored pedestals, a Japanese ceramic sculpture at least five feet tall, and a burnt almond cabinet that dated back a few centuries and appeared priceless. The doll stood on a black lacquer table beyond it.

Felicia's guests milled around her. Koji and Chow were still in the States and they had, of course, been invited. Koji demonstrated the doll's features, his small, smooth face alight with child-like pleasure. A few business acquaintances were present as well, some envious, most pretending not to be. It was a tradition of sorts, despite the fierce competition, to share good news with one's peers.

Irene, Patrick's wife, swatted her fourteen-year-old son's hand as he tried to poke the doll in a spot the average little girl would never contemplate.

"Are you more comfortable with the deal now?" Chow asked, easing up beside Ann as she approached.

"Very comfortable." Ann used the moment to look around for Patrick. And for Jonathan. She liked to pinpoint her vulnerable flanks.

Patrick was hunkered down in front of his mother's chair, his weight braced on his heels, his hands gripped together between his knees. He spoke urgently. Ann kept her gaze on him as she poured herself a Glenlivet at the sidebar in the dining room. Then she headed back in their direction.

A man caught her elbow as she reached the midway point of the large room. Ann flashed an automatic smile. Alvin Pelletier, of Single-Brite Inc. Alvin was a self-made man who had built his company from scratch. Single-Brite was heavily into toddler products, riding the wave of over-stressed moms bent on finding electronic babysitters for their children.

"That doll is beautiful, absolutely exceptional." Alvin let his hand slide down until his fingers linked with hers. His palm was damp.

"Yes. She is." Ann took a moment to consider that nearly everyone she talked to referred to the doll as though she were a living, breathing entity. A very good sign.

"How's business otherwise? Your inventory problem?"

"All tidied away." There are no secrets in this business, Ann thought. "Thanks for asking." She was impatient to get into the pow-wow between Patrick and Felicia.

"We're doing well," he confided as if she had asked. "We'd be looking at sixty million this year if not for that asshole at Swansons."

She knew who he was referring to but didn't want to get distracted by gossip. Patrick was standing now, ending the conversation. "I'd put my money on you any day," Ann said. Alvin may have looked insipid, but he was a vicious businessman. He had a reputation for never employing salespeople directly, thus avoiding the burden of medical insurance and pension plans. Instead, he used independent representatives who covered a specified territory on a commission basis, and she'd heard from more than one angry source that he habitually failed to pay them what was due.

Less than a month ago he'd been predicting sales of forty-eight million. No doubt some of the commissions he'd stolen back made up a part of the sudden difference.

"This guy—this Dean Carlson, the Division Merchandise Manager over there—he wants three thousand dollars for my short-shipping him a hundred pieces of an item," he went on.

"Bet you wish you hadn't done it." Ann tugged her hand free and fought the urge to dry her palm against her thigh.

"It was an oversight! Now it's a fucking nightmare. I've tried to reason with him, but the man won't bend. I might end up cutting him off. There goes five million in orders."

He wouldn't, Ann thought. Even Hasbro or Mattel wouldn't dare cut off Swansons. Ann took a sidestep, grimacing in feigned commiseration. "Excuse me, Al, I've got to—"

"I'd like to talk to you about this guy. How to handle him, get your take on him."

"Give my secretary a buzz in the morning. She'll set up lunch."

"Donna, right?"

"Her name is Dora." Ann left Pelletier and stepped quickly up to Patrick. "Talking about me?" she asked, blocking his way.

He jerked around. "Only in that you've bitten off more than even you can chew."

Ah, she thought. He was already anticipating her pratfall with Baby Talk N Glow. She sipped her drink. "Time will tell."

"I'm meeting with our bank tomorrow, but I'm hardly optimistic. They've been worried about our inventory."

"You well know that problem's been rectified," Felicia said, her voice reedy. It got that way when she was upset.

"So what's your contingency plan?" Ann asked Patrick.

"One step at a time." His brow lowered.

"Not with this doll. I want your back-up plan on my desk before our own bank declines. In fact, let's aim to meet at nine o'clock tomorrow morning."

"Who the hell do you think you're—"

"I'm the president of Hart Toy," Ann interrupted him. She hated to pull rank but had learned a while ago that this was the only way with Patrick. "And you're my vice president of finance. I believe I've just requested the pleasure of your company tomorrow morning?"

"This is the part where you salute, Pat." Jonathan's voice came from just behind her left shoulder.

"I've already signed the deal, Patrick," she said, trying to be more conciliate. "We're not going to go back on our word, not with the Chinese."

"Patrick, please line up interviews with other banks," said Felicia.

Both of them knew that it should have been done already, but Ann held her tongue.

She pivoted to look at Jonathan. "Well, well, the gang's all here. Still keeping an eye on things?"

"I wouldn't miss Francesca's cooking." He plucked a shrimp-and-crab ceviche from his cocktail plate and held it up as though to admire it.

He was keeping his concern over this project from his mother then, Ann thought as he dropped the ceviche onto his tongue.

She turned away. "Where were we?"

"Patrick was just telling me that our advertising director still has the flu," Felicia said.

As glitches went, it was minor. "Then we'll make arrangements to go ahead with the commercial shoot without him," Ann said. "I should be able to clear my schedule and get to Toronto by Wednesday."

"That sort of thing needs weeks of preparation," Patrick argued.

"In Los Angeles, sure. But I'm going with the Canadians on this one. I thought I mentioned that. Yes, I'm sure I did. In a memo. Do you read my memos, Pat? Canada is generally more flexible and I want to get this ball rolling as soon as possible."

"Full steam ahead," Jonathan said conversationally.

Ann fought the urge to look his way again. She still wasn't sure what he expected to accomplish with his agenda regarding the doll. As she turned away from the family enclave, she felt Jonathan's gaze on the back of her neck. She returned to the dining room and was plunking fresh ice cubes into her glass when a hand roughly the size and texture of a bear's paw closed over hers and took the tongs from her.

"Felicia ought to have a bartender here," Sidney Greenspan announced.

Ann felt the muscles in her lower back uncoil and relax. She and Sidney understood each other, despite the fact that they came from completely different backgrounds, his being one of wealth and privilege.

"For twenty guests?" she asked. "Would you waste your precious money?"

Greenspan laughed, a jolting, thunderclap baritone.

"How are you, by the way?"

"Feeling a little upstaged by Baby What's-Her-Name over there." He poured his own drink, ninety percent bourbon. Ann wondered if his ruddy complexion tonight was the result of the liquor or if his blood pressure was up again. Greenspan was a chunky Goliath in his early sixties whose ginger hair was still holding onto its color long after nature had intended. Much of what he had accomplished with his SG Dolls, Inc. had been due more to his inherited wealth than to any talent he might possess. At least, that was the word on the street, and Ann tended to believe it.

She turned her back to the sideboard now and leaned against it to gaze at the doll. "We're going to kick ass with her, Sidney."

"Oh, yeah? Those your knees I hear knocking?"

She sipped and shook her head. "Yours. You're quaking with fear that Hart Toy is going to upstage you."

Greenspan tossed back half his drink. "I'd have grabbed her if I'd had the chance."

"That's precisely why this was kept so quiet."

He glowered at her. "You're too young to be so cagey."

"I was born old." Ann pushed off the sideboard.

"Yeah, well, Baby Pees-Her-Pants is going to take another bite out of your life span."

"That's one talent she hasn't been endowed with."

"Biting or peeing?"

"Make that two."

She didn't get the laugh she anticipated. Greenspan stared at the doll as though she had come to life. "You're taking a big chance with this thing, Ann. You're gambling too much of your resources."

And then some, she thought. "I know."

"Then what the hell are you doing it for?"

"Because I can?"

Greenspan's expression cleared and he laughed.

"What's so funny?" His wife—a woman he privately referred to as Number Four—slid up to his side and tucked her hand in his arm.

His response was rough and abrupt, cutting off any further discussion. "Talking business."

Charlie Greenspan lifted one shoulder in a shrug. She was a magnificent redhead born and bred in the South, maybe thirty years Sidney's junior. She couldn't have cared less about her husband's brusque behavior. She wore a diamond on her left hand big enough to cant her weight slightly in that direction, and a navy Givenchy suit that showed off one of her best assets. Ann thought that Wife Number Four had done well enough for herself, and she knew it. Every woman had her priorities, after all.

Ann placed her empty glass back on the sideboard. "I'll leave you lovebirds to it."

Greenspan snorted, while Charlie gave a smoky giggle.

Ann decided she was tired of pretending she wasn't scared to death about Baby Talk N Glow. She was ready to head home.

CHAPTER 4

Irene Morhardt's priorities were simple. She lived in a decent house in Forest Hills, had a few close girlfriends and two teenage children. She intended to protect these priorities from the preening, self-entitled coward she had married.

"Shut up!" she shouted at Samantha and Timothy in the back seat as they crossed the bridge from the city, heading home after Felicia's party. Her shrill tone worked and it had an added benefit: Patrick winced as it cut through his skull.

"Is that necessary?" His knuckles went white where his hands gripped the steering wheel.

Irene ignored the question. "She's gong to bury you this time, you know."

Patrick released his death grip and slammed his palm against the dash. "What the hell would you have me do? Mom wants this doll. *She's* the driving force behind it."

"Oh, for Christ's sake, Patrick, give it up with a little dignity, would you? Ann's been playing your mother like a fiddle. Stop whining about it and *do* something! Because I'm here to tell you, if Ann does pull this off, you're done. You'll be just one more pencil-pushing rat in her maze."

"I can't take over the project," he said. "Ann's got it under lock-and-key."

"Then *stop* the project!"

Patrick pulled into his driveway with a sigh of relief that he had made it without being stopped. He should have eaten something at the party.

He turned the key in the car's ignition and sat as Irene and the kids poured out of the Volvo wagon. When the doors cracked shut, he winced. Then Irene was rapping her knuckles on his window. Patrick turned the key in the ignition again to lower it.

"What?"

She bent to look in at him, her long auburn hair tumbling forward. He'd loved her hair once.

"If you let Ann do this, Patrick, I swear I'll leave you without a dime to your name. I've had enough of watching you wag your tail every time your mother looks your way. The old bitch isn't going to *give* you anything, don't you get that yet? You don't have a birthright where she's concerned. She thinks you're a fuck-up." She straightened. "And she's right."

Irene stepped back from the window and stalked toward the house. She was a maestro with orders, he thought, laying them down with an aggrandized flick of her wrist, with no idea of the clever effort they required. She was relentless.

Stop the doll? Not likely.

But he had two very good reasons to do so, Patrick thought— although Irene had only mentioned one of them. His mother would rhapsodize the ground Ann walked on if she succeeded with this. And if Ann fell on her face, what good would Felicia's disapproval do him if the company came down in the process?

He felt trapped, caught between a rock and a hard place. The old him would have known what to do. Too many competitors crashed and burned over one promotional item. Thoughts of Hart Toy doing the same crowded his brain, now swelling painfully into a throbbing headache. He wished he had the ability to stay off the booze. He didn't graduate magna cum laude from McGill

University because of his good looks. Sobering up would give him the opportunity to prove his true value to the company.

He could make president if Ann failed with this. But he would be president of … nothing. Hart Toy would be borrowing heavily just to lift the damned doll off the ground. And then, with the vagaries of the industry, of the buyers and the merchandise managers and—God forbid—the whims of the purchasing public, anything could happen. They could be washed up in the space of a year.

Patrick watched the lights in the lower level of his home flick off. A moment later, a golden glow appeared in his own bedroom window. Irene was finally upstairs. He turned the car off for a second time and went inside.

In the den, he poured himself a well-deserved nightcap. Sobering up was easier said than done, he realized. Fucking Ann, he thought as the cognac burned through his bloodstream. He sat in a chair in front of the fireplace and hooked an ankle over his knee. Then he pressed the snifter to his forehead as though it could somehow draw out the pain.

The first time he had seen Ann, he'd been stupefied. His mother had talked nonstop for weeks about the Flower Girl, some urchin selling roses on the corner of 23rd and Broadway. Felicia had passed the girl daily on her way to the office, buying up her wares for some obscure reason Patrick had never been able to fathom. Then the Flower Girl had disappeared. For the better part of two days, his mother had been frantic—until the detective she'd hired to track her down found her holed up in the sanctuary of a church five or six blocks from the corner.

Then Felicia had brought her home. At the time, Patrick had conjured an image of her in his mind—fair, ephemeral, sweet. Instead, Felicia had brought a flu-stricken tramp into their house, one with straw-straight hair, hollow eyes, and cheeks dry and livid with fever.

It had been right after Christmas. Patrick remembered hovering unseen outside the library door, listening to his mother talk about her with Cal Everham, her personal doctor and friend. The man had come by to examine the girl.

"It's a nasty strain of flu this year," Cal had said. They leaned close together, nose to nose, in front of the fireplace. "She should probably be hospitalized. Where did you find her?"

"It doesn't matter. I suspect she's a runaway," Felicia had said. "No parent would allow a child to live this way."

Cal placed his hand over hers. "It wouldn't happen in *your* world, Felicia. But who knows where this girl hails from."

"She won't tell me anything. She seems to hate me even for asking. Cal, I tell you, those begging eyes haunt me."

For what? Patrick had wanted to shout sense into her. *For your money!*

"She's alone in the world, Cal, I'm sure of it."

"I can find her a bed at Bellevue."

"No. She'd only run. I'll keep her here, at least until she's better."

"Felicia, that's a risk."

She gave him a patented Felicia smile. Small, enigmatic. Almost eerily wise. "She can't even stand up without help, Cal. She's hardly capable of robbing me blind."

"You're too trusting."

"I know this child. I've been talking to her every morning, every afternoon for weeks now."

"You just said she avoids all your questions."

Felicia took her hand back. "She's afraid of me. I could turn her in to the authorities. I'm sure she figures that the less I know about her, the better."

"But you keep asking anyway."

"God knows why, but she reminds me of myself at her age. We just have to be patient. I have an instinct about this girl. Time will bear me out." Felicia stood. "I'll have Francesca feed her for a while, put some meat back on her bones, then we'll take it from there."

Patrick had watched his mother pick up a brass snuffer and place it neatly over the flickering flame of a candle. Felicia spoke again after a long beat of silence. "Cal, I was so poor when my Frederick started whittling those clowns. He had a talent for bringing them to life. And that's why they sold as well as they did."

Cal waited.

"One merchant, one man in one out-of-the-way burg in Canada, took them on. He saw something in the clowns that made him willing to take the chance."

"Or he saw something in you," Cal suggested.

"I *was* good," she said wistfully. "In everyone's life, one person must take a chance on them."

"In an ideal world, yes."

"If we don't extend ourselves periodically, then mankind becomes something unconscionably evil. What are we, really, but a snarl of earthbound, frantic souls trying to survive? A hand offered here or there in the dark … it can make the difference in lifting one of us from the morass."

Cal drained his drink and stood. "Well, this frantic soul knows better than to try to talk you out of something you've already decided."

"Did you leave her some medicine?"

"It's on the bedside table. I'll charge your account." They both knew he wouldn't. "I'll want to see her again in a week. If she's been living on the street, God knows what else she's brought into your house."

Patrick couldn't listen anymore. He'd crept back upstairs to the bedroom his mother had given Ann. He'd leaned against the door to find that it was not only unlocked, but that it eased open beneath the pressure he applied. He crossed soundlessly to her bed, staring down at her as she slept.

Her breath had been shallow and putrid, wafting up to him for all its lack of force. At ninety pounds she seemed no threat to anybody. But he knew better. He knew even then that she would somehow manage to ruin everything.

And he had been right. It had taken two more years, but Ann Lesage had struck the first blow toward destroying them all.

Flames rolling in a red-white ball over the water, billowing then playing out like tongues licking the oil-slicked surface. Matthew's scream. Then silence. Jonathan taking hold of Patrick and slapping him, hitting him, harder, harder still, then lifting him by the front of his T-shirt and heaving him bodily into the back of the boat. "Stay there. Just stay there. Don't talk."

Patrick jerked free of the memory with an audible grunt. A wide, wet stain spread over his left thigh where his hand had relaxed, tilting his snifter until the Courvoisier spread over his trouser leg like an indelible mark.

Ann had helped kill Matt and now, after years of manipulating his mother, she had become president of Hart Toy. Irene was right, Patrick thought. He had no choice but to stop her. He had to show his mother who Ann really was. He still had some time. He would make sure Felicia changed her opinion of Ann, and in the process he would end up with what rightfully belonged to him.

CHAPTER 5

The small co-op apartment was his private escape. The single room was spare, dominated by a bed, a California king, draped by a luxurious, silk duvet cover in ruby red. Voluminous curtains in a shocking vermilion, and a large formal desk in cherry wood completed the womb-like interior.

Taking a seat at his desk, he unconsciously drummed his fingers on the blotter. The call was scheduled to take place in ten minutes. Ten more minutes before he knew whether this would be another lead that fizzled.

He closed his eyes for a moment.

His widowed mother's death left him the sole beneficiary of an insurance policy that numbered in the millions. Conservative but intelligent investments, coupled with a frugal lifestyle, had allowed him the freedom to more or less do as he pleased.

He did not consider his approach to women to be a fetish, or even peculiar, for that matter. He liked his ladies to be loose, with few morals. The looser the better. Whores intrigued him. He paid for their services and there were few complications.

Occasionally, hookers weren't enough and he took what he had to have by force. It wasn't rape. Every woman wanted it. Despite their protests—their tears and begging—he read between the words, understanding that no meant yes, that please meant thank you.

His victims adhered to his warning. Most believed him when he said that seeking revenge, or contacting the authorities, would lead to dire circumstances. Except for one young girl in New Jersey, who pulled a knife on him.

He never lost consciousness, but there had been so much blood he thought he had been blinded. The sight of the hellacious scar still enraged him today. Nothing could ease the humiliation of being bested by that girl.

Years of private detectives yielded nothing. Tens of thousands of dollars spent tracking down false leads, from New Jersey to Los Angeles, Maine to Florida. It seemed the girl had disappeared.

Tonight he waited once again, aged fifty-two and running out of patience.

When the phone rang, he quickly snatched the receiver in hand.

The voice at the other end spoke in a monotone. "We found her."

The man practically jumped out of his chair. "I beg your pardon?"

"We found her," the voice repeated.

CHAPTER 6

Ann was mildly out of breath when she reached the Air Canada gate at LaGuardia on Wednesday evening. She dropped into a seat and rested her briefcase on her knees. It occurred to her that if anyone knew its contents, she'd probably be committed. After all, company presidents should not be obsessed with Gameboy, even if it was the original model and dated back a long while.

Opening the case, Ann pushed aside tubes of lipstick and makeup, her wallet, and dug into the back compartment for the Maalox tablets.

She preferred the tangerine-flavored ones, so she took a moment to fish her finger through the bottle, holding it up and tilting it at eye level to look for the right color. She found four of them, put them in her mouth, and chewed diligently.

"You're either considering personal bankruptcy or you're afraid of flying."

Ann's cry of surprise popped out of her like a shot. "What the hell are you doing here?" she asked, jumping to her feet to confront Jonathan.

He stepped around to take the free seat on her right, then made a production of checking the pockets of his leather jacket. He held up his ticket. "I'm on my way to Toronto."

"You're out of your mind."

"I'm a man of my word."

"You're going to this commercial shoot with me?"

"Yes, I am. But I feel compelled to tell you that I resent paying business class."

"I had a free upgrade."

"Well, I didn't."

"Then cash in your ticket and go home." It occurred to her that she'd spoken to Jonathan more in the last few days than she had in the preceding seventeen years. She couldn't believe he was serious about keeping tabs on her and the doll project. What could he hope to gain by it? He knew next to nothing about the toy industry. She could be robbing his mother blind and he wouldn't have a clue.

Ann stood. "I can't stop you from doing this?"

"No. Free country, and all that."

"Well, I won't sit with you on the plane."

"That's ridiculous. You'd rather chat with a stranger?"

"I don't chat when I'm flying."

"What do you do then?"

She played with the Gameboy to keep her mind off the distant ground, but she'd be damned if she'd admit it. "I think highly intelligent, corporate thoughts."

"Spend the time sharing them with me."

Their flight was called.

"Better downgrade to economy while you still have the chance." Ann turned for the gate and left him.

She took her seat on the plane. A few minutes later she was not surprised to find him stopping at her row to stow his bag overhead.

"Care for a drink before take-off?" he asked, snapping his seat belt.

She kept her gaze on the window and the tarmac outside. "Sure. It might take the edge off the possibility of dying next to someone I detest. But I think we have to wait until we're airborne."

He removed a mini-bottle from his travel bag. It had a medical prescription label around it, which explained how he got it past security. Ann watched in bemusement as he divided its contents— Scotch, obviously—into two paper cups.

"Explain this to me again," she said, accepting the drink from him, "your obsession with this doll."

Jonathan held his cup up to the overhead light for some reason Ann couldn't fathom. "This is one time I'm not going to let you operate behind the scenes," he said finally.

Ann bit back on her anger. When had she ever? She kept things close to the vest, certainly. But she wasn't dishonest—never that.

"Why do you hate me?" she heard herself ask.

Jonathan opened his mouth, looking startled then thoughtful, just as the plane's engines rumbled to life. Ann didn't catch what he said. Having finished her drink, she crumpled the paper cup and stuck it in the magazine pouch in front of her. She held her jaw tight as the plane lurched and reversed from the gate. She checked her seatbelt. Again. As though it would do her even a prayer of good if she were coming down from thirty-three thousand feet. Or five thousand, as the case would probably be.

"You *are* scared," Jonathan said, watching her. He sounded surprised.

"Go to hell."

"Not until I know if you ever intended to marry Matthew."

"*What?*"

His expression was benign when Ann's gaze jerked away from the window. It occurred to her that he might have brought the topic up at this precise moment to divert her attention from take off. The sound of the engines became deafening to her over-sensitive ears. She was hurtling, trapped in metal. Then—*oomph.* Off the ground. Higher. Higher.

Ann recalled one other conversation she'd had with Jonathan on the subject of Matthew, going on fifteen years ago. It had been at Felicia's Long Island beach house. Just before Mattie had died.

"I told you I wasn't going to," she said, the scene still vivid in her mind. "I promised you I wouldn't marry him."

"But what did you tell *him*?" Jonathan persisted.

"I didn't have time to answer him, one way or the other."

"Time? What are we talking about here? Thirty seconds?" Any tolerance she'd seen in his eyes abruptly shuttered down. "On the one hand, we have, *Ann, will you marry me?* On the other, we have, *Thank you, Matt, you flatter me, but no.* How much time is that?"

"You bastard." Ann's heart seized, even now, after so many years.

"Spare me the histrionics. Just tell me the truth."

She might have—the why of it all, the hell behind her decision. *Might* have. The Scotch was mellow in her stomach and she felt it loosening her tongue. She could have told him that she had had no right to Matt because his heart had been utterly innocent and kind. He had never been suspicious like Patrick and Jonathan. He'd loved her from almost the start. But he'd deserved so much more than her, someone without the baggage she carried, and the guilt.

"I need another drink," Ann said abruptly. The plane was leveling off at cruising altitude. She loosened her grip from the armrests.

Jonathan caught the flight attendant's attention. "A Molson for me and a Dewars for the lady, please."

The second Scotch promised to go down more smoothly than the first. Ann sipped and thought almost longingly of her Gameboy. But when she opened her briefcase, she withdrew the script and the storyboard for the commercial shoot instead.

"What's that?" he asked.

She slid her gaze to him without moving her head or saying anything.

"Let me see. Please?"

Ann detected a hint of real interest in his voice. She handed him the storyboard.

It was done in color, in sketch form, with fifteen squares. Each of them represented approximately two seconds of film time. He looked at it for a long while.

"Doesn't do a thing for me," he said finally.

"You're not a girl."

"You noticed, huh?"

Only in her most vulnerable moments, Ann thought but dared not say. She snatched the board out of his hands. "I'm trying to educate you."

He settled in his seat, tilting his head back and shutting his eyes. "Educate away. I'm all ears."

Ann rubbed her temples. "Why should I bother?"

"Because I'm interested. And I'm not a novice, you know."

"Really?"

"Believe it or not, over the years I've absorbed a great deal."

"Indeed?"

"Yes, over the dinner table, for instance, when I was a kid."

"You and your father used to leave meals to play pool in the den."

He cracked one eye at her. "How would you know? You weren't around then. And just to set the record straight, it wasn't pool."

"Felicia told me. What was it then?"

"He was interested in my painting. He always wanted to see what I was working on."

For some reason, that stilled Ann's heart "Did your mother know?"

He shrugged. The gesture seemed stiff. "I'm not sure."

Ann had never known Frederick. He'd died a few years before she'd come on the scene, which would have made Jonathan sixteen at the time. "You were a teenage Rembrandt?"

He smiled. "I was an artist in the womb. I remember the finger paints Santa brought me when I was two." He paused. "Did you always want to be a shark?"

It hurt. "I always wanted to survive."

"You're doing more than that, Ann."

"Not at anyone else's expense."

"We'll see."

"Fuck you, Jonathan." The words were torn from her, unpremeditated and heartfelt.

"I seriously doubt if we'll ever get that close." He sat up. "Give me a look at that storyboard again."

She passed it to him.

"I want to know why we're doing this in Toronto."

"Because filming in New York or Hollywood would cost us upward of $150,000," she said, "and I want to control what expenditures I can."

"What's Toronto going to cost?"

"Less than half that. In both time and money."

"Is Toronto as good?"

"The Canadians seem to think so. You were born there, weren't you?"

Jonathan nodded, then gestured at her seatbelt. "Better tighten up. We're getting close to landing."

Ann gripped the belt with both hands and groaned inwardly. What the hell was she supposed to do with him in Toronto?

CHAPTER 7

Cold rain was drumming down when they stepped out of the terminal at Lester B. Pearson Airport.

"Feel testy about sharing a cab?" Jonathan asked.

"You find one, I'll pay for it." Ann ducked back through the doors to wait inside. Pride always came with a price, she thought.

She watched through the window as the downpour flattened his dark hair and soaked through his jacket. He shoved his hands into his jeans pockets and eyed the creeping traffic. Cars stopped now and then to suck in waiting passengers; doors slammed, tires sloshed, and water splattered.

Ten minutes later, Ann hurried into the waiting taxi, while Jonathan stowed their bags in the trunk. Then he got in beside her and pulled the door shut.

Fifty gridlocked minutes later, the cab spit them out in front of the Sheraton Centre. The rain had given way to a light mist that tangled the air. Ann paid the driver and went inside to stand in line at the check-in desk. When she felt his breath on the back of her neck, she spoke without turning. "If I wake up tomorrow morning to find your butt camped in front of my door, look out."

"If they haven't had a cancellation since yesterday, you'll find me on the floor in your room."

She jerked around to face him. "You don't have a reservation?"

"I tried. They were full."

"Well, go somewhere else! This city is full of hotels."

"Can't. That would negate my whole purpose for being here."

"Jonathan, this is asinine."

"I'll probably agree with you after a night on the floor."

Ann whipped back to the registration clerk, disbelieving and incensed. She got her room and took both keys. She dangled them briefly in front of his nose, then dropped them smartly into the pocket of her jacket. His scowl offered her a modicum of satisfaction.

Jonathan stepped up to the desk, his gaze cutting back to her as she took long, sure strides toward the elevator. He wondered if she knew she blushed when she got angry. Until a few hours ago, he hadn't known how easily she could be irritated.

It was well past ten o'clock when Jonathan let himself into his hotel room, pleased that they could accommodate him, after all. He draped his jeans over the shower door to dry and called room service. Waiting for his meal, he considered various long distance calls he could make. He vetoed the idea of touching base with his mother; he didn't want her to know where he was. Then he thought about Carmen Cole.

They had been seeing each other for four weeks now. She was an investment banker with incredible, burnished red hair and skin the tone and texture of ivory. Carmen possessed just enough free-wheeling independence to forestall Jonathan's tendency to feel cornered. Good manners would dictate that he let her know he'd arrived safely, but he couldn't recall if he'd even mentioned the trip.

Jonathan returned the phone to its cradle and went to take a shower. When he finished and stepped out of the bathroom, room service had arrived. He pulled on a pair of sweat pants and collected the steak and French fries. He found the remote for the TV, then began to eat with only half his attention on the screen.

Ann had never really answered his question about Matt, he thought, and now, hours later, he was not at all sure why he had asked it in the first place. Maybe he'd been looking for a response he could live with.

Years ago she had made the promise to him that she would not accept Matt's proposal. They were walking barefoot on the beach, and she was wearing a long, diaphanous dress beneath a denim jacket. She'd fussed repeatedly when the sea had lapped at her hem, stopping to gather it up and wring it out. He'd suggested that they walk farther up the beach, away from the tide, and she'd looked at him like he was incapable of appreciating some fundamental joy of life. To prove her wrong, he'd waded into the water, too, until his jeans were soaked to the knees.

He'd finally had to ask her straight out. "Are you going to do it? Are you going to marry him?" Mattie had told him that morning that he'd asked.

His question had stopped her cold. When he looked at her, he'd found her perfect face tilted toward the sky, framed by moonlight. The opaque glow had caught her tears and they glimmered on her face.

Later, he'd captured that moment on canvas. He'd caught the heartbreak in her eyes, the bitterness, and the fierce, determined hope in the set of her jaw, even without understanding the conflict of emotions. He'd never sold the painting. To the best of his knowledge, the piece was still in storage with other personal works he wouldn't share.

"I'm not going to marry him," she'd said finally, "but I refuse to explain myself."

"I don't need you to. I just want you to leave him alone."

She'd brought her gaze back to his then, and there was a change of countenance. The heartbreak and hope were gone, and all that remained was bitterness. "I might have made him happy. But we'll never know, will we?"

She'd turned and started up the beach again. This obvious rejection had made him feel small. Small and randy. He remembered the twitch of her hips as she'd picked her way through the sand, her skirt gathered up, wads of it held in each fist, showing legs that were tanned and strong. He'd let her move ahead of him because the sudden rush of wanting her was so unforeseen and cataclysmic, he hadn't trusted himself to move forward.

She'd been living with them for two years by then. She'd recovered from her flu but never left. Where had she come from? What did she want from them? Did his mother even know? Sometimes her smile seemed sharp enough to cut glass. At other times, the color would wash from her face, her eyes going stark and vulnerable.

Jonathan could picture Patrick in those days. He had spent nearly every available moment on her heels, waiting for her to do … something. He'd harangued Felicia over the legalities of harboring a runaway. For his part, Jonathan had never expected Ann to cause them harm, but he couldn't help himself from watching and waiting, never exactly anticipating what might come next. He hadn't actually started to hate her until she lied to him.

"Give me your word!" he had shouted after her that night.

"I already did!" She'd answered without turning, the breeze catching her voice and flinging it back to him.

Damn it, it had been a promise. One she'd broken.

Jonathan now returned to the bathroom and ran himself a glass of water, drinking deeply. "What the hell did you do, Ann?" he said aloud. She'd changed her mind, of course, had said yes, had gone back on her word to him, sometime between the night on the beach and the night on the boat, all of two days later.

But what if he was wrong? He paused, then shrugged. He didn't want to go there. At least, not tonight. There was his mother to think about and his reason for being in Toronto. He mustn't lose sight of his mission—to protect his mother's interests at all costs.

No other woman in his life had earned his respect the way Felicia had. Her honesty and compassion, her understanding, even when he explained to her that he did not want any part of the business she had built from the ground up.

Jonathan finally turned out the bathroom light and went to the bed. He picked up the phone and had the hotel operator put him through to Ann's room.

"Hmmm," she answered. Her voice was thick with sleep. While he was prowling his room with memories nipping at his heels, she had been sleeping. That bothered him in a way he couldn't understand.

"Just making sure you're present and accounted for," he said. "See you in the morning."

He hung up midway through her answering growl.

CHAPTER 8

The following morning, Jonathan was already in the lobby waiting for Ann when she arrived downstairs.

"If you slept more often, you might not need this," she said, taking the cup of coffee out of his hands and drinking deeply. "Is there any way I can talk you out of going with me?"

"Why would you want to?"

"Out of respect for Felicia. I wouldn't want to bore one of her offspring to death."

"Good try. Let's go."

He started for the door. Ann drained the coffee and left the mug on the concierge desk. When she got outside, he had a cab waiting.

It was a ten minute ride to the studio. When they got out of the car, Jonathan reached into his pocket and counted out the correct change.

"You know, this really is ridiculous," Ann muttered.

He answered without looking at her. "So you've said at least six times in the last twenty-four hours. Now, would you move aside so I can pay the guy?"

"That's what I meant. There's no reason you should pay for this out of your own pocket. The company will cover our expenses."

He passed the money to the cabbie. When he turned back to her, they were standing too close.

"Ann, I can afford it." He caught her chin in his hand. "You went after the wrong brother."

How could it happen like this? she wondered. One moment they were civil, then everything flared. Ann dropped her briefcase to wrap both hands around his wrist. They stood that way, locked in place, both of them suddenly angry, both unwilling to back off.

"Stop this," she hissed. "Leave him alone, damn it. *Leave Mattie out of this!*"

"Want me to promise the way you did?"

"What on earth is the matter with you?"

"Maybe I've finally decided to get to the bottom of everything, once and for all."

Ann moved one hand to swat at his. But something was jumping in her stomach. "Knock it off."

Jonathan released his hold on her. She breathed in deeply once, twice, trying to get her equilibrium back. Then she bent to snag her briefcase again and headed into the studio.

The building was a converted warehouse. As she signed in with the uniformed guard, she became aware of the musty odor of the place. She glanced at Jonathan, waiting for some comment about cutting corners. She decided not to give him the opportunity and moved forward, up a winding corridor.

It ended at the entrance to a cavernous loft. By the time she reached it, he was behind her again, too close.

"You've used these people before?" he asked as they pushed through a solid metal door.

There it was, Ann thought, the jab. Or at least the prelude to one. "Once or twice."

"And?"

"I was satisfied," she said shortly, and she blushed.

Rattled her again, Jonathan thought. He wanted to wonder about that, but his attention was caught by the set. It was a child's bedroom: a dresser, cupboard, school desk, storage chest. The pinks were vivid, the whites pristine. People swarmed. A man in his mid-forties spotted Ann and pushed out of the crowd. He had spare blond hair and a nose that looked as though it had been punched more than once. Jonathan couldn't get a good read of his eyes through the lenses of his glasses.

"Ann." The guy caught her hand—affectionately, Jonathan thought. The once or twice she'd worked with him had apparently been memorable occasions.

She was wearing that smile again, Jonathan decided, the one that could cut glass. She took her hand back. "Guy Brewer, Jonathan Morhardt," she said, making the introductions.

"Morhardt?" Brewer repeated.

"Felicia's son," Jonathan said. "The other one."

"I didn't know there were two."

"We were able to keep it a secret until just recently," Ann said.

Brewer laughed. "Well, I'm the producer. Good to meet you."

"Likewise. Who's this?" Jonathan put his hand on Ann's shoulder and moved her slightly aside. He felt her twitch at the contact.

The girl who stood behind her was all of seven, Jonathan thought, but she would grow into a woman who would make a man go willingly to his knees. She was blond, with dimples and blue eyes. She was extraordinary and, Jonathan knew in the next moment, she'd been trained to use her looks.

"Hello." She offered her hand perfectly. "My name is Lisette Smile."

Jonathan hunkered down to her level. "And a beautiful smile you have, too."

"Thank you." She kept forcing it.

"Go on now," Brewer said to her. "Make-up needs you."

The girl went back to the set, tossing a coquettish grin over her shoulder—flirting with him, Jonathan realized. He stood. "Where'd you find her?"

Ann rubbed the back of her neck as though it hurt. "Three hundred photographs. We picked forty, auditioned them, narrowed it to five, then gave them camera tests."

"You did all this in less than a week?"

"I started the search before I actually contracted for the doll."

"Malice aforethought. You knew you would sign the deal."

She met his gaze. "Yes."

"Well, what if you hadn't?" he hissed the question at her. "And all these expenses were for naught?"

"That wasn't an alternative, Jonathan," she countered softly.

He watched her move off and wondered about a woman to whom failure was not an option.

Brewer began talking effusively to Jonathan, gesturing at the set before them. "We did all this in the last twenty-four hours, from the wood floor up. It'll take us all day to capture one hour of thirty-five millimeter film. From that, we'll get a thirty-second commercial."

Jonathan scanned the set. To his unpracticed eye, it all seemed professional enough. But Ann had said flat-out that she was taking the cheaper route here. Why? Was she pocketing the difference? That was beneath her, he decided. Too crass.

He watched her stop and lean against a wall to watch the proceedings. Another man—the director, Jonathan assumed—called for quiet. The grip started the dolly moving along the guide rail at a deliberate speed, carrying the camera and the cameraman toward the action.

Lisette touched a hand to the doll's heart and gave the camera a look of bemusement. Jonathan was impressed. The director called for the scene to be shot again.

And again.

Every time it happened, the girl's look of surprise became more wooden. Jonathan could tell that the poor kid was melting. Someone mercifully called for a break and a sandwich cart was rolled out. Jonathan moved over to Ann who seemed preoccupied with her briefcase. "What's that?" he asked, looking over her shoulder.

"It's nothing." She slammed the lid, nearly taking off his fingers as he reached for it.

"It's one of those kids games, isn't it? The electronic kind that we don't sell? And if I hadn't come along, you'd be sitting here, playing with it?" It jived with nothing he knew of her.

"I'm not going to dignify that with a response."

He dropped it because he thought of something else. "Are we paying this idiot by the hour?" he asked.

"Which idiot?" She shook the bottle of Maalox she had removed from her briefcase, held it up, peered into it, shook it again.

"The one in the dark shirt who seems to be running this show."

"Oh. That idiot. Gene Sullivan. He's a genius, actually." Ann found the tablets she was looking for and palmed a handful. She popped them into her mouth as if they were candy and began chewing.

She closed her eyes briefly and rubbed her waist. She was letting him get to her. And for the life of her, she didn't know why. Patrick's barbs usually made her laugh, roll her eyes, dig in. But this was different. She had a very strong urge to take Jonathan by the throat and strangle him.

Ann looked at Lisette. The child was sitting off in a far corner by herself while everyone else ate. Her eyes were too bright. "Oh, shit." She left him and went to the girl.

"Hey, there," she said, kneeling in front of her. "What's wrong?"

"I want my mom."

Ann looked over her shoulder for the woman, and found her bearing down on them.

"Mommy, I *did* it!" Lisette cried as the woman approached. "I tried!"

"You didn't listen to anything that man said! You just took it in your own head to do it your way!" She raised a hand as though to slap the child.

Ann panicked. "Hold on here!"

"Who are you?" the woman demanded.

They were fighting words. Ann stood to confront her. "I'm the woman who hired your daughter."

"Oh." She went flame red. And, like flames, the color crept up from her neck into her cheeks, part anger and part embarrassment. "Well, you talk to her then. Make her see sense."

Lisette wailed as her mother wheeled around and left them.

"Easy does it, chicklet." Ann got down to the child's level again. "Let's talk."

You're hot, baby. Ann tensed, her smallest muscles reacting to the remembered voice inside her head. Her blood started humming. She hadn't heard that voice since she was fourteen years old. But sometimes it still came to life. In her dreams, mainly. Or when little girls cried.

Ann took a breath. "They're outside you, Lisette. Your mom, Mr. Sullivan, all of them. They're not here." She touched a palm to her own chest. "Just pull back into that place inside yourself and everything will be fine. Do you get what I'm saying?"

"I have a place like that," the girl whispered.

"I know you do. We all do. Go inside there and talk to the doll for yourself, okay? Do it for the girl in that special spot. No one will yell at you anymore, not while I'm here."

"Are you important?"

I'm just another little blond girl, Ann thought. She stood and turned away to look for Gene Sullivan. She plowed straight into Jonathan's chest. "Not a word," she snapped, jumping back when they made contact.

"I was just going to ask if everything is okay."

"Right as rain. Leave me alone." She stepped past him and he let her go.

She was halfway across the set, looking for the director, when she saw one of the guards making a lumbering beeline toward her. He was overweight and his face was florid from the rising warmth in the building. "Ms. Lesage?" he asked.

"That's me."

"I have an urgent message for you to call Mr. Morhardt."

Involuntarily, her neck snapped around and her gaze went to Jonathan. He had Lisette on her feet now and was laughing with her. Patrick, Ann thought dazedly. The guard was referring to Patrick, not Jonathan.

She had turned her cell phone off earlier so as not to disturb the filming. Ann headed for her briefcase.

She removed her phone and tapped in the number of the office. Patrick took the call in record time. Generally he played games with her, pretending he was too important, too busy to jump when she tried to contact him.

"What is it?" she demanded.

"Stop the shoot."

She was shocked into laughing aloud. "Have you lost your mind?"

"I'm telling you to cut our losses, Ann. As soon as possible. Our bank turned us down and I can't find another one."

CHAPTER 9

Verna Sallinger raised her hand and felt it hover an inch from Patrick's closed office door. If anyone turned into the corridor, they would assume she was knocking. But it was late and she didn't expect to see anyone. She turned her head to the side and leaned close, listening.

He'd been at her desk when Ann had returned his call. He'd gone back to his own office to take it, moving like a kid who was hurrying to the bathroom. The fact that he wouldn't talk to Ann in front of her, hurt Verna in a spot that was already raw from his other casual insults.

Patrick opened the door suddenly. Verna took a quick step back to save herself from stumbling inside. "You startled me!"

He scowled at her, then looked up and down the hall. "What are you doing out here?"

Verna decided not to answer him. She slid one shoulder between him and the door jamb, moved past, then turned.

The whites of his eyes were threaded with red. The skin beneath them was puffy.

Verna took a breath. "What's wrong, Pat? Talk to me." This time, she thought, he would tell her. He would confide in her and let her into his life.

Patrick laughed hoarsely. "Besides the obvious?"

The only obvious thing she knew was that three banks had turned him down on a doll project he wasn't keen on anyway. "Besides that." Verna touched his midriff and slowly slid her hands up. She used her fingers to knead the tension from his shoulders.

He closed his eyes. "That feels good."

"I know."

She waited but he didn't volunteer anything more. Verna took her hands away and his eyes flew open. She glanced at her watch.

"I thought you might need a sounding board, but I guess not. I'm heading off."

Verna made a move toward the door and caught a glimmer of her reflection in the glass of the framed print beside it. She considered herself attractive, weight held in check, curves in all the right places. Then why this penchant for falling for the wrong guy? Ever since she'd moved to Manhattan from upstate New York. Not that there had been many, but invariably the men she became involved with were either single and jerks, or married.

If at times she found Patrick's touch unpleasant, then Verna simply reminded herself of how much better he was than other men she had known. He had his faults, of course. There was no denying that. Yet, she would give anything to hear him say that he truly cared about her.

"Wait," Patrick said when she reached the door. "Is everyone gone?"

She kept her hand on the knob and nodded.

"Don't go." He caught her free hand to reel her back in.

She let him. And he walked her over to the bar.

His office was huge and pretentious. An impressive oak desk and computer station faced the window. The other side of the room was given over to a black leather sofa fronted by a narrow smoked-glass table. A few pictures of his family hung on the wall, but none of Irene.

Patrick poured himself a snifter of Courvoisier. He held the bottle aloft as though to invite her to join him.

Verna shrugged indifference.

He poured another snifter. She made no move to take it.

"You're angry with me," he said finally.

"I'm worried about you."

He let out a deep, rough breath. "It's been a rotten day."

"What did the banks say?" she asked, finally taking the snifter in hand. "Besides no?"

He groaned and shook his head. "What does it matter? That's the bottom line."

"What did your mother say?"

"That doesn't matter now, either."

Which meant he hadn't told her yet, Verna thought.

Patrick hooked his free hand behind her neck and tried to pull her face closer to his.

She moved away. "How did Ann take it?" She asked.

"I don't want to talk about her," Patrick said.

Verna realized that she was going to have to put more effort into this. "I could help you."

"I know. That's what I'm waiting for."

"I meant with a way to fix the bank mess."

"You?"

"Yes, me." Her anger flared. "We could set a plan down on paper, figure out a new approach."

He took a long swallow from his glass. "I have better plans for you," he said.

"But you don't trust me."

"I *crave* you. That's better."

"Is it?" She stepped further away from him.

"Don't do this. Don't play with me. Everybody wants something from me. Except you."

For a moment she almost faltered, found herself prepared to give in. But too often she'd given herself to him and it proved meaningless. "Pat," she started to say.

As if she hadn't spoken, his arms reached out and he tried pulling her tight.

She struggled against him.

"I need you," he said.

And I need you, she was thinking. But not this way. Not tonight. She pushed hard. He almost lost his balance. She backed up towards the door.

"Where are you going?"

There it was, the insecurity in his voice.

"Home."

"What the hell do you want from me?"

"It doesn't matter," she said, reaching for the door.

"For Christ"s sake, Verna!"

She opened the door and stepped into the hallway.

"Wait! Let me see if I can get you something special. Maybe ... maybe have Ann approve a big, fat raise."

She stood there, feeling sorry for him, feeling sorry for both of them. "I don't need a raise," she said.

"What do you need, then?"

Slowly, sadly, she shook her head. "You figure it out," she said, and she walked away.

CHAPTER 10

"What does 'tire down' mean?" Jonathan asked.

He had spent the last fifteen minutes with her Gameboy, and had gotten pretty good at dancing his fingers over the buttons, when the message 'TIRE DOWN' popped up.

"You've got a flat." Ann kept her eyes on the window as the plane hurtled them back toward New York.

"How'd I get that?"

"You must have run over something."

"I did not."

"Oh, for God's sake, give it to me." She turned from the window and snatched the toy out of his hands. "Was there a crash?"

"Not involving my car. I'm a damned good driver."

Ann glared at him. "In *front* of you. Was there any debris on the track in front of you?"

"If there was, I didn't notice."

She started working the buttons and handed the gizmo back to him. "There you go. You're headed for a pit stop."

"I don't want to go in for a pit stop."

"You have a flat tire. You *have* to go in for a pit stop."

"This is stupid."

"You know, I'm starting to remember why I never liked you."

His attention was already back on the toy. "Why's that?" he asked absently.

"You're argumentative."

"No, I'm not."

"Everything becomes an issue for you. Like the reason why you're here and tracking my every move."

"The doll's a pretty big issue on its own, Ann."

She felt something boom behind her eyes. The headache didn't start slowly and build. It was the kind that was just suddenly there, in full force. She leaned back in her seat and closed her eyes. "What the hell am I supposed to do about this mess?"

"Are you asking me?"

"It was a rhetorical question."

"I'll make a suggestion anyway. Give Pat another chance."

She turned her head to look at him. "Damn it, why did he *lie*?" He'd told her that he'd gone to their own bank and three others, and that he had been refused by all of them. Ann had spent the remainder of the afternoon on her cell phone, calling the institutions herself, trying to pull off a miracle. One of them—Margin Savings and Loan—claimed that they had never even gotten a request from Pat. The officers at the two other banks had confided in her that Pat hadn't been able to answer questions about the doll, and had left the impression that he himself didn't think Baby Talk N Glow was going to fly.

Jonathan turned the Gameboy off and gave it back to her. "Screw it. I don't want to go to pit row."

"Your way or no way?" Ann put the game back into her briefcase.

"Tell me something," he said. "Why's our own bank being so difficult?"

"Because they're stuck on our inventory situation."

"The Moonlight Game business? I thought that was fixed."

She gave him an appraising look. "Osmosis again?"

"Something like that."

"It was. Is." Ann let out a throaty sigh. "Okay. Here's the gist of it. When we bought that company out of Chicago, one of the key products was a successful board game called Moonlight that we could re-release every fall."

"That's good, right?"

Ann rubbed her forehead and nodded. "In theory. But we're dependent on three major accounts—Toys 'R' Us, Walmart, and Target. Last year, Toys 'R' Us got themselves into an inventory bind. They canceled commitments right before Christmas, including ours for the Moonlight game, and we were left holding the bag."

"What happened to the inventory?"

"We sold it. Eventually."

"Could that happen with this doll?"

Things went weak inside her. "Yes."

To his credit, Jonathan didn't comment.

Ann fell silent, too, wondering how to touch on the subject of Patrick again without instigating a fight. She was too tired and anxious to quarrel. "Your brother has got to stop drinking, Jonathan."

"Patrick lets things get to him. It's his way of relaxing."

"You can make excuses for him, but I can't afford to. He has responsibilities to your mother's company."

"So what are you going to do? Fire him?"

"Unfortunately, Felicia wouldn't condone that."

Jonathan studied her face for a moment.

"What are you looking at?" she asked suspiciously.

"You."

"Well, stop."

He continued to study her, then asked quietly, "Tell me, Ann, why did you lie to me about Mattie?"

She fumbled with her coffee cup, then brought her hand back and clasped her fingers together to still them. "I'm going to say this once more, then I want this to be the end of it: I didn't have time to tell Matt that I wouldn't marry him."

She unwound her fingers. One by one. Carefully. "I stalled. I never told Matt anything at all. I never said yes, I never said no. I was trying to find the words, the *right* words. I knew he would be hurt. He and your mother were my only friends in the world…"

There was something hollow in her voice that nagged him into wanting to believe her.

"You're an artist," she said suddenly.

"What's that got to do with it?"

"You of all people should understand that nothing is black or white. There are a million shades of gray."

It was true enough, he thought. So why was he trying so hard to pigeonhole Matt's death?

"I never would have married him," she said. "I told you that. But if you think I'd have held back because I gave *you* my word, you're a fool. I didn't owe you anything. I owed Mattie. And he deserved someone who wasn't so … so…"

She trailed off and made an odd, gulping sound. Jonathan looked at her quickly; it occurred to him that she might be on the verge of crying.

She was just searching for the right word. *"Pretty."* She finally spat out.

Jonathan was startled. There was some kind of wound here, one that did not involve Matt, and he couldn't for a minute imagine what it was. She would never share it, he knew. So he could either believe her … or not. Maybe it *was* simply an issue of gray. Maybe she'd never had time to tell Matt with the kind of words that wouldn't have left his heart broken. And maybe Matt had misunderstood her silence.

Jonathan realized he could accept that explanation and still resent Ann. It remained that if she had told him, if she had been faster, firmer, more definite, Mattie would have likely still been alive today.

"Let it go now," she said finally, quietly.

"Yeah." Suddenly, he was exhausted, and filled with the possibility that by the time this doll business wrapped up, he could have spent enough time to actually get to know her. And maybe even like her more than he would dare to admit.

CHAPTER 11

The man breathed in deeply through his nose and hit the light switch. The apartment was pitched into shadow. He let himself out and meticulously turned both locks on the door.

Downstairs, he undertook the onerous chore of hailing a cab. Autumn was sharpening. The wind had a fractious edge, signaling that winter wasn't too far behind. A taxi stopped for him, and though he detested public transportation, he was grateful to get inside.

"Where to?" the driver asked.

An Armenian or Arab, the man thought. He had absolutely no objection to the ethnic snarl of New York's population. But the way most of them drove was another matter entirely.

"Twenty-fifth and Broadway," he said.

Ann Lesage may not have been ready to give up on her doll, but under the circumstances she would almost certainly have returned early from Canada. He would head over to her office, where he hoped to catch a glimpse of her grim expression.

The cabbie drove, the car hitching, swerving, brakes squealing on grinding stops and near misses. The man held on tight. As they pulled up to the address, fate smiled on him.

A woman he recognized at once came through the lobby doors. She was a brunette of enticing proportions that he could just make out beneath her open, flapping coat. Her stride was choppy in a way that told him she was angry. She drove her long hair back with one hand as she looked right then left, perhaps deciding in which direction she should go. He knew her name, knew her to be Patrick Morhardt's secretary.

Although they had clearly arrived at their destination, the man instructed the cab driver to keep the meter running.

"But you said Twenty-fifth Street," the cabbie protested in broken English.

He handed him two twenties. "You can keep the change if you just hang tight for a minute."

The driver shrugged and did as he was told.

The man knew he had to make a decision. He could follow his intended plan, a rather indulgent one with no immediate consequences, and wait to see if Ann Lesage would show up, or he could make a change. His instincts told him that now that he had spotted Verna Sallinger, this was the more fortuitous path to take.

Verna headed south on Broadway, and he bid the cabbie to follow. They didn't have far to go. She crossed 23rd, strolled a few blocks before turning west and into a bar just past the corner.

Ten minutes later he stepped inside the same bar—finding that it resembled a small Irish pub.

Four patrons sat at the counter, a middle-aged couple, a man in his twenties, and Verna. Fortunately, the stools on either side of her were unoccupied.

"May I?" he asked, indicating the seat on her right.

She picked up her drink, sipped, then put it down.

He didn't wait for her answer and introduced himself.

"Vincent?" she repeated, closing her eyes and leaning back in her seat with a small groan.

"Did I say something wrong?"

"I'd rather be alone, Vincent, if you don't mind."

The man's blood began to boil at the slight. But he kept his emotions in check. The germ of an idea was beginning to percolate—one that was too good to reject. So he swallowed his anger and inquired if it would be alright if he stayed for just one drink before going on his way.

Even that didn't seem to sit well with Verna, but she nodded her head as if she had no choice in the matter.

Neither said a word until his drink—a Belvedere Martini—was served. Then he asked what was troubling her.

"Who said I was troubled?"

"I like to watch people. When you left your office, you were walking mad."

"You saw me leave my office?"

"Yes. I knew who you were. You've been recommended to me, Ms. Salinger. I'm looking for a secretary and I heard you were a good one."

"I'm good and presently employed, thank you very much."

"But I can make it worth your while."

He watched her mull over his comment. It always came down to money. He believed everyone had a price, no matter their self-esteem or determination.

"Sorry. Not interested."

The little bitch. *Not interested, my ass.* He heard her but pretended he hadn't. He continued to drink in silence, focusing on the fulfillment of his idea, which was beginning to delight him. When he finished his drink, he stood from the bar and said good night. The smile was back on his face and it was no longer forced.

He was confident that he could persuade Verna Sallinger to become a foot soldier in his cause. Her personal relationship with Patrick Morhardt—the drunken fool—would prove invaluable. Once Patrick was trapped and Verna Sallinger gone, he'd be left with Ann Lesage, and oh what wonderful surprises he had in store for her. His blood rushed with the thought of it. He could hardly wait.

CHAPTER 12

"Your mother called."

The news soured the coffee Patrick had just swallowed. He put his cup down on the kitchen table. "When?"

"While you were in the shower." Irene lifted his cup and set it on the sink counter with a thud.

"What did you tell her?" Patrick asked warily.

"That you'd already left and I didn't know if you were heading straight in to the office this morning or not."

He should have been out the door an hour ago. He had planned to stop at the office before his morning appointment, but last night had done him in. He'd spent most of it in the den, thinking, drinking. He lifted a shaky hand to his eyes, rubbing until they were sore.

"And what's with your brother lately, anyway?" she demanded.

Patrick frowned at the change of subject. Even that reflex hurt, and he had to think hard to change gears. "What are you talking about?"

"Jonathan. He's been stuck up Ann's ass like an enema all week."

"Christ, Irene, that's crude."

"I'm running out of niceties, Pat. I'm sick of this."

He took his briefcase from the counter and stepped toward the door to the garage without answering.

"Talk to me, damn it!"

Patrick looked back at her, his gut churning. It occurred to him that he hated her. He wished he had it in him to hurt her, physically *hurt* her for all her derision and complaints over the years. Nothing had ever been good enough.

"I didn't get the financing," he said. "That should have been it, but Ann went ahead with the commercial shoot anyway. Mom's pissed. She blames me. She wants this bloody doll and she expects me to find the money to pull it off. We're out the cost of the commercial because Ann wouldn't back down. And they've both got their drawers in a twist over going back on our word with the Chinese. So I'm going to have to think of another way."

Irene stared at him, then she groaned as she leaned against the refrigerator. "You can't do anything right," she said.

He thought again of putting his hands around his wife's throat, tightening, squeezing. Patrick took a deliberate step into the garage instead.

"What do I tell Felicia if she calls back?" Irene called after him.

"That I told you I was going to try one more bank before I went to the office."

He was bone-tired and the day hadn't even started yet. Patrick closed the door behind him. A minute later, he was in the Volvo wagon, heading for the train station.

He wasn't going to a bank. He was going to a lawyer.

He had worked with Ann for too many years. She wouldn't have taken his word on the bank situation. By now she would have contacted them herself and checked his version of the story. She had probably even figured out that he had never spoken to Margin at all. She'd call him on it if he couldn't sidetrack her by miraculously producing the money she needed.

How the hell had she done it, he wondered as he left his car in the lot and headed for the train. How had she usurped him so completely over the years? He'd kept his eye on the little bitch from the first time she'd set foot in Hart Toy's mailroom. But it wasn't just Felicia she had wowed. She'd taken everyone by storm. Part of it was that chilly intelligence. The rest was the I-could-like-you-if-you-really-wanted-me-to vulnerability she let peek out now and then.

He'd seen how she'd done it with Matthew. Snuggling in, touching the kid's neck, his hand. Grinning into his eyes, then backing off. *I'm no good for you.* He'd overheard her say that to Matt once, full of regret and shame and hopelessness.

Patrick had almost respected her then for realizing that she didn't belong among the Morhardts. He'd cornered her coming back from the beach one night in Long Island, just before Matt had died, and he'd taken that fantastic blond hair of hers in his hand, pulling her head back, kissing her hard. He had been prepared to accept her on her own terms that night. He thought he knew what she wanted. Barefoot in the sand with that dress all fisted in her hands, she would be the perfect receptacle for his disdainful love. But she'd kneed him in the balls, showing herself to be a vicious little street fighter who would feign insult and injury. He had been enraged.

Two weeks later, she'd gone to Felicia with her pirate ship idea. They'd been planning to go big that year with his idea of a jumbo-sized model boat, but she'd coopted the concept and turned it into a ship, complete with rigging, tiny holds with gallows for the prisoners, cannons that fired ammunition, and treasure chests filled with gold coins and jewels. She'd created a map of the Caribbean circa 1560 that converted into a board game. The ship was a stand alone toy, but any kid who owned one would want an opponent to play against, and that meant another ship sold. The proceeds from the product had pretty much funded the acquisition of the game company from Chicago.

After that success, there had been no stopping her. She was creative. She was cunning. And she had a way of smiling that made men hurt.

What the hell was Jonathan doing sniffing around her these days? What was *that* about?

The train disgorged him in the city. Patrick stood on the platform for a woozy moment, his mind seizing on the conviction that he had to call his brother before the day was over. He had to find out what was going on with him and Ann.

Jonathan had always hated her, too. Because of her, Jonathan had lied to the authorities. Because of her, his right hand—his painting hand—had been in a cast for six weeks. Part of him wished he could let go of that horrible time, the circumstances leading up to Matt's death, but he continued to obsess about it, year after year. He was like a dog with a bone—unable to leave it alone and let it lie forgotten.

Patrick found a cab outside the station and ordered it in the direction of Park Avenue. The office he stepped into thirty minutes later was extravagant, all dark wood and leather.

He settled into a deep chair that supported and cushioned his back, then began to consider what it would be like to redesign his own office in the style of this reception area.

The secretary jolted him out of his reverie, speaking in a voice that was silky and seductive. "Mr. Morhardt? Mr. Salsberg will see you now."

Patrick went into the man's office. The carpet was so thick he actually felt himself sinking into it. The incandescent lighting put him in the mood for a drink. The wet bar reminded Patrick of the pubs his brother favored, brass rail, swivel stools. And damned if there wasn't gold-plating on the chandelier.

Three-quarters of a million a year in rent, he estimated, at the bottom side. He should have gone into law and left his mother holding the Hart Toy bag on her own.

THE DOLL BROKERS • 63

"Patrick. Good to meet you, finally." Richard Salsberg rose to shake his hand. Patrick had gotten the man's number years ago, when his third drunk-driving charge had put him at risk of serving jail time, but he had never used it before now. "I have good news for you."

Patrick's adrenaline spiked. He had dreaded this meeting, but had still prayed for the result. "You found a bank willing to cooperate?"

"It depends somewhat on how much you really want the loan."

"What's the figure?"

"Fifty thousand."

Patrick's stomach heaved. "Fifty thousand? What does it buy me?"

"A new bank, just as I explained on the phone."

It had been a cryptic conversation, but Patrick had gotten the gist of it. "Just like that? No questions about our inventory, or what we're planning to do with the money?"

"Not a one."

"How much of the fifty is yours?"

The man's congenial smile melted like ice cream in August. "Look, you produce fifty thousand dollars and I'll give you a bank. That's how I fit in."

Patrick felt more nauseous than he had at dawn, when he had upchucked the last of the cognac. He wanted the deal spelled out. "You're saying you know of an account manager who would take a bribe?"

"I'm saying no such thing, Patrick. And none of this should concern you."

But it did. It concerned him very much. Not the ethics actually, but the fact that he could get caught. "I haven't gone this way before. I'd like some idea of how it works."

"It's strictly a matter of setting up guarantees. The account manager doesn't want to get burned. I'll be the one to insure his neck."

"Right." Patrick suddenly saw his mother's face, her judgmental frown looming in his mind's eye.

Salsberg stood preemptively. "Apparently you're not ready to make a decision."

"No, I have to." Patrick heard himself speak the words aloud. *Damn Ann Lesage.* "You want cash?"

"That would be best. I'm authorized to offer you terms but … you get what you pay for, if you catch my drift."

"Cash or questions?"

Salsberg didn't reply.

"Which bank is it?"

The lawyer made a show of looking at the papers on his desk. "Atlantic S and L."

"I'll have the money to you by the end of the day, at the latest first thing tomorrow."

"Good, Patrick. I'm always willing to lend a hand."

Patrick left the office wondering how in hell he was going to siphon fifty grand out of the company.

By the time he got to his office, his bowels were churning. Ann was standing outside his door, looking rabid.

"Well?" she demanded. "Irene told your mother that you were looking into another bank this morning. What happened?"

"I got the money from Atlantic Savings and Loan."

She seemed to explode with relief. He wished he could have made her suffer more.

"I'd like to hear the details," she said, pushing off his door.

"Give me ten minutes." He needed a shot of something first, to calm himself. He had pulled off a near-miracle. By nefarious means, of course, but a miracle nonetheless.

CHAPTER 13

When the cab dumped her off at West 85th and Broadway, Ann simply wanted to collapse in front of The Savannah. *Home.*

She had never learned the art of letting tension roll off her. By the end of the day she was exhausted from waging war against it, as it burrowed into her, dug into her muscles, and went deep into all the visceral parts of her.

She stepped inside the lobby, moving past the concierge, her back slumped, her heels slowly clicking on the floor. By the time she made it upstairs and into her apartment, her only thought was of a Glenlivet and water.

She uncurled her fingers and let her briefcase drop. She slid her shoes off and stepped over them, padding barefoot. On the way to the kitchen, she dropped pieces of clothing and various accessories on the furniture: her suit jacket falling on the back of the bulky, bronze Telegraph Hill sofa, her earrings landing on a knobby-legged, glass-topped table with brass rim.

In the kitchen, a jarring early-eighties flashback, she plopped ice cubes into a chunky, cut-crystal glass that had been a housewarming gift from Felicia, and made herself a drink. She unzipped her skirt, twitching her hips a little so it would slide to the floor. When it puddled at her feet, she bent and swiped it up, carrying that and the Scotch back to the sofa.

She snuggled in, her feet drawn up beneath her. When the telephone rang, Ann looked down at it, squinting to see the Caller ID.

Felicia. She picked up the telephone. "Everything's fine," she said without greeting. "He pulled a rabbit out of his hat." They rarely referred to Patrick by name. Although their trials broke Felicia's heart, and Patrick had more than a few extra strikes against him, her love for her children was unwavering.

The woman released a sigh of relief. "Sounds too good to be true. Tell me, Ann, are you still leaving for London in the morning?"

"Mid-afternoon."

"It's going to be grueling."

"I'm up for it." *Lie.* Her stomach was bothering her constantly now. The back of her neck had been a knot of pain for more than a week. The idea of facing down various European distributors and convincing them to take on Baby Talk N Glow brought the tension back to her skin in a flare of heat.

"Ann, do you believe in this doll?"

She hesitated only a fraction of a second. "I do."

"Then we're doing the right thing. We'll succeed with this."

Ann's gaze went to the window, where dusk was drawing closer to the glass. "Everything's going to be fine," she agreed. "Have some dinner and get some rest. What time will Cal be there?" Felicia had enjoyed a close, circumspect relationship with her doctor for too many years to count.

"Any moment now," Felicia replied promptly. "However, I hurt too much tonight to kick up my heels."

Ann's heart did a quick, sharp hop. *Don't tell me this. I don't want it to be true.* "He won't complain."

"May I do so?"

"Oh, Felicia…"

"Well, then. That's enough of that." The woman's voice went abruptly brusque. "What about the golf tournament?"

The Toy Industry Association sponsored it once a year. It was a horrible time to be away from the office, but the proceeds went to quality charities. Ann took a quick mouthful of Scotch. "I can't do it this year. I'll be somewhere in Paris by tee time." This was edging near shaky territory. Patrick would be the obvious choice to send in her stead, but she could not, *would* not, remind Felicia that the man wasn't likely to stay sober long enough to do any good.

"What about Jonathan?" Ann heard herself ask. The tempo of her pulse quickened and she sat up straighter on the sofa. There was a thought. It would keep him from following her to Europe.

"He's a worse golfer than you are," Felicia said. Then, after a pause, she added, "You've been spending some time with him lately."

That woman didn't miss a trick. "He seems interested in the doll."

"That's odd."

Ann tried to think of something to say, then she got a reprieve.

"Ah, there's the door. Dr. Everham is here."

"Francesca will get it. Don't push yourself."

"I will answer my own door for my guest, and I will be on my feet when I do so."

Ann suppressed a shudder. "All right, then," she said. "You take care." She half stood before she dropped down again, laughing hoarsely. The irony of it was that Felicia, with her cancer-wasted body, would enjoy a touch tonight, a caress, a warm smile. Yet she, in her prime at thirty-three, was alone.

"Bed," she said aloud. She'd skip dinner, along with the basement gym, though she'd planned one last visit before her trip tomorrow. She was just getting into the Steve Jobs biography autobiography. Ann decided that she'd snuggle down with the former-CEO of Apple and a nightcap.

She got to her feet and strode into the single bedroom. It was the one room she *had* finished. When she had first bought the co-op, she had intended to do the whole apartment in layers of ivory, eggshell, and pear. She'd stopped herself because she didn't like what that said about her psyche. But her bedroom ... this was white. It was where she needed the white in her life to be. Bedspread to bureau to makeup table. The only real color was in the paintings—a triptych inlaid in the wall opposite the window and a huge Picasso copy opposite her bed.

Ann unbuttoned her blouse and shrugged out of it. She yanked back the pristine eiderdown comforter, whaling her fist into all the stark, crisp pillows that were more than any one woman would ever need. Then she swore. "Damn him. Damn him all to hell."

She'd get it out of the way now, she decided.

She couldn't find her personal address book since it was not resting in the usual place—the kitchen junk drawer—so she grabbed her BlackBerry out of her briefcase and scrolled for his number.

A woman answered.

"Jonathan," Ann said. The single word squeezed through her clenched teeth.

"May I tell him who's calling?"

"No, you may not. He probably won't come to the phone if you do."

There was a beat of silence, then the woman's voice echoed back as she seemed to tuck the phone aside and speak away from it.

Ann thought she heard sheets rustle. He was in bed at a quarter past eight on a weekday night? The son of a bitch was having sex.

"What do you want, Ann?" he asked, his voice coming into the phone.

"How did you know it was me?"

"Most of my acquaintances have some semblance of phone etiquette."

"Then it's time you moved down in the world."

His chuckle was dark and somehow warm, but she wasn't sure if it was meant for her or his companion. As she sat alone on her iron bed big enough for two, Ann thought she despised him more at that moment than ever before. She sucked in breath. "You're going to do it again, aren't you?"

"Do what?"

"Appear at the airport tomorrow like … like some kind of ghost rattling chains."

"I never got into Dickens."

"Because you were too busy slapping around purple and black paint. Dickens has a lot going for him."

"Why are we talking about this?"

Because when it came to Jonathan, she had a strong stake in being combative. "I'm just calling to ascertain if I should hold a seat for you on the plane."

He let out a sigh. Maybe the woman was touching him.

"What?" Ann said. "What did you say?"

"I'll pick you up at 1:30. We might as well ride to the airport together."

Ann disconnected without answering.

He was going to Europe with her, then. She'd known it. It was going to be a very long week.

CHAPTER 14

Mark Twekesborough met them at Heathrow as dawn peaked over London's horizon. He was a rawboned man with a ruddy complexion, dark eyes, and a steady gaze. His sandy hair tended to be perpetually shaggy. Twekesborough owned one of the larger distributorships in the U.K., handed down to him by his father.

Ann had first met him at the Toy Fair in New York years ago. She'd been young, excited, bug-eyed at the commotion. Mark, a few years older, attending with his father, had pretended to be jaded. They'd hit it off immediately, and Ann had enjoyed a heart-tickling week of good food and interesting conversation—most of it revolving around the industry she was soaking up.

She smiled inwardly at the memory as he dragged her into his arms, hugged and kissed her. "Good to see you again, kiddo," he said.

Her last business trip had been five months ago. Over the years she had progressed through the company ranks, and she and Felicia had spent time traveling together, not only across North America, but to the Far East and here to Europe as well. All for business, with few if any moments allowed for personal relaxation.

'How is the old girl?" Mark asked reading her mind.

"She's sick," Jonathan said shortly.

Ann's gaze shot his way. Damn it, that information was for Felicia to disclose.

Jonathan's expression was deliberately bland. She took a steadying breath and glanced back at Twekesborough. "Forgive him," she said. "He doesn't travel well. Felicia is a little under the weather."

"I'm sorry to hear that. Nothing serious, I hope."

"We're all hoping." She left it at that and turned a palm in Jonathan's direction. "Allow me to introduce my cranky traveling companion."

"Actually, I believe we met years ago. You were still in knickers at the time." Twekesborough held a hand in Jonathan's direction.

"And you were trying to figure out how to shave." Jonathan shook his hand hard and fast.

Mark shrugged off his comment. "Shall we go?"

Ann nodded and began moving up the concourse. "It's incredibly thoughtful of you to meet us at such an hour."

"Why wouldn't I, for an old and dear friend?"

He fell into step beside her. Jonathan was behind them. Ann refused to look back.

Twekesborough dropped them at the Berkshire in the Baywater district. While the valet wrestled with their luggage, Ann leaned down to look back into the car at Mark. "Two o'clock, then?" Their meeting had been scheduled to allow her to catch some sleep first.

"I'll have you picked up."

"Thanks." Twekesborough pulled away from the curb and she entered the hotel. Jonathan was already at the registration desk. She stepped up next to him. "Would you like to explain the cause of your sudden, despicable mood?"

"No. He's got us sharing a room."

"*What?*" Ann felt her heart knock.

"Your friend reserved us a suite."

"I don't give a damn if it's a villa on the Med! Change it."

"I'm too tired." He took the key.

"How can you be tired? You were in bed by 8:30 last night."

"Ah, but I wasn't sleeping."

Ann felt her hand curl into a fist. She relaxed it deliberately.

"Maybe he figures we need to be in close proximity to plot our strategy," Jonathan said, turning away from the desk.

"Like you could."

"Now, now. Try to be nice."

Ann headed for the elevator. A suite meant that there would be at least one door she could close on him.

They went upstairs to find tea waiting for them. Ann took in her surroundings. Typical for London, there was not a generous amount of space. Even the windows were on the smallish side, partially hidden by half-open velour drapes which had gone out of style in North America years ago. Mauve wallpaper with a butterfly pattern covering most of the walls. A twin, gaudy blue couch sat facing an antique wood cabinet that contained the mini-bar and television. The bedrooms were located on either side; the washroom closest to the entranceway.

The lack of privacy made Ann shiver. How did she feel about being so close to Jonathan? Part of her was intrigued, but the other part wanted to put up as many barriers as possible.

The bellboy asked if he could order them breakfast. Ann told him they'd wait and sent him on his way.

When she turned from the door, Jonathan stood in the middle of the room, arms loose at his sides, working up a scowl. "What did you just do?" he demanded.

"What do you mean," she said, "I tipped him."

"No, damn it, before that. You sent him away ... and I'm hungry."

She went to the tea service, turned her back on him, and deliberately poured only one cup of the steaming brew. "Jonathan, please try and control yourself. This is going to be unpleasant enough without your vile mood. Don't worry, you'll be home with what's-her-name in a week."

"With who?"

"With whoever you weren't sleeping with last night."

"Carmen," he said, following her to the tea table.

"I wasn't fishing for a name."

"Why would you?"

"That's my point. I wasn't."

He picked up a scone, chewed, and grimaced. "This is disgusting."

She clapped her hands over her ears. "Enough! If I'm stuck with you in this room, the least you can do is be civil."

"It's not my fault you're stuck with me. Take it up with Mark. By the way, I thought the English were supposed to be reticent. Stuffy. My God, I thought he was going to swallow you whole when he hugged you."

Ann picked up a scone and chewed with sharp, strong bites. "I'm eminently huggable."

Jonathan nearly choked. "Like a porcupine."

"Screw you." She picked up her cup again and carried it to the door of the bedroom closest to her. "I'm going to take a nap. I'm exhausted."

"It's barely eleven our time."

"I'm used to turning in early. And when I go to bed, I sleep."

"Stop. You're going to break Twekesborough's heart."

Her heels nearly skidded beneath her as she broke stride and turned back to him. Then the air went out of her. "Please, let's not fight."

Jonathan wasn't sure exactly what was behind his bad temper. He only knew that something in his chest was knocking like a broken piston in an old sports car. Twekesborough had seriously gotten his dander up. "Could be a week is the maximum exposure to each other we can stand."

She lowered herself into a chair and looked at him, then quickly turned away. For a fleeting moment she imagined that she and Jonathan were not adversaries but lovers. And the room transformed in her mind's eye. What was gaudy was attractive, what was small was now quaint. And she wished with all her heart that she could live this dream one day, of having someone she could fully trust, someone she could be honest with, confide in. Of course, it could never be Jonathan. But the experience of sharing space with him, seeing her reaction to having him in such close proximity, told her that it might finally be time to allow a man into her life.

Ann blushed at the thought, immediately forced her mind to clear. "Something occurred to me while you were sleeping on the plane," she said.

"I wasn't sleeping because you wouldn't let me." His arm was probably going to bruise from the grip she'd laid on him when they'd hit turbulence.

"You were snoring."

"I don't snore. And what were you thinking about on the plane while I wasn't sleeping? Giving up on this doll business?"

"I can't do that. You know I can't."

There was something in her voice that made him pause. "What, then?"

"We have one thing in common, Jonathan, and *only* one thing. That's Felicia."

He found he had absolutely no argument with that, though he would have liked to have found one. "Okay."

"We should be working together to give her what she wants before she … well, before. If you continue to divert my attention with this petty behavior, I could make some crucial mistake that could unhinge everything."

"If this is your way of asking me to leave, don't bother. I'm not going to let you run around unchecked."

Ann sat back and closed her eyes. "I'm not asking you to leave. Follow me around if that's what you feel you have to do. But you've got to let me focus on the business at hand. For your mother's sake. We're the only two people who seem to really take her into consideration."

Jonathan found himself almost believing her, or was it that he *wanted* to believe her? He didn't respond and instead moved toward the far bedroom.

"We're on the same side here," she called after him.

He paused in the doorway and looked back. She was sprawled in the chair with her long legs stretched out, one ankle hooked over the other. She looked mussed, tired, vulnerable. Her skin was parchment, but just underneath her eyes was a bruised look. He thought again of that behemoth of a Brit crushing her in his arms.

"Yeah," he said finally. "That's what scares the hell out of me."

CHAPTER 15

At 2:00 that afternoon, with mixed feelings of trepidation and hope, Ann marched out of the hotel and into her meeting with Twekesborough.

She recalled a time when the toy industry was different in Europe. A handshake could solidify a deal and the deal was rarely broken. Courtesy and respect for relationships and history took precedence over the almighty dollar. Not any longer, unfortunately. Today, some of the worst elements of doing business in the United States were gradually seeping through here, and few of the old values continued to thrive.

Still, Ann had come to London first because of England's potential. With a population of slightly over sixty-three million, she figured the volume on the doll could run anywhere from seventy-five to a hundred thousand pieces. She wanted to get off to a good start.

Twekesborough's second welcome in the last number of hours remained effusive. He ushered Ann into his office in the same manner as he had greeted her at the airport—with a big, sloppy hug. Ann glanced warily at Jonathan, who glared at them, pouted, stalked to a chair and sat. Ann couldn't believe her eyes. What the hell was wrong with him? Suddenly she felt grateful to be sitting across from Twekesborough. He would make everything easy.

"Tea?" Mark offered.

"No, thanks," Ann said. "I had my fill at the hotel."

"None for me," Jonathan said, hooking an ankle over his knee. "Real men don't sip from china."

Ann stared at him. He was at it again.

Twekesborough dragged up a smile, then looked at Jonathan and fought back a little. "You know, you used to be good company."

"I still am. In my element."

"As I remember, you were never enthralled with the business."

"Let's just say it currently has my attention."

"Well, then." He turned back to Ann. "Show me what all the excitement is about."

Ann placed the box she was carrying in her lap. She removed the doll and lifted her above her head. Baby Talk N Glow giggled.

"Clever." Mark said, a grin on his face.

Ann moved around to the other side of Twekesborough's desk and stood next to him. As if cradling a real baby, she gingerly laid the doll down on the teak surface. When Baby Talk N Glow left her arms, she cried. Then Ann tickled her stomach and the doll laughed. She touched her cheek and Baby Talk N Glow blushed. Ann tried to contain the evident pleasure she felt at the doll's performance.

"Whoa," Twekesborough said. "Impressive."

"Put your hand on her chest, her heart beats. And there are no discernable wires. It's all controlled by a computer chip, powered by a miniature nickel cadmium battery that will last five years." That, she thought, was the technology that set the doll apart.

Twekesborough reached for Baby Talk N Glow. He touched her nose.

"That's my nose," the doll said, and Twekesborough jumped a little in surprise. He gripped her foot.

"That's my foot," she said.

He tweaked one of her toes.

"That's my toe."

"Kids will love this." He was practically gushing.

"I know." Ann sat down again, pleased. She didn't look at Jonathan but could feel him leaning forward in his own seat.

"Of course, the voice would have to be changed for us, to get a British accent," Mark said. "We can do the digital master here and forward it to Hong Kong." He paused. "And how much will this little baby cost me?"

Ann took a breath before forging ahead. "Ten dollars and fifty cents." They both knew that the doll would ship directly from China to England, and that her company's profit was included in the price.

Twekesborough fumbled with the doll as though she had bitten him. "Lord, Annie. That's high."

"*Annie?*" Jonathan repeated.

Ann ignored his comment and focused on Twekesborough. "Retail in the States is going to be ten dollars higher than what you would normally pay for this type of doll," she said. "Twenty-nine ninety-nine."

"Oh? And how are your American customers reacting to that?"

"I'm still about two weeks away from approaching them."

"What if they won't go for the price?"

"Then I'll cancel the project, and you'll be the first to know."

Jonathan made an odd sound in his throat. Ann's brow furrowed. Her tension was starting to go sub-dural now. Unconsciously, she rubbed her neck.

"How many pieces would you like me to commit to?" Twekesborough asked.

She needed a strong commitment from England; there was simply no getting around it. "A hundred thousand."

"Bloody hell!" Mark exploded.

"Not that infatuated with her, are you?" Jonathan asked, inclining his head to let it be known he was talking about Ann, not the doll. Ann gasped at his rudeness, but Twekesborough only laughed.

"Actually, I am," he replied. "And I know what she's capable of." He paused. "All right, Annie. I'm in."

Ann gave him her warmest smile.

Twekesborough rose and reached for her hand. Ann stood as well and gave it to him. Rather than shake it, he took it and pressed it to his lips. "Please let me know how it goes." He said. "I think she's a winner."

"Mark, thank you for your confidence. It means the world to me. And of course, I'll keep you posted."

"Do you have time for an early dinner?"

"Normally that would be lovely, but I think we'd better grab something at the airport." She stopped his protest before he could voice it. "These trips are so grueling, Mark. I appreciate the offer, but I don't want to rush anymore than I have to.

He seemed genuinely disappointed. "I'll have my car drop you off, then."

"Wonderful. Thanks."

Ann turned from the desk and found Jonathan was already gone. By the time she got downstairs and outside, he was in the car. She slid onto the rear seat beside him.

"Let's go, *Annie*," he said.

Ann's jaw was tight enough to hurt. "Your behavior was an outrage."

"Yeah. Well, his fawning was pretty nauseating."

"*Fawning?*"

He caught her hand and kissed it hard. "Fawning," he defined.

Ann snatched her hand back. "Stop it."

"What kind of personal relationship do the two of you have?" he asked.

Ann fumed. "Explain personal."

"Did you sleep with him?"

She had to choke back her anger. This was something she always had to fight her way around. "No."

"Well, you do *something* to him. He's all ga-ga over you."

"And how is that any of your business?"

"I'm just curious."

"Did you ever think I might not have gotten the commitment we needed if I'd looked more like you … and displayed your disposition?"

He shot her a wry look. "That doll is pretty impressive. I didn't realize she could do all that."

"Felicia's no fool. The doll is amazing and Felicia is crazy about her. She sees her potential."

"Will you really scrap the project if you meet with resistance on the price in the States?"

"Of course not."

"Okay," he said finally. "Then let's make sure this doll flies for my mother."

Ann hesitated, then nodded. She felt some of the tension slide off her skin. A truce had been called. She hoped it could last for more than one afternoon.

CHAPTER 16

Octber in Madrid dripped with sunshine, snug beneath a cloudless sky that was a quintessential blue. This time they were met at the airport by Seve Marques.

In direct contrast to Twekesborough, there was nothing endearing about Marques. Ann watched him approach, feeling herself stiffen. He was thin and sharp-edged, with a pencil-slash of a mustache. His hair was full and perfectly black despite the fact that Ann knew he had at least twenty-five years on her.

He stepped between her and Jonathan when they passed though the gate, shutting Jonathan out as insignificant to the equation. He might well be, Ann thought, but it was still disrespectful. "Welcome. Your trip was good?" Marques caught her hand and kept holding it. They took four, five, six steps into the concourse before Ann managed to slide her fingers free.

"Madrid is our third destination in as many days," she answered. "You know how it is."

"Ah, you should relax then before we talk business. Let me take you to lunch."

Ann thought of wine at mid-day, of four courses and paella. Her stomach lurched at the thought. She was exhausted, but she knew Spain was going to be tough. There was no sense antagonizing

Marques by refusing his offer. "Wonderful," she murmured.

They piled into a small black sedan with seats as soft as butter. Ann wanted to draw her feet up beneath her, snuggle in, but she and both men were cupped together like triplets in a womb, and there wasn't enough space. Marques sat between her and Jonathan. He shifted his weight until his hip slid closer to hers.

"Jonathan, how are you doing over there?" Ann asked to forestall any cute or caustic comment he might have. His behavior with Twekesborough was still fresh in her mind.

"Real peachy, *cara mia.*"

"Any particular reason you're speaking Italian in Spain?" she asked.

"We're in Spain? When did we get here?" he responded.

Ann smiled. She knew what he was feeling. The three days they'd spent in Europe felt like twice that amount. She eased her weight against the door, trying to escape the press of Marques's body. The car inched up in front of a restaurant that offered *al fresco* dining. Wrought iron tables under a red canopy. Flower boxes spilled leaves and petals over a barrier rail.

"I'm sorry—what?" Ann glanced at Marques. He had said something to her while they were being seated.

"May I see the doll?" he repeated. "Perhaps I am being premature. We should wait until after we dine. But you've piqued my curiosity." His hand moved to her thigh to coax her.

Ann crossed her legs the other way to avoid his touch. She reached for the box she'd placed under her chair.

"You're a skittish American lady." His voice was an undertone, meant only for her ears.

She wanted his business. Desperately. But her thigh wasn't part of the deal. Ann crossed her legs again when his hand came back.

She was shaking a little. She opened her mouth, but no words came out. She was too tired to deal with this sort of thing right now.

Jonathan reached across and took the doll off her hands. "She's a barracuda," he said.

Marques shifted in his chair, more or less acknowledging him for the first time. "Your baby doll?"

"No. The American lady."

"Ah." Marques's grin showed teeth. "She is *your* lady?"

"Do I look suicidal? But you're not buying her, right? You want *this* little girl." Jonathan held up the doll.

"Yes, of course."

He went through Baby Talk N Glow's routine, going so far as to add a few of his own improvisations.

He'd picked it up well, Ann thought. In spite of herself, she was almost grateful to Jonathan for taking over, and she smiled slightly at the sight of him, the macho artist, with a doll in his hands.

When Marques asked about the doll's battery and location, Ann found Jonathan's foot under the table and pressed down hard to warn him not to answer. To her astonishment, she felt him kick her. She winced with pain, but before she could field the question herself, he answered.

"It's a secret." Jonathan reached and took the doll back from Marques' hands. "It's tucked up so neat and tidy, even I don't know where it is."

"And who are you?" It finally occurred to Marques to ask.

"A genuine, bona fide Morhardt."

Marques looked to Ann doubtfully. "So who knows where the battery is?"

She suddenly felt playful. "I do," she said, "and if you commit to a hundred thousand pieces, I promise to tell you." Ann knew where Marques was going with this.

"One hundred thousand pieces? For that amount, I would need a sample. I have associates. I cannot make such a decision myself."

"Sorry. No sample," she said, knocking his hand off her knee again. He looked startled, then frowned.

The waiter came for their order. For the next thirty minutes, Ann sipped wine and picked at the rich paella which, under different circumstances, she would have enjoyed immensely. She declined desert and when the meal was over, she stood to stretch and found she was suddenly woozy. She started towards the ladies' room when she felt a hand on her elbow and tried to jerk it away. The hand held fast.

It was Jonathan next to her, steadying her. "You okay?" he whispered.

"Just peachy, *cara mia*."

He noted the look in her eyes. "You're buzzed," he said. Then he added, "Let's get out of here. We're wasting our time."

Ann shook her head. "We've got Lothario's car—which, I might add, contains our luggage. And we have to preserve appearances with him for the next time around. There's a future beyond this doll, Jonathan."

"Is there?"

She thought about it for a fraction of a second. "Well, actually, maybe not."

"Okay then. Lothario can kiss my ass."

He kept her elbow and steered her toward the street. He found a cab and pushed her inside, then he went back to get their luggage from Marques's driver. Marques was still in the restaurant, taking care of the bill.

"Where are we going?" he asked Ann when he got in the cab.

"Damned if I know," she muttered. "Old Seve made our hotel arrangements."

She leaned into him a little when the cab turned a corner. Jonathan caught her shoulder and shoved her upright. "Okay. I know Madrid pretty well."

That surprised her. "You do?"

"Of course. What do you think? I've never traveled before? I was here last spring. A group of artist friends decided it was time to stir the muse in all of us." He turned to the driver. "To the Melia, *por favor.*"

Ann settled back in her seat, rubbed her forehead and stared straight ahead. "We've got a great product. This stop shouldn't have gone so badly."

"You've got Markie-Poo in London wrapped around your finger."

"And I just lost Spain." She thought about it. "No, I didn't. Marques never intended to give us a commitment."

"Is that why you wouldn't let him have a sample?"

"If I had, within ten weeks every store shelf in Spain would have been stocked with a Baby Talk N Glow replica. They're famous for their knock-offs. He was trying to angle something out of me that he could copy."

"Or you bailed," he said.

"No, I didn't. I wanted to stay. Except for the fact that he was groping me."

Jonathan felt something hard prod him in the chest. "Where?"

"In the restaurant. Under the table."

"No, I meant which part of your … anatomy."

She cut him another look. "This interests you for some reason?"

"Yeah."

"My leg."

"And you let him?"

She elbowed him lightly in the ribs.

"This is bad, right?" he asked finally. "Losing Spain."

"It's bad."

The car stopped in front of their hotel, but he didn't open the door. "What are you going to tell Felicia?"

She never hesitated. "Not a word."

"You're going to lie to her about it?"

"Of course not. I'm going to evade her."

"Can you do that?"

"Until I have some good news to tell her, yes."

Her skin seemed stretched over her cheekbones and wore an almost bluish cast. Then her eyes sparked again with that familiar grit. "Are you going to sit here staring at me all day or can we go inside?" she snapped.

There, he thought, was the Ann he knew. "Where are we off to tomorrow?"

"It's a secret," she teased. "You'll have to wait and see."

"I think I'm going to pour more liquor into you tonight and get your secrets out onto the table."

"After I sleep. I need a second wind, then maybe I'll dance on a few tables for you."

She pushed on her door and got out of the car. Jonathan retrieved their luggage. He kept his gaze slanted her way as she strode into the lobby. Her legs were steady enough but there was definitely something off in the set of her shoulders. It was the kind of detail his painter's eye would catch. The arrogance was gone, he thought.

She was scared, he realized. What had she said? *Spain shouldn't have gone this badly?*

Yeah, he thought, he'd ply her with liquor and dig into her for details. But was that all he really wanted? Details of their itinerary? An explanation of why she was so worried? Or was he hiding the truth of his true motives, even from himself?

CHAPTER 17

Ann was halfway across The Melia's mammoth entranceway when she heard her name being called. She couldn't place the voice so she looked around. She spotted Sidney Greenspan, tall and corpulent, hurrying toward her from a bar off the hotel lobby. In Madrid. In the same hotel Jonathan had chosen. Ann felt her chances at sleep sliding through her fingers like sand.

Greenspan took her hand in his and gave it a vigorous pump. "What in the world are you doing in Spain?"

He knew about Baby Talk N Glow, she thought. He had been at the coming-out party Felicia had thrown for the doll. "We've been to see Seve Marques."

"How did it go?"

"It went."

"I heard you couldn't get financing," he said.

Her heart kicked. How had word of *that* gotten out? "A nasty rumor, nothing more."

"You did get a bank, then?"

"Of course, we did."

"And Marques was enthusiastic?"

"Exactly the reaction I expected," she said without lying. The last thing she needed was for rumors of this trip to get back to the States before she did.

"We just arrived," Greenspan said. "We're making a little vacation of it."

Ann looked towards the bar and saw his wife's face peering out at them through a trellis-like partition. She was as pretty as ever, with her abundance of red hair partly shadowing her overly made-up face.

The woman wiggled her fingers at her and she gave a wave back. God, she's young, Ann thought, not for the first time.

Jonathan stepped up to shake Greenspan's hand. "Good to see you, Sidney."

"You two are here together?" Greenspan asked, sounding surprised.

"We're just one big happy family," Jonathan offered, placing a possessive hand on Ann's shoulder.

Now what the hell was he up to? Ann half turned to him. "Have you lost your mind?" she breathed in an undertone.

"I'm just eccentric," he murmured back.

Greenspan's mouth gaped. "I didn't realize you two were … close."

"We're not," Ann said. "Jonathan is interested in our new doll, so he made this trip with me."

"Ah—I see." He paused. "Have you both eaten? Charlie and I were just about to grab a bite in the bar. Why don't you join us?"

Ann heard her stomach grumble. She pressed a hand there, embarrassed. "Maybe a drink," she said.

Jonathan made a sound in his throat. But to his credit, she thought, he swallowed whatever he'd been about to say. She pivoted to face him. "I've gotten my second wind," she whispered.

"You're whacked." He dropped his voice as well so Greenspan wouldn't overhear. "And you don't need one more guy slobbering over you."

"Sidney doesn't slobber," she said. "He's married."

"Sure, that'll stop him. Let me make our excuses."

Something caught in her chest. It was the second—maybe even the third—time in as many days that he had tried to step in to save her. "I wish I had a choice, Jonathan, but I don't. I have to show strength. If I slink out of here now with my tail between my legs, word of it will spread."

She turned back to Greenspan. "We've got a little while," she said. "I'd like to say hello to Charlie."

"And I'll take care of checking us in," Jonathan offered.

She flicked a glance back at him. "Thanks. What should I order for you?"

"I'll take a Sierra, if they have one."

She followed Greenspan into the bar and endured a momentary hug from Charlie. The younger woman was overripe with perfume and she didn't seem to want to let Ann go.

Ann sat. "Is any part of your trip business?" she asked. "Or is it strictly a vacation?"

"A little of both," Greenspan answered. "I'll move on next week and take care of business, while Charlie will head home."

A waitress approached. Ann ordered a Sierra and her usual.

Sidney began pumping her for information. He was usually the nosy type but something felt strange here, listening to what was starting to sound like an inquisition. She ignored him for the most part and engaged Charlie in conversation instead, asking if this was her first trip to Spain.

"Me?" The younger woman laughed. "Why, no, darling." She placed a hand on her husband's arm. "Sidney enjoys taking me practically everywhere. Isn't that right, honey?"

Sidney tried to steer the conversation back to where he obviously wanted it to go, just as Jonathan showed up.

"What did I miss?" he asked, pulling a chair out beside Ann. She had never been so glad to see him.

He caught her expression and winked. Then he grinned at the

beer that was waiting for him. "I love Madrid," he said. He took a long sip, then turned to Ann. "Want to dance?"

She looked up at him, startled. "Are you serious?"

He nodded. "Table-top, or will the floor do?"

"I'd prefer the floor."

"Glad to hear it. Let's go see if they know any good funeral dirges."

"I don't understand," Sidney said.

"You're not meant to," Jonathan answered. He stood and Ann let him take her hand. He helped her to her feet and she followed him onto the tiny dance floor.

Whatever the musicians were playing sounded moody and sweet. Ann had no idea what the Spanish words meant, but to her ears it felt like heartache and love. Jonathan's hand found her waist. She wondered what exactly was going on, but she let her body flow into his. A not entirely unpleasant heat seemed to radiate between them.

She really despised him for making her feel so good, for the sensation in the pit of her stomach that made her want to settle in and stay there, rather than pull away.

"Thanks," she said, interpreting his gesture. "I couldn't bear Greenspan's company for another minute."

"Me neither, *cara mia*."

She felt a laugh tickle her throat. "When did you get to be so nice?"

"Along about your fourth glass of wine. Or maybe it was the first Glenlivet."

"So it'll pass by morning?"

"Let's hope so."

Ann laughed. Then she groaned and rested her forehead against his shoulder. "God, I'm tired."

"We'll be home before you know it, and this'll all be a memory."

She thought she felt his hand stroking between her shoulder

blades. She had *definitely* had too much to drink. "No, it won't," she said. "We've got to do the rounds of the American retailers next." *We?* Had she actually said *we?*

"When does this happen?"

"Week after next."

"You've got to be kidding."

"You don't have to go."

"Wouldn't miss it for the world." He moved his other arm to her waist and coaxed her even closer. "Ann?"

"Hmm?"

"How do you feel about dancing with Mr. Greenspan?"

"Why?"

"He's heading this way with a cut-in look on his face."

"Are your Sir Lancelot instincts still in place?"

"They're the best part of me."

She snorted. "Prove it."

He caught his foot around her ankle and tripped her.

She almost went down. All that saved her was his arms around her waist. Ann tightened her grip around his neck long enough to grab back her equilibrium, then she let go and punched him. "What ... was that?" She was so angry she was sputtering.

"Are you hurt?"

"I—"

"Can you dance?"

She felt a hand on her shoulder from behind. "What?" she snarled, turning about.

Greenspan took a startled step back. "Ann, what happened? Are you all right?"

"Of course, she's not," Jonathan said. "Look at her. She can hardly stand."

Ann listed quickly in his direction.

"I'm going to take her upstairs so she can get off her feet."

Ann nodded, not trusting herself to speak.

Greenspan made sympathetic clucking sounds. When they returned to the table, Charlie looked like she could cry. Was it out of sympathy for Ann's injury or because she would be left alone with her husband?

"Don't forget to limp," Jonathan whispered as they left the bar.

"I don't have to fake it." She gave him another shot in the arm for good measure.

"Hey, I saved you from having to dance with those sweaty paws of his. Where's your gratitude?"

She gave a little shudder at the thought of Greenspan's hands on her. They stepped off the elevator on their floor. "You know, he's going to tell everyone in New York that we're having an affair."

"Well, we're not. Hold up there." He caught her elbow and pulled her to a stop. "This is your room."

"If word gets back to Carmen, you could be in trouble."

"You have a hell of a memory for names."

She grabbed the key from his hand and opened the door. She thought of saying something profound but found herself at a sudden loss for words. "Good night," she said abruptly. And she stepped inside her room, quickly closed the door behind her.

CHAPTER 18

"I am sorry, *monsieur, madame,* the plane has had mechanical difficulties in New York. You are rescheduled for tomorrow morning. We have arranged..."

Ann blocked out the rest of the words. This couldn't be happening. Not after the kind of week they had had. She looked at Jonathan, then back at the airline clerk. She wanted to scream, at the very least throw something at somebody.

They had left Spain without a commitment for Baby Talk N Glow, which had not been a surprise, but disappointing, nonetheless. And she could almost accept their Italian distributor's commitment of forty thousand pieces, pre-warned as she was that the doll's skin coloring might be too light to afford a huge success in his market. But Germany's forecast of one hundred and twenty thousand reduced to eighty rubbed her raw. And here on their last stop, in France, Ann had been nearly driven to distraction. Charles La Croix, who had always been a strong ally of Hart Toy, had spent their entire meeting decrying the state of the toy industry, and the doll segment in particular. Ann had counted on a commitment of one hundred thousand pieces—the French population was almost as large as that of the U.K., with a potential toy volume to match— yet all they could squeak out was a mere fifty thousand.

"Ann—what do you think?" Jonathan was asking her.

"Huh?" She tried to refocus.

"Oh, never mind." He turned back to the clerk and took something from him, then proceeded to lead her away.

"What was that all about?" Ann asked, shrugging off the hand that was gripping her elbow.

"What was what about?"

"What did the clerk just give you?"

He took note of her tone, the wiped look on her face, and he knew it was time to take charge. Much of their trip had been eye-opening for him. The business of toys had paralleled the makeup of too many other industries in the twenty-first century. Consolidation and staff reductions, greed and unethical behavior, had stripped it of its humanity and decency. But what had really surprised him was the numbing risk involved. His respect for his mother—a true survivor—and for Ann, was enhanced. The woman was suffering. Something inside him wanted to console her, to tell her none of this was her fault, and to somehow make her pain go away.

"Jonathan—where are you taking us?"

She looked strung out and her voice was shrill. He knew he was doing the right thing. She would have to go along with it. He would give her no choice.

"Jonathan—"

"Trust me," he said and continued to guide their luggage trolley through the departure level of the airport, outside, and into the queue for a cab.

They were no sooner strapped into the back seat of the taxi when he instructed the driver: *"L'hôtel Le Régent, s'il vous plait. La rue Dauphine. C'est près du Boulevard Saint Germain des Prés."*

Ann sat up with a start. "What the hell! You haven't lost your French?"

He smiled. "And why are you surprised?"

"I ... never thought. After all this time. I—"

"Just relax. You are in good hands, *Fraulein*."

"*Fraulein*? Oh dear God. Jonathan, where are we going?"

Jonathan turned to the driver. "*A peu près combien de temps vas t'il prendre pour se rendre à l'hôtel?*"

"*Environ quarante cinq minutes, monsieur,*" the driver replied.

Ann punched Jonathan's arm. "Now you're showing off."

His smile grew. "Just wanted to prove I know the difference between German and French."

"And where are you taking me, exactly."

"This is what United Airlines expects us to use tonight." He waved a hotel voucher in her face. "Check in at three p.m. at a hotel convenient to the airport. I refuse to be stranded in Paris in some dumpy, fleabag hole-in-the-wall."

Ann instinctively looked at her watch. It was still early, not quite nine in the morning. "But doesn't the voucher mean our rooms would be comped?"

"*Absolument, ma chère.*"

She was hardly proficient in French, but that much she understood. "I am not going to waste money by staying somewhere else," she said.

He took her hand in his. "Sometimes you do what you've got to do. Now—would you just relax. We've been on the go for the better part of a week. I've seen what pressure can do to people, and I see what it's doing to you. Relax and enjoy. I am going to show you the Paris you have never seen before. Not with the schedule you keep. Today and tonight is on me, so no more complaints."

"Complaints?" she said, somehow already feeling restraints being lifted. "I never complain."

"No, how silly of me. The great Ann never complains."

"But I have a question for you."

"Okay. Shoot. But this is the last one you're allowed."

"If this day is going to be on you then why splurge on a fancy hotel?"

He shrugged. "Who said it was fancy?"

"Please, I know your expensive taste."

"For your information, we are headed towards an area favored by writers, actors and musicians. It is also home to the oldest church in Paris. The tour will commence later. No more talking. Feast your eyes."

Ann obeyed, forcing further protest from her lips. And by not talking, or even thinking for that matter, she was able to do what she had never done before. During all her business trips with Felicia, to so many varied and far-off countries, she had never truly gotten away. There was never the time, the money, nor the inclination. Seated now in the back of the taxi she willed her mind to pretend, to act like a person on vacation, a person without a care in the world.

After checking out of the Hilton Hotel in Paris this morning, it had never occurred to her that she would be returning so soon to the one city in the world she preferred above all others. She opened her eyes and gazed out the window at the countryside whizzing past. All those quaint towns and villages, with their oh-so-many church steeples. She could almost smell the baguette and cheese she suddenly craved.

By the time the cab wended its way through the intricate, narrow streets of *St-Germain-des-Prés*, she was sitting wide-eyed and filled with wonder. This was the Paris steeped in tradition, with block after block of crowded cafés and hip boutiques. The architecture of a bygone era appealed to her most, and she imagined herself remaining here for weeks and months, not just hours.

"Is this where you painted?" she asked Jonathan.

"Uh-uh. Most of my time was spent in Montmartre," he said. "Where else? But this area of Paris is where I hung out."

When they finally pulled up to a stop at their hotel, Ann cried out with pleasure. Le Régent was nothing she expected. Un-Americanized, unpretentious, small and unassuming, she loved it at first sight. For once in her life she did nothing. She stood by as Jonathan tipped the cab driver, stepped up to the tiny check-in counter to register them, then attempted to squeeze not only their luggage but the two of them into an elevator built for one.

She continued to hold her tongue as he fought first with one bag, then the other, cursing aloud in frustration, banging the narrow carriage walls, until he finally gave up in despair.

"May I ask you something?" she said.

"No, you may not." He ignored her and continued his efforts.

Finally, she picked up her bag that was not very heavy to begin with, slipped her room key out of his hand, and turned towards the stairwell.

"Hey—where you going?"

"To my room. Do you mind?" She did not look back.

"I'll meet you in the lobby in ten minutes," he called after her.

She began to mount the stairs, only to find that they were so narrow, by the time she reached her destination on the third floor, she was struggling a bit herself. She turned the key in the door and immediately broke into hysterical laughter. Seldom in all her travels had she been faced with such a small room. The walls were painted a flowery pink. The single bed looked like it barely fit. The dresser opposite only had a few shelves, no drawers. And the bathroom, which she had to squeeze into, had a bath with a self-adjusting shower head but nothing to hold it in place and no shower curtain to keep the water from running onto the floor.

Yet, she loved it, realized she wouldn't change it for the world. The entire week had been filled with Hilton hotels or their ilk. It was time to be brought back to reality.

When Jonathan met her in the lobby she was ready to get out and see the city.

He took her by the hand and led her to the Metro. One glance at the huge map on the wall by the ticket booth and he knew exactly which train to take. Fifteen minutes later they arrived at their destination. They rode the escalator to street level and the warm sunshine of a cloudless day washed over them. There was a bit of a breeze in the air but the temperature, Ann guessed, was in the high sixties. As they started on their way, she could see the *Arc de Triomphe*. The closer they got, the more majestic it appeared. "Built in honor of Napoleon's most celebrated victory," Jonathan explained once they stood across from it.

"Wonderful." Ann paused. "But how do we actually get there?"

Jonathan laughed, although he could see her conundrum. There were two ways to cross the always bustling traffic circle— one was to follow most of the other pedestrians and use the underground passageway—the other was to chance injury to life and limb and dodge the traffic. He chose the latter, taking hold of Ann's hand and guiding her in-between the mad rush of vehicles.

"Watch out," he warned with some amusement in his voice. "Easy does it…"

Somehow, Ann found herself being led across the precarious thoroughfare, too nervous to voice a complaint.

They paused at the entrance to the *Arc* to catch their breath. When Ann tried to speak, Jonathan hushed her. "Shh," he said and pointed downwards.

"Why are you whispering?"

"We don't want to disturb him."

"Who?"

"Victor Hugo. He's been lying in state down there since the late 1800s."

She ignored him and moved away.

"Hey," he called after her. "The guy needs his rest."

She laughed despite herself.

"But let me tell you something else," Jonathan quickly added.

She turned towards him again. "You're just a font of knowledge, aren't you?"

"Better believe it. But this story might even appeal to the hard-hearted you."

She flinched.

He took her hand and shook it playfully. "Relax. I'm only kidding. The *Arc de Triomphe* was conceived in 1805 but took some thirty-one years before its completion. However, Napoleon was getting married for the second time and he couldn't wait, so he did what any red-blooded Frenchman would do—he had the architect build a temporary replica on this very site, so that he and his bride-to-be could pass beneath it on the way to their wedding at the *Louvre*." He paused. "Nice story?"

Ann shrugged. "Yeah. But I'll bet you made it up."

"No, I didn't. You can ask anyone. Here—" He made to stop a passerby, a middle-aged gentleman wearing a black, wool beret.

"Jonathan!" She pulled him back, embarrassed. "I believe you, okay? You don't have to do that."

He hesitated, then motioned towards the top of the Arc. "Elevator or stairs?"

"Stairs," she told him. The climb didn't appear very steep and the exercise would do her good.

At the top they strolled to each observation post and admired the view. Jonathan pointed out the sprawling thoroughfares: *L'Avenue de la Grande-Armée* leading toward *La Défense, le Bois de Bologne* and *les Grand et Petit Palais*.

Before Ann knew it—and as Jonathan promised—they were soon strolling side by side along the *Champs-Elysées*, passing stores of the famous designers, from Chanel to Louis Vuitton, from Yves St Laurent to Christian Dior.

They stopped for lunch at one of the smaller restaurants along the magnificent boulevard and each had a *croque monsieur* with a Perrier. Then Jonathan continued his history lesson with explanations of everything from Napoleon's rise to power to the zealous, French royalty and their notorious behavior.

Ann found herself completely enchanted by this side of Jonathan, finding him somewhat magnanimous and engaging.

They continued to walk until it was mid-afternoon. Jonathan led them into a hotel bar where he ordered two glasses of Dom Perignon. Halfway through her drink, Ann began to hear a little voice hissing a warning in her ear: to remain on guard, to not be gullible.

The voice followed her throughout the remainder of the day. She ignored it as best she could and time passed quickly. Ann delighted in a stroll along the *Seine* with its artist easels and book stalls, and the ride on the *bateau mouche*, which gave her a far different view of Paris by water. Then her second subway ride—or was it the third? Disembarking practically next door to the *Tour Eiffel*. Joining hundreds of tourists in line for one of the elevators. Riding to the top of the steel masterpiece and realizing that the view from the *Arc de Triomphe* was nothing compared with this.

The city spread out before her in all its color and grandeur. The view of the *Seine* from here reminded her of a necklace of diamonds, while the crowds filling the cobblestone streets reminded her of a colony of ants. She was quickly overwhelmed with the romance of the city, the ancient history etched into its very fiber.

"Look—" Jonathan pointed north, "—that's where we came from, and if you look east," He pointed again, "you can see our hotel."

"Honest?" Ann looked, but they were so high up and so far away she couldn't be sure of anything.

"Certainement, madame," he said.

She smiled at his French, and found delight in his attempts to please her.

"Imagine this structure," he told her, "built around 1889. It was meant to attract people to the Universal Exhibition being held in Paris that year, and was to be dismantled afterwards. But shrewd minds prevailed and here it still sits. Crazy things have been attempted, however, from people climbing it, girder by iron girder, to men parachuting from it, to one poor soul in the early 1900s who tried to fly from it, using a cape for wings, and plunging to his death in front of a horrified crowd."

Ann glanced at him. "And you know all this, how?"

"Hey—I used to live here. Remember? The history of the city's landmarks always intrigued me." He looked at his watch. "Uh-oh. I hope you've seen enough. It's time to go."

Soon they were in another subway, with Jonathan anxiously looking at his watch for the fifth or sixth time, until Ann finally had to point out to him that if the order of the day was relaxation, he seemed awfully fixated on a predetermined schedule.

Instead of a reply she was met by a silent shrug.

Their next stop was the *Louvre*, but it was getting late, almost closing time. They hurriedly purchased their tickets and walked inside. Jonathan started off in a slow jog, with a tired Ann following closely behind.

Finally, he paused, instructed her to close her eyes and not open them until told to do so. She protested that she was too old for this kind of thing, but went along with him, allowing herself to be guided forward.

"Okay," he said in a hush. "Now open."

When she did, she drew in her breath. The Mona Lisa was so small it took her a moment to realize that this truly was the real thing and not an imitation. Even Jonathan's exultations about the colors, the brush strokes, the genius of the piece, did little to assuage her temporary disappointment. But the longer she examined it the more she came to appreciate it.

"Da Vinci painted this around 1504," Jonathan said. "He'd probably turn over in his grave if he knew of all of the fuss caused by the book, *The Da Vinci Code*."

One of the security guards approached and reminded them that the museum was closing. Ann reluctantly lowered her gaze from the painting. She was tempted to salute or at least wave, wanting to somehow advise the lady that she would not be soon forgotten.

Nightfall was upon them, and while Ann would have been satisfied to return to their hotel, she quickly realized that Jonathan had further plans. Into a taxi this time, not the Metro, and back to the heart of *St-Germain-des-Prés*.

Le Fermette Marbeuf was established in 1895, Ann read in the menu. The stain-glass mural for which restaurant was famous for was commissioned at the time of its opening. Every table, although small, was adorned with embroidered rose tablecloths and matching linen napkins. The ambience, helped by the glowing candlelight and mostly mixed couples speaking in hushed tones, was seductive in its intimacy.

Jonathan looked at Ann and broke into a grin, reminding her of how much he resembled a little boy. "What?" she asked.

"You," he said.

"What about me?"

"Do you realize you haven't cursed or complained once today?"

"Haven't I?"

"Not once."

"And this means?"

"That you had a good time."

She shrugged. "Well, maybe I did."

"This is the kind of Ann I think I'd like to get to know."

"And you," she countered. "No more Mr. Belligerent. Tell me, Jonathan, which is the real you?

"Which do you prefer?"

Despite her intentions, she blushed. She would never admit it, but the Jonathan of today was someone she could really like.

"Ann?"

She forced her smile and changed the subject. "I'll tell you what I'm curious about. The Jonathan who speaks French like a trouper but won't admit to dating anyone here, in Paris."

"That's what's on your mind?"

"You betcha, *Mon-sewer!*"

The waiter interrupted with the wine—a *Chateauneuf du Pape* dating back fifteen years. Once it was poured, Jonathan recounted for Ann how his stay in Paris was so hectic he seldom had time to socialize.

"You mean, painting is all you ever did?" Ann asked. "No dating?"

"Well, I did go out from time to time," he finally confessed.

"Uh-huh. Tell me more."

Their appetizers arrived: *fois gras* for her, *escargots* for him. The waiter no sooner left when Jonathan burst into laughter.

"What's so funny?" Ann asked.

He pointed at the sizzling plate in front of him. "A friend of mine used to call these tiny pieces of Michelin tires in butter sauce."

She smiled. "Did it ever get serious with one of your dates, by the way?"

"Eat your appetizer, Ann," Jonathan said, which was enough of an answer for her.

They tended to their food, both finding it delicious. The waiter cleared their plates and poured more wine. Further conversation was interrupted by the serving of their main course, which was *entrecôte de boeuf.* Ann was halfway through her meal when a couple near to them caught her eye. The man seemed in his early forties, the woman in her mid to late thirties. She wasn't particularly pretty, but she was smartly dressed, and the glittering diamond necklace was definitely not fake. Ann suddenly felt self-conscious in the plain sweater and skirt she wore. There had been no discussion of dining out, and she wasn't the only patron simply attired, yet she felt out of place. She glanced back at the couple, caught them in a kiss, and turned away.

She took in Jonathan seated across from her, and for a fleeting moment imagined his lips on hers. Relishing the sensation, she let down her guard, and the warning voice she experienced earlier in the day came back, this time with force. She knew at once why this day had not been such a good idea. Yes, it had been wonderful, one of the best of her life. But it was only a tease, forbidden fruit that would be imprudent to savor.

The wine suddenly tasted bitter. Her appetite of only a minute ago disappeared, and her stomach grew sour.

Jonathan began to talk about their trip and some of his observations. After watching Sidney Greenspan and Seve Marques with her, he had come to understand how difficult it could be for an attractive woman in her position.

"You're absolutely right," she said. "Some things have changed for women in business, but not many." She forced herself to carry on their conversation, yet to her ear, every word she uttered was stilted.

"I can just see you and my mother traveling together. An unbeatable duo."

"It wasn't always easy." She paused at the memory, recalling their numerous trips, especially to Japan and China, where men looked down upon them simply for being women, making it impossible for them to be treated as equals.

"Yet, you thrived." Jonathan said.

She nodded, feeling like a fake. While the subject was one she usually could warm to, now she could only respond with silence, too aware of how she was spoiling the mood for both of them.

Jonathan seemed to notice the change in her, but was too sensitive to comment any further. Ann pushed her plate aside. Jonathan paid the check, then pulled back her chair and waited for her to stand. He did not try to take her hand. The taxi ride took less than ten minutes. They said goodnight in the narrow third-floor hallway of their hotel. Ann washed her face and brushed her teeth, then went to bed. A melancholy settled upon her that she couldn't shake loose. She lay on her back, staring at the ceiling. It was sheer exhaustion that brought sleep, but it lasted less than two hours.

It was her own scream that woke her. She shot upright in the narrow bed, found a cold sweat creeping down her shoulder blades. Her neck was stiff; she tried to loosen it by stretching it from side to side. Then she lay down again.

Mad Dog was back with a vengeance. He was not the first of her mother's so-called boyfriends, but he was the one who frightened her the most. She was a kid really, barely into her teens, when they would come to her bed and observe her in silence as she pretended to sleep. Sensing them standing above scared the daylights out of her.

Too often she would hear her mother's screams, not from passion but from the beatings she took, as evidenced by the bruises Ann saw the next morning. She did not want to end up the same way, to be beaten, maybe killed.

Mad Dog was close to twenty years Ann's senior, and unlike anyone she had ever known. Her mother had a nickname for all of her gentlemen 'friends' and this one was called Mad Dog because of his violent temper that bordered on insanity. That and his cold, dark looks, with deep brown—almost black—eyes that were so menacing they could cut to the bone. He too would approach her bed when he was finished with her mother. But unlike the others, he'd always move in close, so close that she could practically taste his liquored-up breath. So close that she was afraid he could see her heart beating through her skin.

When he caught Ann around her mother, he would stare at her in a way that would make her feel dirty and ashamed. At night that shame turned to the worst fear imaginable.

Inevitably, the time Ann always dreaded came, and Mad Dog not only approached her bed, but slowly lowered himself onto her, turned her towards him, and placed a hand to her breast...

Ann shivered at the memory. "I'm okay," she repeated aloud. "I'm in Paris and I'm fine."

As if to test her own words, she bounced up and snapped on the bedside light.

The room was void of ghosts.

She glanced towards the phone sitting on the bureau opposite her bed. She quickly got to her feet, approached and lifted the receiver.

Coward, a voice teased.

She was about to ask the operator to connect her to Jonathan's room.

What good will he do you? the inner voice taunted.

But Jonathan had proven himself today. Why shouldn't she lean on a friend?

Coward!

She looked at the phone a moment longer, then hung up.

She was alone; she would always be alone. As much as she might want to fight against it, it was her destiny.

She lay back down but kept the light on. She let the tears fall without making an effort to brush them away. Hours passed before she fell back asleep.

CHAPTER 19

The flight home from Paris seemed to take forever. Jonathan was filled with thoughts of Ann and the change that had come over her yesterday. He racked his brain to find the trigger point, the one thing he might have said or done. Finally, he concluded he was blameless, that Ann's mood swing was more a reflection of her than it was of himself.

Still, earlier this morning, he had tried to do his best to cheer her up, ignoring the dark circles under her eyes, making every attempt to get her to smile. When they hit turbulence two-thirds of the way through their flight, he not only allowed her to grip his arm, he put his free one around her shoulders and held her.

They said their goodbyes at JFK, with Ann refusing his offer to share a cab. An hour after he left the airport, Jonathan unlocked the door to his loft and nudged his suitcase inside with his foot. He stood in the entrance for a moment, taking in the 2500 square feet of mostly open space before him. It was all his and he was proud of it. He had spent months toiling, scraping layers of paint, laying bricks, converting it into a home and studio—a place he could both work and live in. The splay of light from the floor to ceiling windows brightened his mood. He stepped inside, closed the door and made his way to the kitchen for his welcome-home beer.

The kitchen was in a corner behind a diagonal brick divider that rose some five feet. The opposite end—where most of the windows were—was taken up by his work. The walls were dotted with it, various pieces of art he was living with before deciding if he wanted to sell them, keep them, or ditch them entirely.

The loft had a vaulted ceiling which gave a soaring sense of height—almost cathedral-like—that complimented the floating staircase that sat left of center in the room. It was all polished oak with gold copper trim that had taken him weeks to complete. It rose boldly to reveal the master bedroom, small den and bathroom.

He got the Sierra from the fridge, opened it and drank deeply. He felt tired but he had an idea that Ann was feeling worse. Unless Jonathan badly missed his guess, she'd dropped three or four pounds on the trip.

"Hey, I'm an artist," he muttered at his reflection in the black gloss of a window. He knew the human form. He caught it almost subliminally when curves started to turn to angles. She'd lost four pounds, he thought, drinking again. Easy.

The phone rang. Jonathan veered around the divider, back into the main living area, and made a grab for the receiver.

"Cut me a break. I just walked in the door."

Felicia sighed. "Manners, dear. Have I taught you nothing?"

He grinned at her voice. "Sorry. I thought you were someone else."

"If your tone is any indication, I believe you're about to part ways with her."

She knew him too well. "Carmen is smart, savvy"—*great in bed*, he added silently—"and developing a possessive streak."

"Perhaps it's enough then, dear. Time for a change. Life's too short. So tell me, how did the trip go?"

Shit. He wouldn't be able to keep a whole week's absence from her. A quick trip to Toronto was one thing; Europe was something else entirely. "Good, I guess," he said vaguely. "But what do I know?"

"That raises another interesting question," Felicia replied. "If you know nothing about the business, why *did* you go to Europe?"

"Can you hold on a minute while I grab another beer?" He needed a few seconds to figure out how he would respond to the question.

"Of course."

He placed the phone on the table while he returned to the kitchen. She'd still be on the line when he got back, but he could hope.

"Okay. What were we talking about?" Jonathan asked when he returned to the phone.

"Why you went to Europe."

"This doll is a big deal, right?" Jonathan said.

"She is. And I have the utmost confidence in Ann to handle her. As opposed to a man who has not set foot in our offices in six years, and then only to take me to lunch."

"I remember that. It was your birthday, right?"

"Stop trying to change the subject."

"I hadn't been to Europe in a while. I just thought, you know, what the hell. I'll go."

"Jonathan, you're behaving strangely these days, to say the least."

"I'm an eccentric. You know that. An *artiste…*"

"I beg your pardon?"

"Never mind." He was over-tired.

"Well, at least tell me how the trip went?"

He stalled. "Have you spoken to Ann?"

"She wasn't answering her phone. Probably soaking in the tub."

"That sounds about right," Jonathan said. "We parted at JFK a little over an hour ago."

"Didn't you see her home?"

His mother was tough to slip around, Jonathan thought. In thirty-five years, he'd never quite gotten the knack. "She wouldn't hear of it. Look, Mom, I'm bushed—"

"I'll let you go then. But first, please tell me how it went in Spain. I'm dying to know. They're always the hardest sell."

"Spain?" His heart gave an odd thudding sensation against his rib cage.

"Seve Marques."

"Weaseled old guy with a lot of hands?"

"That's right, at least the weaseled part. I never became acquainted with his hands."

"Uh … we met him over lunch. He seemed to like the doll." Enough to want to knock her off, Jonathan thought.

"What kind of an order did he give us?"

"I'm not sure of the numbers. I spent a week listening to them, Mom, and they all run together in my head. A hundred thousand here, fifty thousand there." He was aiding and abetting Ann in lying to his mother, he thought.

Evading. They were evading her.

Felicia sighed. "It was bad."

"I didn't say that. Ann didn't seem to think so. Seriously, Mom, you've got to get the exact figures from her. She was doing all the talking and negotiating. It went right over my head."

"Which brings us back to why you went in the first place."

"I like Europe!" He almost shouted it this time.

"You told me you had your fill, after living there."

"I changed my mind about it."

"Yes, dear." She paused. "You know, I always find out everything anyway, so you might as well fess up. Of course, in this instance, I'm running out of time."

"Damn it, Mom—"

"Good night."

The phone clicked. As Jonathan stood staring at it in his hand, a thudding fist hit his door. There were Third World countries who enjoyed more peace than he was having tonight. He dropped the phone and went to yank the door open. "What?" he demanded.

It was Patrick. And he was sodden. "I wanna know what's going on with you."

"Ah, hell," Jonathan muttered.

His brother pushed past him, stumbling a little. Jonathan winced as Pat dropped onto the sofa, legs akimbo.

"By all means," Jonathan said. "Come on in."

"You went to Europe."

"Yeah, and I've already heard from Mom about it." He closed the door. "So what?"

Patrick lurched up, then stood swaying. "You went to Europe with *her*."

Jonathan decided not to address that. "What are you doing on this side of the river at this hour?"

"Where else would I be?"

"Home? Last time I checked, you had a wife and kids."

"Worked late." Patrick veered toward the kitchen area.

Jonathan went after him. "It's eleven o'clock, pal."

"I was waiting for you to get home." He yanked open the refrigerator door, then some cupboards. "Don't you have anything to drink besides beer?"

"It's what I like."

"You have the taste of a peon."

"Yeah, but I can afford it."

"What's that supposed to mean?" He turned and looked Jonathan's way, his jaw jutting. "I can't afford what I like?"

"I don't know. Can you?" Jonathan rubbed his eyes. "Pat, if you came here looking for a fight, I've got to tell you, I'm not going to join in."

"You went to Europe. With *her*," Patrick said again.

He still wasn't going to rise to the accusation. He turned his back to Patrick and moved into the living room, his brother following him.

"Have you forgotten what she did?" Pat demanded.

"No." Jonathan sank down in one of the chairs.

"Are you screwing her?"

He felt all his facial skin pull tight. "Watch yourself there."

"You are, aren't you? Wasn't one brother enough?"

Jonathan paused, stroking his jaw. His mind rolled back, over bumpy memories of that last vacation they'd all taken together on Long Island, to the night in the boat, the night Matt had died. Matt had been standing at the windshield, the wind flattening his dark hair, whipping the fringes of it behind his head. Laughing, Jonathan thought, with every bit of glorious exhilaration in his young soul.

"She's going to marry me!" Matt had shouted. His voice had belted out over the growl of the engine. The wind had whipped it and carried it, pitching it and turning it until it had sounded almost manic.

That's not true, Jonathan had thought. She told me she wouldn't. But before he could answer, Patrick had shouted back.

"Mattie, wise up! We both fucked her! She's making the rounds, trying to wrap one of us around her finger!"

Jonathan had thought, wait, wait, no, not true. That family vacation at Felicia's request had been the most extended time they'd all spent with Ann. He couldn't deny that for a moment during their beach walk, he had felt an unmistakable attraction toward her, but it had never been acted upon.

The rush of these old memories opened a wound, and Jonathan felt the pain of Matt's loss. He turned to Patrick and told him to take his sorry ass home.

His brother gave a guttural sound and lunged, gripping Jonathan's sweater in his palms and trying to lift him out of the chair. Jonathan wrapped both his hands around Patrick's wrists, twisted, breaking his hold. "Back off," he said, too quietly.

"I want to know what happened in Europe. Irene says you've been stuck up Ann's ass for weeks."

Jonathan stared at him. Patrick's eyes were bloodshot, runny. His complexion was splotched. *He had lied to Mattie.* Matt had died with that twisted untruth in his mind.

He let one of Patrick's wrists go. He brought his fist back and fired it hard into his brother's gut. Air shot out of him. He looked stunned.

"Get out of here," Jonathan said. "And we'll forget tonight ever happened."

Patrick swung back.

As fights went, it was pathetic. Jonathan thought about that as he shifted cleanly to one side and avoided his brother's fist. Then he lowered his head and came up out of the chair, driving into him, knocking him flat. Onto the coffee table. The glass top was upended but somehow didn't break

They rolled. Patrick swung feebly. Jonathan pinned him to the floor.

Now he was fighting over her, he thought. He was aiding and abetting her one minute, throwing his fists around the next. With his own brother.

But Patrick had lied to Mattie.

"You never had her." He used his weight to hold his brother down.

"I didn't want her!"

"You lied to him, damn it! You broke his heart on the last night of his life!"

"I was trying to save him! I was trying to stop him from being a fool! Nothing else would have woken him up!"

It would be too easy to slam his fist down into that florid, drunken face, Jonathan thought. Instead, he deliberately eased his weight off his brother.

Patrick grunted and rolled onto his stomach. Then he heaved.

"Ah, man," Jonathan said. "Good show."

Patrick scrubbed his hands over his face. "Don't get tangled up with her, Jon. Don't let her get to you, too."

"Nobody's tangled up with anybody, you idiot." He got to his feet and went to get a towel. But the words he'd just spoken rang hollow in his ears.

CHAPTER 20

The days between Europe and visiting the American retailers passed like dominoes falling, one onto another. There were details to take care of, logistics to manage. The rough draft of the TV commercial had to be dubbed into each country's language—and the balance of international territories to be contacted. Ann needed to fill the holes left by Spain's lack of support and Germany's meager order. In between, she saw her doctor for a prescription antacid that put the Maalox to shame.

Jonathan came by the office twice, but lavished most of his attention on her secretary. Ann couldn't quite figure out the purpose of his visits, but she didn't have time to dwell on it. She barely saw Patrick at all, and *that* worried her. As for Felicia, she was doing the best she could to dodge her, making only short visits to her home. She refused to burden the woman with premature news, hoping she would soon be able to paint a prettier picture.

Before Ann knew it, her travel date had arrived.

She was in her bedroom, folding a sweater into a suitcase, when Jonathan's knock came at the door. She finished what she was doing, smoothing a hand over the soft cashmere, and picked up her coffee mug before she went to answer it. She grinned a little when a second thumping sounded, harder and more impatient than the first. She was deliberately goading him, forcing him to wait for her. Finally, she pulled open the door and ushered him in.

Instead of saying hello, Jonathan nodded at the coffee in her hand. "That stuff can't be helping your stomach."

"Neither do you, but I can't seem to kick you out of my life, either."

He stepped past her into the living room. Looking pretty damned good, she thought.

"Why aren't you ready?" he asked.

"I am."

"You're barefoot." He stared at her feet as though they were an affront.

"I can fix that. Will boots bother your sensibilities, or should I wear pumps?"

Jonathan had an unnerving flash of her in black leather. A lot of it. Not just boots, but head to toe with strategic gaps. And all that blond hair. What was he thinking? *Shit*. This trip was definitely a bad idea. How could he explain it to his mother and brother, let alone to himself? But he couldn't bow out now.

"I need to use your bathroom," he said suddenly.

Ann frowned. "Down the hall. The only door to your left."

He found his way, closing the door behind him. He looked around. There was a rug on the floor, a geometric pattern of ultramarine and turquoise and sea-green. The walls wore a delicate tint of sky blue. There was a sunken tub of warm ivory, surrounded by urns of dried lavender and grasses, wire baskets of thick rolled towels, a pedestal sink matching the ivory of the tub … and a wine bucket perched on the tub ledge. With two glasses.

Jonathan returned to the front door where Ann was waiting with her suitcase and a garment bag. Her boots were brown leather, not black; her skirt was long, calf-length, but slit up the front. Nice, he thought, but instead of complimenting her, he brusquely picked up her suitcase and barked, "Let's go."

"You know, you don't have to make this trip. No one is holding a gun to your head."

"Keep trying to talk me out of it and I'll start questioning your motives again."

Her stomach jumped. Ann pressed a hand to it. "Is that your way of telling me that I am beginning to earn your trust?""

Damned good question. "I've got a cab waiting, Ann. Can we get to it before it costs me my entire portfolio?"

"I guess you don't have much of a portfolio, then," she said lightly, and she plucked her keys off the entry table.

"I, at least, can buy furniture."

"So can I."

"Your living room is empty."

"I want perfect pieces." She stepped out into the hall after him and locked the door.

"There are furniture stores all over the city."

"I said perfect. Not adequate. Each piece has to speak to me. That takes time."

"Yeah, well, if you're planning another shopping spree, let me know so I can stay home."

Ann bit her lip against laughing. Then she almost stoked the furnace of their old feud when they got into the cab. "Have you seen Patrick lately?" she asked.

His response was quick and too harsh. "Why?"

She turned her head to look at him as she buckled her seat belt. "He's been laying low."

"Not low enough."

"What does that mean?"

"Nothing." He changed the subject. "What's the purpose of this trip, by the way? Same as Europe?"

"More or less. Think of Toys 'R' Us and Walmart as small countries."

"Are you still avoiding Felicia?"

"I told her the truth about Spain this morning. But I caught a real coup with Australia to make up some of the difference."

He looked at her sharply. "Australia? You're selling dolls to Australia and we didn't get to go there? You made me go to *London* instead?"

"I like London. I'm afraid of kangaroos."

He poked a finger in her direction. "You're afraid of *flying*. It has nothing to do with wildlife, and everything to do with twenty-one hours in the air. Ah, man. *Australia.*"

"Stop complaining. I'm about to knock your socks off with Bentonville."

"Where the hell is Bentonville?"

"Arkansas."

"Can't hardly wait."

By the time they got to the airport, she thought he was his irritating self again. Then they ran into Alvin Pelletier.

They were heading up the concourse when his bellow came from behind them. Alvin's voice had a way of demanding that people stop, then salute. Ann did the first, waiting as he closed the distance between them.

"You guys running off to Vegas to get married? You sure as hell got some tongues wagging around this city."

"We're headed for the Dominican Republic for a quickie divorce," Ann replied. "The marriage lasted about as long as I thought it would."

Pelletier laughed, a robust sound that drew the attention of passers-by. "That's what I said to everybody. Hell's going to freeze over before you two crawl into bed together." His eyes went shrewd. "So where *are* you going?"

"Retailers," Ann said. They all began walking again.

Alvin cut a glance at Jonathan. "And how do you fit in?"

"Trying to answer those rumors, Alvin?" Jonathan shrugged. "I've developed an interest in my mother's business, and particularly our doll."

"Why?"

"Because people like you wish you had her."

"Not me," Pelletier said, stopping at a gate and turning to Ann. "The gamble you're taking is crazy. You can't spend five million on television advertising, hoping you'll get support from the major retailers. I hate to see you put Felicia's company under this way."

"This is Felicia's baby, Alvin," Ann said. "I'm just pushing it through for her."

"You're going to fall flat on that pretty face of yours."

"It's been scraped up before."

"You should get out before it's too late." He took hold of her arm in a gesture of intimacy.

It already is, she thought. "Is this your way of saying 'break a leg'?"

"Hell no." He let go of her arm and waved a hand. "That's my flight being called."

Ann looked up at the sign over the check-in desk. "Why are you going to Milwaukee?" she asked.

"Got a meeting set with that asshole at Swanson's."

"Dean Carlson? Isn't he the one you were going to cut off?"

"Yeah. I still may do it."

Bull, Ann thought as she watched Pelletier turn away.

"Who's Dean Carlson?" Jonathan asked once the man was out of ear range.

"The divisional merchandise manager at Swanson's."

"And what did he do, exactly?"

"Fined Alvin's company a few thousand dollars for shipping early."

"What?"

Ann laughed at his expression. "He does it to all of us. Fines us for shipping early. Fines us for shipping late."

"And you accept it?"

She shrugged his comment off. "He's not the only one. Just a cost of doing business today."

"Jesus. No wonder you're popping stomach pills all the time."

"Oh, really? You mean, you're finally starting to understand?"

He let her pull a bit ahead of him. Understanding all of the ramifications of the toy industry was one thing; fitting the puzzle pieces of Ann together, quite another.

CHAPTER 21

Ann always found herself unnerved by Walmart. Entering their headquarters gave her the feeling that she was consigning herself to the Army. The building was flat and drab, and stretched for at least a city block.

She gave their names to the receptionist, then guided Jonathan to a seat. The chairs were hard metal, lined up classroom-style. She knew from past experience that her back would begin to ache if they were kept waiting for too long.

"This is rather austere," Jonathan said.

"No kidding."

He slouched in his chair. "So what's our situation, now that you got Australia in the fold?"

"Internationally, we ended up okay. Not great, but okay. A lot rides on this trip, this stop in particular."

"Really?"

Ann lifted her shoulders and sighed as she dropped them again. "Hasbro and Mattel control the manufacturing side of things. Toys 'R' Us and especially Walmart are the retail gods. Walmart, in particular, more or less has its own set of rules."

"What kind of rules?"

"If you want to do business with them, they prefer the top gun. So in our case, I'm it."

"Hey, I'm a Morhardt. I ought to count for something."

"Seve Marques wasn't impressed with you."

"Only because I don't have your legs."

Damn it, he always managed to turn things around, just when she was starting to feel semi-comfortable with him. She re-crossed her legs carefully. "Walmart forbids their buyers to be entertained by company reps."

"Seve would weep real tears."

"Seve joined us for lunch. Walmart buyers aren't allowed to." Suddenly, an image came to mind of the dance she and Jonathan had shared in Madrid, of their tour of Paris. She blinked until the image went away. "Walmart's gone digital with a neat little program called Retail Link," she said, changing the subject. "It's connected by a password through the internet. Suppliers are expected to monitor the sales of their own products on a weekly—even daily—basis, and alert Walmart when sales are either picking up or slowing down. It's become our total responsibility."

"I'm not surprised, Ann," Jonathan said. "It's called bowing to the god of higher profit margins. It's not just toys, and it isn't only Walmart. More and more jobs are being eliminated and more and more pressure applied on those people whose jobs remain."

"Really, smart stuff? And you're a painter?"

"Good thing, too."

She felt an odd sensation in her chest. "Still interested? You haven't been doing much of it lately. Not since you started following me around."

"The muse is in Bangladesh," he finally answered.

Ann frowned. "Bangladesh?"

"It's where he goes when he's not with me."

"Are you serious?"

"I have to think of him as vacationing, or I'd lose my mind."

"But *Bangladesh?*"

"Ever been there?" he asked, shifting his weight in the hard chair.

"No."

"Neither have I. But I really can't see him lunching with Seve in Madrid."

She hated it when he made her laugh.

An announcement over the PA system declared that all ten o'clock appointments were to proceed to their pre-assigned meeting rooms.

Ann stood and Jonathan followed her. He wasn't sure what he was thinking anymore. But the image of her slumped shoulders heading into The Melia still made him itch. *This trip shouldn't have gone this badly.*

It didn't take long—perhaps a minute or two—before the buyer showed up. Jonathan took a seat and wondered if this was a good sign. He watched Ann turn on.

"Jonathan Morhardt, Byron Young." She made the introductions as she removed the sample of Baby Talk N Glow from her travel bag. The guy was fresh-faced, freckled, probably of an age that entitled him to wear a varsity sweater with impunity, Jonathan thought.

"How are you? I hear Moonlight is still near the top these days," Young said with a southern drawl.

"Moonlight's a great game. But what I'm about to show you is revolutionary." Ann took the doll out and began the demonstration.

"That's pretty cool," Young said when she was finished. "What's my cost?"

Ann dodged the question. She was good, Jonathan thought. "We're investing five million dollars in television advertising, plus another million for posters in subways and bus shelters."

"Great. But my cost?"

"Trade cost will be twenty-six seventy-five."

"What's *mine?*"

"Twenty-four dollars and eight cents."

"Hmmm…" He sat back in his chair.

Ann could see him doing the arithmetic in his head. At a retail of twenty-nine ninety-seven she knew his margin was twenty percent. Not exactly what he'd prefer, but he could live with it. And this was why Walmart stood apart from everyone else. Other retailers insisted on advertising rebates, warehouse allowances, defective allowances, yet directed this package of discounts to their company's bottom line. Walmart, on the other hand, asked for a price that had all the discounts netted out, so that whatever savings they received could be passed on directly to their customers.

"Twenty-two dollars would make a lot more sense," Byron said.

"I'll tell you what," Ann started to say, pleased with herself for saving this tidbit for the end. "We'll throw in a five dollar consumer rebate. That'll help both of us in a far more significant way."

Byron paused. "Two hundred and fifty thousand," he finally announced in a casual voice.

Ann felt Jonathan's kick under the table. She was encouraged herself until she heard what came next.

"That would be my estimate … if you were Mattel."

"I beg your pardon?" She blanched.

"I'd commit now, on the spot. But how do I know that Hart Toy can pull it off? Anything can happen to a small company such as yours. I've seen it before. That's why we're being asked to narrow our vendor base. I mean, if this doll is so good, how come Mattel didn't end up with her in the first place?"

Ann's color was heightening. Jonathan knew, without a doubt, that she was seriously upset.

"Mr. Young," she said, not caring if her anger showed or not, "how many years have you been buying toys?"

The buyer's voice faltered. "A year and a half, or so."

"A year and a half," she repeated in a dismissive way. "And Hart Toy is now in its fortieth year. Not one of our executives has less than ten years experience. Would you say we're a flash in the pan, Mr. Young? Some of the most innovative product in the toy industry has been generated by small companies such as ours. Where do you think Cabbage Patch came from? Or Trivial Pursuit? I know, I know, they were before your time. But the point is, when I said we'll be spending five million on television advertising, that's two million more than Mattel or anyone else would likely spend on any one product. If you want affidavits from the TV stations, we'll supply them to you. If you want a letter from our lawyer guaranteeing our advertising commitment, I'll give it to you. But don't tell me that a small company like Hart Toy can't be as effective as Mattel."

Jonathan had the urge to stand up and cheer. Young apparently didn't share the sentiment. He remained silent.

"Do you like the doll?" Ann asked.

"It's very good," the buyer acknowledged.

"And?"

He shrugged.

"Are you saying you still won't give us a commitment?" she asked incredulously.

Byron Young's face turned red. "Well—" he managed.

"You're falling into a trap," she said. "Don't you see?" Her voice softened. "Mattel and Hasbro have been on this kick for years. Swallowing up one competitor after another. For power. For control. Does this make them better innovators? Does it make their sales and marketing people more savvy? More talented than my own? You know and I know that Walmart is more sophisticated than most. You buy by category and subcategory, with so many dollars allotted to each one. Mattel and Hasbro intentionally load each of your categories to the point where you have no room for anyone else. When word gets out about our doll—and I assure you, it will—Mattel will suddenly introduce two or three new baby dolls of their own. They'll lock up that sub-category and your open-to-buy will be gone for the year."

"I'm familiar with their methods," Young said tightly. "But my guidelines are laid down by management." It sounded like an apology. "I like the doll," he continued. "I'm sure we'll carry her…"

"But you won't give us a commitment today?" Ann interrupted harshly.

The buyer shrugged. "I can't. I'm sorry."

Ann swallowed as she felt the acid in her stomach churn. She was aware that Young was fairly new at his job; it made sense that he would want to protect himself. If management said beware of smaller firms, he'd take it as gospel. No matter how good their doll was, he'd want to wait before making his final decision.

She began to put the doll away. And then it dawned on her that she had made a terrible mistake. By not treating the buyer more diplomatically, by belittling his experience while boasting of her own, she had undermined him. This was something he would not soon forget. Besides, she had allowed her pride to come into play and that was unforgivable. Integrity in dealing with each buyer, honesty and persistence—all were earmarks of a true professional. Sales had turned into an art form. Instead of swallowing her own ego, she had become consumed by it.

She stopped what she was doing and turned to face Byron Young. "I've been thinking of your position," she said, "and I want to apologize. I guess I've become so wrapped up in this doll I've lost sight of what really matters. You've supported my company from the time you started with Walmart. I have no right to preach to you, let alone question your experience. I truly am sorry. If there is—"

"Ann," he interrupted with a boyish grin, "no offense was taken. "Y'all have to fight for what you believe in, and I understand that." He extended his hand. "Thanks for coming in today. I'll do my best to fit your doll into next year's program. I really do like her."

And with that, he left them. Ann waited a moment, then heard Jonathan approaching behind her.

"You apologized," he said. "I never thought I'd hear an apology from you."

She turned on him as though he was single-handedly responsible for everything that went wrong. She grabbed the front of his sweater with a fist.

"Drop it," he warned. He looked down at her hand.

"Or you'll do what?" she asked, without letting go.

"Show you what happened to the last guy who tried this. I spent some time on top of him."

Something hot gathered in her belly at the image that brought to mind, something she didn't want to contemplate. "*Him?* Why, Jonathan, you surprise me."

The color in his eyes changed. "If it had been a she," he said slowly, "I wouldn't have gotten up."

"That's reassuring." Her heart was gallivanting. "For your mother's sake. She'll be glad to hear your sexual orientation is mainstream."

"I'm not sure Felicia belongs in this conversation, Ann. I think this might be between you and me."

She couldn't breathe. Her stomach burned. First Byron Young, then this … whatever this was.

You know what it is and it's scaring the hell out of you, whispered a nasty voice in her head. Ann sucked in air. She finally dropped her hand and stepped back. "Let's go."

He didn't answer for a long time, and that scared her even more. She'd been waiting for one of his quips, needing it. But all he finally said was, "Right."

They turned together and stalked, shoulder-to-shoulder, out of the Walmart building.

CHAPTER 22

Ann woke Wednesday morning with a pounding headache. She was in Chicago and had no choice but to get up and face the day. There was no way she was going to be able to hide the Walmart disaster from Felicia, she thought. So she would have to fix it. Somehow, she would fix it. She noticed that the room was frigid—apparently the heat had conked out overnight—and she craved coffee with an almost physical ache. For the first time in years, she contemplated combining her caffeine fix with a cigarette.

It was barely six-thirty. She'd eat something now, Ann decided, then she and Jonathan could head straight out to Kmart without cozying up together over breakfast. Although that would probably anger him. He didn't seem to take it well when she interfered with his meals.

She called room service and settled for fruit and coffee, then she went to take a shower.

She stripped her nightgown over her head on her way to the bathroom. Her naked reflection suddenly assaulted her from too many mirrors as she stepped over the threshold onto cold tile.

Ann hesitated, her eyes darting from one image of herself, to the next, to another. She looked like hell. Her skin was flaky and dry from too much pressurized, recycled cabin air. Her hair was limp and her eyes were clouded. She stepped back and dropped her arms, forcing herself to look down the length of her body. How long had it been since anyone had touched her, since she'd felt any real sense of life in those limbs, inside?

Mark Twekesborough had been kind in his attentiveness, she thought. Seve Marques was a bastard and would go after anyone in a skirt. Ann looked at herself gravely, searching for something worthwhile, and came up empty. She knew she had nothing inside to give. Still, remarkably, she felt the urge for intimacy. For the first time since Matt's death, she wanted to offer herself to somebody. She longed for the give and take, the feel of a caress on bare skin.

Jonathan was responsible for this, she thought. Jonathan, with that sliding, speculative gaze that had edged toward her mouth on Monday. *Jonathan?* On one level, it seemed absurd. On another, it made her ache. Impossibly, he had made her want again. He had made her want to give all the things that had been ripped from her years ago and were no longer hers to relinquish.

"Damn him," Ann breathed. Her voice shook. She turned away from the mirror and got into the shower.

When her coffee and fruit arrived, she still felt bruised. She settled at the table in her room, thinking once more, fleetingly, of a cigarette, then she flipped open her briefcase. Instead of going for the hidden pack, she took out her calculator and a notepad, and began running numbers.

Without Walmart, her goal of a million pieces was shattered. A ripple effect would result that would end up hurting their advertising campaign, as well as their profit margin. She didn't see any way around it. The entire project—out of necessity—would have to be scaled back or canceled.

Ann got up for her cell phone and called their advertising agency.

On the east coast, Bob Turnbull was just arriving at the office. She could tell by his aggravated tone. Nothing like being hit with a panic call before you even sit down at your desk, she thought.

"We've got to trim back," she told him.

"Ah, Ann." She heard pure frustration in his sigh. Turnbull didn't like glitches. "Be reasonable. We purposely booked the television campaign this far in advance to get a jump on your competitors. Cancel or change something now and you'll never get it back."

Ann thought about it. With so many burgeoning satellite dishes and cable companies, it was tough to build a worthwhile campaign. She *had* to spend the money to reach her target audience. Some ten or fifteen years ago there were barely four hundred half-hours devoted to children's broadcasting. It had been easy to choose the meaningful programs. Today it was more like eleven hundred hours.

"What about the billboards in subways and busses?" she asked.

"I've got a better question. What's happened since the last time we talked?"

She couldn't tell him.

There was a knock on her door. It had to be Jonathan. "Look, Bob, I've got to go," she said. "I'll call you back later." Ann got off the phone and went to the door, jerking it open.

"It's not even 7:30 yet!" she snapped. "Don't you ever sleep?"

His gaze started at her feet, came up over her bare legs, and slid over the silk of her robe. Ann pulled the lapels together and kept her arms crossed over her chest. His eyes finally settled on her tangled, wet hair.

"What?" she asked defensively.

"Hell of a way to answer the door. What if I had been room service?"

"He's already been and gone."

Jonathan's brow furrowed as he stepped past her into the room. "You ordered breakfast without me? What the hell am *I* supposed to eat?"

"There's plenty of fruit left over, if you want some."

"That's right up there with scones. I need eggs. Bacon."

"Bad for your arteries." She closed the door behind him.

"I'll worry about it in five years. Right now, I want furnace food for the day ahead."

"There's a restaurant downstairs." *Why was she arguing about food when her world was coming apart?* But somehow, she realized, it felt good. "And you're not that young. Go look in the mirror." She twirled a finger at his temple. "You're going a little gray there. No big deal, but it shows because your hair's so dark."

He moved off for the bathroom and Ann smiled to herself.

"You can hardly see it," he said when he returned. "And nobody's ever complained."

"I'm glad for you. I'm just saying that you don't need bacon. The end is closer than you think." She picked up her coffee and drank.

"You're in a hell of a mood." He started for the door. "Let's go to the restaurant. Put something on first."

"You think I should? I was going to stroll in like this—or better yet, naked."

His gaze shot back to her, heating. "Are you trying to instigate something here, Annie? Are you playing games with me?"

Things shook inside her, then steadied. She turned away. "No, I'll meet you downstairs."

She kept her back to him until she heard the door shut. Then she spun around, hurried over to it and threw the lock. She let her breath out.

Annie.

He'd only called her that because Mark Twekesborough had. He'd made his point, though.

She threw things back into her briefcase. She wiggled into pantyhose, then chose what she wanted to wear. Make-up and an attack with the blow-dryer restored her a little. Ann added more blush and decided to tuck her sweater in to take up some of the loose space in her skirt. She'd lost quite a bit of weight, she thought, since she'd signed the deal on the doll.

By the time she got downstairs to the hotel restaurant, Jonathan had eaten. The only thing left on his plate was a sprig of parsley and a streak of something that looked like Hollandaise sauce. "You had *Eggs Benedict?*" She gaped at him.

"Canadian bacon is leaner, right?"

Ann shook her head as she took a seat across from him. "Let me finish off your coffee, then we can go." She took his cup and poured in sugar.

Jonathan sat back and watched. "You know, I'm not going to let Felicia bury you in our family plot."

"What?" Ann jolted.

"At least what I consume doesn't cause me physical pain. You're wrecking your stomach with caffeine."

"You'll go first. And you won't even know about it." Ann drank coffee and girded herself. "Okay. Let's get this show on the road."

They left the hotel. They had a rental car and Jonathan drove. Ann turned on the radio. He changed the station.

"What's this?" she asked, recoiling from the burst of sound.

"Rock 'n roll, baby."

"You're doing this to irritate me. You like jazz. Blues."

"Depends on my mood. This gets my adrenaline up for the fight."

"What fight?"

"The one I assume we've got coming with another twelve-year-old buyer. Are you going to take his head off like you did with Byron Young? Great speech, by the way."

"Thank you." She let herself smile. "No. We're going to Kmart today, and that's Tom Carlisle."

"Which means?"

"He's one of the good guys. Been around for a long while."

"But isn't Kmart in bankruptcy?"

"They were. They've since amalgamated with Sears."

They gave their names to the receptionist and were kept waiting for a half-hour. Carlisle finally appeared, hitting the meeting room with high energy, kissing Ann on the cheek.

"Here we go again," Jonathan muttered.

"I'm simply irresistible," she whispered back. It was safe to play games when a pudgy, fifty-year-old black man was watching them curiously.

"Jonathan, right?" Tom shook his hand. "I remember you."

"We've probably met at one of those Toy Fairs, right?"

Tom laughed. "No. I think it was a Vegas golf tournament. You were terrible."

Jonathan rubbed his jaw. "Jeez. That had to be ten years ago. I stepped in for my mother."

"Has your game improved?"

"Not a lick."

Tom nodded. "I like an honest man." He looked at Ann. "What have you got for me today?"

She handed Baby Talk N Glow over to Carlisle without going through the doll's repertoire. She remembered Mark Twekesborough's startled delight when the doll had begun talking to him. Maybe Walmart had been an aberration. Today would be different.

Carlisle handled the doll, not making any comment. He touched her nose, her toes, her ears. She chatted away. But when he felt her heartbeat, his dark face seemed to shine. When the doll's own skin began to glow, he laughed out loud. "This is incredible," he said. "How long will her battery last?"

Ann breathed again. "No less than five years. It's a new technology. We'll guarantee it on the package."

He put his hand on the doll's heart again. "How does it do that?"

Ann remembered what she had told Seve Marques. "Magic."

Carlisle smiled. "Meaning you're not going to tell me."

"Right."

"What do you want from me?"

Ann answered baldly. "A commitment for about a million pieces."

"No, seriously."

"How many do you think you can sell?"

"What support will you give it?"

She outlined her advertising plans while Carlisle sat back in his chair. The doll was still on his lap. He stared at her for a long moment, his face void of expression. Tom Carlisle was admired and respected by everyone in the industry but, often, he had this fugue thing going on. It was his quirk. He never bought a toy until he'd zoned out on it. He was zoning now, staring at the baby doll hard. Minutes ticked by. Ann didn't dare look at Jonathan, though she could hear him shifting impatiently in his seat.

This was good, she decided. *Oh please, God, let this be good.* The buyer was running numbers in his head. She had never known him to behave like this and *not* give them an order.

"I'm sorry, Ann, but I just can't commit right now."

She would have sprung out of her chair if the room hadn't suddenly tilted around her. "I beg your pardon?"

"I just want to clear it with a few people first. The doll's great. She's fantastic."

"Then what's the problem? Why wait? You never had to clear your buys with anyone."

"Times are changing, Ann. I'm sorry. With any amount of luck, I'll be able to get back to you as soon as tomorrow."

"I'll be in Minnesota tomorrow." Her voice had a hollow ring. Everything was pouring out of her. All her hope. Her determination. This was unbelievable.

"Give me your cell phone number and I'll catch up with you. I need twenty-four hours."

"Right. Of course." She rattled her number off as he wrote it down.

She didn't remember leaving the building.

They were back at the car before her knees locked and she couldn't go any further. She gripped the door handle, holding on, looking at her own knuckles almost dispassionately. They were white.

"We're in one of those shut-up zones, aren't we?" Jonathan asked.

Ann closed her eyes. "Please. Don't joke. Not now."

He shrugged and reached around her to open the door. Then he looked at her and felt his soul shift.

She was crying. It was nothing ugly, not devastating—not Lady Ann, he thought—but her eyes were swimming. And somehow that was worse.

"Ah, hell." He pulled her into his arms. "Take it easy." She resisted, swatting at him blindly, then she went limp. She was trembling to the bone.

CHAPTER 23

They were back in New York by Friday night after zigzagging from Chicago to Minnesota, then Detroit, and finally to New Jersey. This time they shared a cab. Jonathan found himself carrying Ann's luggage upstairs to her condo. He dumped her bags on the floor. "I guess you don't have any beer."

"Beer?" Ann seemed confused. She looked at him while she chewed her lip. She'd been acting vague and distracted ever since the Kmart disaster.

"Beer," he said again. "Barley? Hops?"

She kicked her shoes off. "Oh. No." Then she added suddenly, "Damn it, I've got suits in there." She picked up the crumpled garment bag, then, looking lost, went and hung it on the kitchen door frame. She ducked beneath it into the other room. "I have wine."

"That's good." He said, trying to be funny. "But is it still fermenting?"

She poked her head around the garment bag again. "What?"

"Never mind. I'll drink it. But I'm keeping my clothes on."

She frowned. "I think that would be best."

Jonathan wasn't sure if he had just been shot down or not.

A few minutes later she came back with a bottle of Chardonnay in one hand and two glasses hooked in the fingers of her other.

She set everything down on the glass-topped table, then stared at the wine as though she had forgotten what it was for. Jonathan crossed the room, pulled the cork out of the bottle, and poured.

Ann looked up at him. Helplessly, he thought. He had never seen her this way. The crying in Chicago had been bad, but it had definitely gone downhill from there. Now he felt a sense of shifting, unwelcome changes happening to him with this woman who was staring at him now as though she'd just lost her soul.

"What am I supposed to do?" she murmured aloud.

"I don't know." He handed her one of the glasses. "You're the business whiz. I deal in paint, remember?"

"I liked that cityscape you did," she said suddenly, her mind jumping fretfully again as it had been doing all day. "The one with the vivid green and blue slashed across the canvas."

He thought of the colors in her bathroom. So she liked green. He moved to sit down on the other end of the sofa.

"I've done a lot of cityscapes," he said. Safe topic.

"The one I'm thinking of was ... I don't know. Bleak."

"That's the moody side of me."

"I bought it."

"What?" He almost choked on his wine. He looked around the room, but the painting wasn't there.

"I sold it not long afterwards," she said, reading his gaze. "Someone offered me a really good price."

For some reason, that struck Jonathan as amusing. It was so like her, he thought. Sensitive enough to have bought the piece in the first place, savvy enough to have unloaded it for the sake of a profit.

"Why are you here?" Ann asked suddenly, startling him with another change of topic.

He could have played dumb, could have offered excuses, but he decided against it. "I'm worried about you. The fact that you look like road-kill."

She swiped her hair back from her forehead with her free hand. "That bad?"

"Worse."

She shook her head. "I don't know what happened to us this past week, Jonathan."

"You want my take on it? Unqualified, unmitigated disaster."

"But *why*?" She launched to her feet and paced.

He watched her: a statuesque blond, barefoot, and in a short leather skirt. Maybe she didn't look entirely like road-kill, he thought, and he shifted his weight uncomfortably.

He'd been okay with wanting her—a little. If he hadn't wanted her—a little—he could have handled starting to like her. Tangle it together and—

She'd said something.

"What?" he asked, his voice a little too harsh. "I can't follow you." He patted the sofa. "Why don't you have a seat, Ann."

She ignored his request and continued to pace. "Something about this is too wrong," she said.

"About this past week? You've been bitching about the industry since we landed in Arkansas. I'd say you were right on the money. You—and I'm not saying you, specifically, because I know Felicia was a big part of this—but you took a gamble and got kicked in the teeth."

"Jonathan, for God's sake, they bought my *pirate ship* a number of years ago!"

He shook his head, out of his depth. "Was there a bigger market for that? Was it especially clever? I don't know the answer. Tell me. What's the difference between then and now?"

"This doll is *better*."

He put his glass down slowly.

"I've worked for Hart Toy in one capacity or another for almost seventeen years. Not once have I ever—*ever*—batted zero with Walmart, Kmart, Target *and* Toys 'R' Us." She shook her head.

"Something is wrong here. It simply doesn't make sense." She continued to prowl around the room.

"This sort of thing has never happened before?" he asked.

"No. Not with all four major retailers at the same time."

He thought about their just completed trip. Their meeting with Linda Figgures at Target had been abruptly derailed by the intrusion of her boss. Figgures had been thrilled with the doll and then her reaction changed. After a quick powwow out in the hallway, she'd told them that there was new pressure afoot to more effectively manage their vendor base. By consolidating, they could get better deals, with lower discounts and longer payment terms. She ended the conversation by saying that she'd pitch Baby Talk N Glow to the powers that be, but she couldn't make any promises.

Then they had batted out with Browns, a two-year-old chain that had sprung up in the Detroit area and had mushroomed quickly into two hundred and fifty stores. Their buyer—Gerry McGuire—had been his coarse, bitterly negative self, almost outlandishly obstinate. At first he'd lectured them on the feasibility of a doll retailing for ten dollars higher than the popular and proven price of $19.99. Then he went on about the ridiculous margin he would make, despite the ten percent package of discounts, continuing to berate them until it became clear he'd really been looking for some kind of cut he could slide into his own pocket. Ann had gotten righteous and stubborn. Another commitment lost.

Finally they'd arrived in Wayne, New Jersey, the home of Toys 'R' Us, in many ways still the most vital retailer in the toy industry. Ann explained to Jonathan how years before, the core of Toys 'R' Us' existence had been variety. Close to twenty-two thousand items in all had been offered for sale. But not anymore. Today, instead of cutting their vendor base as Walmart and Target were threatening to do, they narrowed their selection down to nine thousand products which, for all intents and purposes, was the very same thing.

The sound of the buyer's voice had brought them to attention, and Ann and Jonathan followed her to her office. Alison Steinfeld had gushed and cooed over the doll. The five-year-old business with the battery had delighted her. She'd been ecstatic. But the cost of the doll became an issue. Steinfeld insisted they come up with extra money to purchase an end-cap program, meaning the doll would have feature space at the end of an aisle in a four-foot section in each store. This was something Ann was prepared for. If other retailers got wind of it, she would definitely be held liable. Still, it would not be the first time that one major account received an advantage over another. She reluctantly gave in to the cost of the end-caps—to walk away with a commitment of only fifty thousand pieces, which was not even half of what it should have been.

Tom Carlisle of Kmart had never called back, and he hadn't taken any of her calls.

Jonathan now watched Ann move around the room. "Okay," he said. "What do we do? And for God's sake, don't make me lie to my mother again."

Her gaze bounced, then settled. "You lied to Felicia?"

"I pretended I didn't know how bad Spain was, that I was in the ozone about the details."

"Not a stretch."

He hooked an arm over the back of the sofa. "Mock me now, but this has been a crash course in everything I never wanted to know about toys. Soon I'll be taking over your job."

"Please? Tomorrow?"

There was a thinness to her voice that made him want to … do something. But, what? Get to his feet? Comfort her? Slay the dragons while she resigned herself to the inevitable? But she wasn't the resigning kind.

A minute or two passed. Then Ann scraped fingers through her hair and glared at him. "Okay, tomorrow I'll call every single one of them again," she said, her voice strengthening. "Every retailer."

"Tomorrow's Saturday," he pointed out.

"Then I'll do it on Monday. We have time."

"We do?"

"Of course. Nothing will be decided until New York Toy Fair in February, at the earliest."

"So why are you so concerned?"

"You know the saying about first impressions lasting longest? Well, it's no different here. And the vibes I've been getting back from the buyers are baffling me, to say the least."

He swallowed the last of his wine. "You'll just have to be patient."

She looked somehow lost and driven all at once. "I know," she said, and collapsed onto the couch next to him.

CHAPTER 24

Ann Lesage would soon be on her knees.

Vincent opened a bottle of celebratory wine, a Spanish rosé. Hart Toy would inevitably have to default on their contract, he thought. And that would set the rest of his plans in motion.

When his cell phone rang he looked at it as if it might be a foreign object.

"What is it?" he demanded.

There was a short silence that Vincent didn't like. "I just heard from Tom Carlisle."

"And?"

"He says he can't go through with it."

"I beg your pardon?" Vincent stiffened.

"Claims his conscience is getting the better of him."

"Did you tell him that you would have full rights to the doll within a matter of days?"

"I did. But waiting for me to put out the doll just so he can have a better price is not something he wishes to pursue. Quote, unquote. Ann's been calling him two, three times a day. He no longer has the heart to disappoint her."

"Sonofabitch! I thought you said your relationship with this guy was a strong one?"

"It is, but he's got some scruples."

"Fuck his scruples!" Vincent exploded.

"It's only Kmart. There are others in the running."

Disbelief charged Vincent's fury. "I want you to listen to me," he said quietly, his voice turning to steel. "I suggest you call Tom Carlisle and ask for a favor. I will not accept no for an answer. Do I make myself clear?"

The pause was underscored by the other man's breathing.

"Hello?"

"Yes, I hear you."

Vincent snapped his cell phone shut. Then he hurled it across the room. It hit the bar, sliding into the glasses there. It whirled over the smooth surface like a demented figure skater, finally knocking a few pieces off. They fell over, some shattering on the bar, others bouncing on the carpet.

Vincent left the mess as it was and went to pour himself another glass of wine.

CHAPTER 25

Ann was working in her office when her secretary knocked and walked in. "Jon's here," Dora said.

Jon? Ann came to her feet and stalked into the anteroom. Jonathan sat with one hip on her secretary's desk. "Well," she drawled, "if it isn't Prince Charming."

"What's up?"

"Nothing." *Everything.* "Come on in. And leave Dora alone."

He winked at the woman. Ann grabbed him by the elbow and guided him into her office.

"Watch it," he complained. "This is a good sweater. You're getting it all stretchy."

"It's nothing compared to what I'm going to do to your neck."

"What's got your panties in a twist?"

"She's young enough to be your daughter." Ann thrust a thumb in the direction of the anteroom.

"If I copulated at thirteen."

Ann skewered him with her eyes. "No wonder Carmen is history. You're a pain in the ass. I don't blame her for dumping you."

"How do you know Carmen is history?"

"Your mother told me."

"You talked to Felicia about Carmen?" That got his attention. "And for the record, *I* dumped *her*." He went around and sat behind her desk, just to gouge another reaction out of her.

Ann was wearing blue today, he noted, a long, soft sweater and leggings. And she was barefoot again. He picked up the legal pad on her desk. "What's this?"

"I just got a commitment from Kmart."

"You're kidding?"

"A hundred and fifty thousand pieces."

"That's a lot—right?"

"It was what I had penned in for them, before everything started to go to hell in a hand-basket."

"Which guy is this? Carlisle, right? The one who zoned? You changed his mind?"

"I don't know *what* changed his mind, but I never look gift horses in the mouth."

Jonathan leaned back in her chair. "I'll buy you lunch to celebrate."

"It's only ten-thirty."

"Okay. Brunch, then."

He saw something in her eye twitch. "Why?" she asked.

Because, he thought, he'd been staring at a blank canvas since 5:30 this morning. Because his muse was Bangladesh-ing in a very big way. And his thoughts of her had been relentlessly filling the void. He'd come to her office without plan or provocation, or a lot of consideration. Maybe because he just didn't want to understand what he was thinking about, or why. "I'm hungry," he said.

Her intercom buzzed. Because she was closer to the door than to her own desk, Ann simply turned around and opened it. "Who is it?" she asked her secretary.

"Gerry McGuire from Brown's."

Ann spun back into the room and nudged the door closed with

her backside. She hurried towards her desk. "I need my seat." She caught Jonathan's sleeve and started to pull.

He came out of the chair. "Damn it, will you watch the sweater?"

"If I can salvage this disaster, I'll buy you a whole closet of sweaters." She sat and reached for the phone.

"Do the speaker thing." Jonathan said. "I want to hear this."

She hit the button and said hello.

"Ann," McGuire said into the room. "You didn't hang around Detroit very long. I tried to reach you after you left my office but you were already gone."

Jonathan settled down next to Ann, laced his fingers together behind his head and watched her.

"Why?" she asked McGuire.

McGuire stammered into the quiet, then started again. "Look, your new doll has some interesting possibilities. I'd like to carry her. But come on, I can't compete with Walmart."

"No one is asking you to. I don't expect that size of a commitment from you."

His voice went sharp. "How many did they give you?"

Jonathan listened to her jump the question. "Kmart is in for one-fifty."

"Damn it, Ann, I'm not them, either. I have some constraints."

"Such as?"

A new silence beat into the room. It made Jonathan curious.

"I need a bigger discount," McGuire said finally. "One up front."

Jonathan's antennae tweaked, but he wasn't sure why.

"Gerry," Ann said flatly, "our policy hasn't changed. You get ten percent on Moonlight and everything else we do. Why should Baby Talk N Glow be any different?"

"She's more high profile."

"You said she was too expensive."

"Ah, Ann. Come on. That's an old buyer's ploy. Emphasize the negative. You've been around long enough."

"Don't remind me."

"I need an extra discount. Say … three."

"Three," she repeated.

"If it's now, on the early end, I'll settle for three. I'd just want to structure it so I'm not looking at it a year down the road."

She frowned, looked at Jonathan, then shrugged.

"Okay," she said finally.

Jonathan brought his hands down fast. What the hell? She gave a little shake of her head to keep him from interrupting.

"Okay?" McGuire sounded equally surprised.

"Brown's has been in business—what? Two years now?" she asked, seeming to change the subject.

"About that," McGuire said cautiously.

"In that time, they've instituted a series of fines that's unprecedented in the toy industry. For God's sake, Gerry, you charged me a hundred dollars for sending one invoice through the mail instead of electronically!"

"Damn it, Ann, that's company policy. I can't—"

"Listen to me, Gerry. You got me for *five* hundred dollars for using the incorrect freight forwarder. You hit me for a thousand for shipping three days early. And when I was a day late, you nailed me for *another* five hundred."

"Walmart does it."

"Their volume is much higher than yours. They have cause to be demanding. And they're still not as bad as you."

"What's your point?"

The guy sounded like he was whining. Jonathan thought.

"I'll give you three percent up front, paid to your company," Ann continued. "But I want something in return."

Jonathan sat up straight.

"I want you to reverse all those fines I just mentioned," she said, "and a guarantee that there won't be anything similar for the next two years."

"I can't—"

"Then no deal. I've got to run, Gerry. Sorry, but that's the best I can do. The three percent has to come from somewhere."

"Wait! Just wait."

"I don't have time for this. Take it or leave it."

The pause didn't last long. "All right! I'll fix the fines and go for seventy-five thousand pieces."

"Duly noted."

Jonathan watched Ann go limp in her chair after she disconnected.

"Now I have Brown's, Kmart, and Toys 'R' Us," she gloated. "The extra three percent will be negated somewhat by those fines. It'll come out in the wash."

Jonathan thought about it. "That was good."

"*That*," she answered, standing, "was a girl from Newark."

She was halfway to the door before Jonathan thought to stand as well. *Newark*? He'd known her for seventeen years and never figured out where she'd come from. Felicia had never told them, if she even knew herself.

Ann had just gambled and won. And she hadn't batted an eye while doing it. Tough streets there, he thought, in Newark.

"Where you going?" he asked.

"To brunch. Bring your credit card. I just worked up an appetite."

By the time he got to the hallway, she was well ahead of him, knocking on Patrick's door. He watched her turn the knob. Jonathan stepped up behind and peered over her shoulder.

Patrick's secretary was sitting at his desk. Jonathan remembered her as a knockout—he'd met her at last year's company Christmas party. At the moment, however, she was wan and seemed out of sorts.

"Where's Patrick?" Ann asked.

"Um … oh, Ann. He's—uh—at a meeting."

"Here? In the building?"

"No. Somewhere else."

Jonathan felt renewed tension coming off Ann like something palpable.

"Look, Verna, when he gets in touch, could you tell him I'm looking for him?"

"Will do," the girl promised.

Ann turned to face Jonathan. He was too close. She couldn't back up because the door was against her spine.

"You've made the girl nervous," he said. "Is this the Newark thing again?"

"She was nervous before I walked in." He was leaning close. What was he doing? Ann tried to ease around him. "Are you going to feed me, or what? There isn't a restaurant behind this door you're trying to push me through."

"You're nervous yourself, Ann. Why is that?"

She was dying. She wanted him, and she was dying over it. "Back off."

"It's never wise to bite the hand that intends to feed you, so stop snarling."

He finally moved. He was five steps ahead before Ann got sufficient balance back to follow. Her pride wouldn't let her hurry to catch up.

CHAPTER 26

Verna waited a long time in the same position, afraid that Ann would return.

Then the shakes began to course through her body, making her flesh tingle and causing something unpleasant to catch in her throat. That had been close, too close for comfort.

That bastard, that …Vincent, or whoever the hell he was. From a chance meeting in a bar to this, whatever this is. She didn't know; didn't want to know.

She was in love with Patrick. She would never hurt him. But she had run out of options at midnight last night, when Vincent had showed up, pounding on her apartment door. Still fuzzy with sleep, she had peered out into the darkness at his hulking presence, recognizing him immediately, no matter how brief their encounter in the bar had been. It was his scar and a menace in him that was not easily forgotten.

Suddenly, he was inside and she was lying flat on her back, with Vincent on top, straddling her, pinning her down. She yelled for him to get off of her, to get out, that she would call the police. But he had laughed in her face.

When he rose to his feet and ordered her up, she obeyed, wrapping the housecoat she had hastily put on before answering the door more tightly around her. He moved to the small table against the scarred kitchen wall and took a seat, motioning her to join him. Nervously, she pulled back one of the hardback wood chairs and sat down. Without uttering a word, he removed some eight-by-ten photographs from his briefcase and placed them on the table in front of her.

Verna hardly made a sound, but her eyes sped to the table top. He pushed the photographs closer. Her gaze dropped. They were photographs of her mother, the only person whose safety and wellbeing meant more to her than anything in the world. Her mother, who had carried on penniless after her father's sudden death in a car accident; after her brother's trouble with a series of drug arrests; and after Verna's own missteps through the years. Her dear mother, who had never failed to be there for her. Verna could not, would not, allow her to be harmed in any way. She stood abruptly, a stricken look on her face, and sent her chair flying to the floor with a thud.

"Relax," Vincent said. "Nothing's going to happen to her. You just have to listen to me. And do as I say…"

Verna remained standing, trying to envision an escape route from her apartment.

"Sit down," he demanded.

When she failed to respond, he jumped to his feet, gripped her shoulders tightly, and turned her towards the table, forcing her back into the chair. Then the tears came. As the minutes passed, she made no move to dry her eyes.

Vincent began to speak. Although she was only half listening, she heard his message loud and clear. She was to take the envelope and pouch he was about to give her and place them in Patrick's briefcase. Then she would be contacted with further instructions. Once it was done, she would never hear from him again. "I assure you this will be over in a matter of a day or two," Vincent said as he stood and made his way to the door. Then he turned back and issued his final warning. "But if you go to the police, or anyone else for help, don't count on seeing your mother again." With that, he turned on his heel and left.

Seated alone in Patrick's office now, the memory of Vincent's threat caused Verna's shaking to intensify yet again. Too numb to contemplate the contents of the envelope and pouch, she forced herself into action, opening Patrick's briefcase and dropping them both inside.

Verna was about to leave the office, when her cell phone rang. Suspecting who it would be, she reluctantly placed the phone to her ear.

"I want you to get Patrick to take you home at the end of the day," Vincent said without a greeting.

"What do you mean?" she responded. "He has an appointment this afternoon at the warehouse."

"Then you'll get him to take you with him."

"To the *warehouse*?"

"To a bar," Vincent said. "Get him drunk. As drunk as he's ever been in his life."

Verna listened without saying a word.

"Then send him on his way. Once he drives off, call the cops and report him, give them the license plate and description of Patrick's car, then tell them that unless they do something he won't make it home in one piece."

She cocked her head to the side and realized all too clearly that when the police pulled Patrick over, they would find what she had put in the briefcase. "I can't," she muttered. "I can't do this to him."

"Fine," came the bloodless voice over the phone, "then call your mother and say goodbye."

CHAPTER 27

By twenty past seven, Ann was feeling good enough to toe her shoes off and put her feet up on the desk. She closed her eyes and let her head fall back against the chair.

"Ah." Her voice hummed. With relief and yes, she thought, with pride. An acceptable reaction when you went to war with all your guns blazing—and won. But she was too drained to appreciate the full scope of the emotion when there was still one more thing she had to do.

She leaned forward to press the speed dial on the phone.

"Are you now ready to tell me the whole truth?" Felicia asked when she picked up the phone and heard Ann's voice.

Ann winced. So much for keeping her in the dark. "Of course."

"Good. Then how *are* my boys doing?"

Ann blinked in confusion. She'd thought Felicia was asking about Baby Talk N Glow. "They're fine, to the best of my knowledge. But we all know that my knowledge is limited where they're concerned."

"Pat?" Felicia persisted.

"He was in meetings all day. I didn't see him."

"Jonathan?"

Ann opened her mouth and closed it again.

"Are you still there, dear?" Felicia asked.

"I'm here. The last time I saw him he was pretty absorbed in the welfare of his favorite sweater."

"I beg your pardon?"

"Never mind. I called to give you an update on Baby Talk N Glow. Kmart is in for a hundred and fifty thousand, and Brown's gave us seventy-five."

Ann got off the subject of Jonathan fast. Everything was changing with him and she didn't know what to do about it. She didn't know what she *wanted* to do about it. Every instinct she possessed told her that he wasn't going to go away long enough for her to figure it out.

"That's high for Jerry McGuire," Felicia said, bringing her back.

"He was motivated."

"Ah, Ann." There was amusement in Felicia's voice as she read between the lines.

"I got him to eradicate those fines."

There was a pause, then Felicia laughed. "There's my girl. What about the other chains?"

"I'm still waiting to hear from Target, but they should come in for a hundred and fifty, if management doesn't interfere."

"And Walmart? No change there?" Ann had finally had to tell her the truth.

"You know how they are. If we were Mattel, we'd have an order in our hands for two hundred and fifty thousand pieces."

"But we're not Mattel," Felicia said.

"So we'll have to wait. But they'll come around."

"Toys 'R' Us?"

"Hedging their bets, but they're in. By the time I wrap up Meijer and some of the other regional chains, we ought to have at least another couple hundred thousand."

"Our breakeven point is just over six hundred thousand pieces."

Ann rubbed her stomach. Anything less, and they'd show a loss. Felicia was sick, but she was still sharp as a tack. "I know. The numbers dance through my dreams."

"One would think we'd have buyers falling over themselves to get their commitments in," Felicia fretted.

"You know how it is. Most of them just don't care anymore. One product is the same as any other. The buyers who are experienced and old enough to know better are being shipped out." It was the only way she could justify how spectacularly bad their trip to the American retailers had been. Nothing else made sense. Their doll was just too special.

"Well, Ann," Felicia said, "I have one more question before I let you go."

"Shoot."

"Are you seeing Jonathan?"

"Am I *what*?" Ann's feet hit the floor hard.

"I'm just wondering about all these trips the two of you have been taking."

"That's business."

"Of course it is, dear. And it's explained perfectly by his avid interest in toys." She disconnected.

Ann stared at the telephone. Wiley old coot. She'd been gearing up for that question through their entire conversation.

A knock came at her office door. It was late and the sound made her jump. She padded barefoot to answer it. Could it possibly be Jonathan, twice in one day? Who knew with him? He was the most contrary, unpredictable individual she'd ever gotten tangled up with. She flung the door open expecting to see his face.

"What now?" she demanded. "You've fed me, harassed me— oh."

It wasn't Jonathan. Her senior accountant all but leaped back from the threshold.

Everly Bingham was holding a computer print-out in his hands. He dropped it when she startled him. Pages fluttered to the floor. He dove to get them, the overhead lights gleaming on his bald pate between spare strands of pale, blond-gray hair.

"I'm sorry, Ms. Lesage. I saw the light on under the door and I thought, well, if you were still here, maybe you'd have a moment."

"Of course." Ann stepped back, embarrassed. "I'm sorry. I thought you might be someone else."

"No problem." He had his papers together now and he skittered inside. He had always reminded her of one of those little shore birds, the kind that darted in and out of the white-fringed scallops of surf.

Ann went back to her desk. "You're looking for me? Not Mr. Morhardt?" Bingham's job technically fell under Patrick's domain.

"I met with him earlier today."

Ann felt her stomach shift uneasily. "And?"

"He told me not to worry, but I ... well, I'm simply not comfortable with that."

His narrow face heated. Small wonder, Ann thought. He was going over his boss' head. "Not to worry about what?" she asked.

"We seem to be missing money."

"We?"

"The company."

Her heart dove. "How much?"

"A hundred thousand dollars."

Compared to the five million she'd committed in advertising dollars for the doll, it was spare change. But the fact that it was—what had he said? *Missing*—was boggling. "Where did it go?" she asked stupidly.

"That's precisely the problem, Ms. Lesage. I don't know."

"A hundred thousand dollars," she repeated.

"I could show you."

"Please do."

He came to her desk and spread the pages out. Ann stood to look down at them. He took a pen from behind his ear and began explaining. Drawing lines. Showing transfers. Fifty thousand dollars jumping around and ultimately disappearing. It had happened weeks ago.

"I am terribly sorry to have to bring this to your attention, Ms. Lesage, but in my estimation, someone ... well, took it."

She felt lightheaded. Ann sat and dug her fingers into her temples. She pressed hard. Bingham's calculations had been stellar for eleven years now. She didn't doubt him, but... "You said a hundred thousand. That was fifty."

"Yes, well, we're looking at two separate incidents. I noticed the first one some time ago. I ... well, it occurred to me..." He trailed off, his gaze jumping around the room.

"You thought it was your mistake," Ann finished for him.

Breath gusted out of him. "Yes. Nothing like this has ever happened before, not while I've had control of the books."

She nodded. It didn't seem to comfort him, so she added, "I know that."

"I became more diligent. Checking our balances online daily. I believe that's what enabled me to notice this second discrepancy right away. It's not my error. Someone would have covered this up as well if I hadn't immediately become aware of the transaction. It happened today."

Ann grabbed a page and looked at it. The first transfer had taken place on the same day Jonathan had been trailing her around Toronto. *What was she thinking?* That his sudden interest in the business coincided with the leapfrogging activity of fifty thousand dollars? He'd been here today, too, she thought, when the other fifty thousand had vanished.

Her stomach rolled sickeningly, then it steadied.

No. She might have believed it a month ago, but she knew him better now. Or so she thought. At least she knew that he didn't need a hundred thousand dollars. And if he *was* pressed for that kind of cash, Felicia had ample to loan him. He was irritating, frustrating, often outrageous, but he was also brutally honest.

And he couldn't have been moving corporate money around if he was with her in Toronto.

Not Jonathan, then. Patrick.

She'd fought for weeks to get this doll project on reasonable footing so she could give Felicia some halfway decent news. And now … this.

Someone had *stolen* from the company, at the worst possible time.

Bingham's face had gone pale as milk. Sweat had broken out on his forehead.

"You're fine," she told him. "You did the right thing, coming to me."

She tried to stand. Her legs didn't want to hold her. *Patrick*, she thought again. In so deep, with the liquor and who knew what else? Obviously into something he couldn't go to his mother about. So he'd just taken it instead.

"Mr. Morhardt told you not to worry?" She had to be sure.

"Actually, he told me he'd meet with me later in the week, that his schedule was tied up for now. But not to … uh, sweat it."

That would give him time to cover the second transaction, Ann thought.

"Maybe this is why you have no furniture," said a voice from the door. "Why bother? You live here."

Her gaze flew up. *Jonathan*. She had the single, almost giddy thought that she'd known he would show up tonight. It took her another moment to realize that he looked as bad as she felt.

He cocked his head in the direction of Bingham. Ann opened her mouth to ask him to leave, but Bingham was already hurrying to gather up his papers. He fled the room, muttering apologies for the intrusion.

"What is it?" Ann asked when he was gone.

"I need you to come with me. And bring the company checkbook. We've got problems."

"The company checkbook is a little shaky at the moment."

His eyes went thin but he didn't ask why. And that, she thought, was unlike him. "It's Pat," he said. "He's been arrested."

Ann gripped the edge of her desk, pictured her life exploding into tiny shards, raining through the cosmos. "For what?"

"DUI."

That didn't surprise her. "Okay. Is Irene digging her heels in about coughing up the bucks? I'm sure I have enough in my own account to bail him out."

"Irene says she doesn't have the money. And Mom doesn't know about this yet."

"So?" Ann said.

"God!" He paused. His face was haggard, she thought. His eyes were stricken. "They're also holding him for possession of cocaine … and conspiracy to commit fraud."

CHAPTER 28

Vincent waited in the dark shadows, far from the reach of the streetlight, watching the entrance of the precinct where Patrick had been taken. He felt a cold thrill at the thought of Ann arriving here, and couldn't wait to catch a glimpse of her face.

It was a risk, the type of risk that fed a kind of sexual excitement into his blood. She'd come here, he knew. She'd rush to try to save Patrick, even though she despised him. She'd do it for the old woman, and because of her own galling self-righteousness. But soon he would delight in her denigration, the slow but meticulous tearing apart of everything she believed in and held dear to her heart.

Ann's upbringing should have twisted her. Would have turned most women rabid. But Ann had become staunch. Perhaps her survival could be attributed to some misshapen gene at odds with the others. Or maybe to the debt she thought she owed to the hand that had pulled her out of the quicksand. Regardless, Ann Lesage had matured into a canny but moralistic force of nature, and he hated her for that alone. She would soon find out that honesty and a rigid work ethic meant nothing in the world today, and it would give her no protection from her past.

Patrick Morhardt and his petty weakness had ruined everything for her. He hoped that something vicious would squirm its way into her heart so she would finally learn to hate.

Vincent smiled into the night, savoring all the moves he had made. Discovering the source of Patrick's financing had presented even greater complications than just having the loan called due. He'd put pressure on the loan officer at Atlantic who had in turn given him Richard Salsberg. He'd convinced the attorney that it was in his best interest to demand another fifty thousand dollars from Hart Toy. Let's see her fight back now, Vincent thought.

Her vice president of finance was about to be indicted on the basis of the evidence slipped into his briefcase. The cocaine only added a diversionary complication. No matter the outcome, Ann would lose her precious baby doll ... and a great deal more.

Then she would be his, and he would make sure she understood that she could never escape her past.

Vincent stepped further into the shadows as a cab pulled in front of the precinct. Ann Lesage stepped out, as sure of herself as always and—as he had hoped—very angry. The color of her cheeks gave her away. That, and the fury in her eyes.

Then Jonathan Morhardt emerged after her.

Vincent frowned. He'd never entirely gotten a handle on that man. The younger Morhardt brother tended to be unreadable. His sudden collusion with Ann Lesage was not something Vincent had foreseen. He'd initially dismissed it. Now it caused him some concern. But in the end, the odd hitch was always to be expected. And he was confident that, in time, he would turn it to his advantage. For now, he would allow himself the luxury of savoring this desired change in Ann, seeing her unnerved, shaken to the core and about to unravel.

CHAPTER 29

P anic rushed through her veins. Patrick had really done it this time; it was doubtful whether she, or anyone else, could save him. Just the thought of arraignments and bail hearings was enough to drive her to distraction.

"Want some coffee?" Jonathan asked.

She jerked around and stared at him. An hour ago, maybe two, one of her biggest concerns had been the things this man was suddenly making her want. Now—irrationally, perhaps—she saw him as the enemy.

"I guess not," Jonathan said. He didn't need a direct response; he could read her expression.

Ann scrubbed her palms against her cheeks, trying to create friction that would bring some warmth back to her skin. "Did you honestly think we would be able to spring him free? From this, Jonathan? He's gone over the edge."

He turned away from the coffeemaker to face her fully. They were waiting in a twelve-by-twelve precinct room overlooking the detective's bullpen on the other side of the drawn blinds. The air smelled of sweat and smoke.

Jonathan moved to a cork board, yellow pages with curled edges affixed to it. "Pat didn't commit any of these offences," he said finally.

Ann gave a shrill laugh. "Sure. Go tell that to Detective Whatever-the-hell-his-name-is. I'm sure he'll take your word for it and let Pat go."

"We'll straighten this out."

"You came to get me instead of calling a lawyer! What were you thinking?"

"My first impulse was to try to contain the situation. If it can be contained."

"We're talking trafficking in cocaine here, Jonathan!" She heard her voice screech and she pressed a trembling hand to her mouth.

"Calm down," he said. "Emeril will be here soon." Emeril Lacey. Their lawyer. They'd called him from the cab on her cell phone. But he was their corporate counsel, not a lawyer capable of dealing with a situation like this.

"You're blind where Pat is concerned." She didn't want to fight with him, didn't have anything in her to fuel a fight, but the words spun out anyway.

Jonathan turned back to the cork board. "You always want to paint him black, but he's just a weak shade of gray."

"This isn't some damn canvas we're dealing with here!" she shouted. More fighting words, unstoppable. She was helpless to change the course of them. "I need you to wake up and see the facts."

"The facts," he repeated. He rubbed his jaw. "Okay, how's this? There's not a doubt in my mind that he was drunk to the gills when he got stopped. He has a drinking problem."

"Eureka."

"I might even be inclined to bite on the possession charge."

"What's another addiction or two?"

"You're pissing me off, Ann."

"I'm trying to get through to you!"

"I know my brother. There's no way that man is capable of fraud and extortion."

Ann waved a fist at him. *"He stole a hundred thousand dollars from the company!* Would you have thought he was capable of *that?"*

Emotion played over his face like a film on fast-forward. A mottling anger. And that same distrust that had marked most of their early days together. "You're out of your mind," he said finally.

"I'm not." She began to pace. "I found out just before you sailed into my office. That's what Bingham was doing there."

"And you can prove this." His tone was flat.

Ann shoved her hands into her hair hard enough that the clip holding it tore free. "I will."

Jonathan gave a bark of ugly laughter. "A hundred grand is missing so you're going to find a way to pin it on him?"

"In light of all this, don't you think he invites just a little suspicion?"

"In light of all this, I think he deserves a little compassion!"

"People need to earn compassion!"

"Did you, Ann? Did you earn it when my mother dragged you off that church floor?"

His words stunned her. Cold rolled through her, chased by something unbearably hot. Ann dropped her hands and stared at him. "You bastard." She was shaking.

"Were your wilted flowers a fair trade for a cushy job and years under our roof?" he persisted. "You took all that, then you killed a piece of her. She never recovered, was never the same. Now you think you can just take the rest?"

As soon as the words left him, he wanted them back. Her face went the color of ice. She didn't know what had happened that night on the boat. Only three people had ever known, and one of them was dead. The only sure way to keep the truth from Felicia had been to hide it from everyone, even Ann. And it had been the only way to keep Patrick out of jail all those years ago.

"What…" Ann trailed off to swallow convulsively. "What do you mean?"

Jonathan turned back to the notices on the wall without answering. He hated the gripping feeling in his gut.

"You meant something," she said. "That comment had intent."

"Jesus, Ann, I just get tired of you lambasting Pat all the time. What do you think that does to Mom?"

"I never say it to her."

He knew that. At least he had never heard her. Things inside him twisted harder. "Whatever."

"No. Not *whatever*. I want to—"

A sharp knock on the door interrupted her. Emeril Lacey came into the room.

Ann moved automatically to meet him. She glanced at Jonathan as she passed him, trying to tell him with her eyes that they'd finish their own business later.

"Thanks for coming," she said to the lawyer.

The man shook her hand, then strolled a little further into the room, stopping at the table. He was broad and tall. Ann had never seen him in anything but a charcoal-gray suit, but tonight he was in jeans and a sweatshirt.

"It's what you pay me for," he replied. "Though, under the circumstances, I've brought someone a little better versed in this sort of thing."

She felt her knees go soft with relief. He had brought a criminal lawyer. "Who is it? And where is he?"

"His name is Frank Ketch and he's with Detective Rondgrun now. I went to law school with him. He's one of the best in his field." Lacey pulled out a chair and sat. "I've got to tell you that Patrick is going to need him on this." His gaze moved to include Jonathan as well. "It looks like the D.A. has managed to put together some substantial evidence already."

It occurred to Ann then that she didn't know most of the details. She sat, lowering her head into her hands. "Tell us."

"Starting with the least serious of the charges, his blood-alcohol level was 2.2 when they picked him up. He should have been comatose. He says he was at Amoroso's on Fifth. He left there late this afternoon and was headed out of the city."

"He doesn't drive in the city," Jonathan interjected.

"The authorities have impounded a pearl-gray Volvo wagon, registered in his name."

Jonathan sat. He did it hard. "Yeah, that's his."

"He was going out to the warehouse late today." Ann pushed a few strands of hair away from her face. "He'd want the car for that."

"Well, he never made it," Lacey said. "He got maybe ten blocks before they pulled him over. Someone called in to say that Patrick was driving under the influence. The call was traced to a pay phone in the bar. A patron obviously watched him stagger out of there."

Ann hadn't meant to glance at Jonathan again. Maybe it was the sound he made. A grunt that broke off too fast.

"Go on," he said to Lacey. "I want to hear the rest."

"A patrol unit stopped him and he was reportedly belligerent. He tried to run, to take off on foot. The ensuing fight gave them cause for search-and-seizure. They found cocaine in his briefcase—in the car—a quantity that puts him in the area of intent-to-distribute. And they found a warrant issued in Hong Kong for his arrest."

"Huh?" Ann looked at the lawyer and waited.

"What does it say?" Jonathan asked.

Lacey turned back to him. "Apparently your brother finagled the rights to some doll that he had no business negotiating for."

Ann felt the room reel.

The lawyer shuffled some papers aside. "I have the name of the doll," he said. "Oh, yes. Here it is. Baby Talk N Glow."

CHAPTER 30

By the time they accompanied Lacey out of the room and were told they could see Patrick, the tension between Ann and Jonathan had reached the saturation point. It was after midnight and Ann was exhausted and on edge. Filled with hurt and confusion, she grappled with the idea that Patrick might have been trying to sabotage Baby Talk N Glow.

"Right down there," the policeman said, pointing at a narrow hallway leading off the bullpen.

Patrick was being held in a room with a cage. There were four green plastic chairs, a single, barred, grime-streaked window. The walls were shades of old concrete, mottled gray and brown. As soon as Ann stepped over the threshold, the reek of him hit her—the sour sweat of fear and vomit laced with cognac. He'd taken off his suit jacket; it was hanging on the back of a chair. His white shirt was torn at one elbow, while a streak of something black cut a diagonal line across his chin.

With seventeen years of pent-up anger, Ann moved close and slapped him. "What the hell have you done?" she demanded.

Jonathan came up behind and gripped her shoulders, pulling her back.

"Don't touch me," she warned, twisting from his grasp.

To her disgust, Patrick began to cry. His face contorted and he dropped his head so his chin hit his chest.

"Maybe we should all calm down," said the other man in the room, someone Ann had barely noticed.

Now she looked at him. He was scarecrow thin and very tall. His clothing seemed to both balloon and bag on him. He had wispy, straw-colored hair, and he wore heavy, dark-rimmed glasses. His eyes blinked myopically behind the lenses, but his gaze was steady.

"You're Frank Ketch," she said.

He nodded. "I think I can help, if you'll let me. Patrick tells me he doesn't have the funds himself to retain me."

Ann's gaze jumped to Pat again. "What did you do with the hundred thousand?"

His head snapped up but his gaze cut away guiltily. "Ah, Jesus," he said. "Jesus Christ."

She heard Jonathan's intake of breath behind her. Patrick *had* taken the money. But why?

Ann couldn't stand the smell of him, but she went down on her haunches beside his chair. She had to see his eyes. "Look at me," she said. "Where is it? Damn it, what did you do with it?"

"That's not the issue here, Ann." Jonathan's voice was raw.

"It is," Pat said hoarsely. "I mean, it could be. I think someone is trying to … ruin me."

Ann felt woozy, as if she could keel over at any moment. "What are you saying? That someone is *blackmailing* you? Who?"

"Richard Salsberg. He's a lawyer I went to for help in arranging the bank loan. I gave him the first fifty. It should have been done. He called today and wanted more." He was still drunk. He was slurring his words and rambling.

"What kind of a bank would—" Ann broke off, the words gathering like thorns in her throat. "Oh, dear God." She spun away. She couldn't look at him.

A whining tone came to Pat's voice. "Every other bank turned us down. I had to do something drastic."

Ann jerked back to him. She hadn't known it was possible to be this angry. "No, everyone else did *not* turn you down! You never even went to Margin! You had an appointment with them that you didn't keep!"

"Fuck you, Ann," he spat suddenly. His gaze went feral and shot to Jonathan. "Or is that your job?"

She didn't actually see Jonathan move. There was a blur in a corner of her vision. Then Patrick was out of his chair, hoisted in the air by his shirtfront. Jonathan shook him viciously, then thrust him back down.

Ketch took a step as though to move between them, then apparently thought better of it.

"Pat." Jonathan's voice was a low, dangerous vibration. "You're not exactly in a position to be alienating someone who might be willing to help you."

Patrick looked in Ann's direction. "If she had just backed off on the doll, none of this would have happened! It's *you*, Ann. It's always about you, from the day you walked into our lives!"

"Knock it off!" Jonathan warned.

The room pitched into silence. Jonathan had come to her defense again, Ann realized, and she didn't know what make of it.

"What do we do now?" Jonathan asked Ketch.

"First, you retain me," the lawyer said.

"Of course. How much?"

"Twenty-five thousand to start. It's non-refundable, even if he's not held over for trial. If he is, I'll need another twenty-five. Then ten when half of that is whittled away, and so on until this is resolved."

"Give me until the end of business tomorrow."

Ketch nodded. He looked at Patrick. "I'm afraid you'll be staying here tonight."

Pat had folded into his chair. Now he came out of it like someone had set it on fire. "No, I can't! I didn't do anything. The cocaine isn't mine. I know nothing about that subpoena from Hong Kong!"

"I could get a judge to hear this tonight on the DUI but not on the cocaine charge. I'm sorry. These things take time."

Ann thought Patrick was going to grab the lawyer. "I keep telling you! I don't know where that cocaine came from!" He looked like he was going to cry again. "Salsberg is doing this to me. I don't know why." He turned bleeding eyes to Jonathan. "Don't leave me here alone."

Jonathan stared at him for a heartbeat. "Well, I'm sure as hell not going to cozy up to you in that cell," he said, sticking a thumb in the direction of the cage.

Patrick focused on the wire mesh. He blanched, covering his face with his hands.

"Look—may I speak to you in private?" the lawyer said, motioning Ann and Jonathan to step outside.

Once in the hallway he advised them that Patrick was in no condition to respond to their questions tonight. "Let him sleep it off," he suggested. "Once he sobers up I'll get more out of him."

Ann turned, abruptly began to walk away. Her head was splitting. Her world was coming apart, yet she regretted her impulsiveness. She shouldn't have struck Patrick, shouldn't have allowed her feelings to get the better of her.

Her footsteps echoed. Despite the harsh words between them, she half-wished Jonathan would catch up to her, whisper something kind in her ear.

But silence followed her outside. Ann stood quietly for a moment, feeling completely alone, wondering what the future had in store for them all.

CHAPTER 31

Jonathan watched Ann walk out of the precinct and was tempted to go after her. It was late and he was past the point of being tired. Too much had been spoken in the heat of anger. He wanted to apologize. But the predicament his brother had put them in weighed heavy on his mind. Personal feelings would have to be ignored.

He said goodnight to the lawyer and went outside to hail a cab. It was getting colder. Winter wasn't too far away. He didn't need to think twice about where he had to go. If he was going to find a way to exonerate his brother he would have to do so fast.

The street was deserted when the taxi left him off at Hart Toy's office. He reached into his pocket to retrieve a set of keys his mother had recently provided him, then entered the elevator and pushed the button for his floor. What would he find? Would it be worthwhile? He didn't know, but anything was better than just sitting around, waiting for events to play themselves out.

He hit the light switch, walked into Patrick's office and right over to the three-drawer gray file cabinet next to his brother's desk. He put the key in the lock and pulled the top drawer open.

Almost an hour later, having waded through file after file of bank dealings and financial reports, Jonathan was past the point of boredom. He finally removed his coat and sat down in the chair behind Patrick's desk.

Leaning back, he allowed his mind to drift. It didn't take long for him to remember the horrible look on Ann's face when she confronted his brother at the police station. It only made matters worse that Jonathan had wrongly insinuated that she had never pulled her own weight, or that she was somehow implicated in Matthew's death. What the heck was he trying to pull?

That damn pride of his. Familial loyalty overriding his feelings for Ann. Sooner or later he would have to come to grips with those feelings. Sooner or later he would have to face the truth. But not now. Now he had to focus on the situation at hand.

New York was the least likely city in the civilized world where someone would call the cops because a man staggered out of a bar drunk. After all, there were always cabs available. So Patrick had to have been drinking with someone, someone who set him up. His brother admitted taking the hundred thousand dollars to pay off the lawyer who had helped him solidify the loan with the bank. But he vehemently denied any knowledge of the cocaine and whatever it was that the Hong Kong authorities were trying to implicate him in. It was a stretch to think that Patrick had suddenly gone from being a common drunk to a drug dealer and conspirator.

Reluctantly, Jonathan stood and went back to his chore at the file cabinet. He began examining each of the bank covenants they had agreed to over the years, the lines of credit that had been approved or disapproved. This took the better part of another hour. The second drawer revealed the agreements they had signed with the retail trade, be it Walmart, Toys 'R' Us, Target, or Browns. Warehouse allowances, advertising allowances: all documented and set in stone. The only time he paused was when he found the letter from Gerry McGuire, about Hart Toy being fined because they had shipped one day early. He remembered

Ann's conversation with the man, and McGuire's promise that this fine and others would be reversed.

The third drawer contained most of the contracts they had signed with inventors and manufacturers. There was one for their line of basic dolls. Another detailed the acquisition of Moonlight, their hugely successful board game. It was no surprise to Jonathan that most of what he was looking at originated in Eastern Asia, predominantly China. While Hong Kong still contained many of the head offices, manufacturing facilities had gravitated to areas that had sprung up and blossomed in recent years: Shenzhen, just across the Hong Kong border and designated as a Special Economic Zone, being the most notable.

Baby Talk N Glow had come to them from an inventor in Hong Kong. Despite the doll's many merits, they had encountered serious problems. Still, Ann had persevered. And with each additional step taken, the obstacles had become greater. And now this. It suddenly occurred to Jonathan that this latest incident involving his brother may have been another attempt to keep this project from moving forward. Perhaps Pat's situation had nothing really to do with Pat at all, and everything to do with Baby Talk N Glow? Jonathan realized how crazy that seemed. Did it have something to do with the inventor? The competition? Or was someone out to get Pat, as he suggested? That did seem to be the most viable scenario. Pat had alienated a lot of people over the years. Not only in business, but in his personal life as well.

Jonathan shook the cobwebs free. With some speed he took hold of the remaining files in the bottom drawer. He slapped them down on Patrick's desk and reclaimed his seat. Then he began to thumb his way through, uncovering one contract after the other. He was nearing the end when he pulled out the Baby Talk N Glow file. Opening it, he practically jumped back in alarm. The folder that should have contained the contract was empty.

CHAPTER 32

Ann woke at twenty past three in the morning with screams slicing her throat like razors. The dream always came when she felt most vulnerable. Not since Felicia picked her off the street could she remember a time when she was this defenseless. She had forestalled sleep as long as she could—pacing, drinking Scotch. At some point in the night she had finally dragged herself into bed. Now she fisted the comforter in her hands and threw it to one side. She flew from her bed, almost tripping on her way to the bathroom. She made it to the toilet, fell on her knees, and heaved. *You're hot, baby.* It hadn't—not really—been a dream.

It was a memory. He'd stunk the way Patrick had smelled tonight, of sour liquor and sweat. He'd had perfect teeth but a very mean mouth. His hand had gone to her breast and she froze. Unlike the other times, when he would simply stand and stare at her, his intention was obvious. She wanted to reach for the butcher knife she kept sequestered beneath the mattress. Yet fear paralyzed her limbs. It was only after his other hand went between her legs that she tried to reach out for it, but it was too late.

His first blow struck her forehead because she'd ducked. Some survival instinct had made her dive under his hand. He'd connected near her temple, however, and it had stunned her, flattening her.

She'd gone belly down on the dirty plank floor and he'd taken her right there, from behind, shoving up her nightgown and ripping off her underpants. The friction had been bone-dry and excruciating. He continued to pound at her until she passed out.

She'd never even known his real name, Ann thought now, spitting into the toilet. Her mother had referred to him as Mad Dog, and the name had stuck. After that terrible night, Ann berated herself for being a coward. She had been sleeping with the butcher knife for months. Yet, when it came time to use it, she was unable to act, unable to protect herself.

Ann now flattened her palms on the bathroom rug and pushed herself to her feet. She tugged her sweat-soaked nightgown over her head and turned on the shower. She would not go back to bed. She never went back to sleep once Mad Dog bit his way into her mind. She brushed her teeth and stepped into the shower, letting the hot water pelt her skin. When she got out she felt clean but unsteady. She was standing in the kitchen with a towel wrapped around her, taking her first strong, sweet mouthful of caffeine—black with three sugars—when the phone rang.

It startled her and she swallowed wrong. Coughing, she moved to the living room to answer it. It wasn't until she reached for the phone that she noted that it was close to four o'clock in the morning. Worry creased her brow as she lifted the receiver.

"Wake up," Jonathan answered to her hello.

Ann closed her eyes. Damn it, she would *not* show that she was glad to hear his irritating, familiar voice. Instead, she said, "How dare you call me in the middle of the night?"

"I wanted you to know what I've found," Jonathan said.

"Found where?"

"In your off … or at least, Patrick's office."

"Patrick's office? Jonathan, how did you get in there?"

"My mother gave me a set of keys a few weeks ago. I came here right from the police station. I wanted to see what I could dig up on this whole mess."

Ann rubbed her temples. "And?" she asked.

"Well, I didn't find anything, except for the fact that the Baby Talk N Glow contract seems to be missing."

"Missing? What are you talking about?"

"Would the contract be kept in the file cabinet in Patrick's office?"

"Yes, he keeps all of our contracts. It's up to his department to see that royalty payments are made on time, et cetera. Are you sure you looked in the right place?"

"No," he said, obviously taking her question as an insult, "I took one perfunctory glance around his office and then called you."

"Jonathan—"

"I found the file folder, goddamnit! It's empty."

"Okay, okay." She chopped off her next thought, trying to avoid confrontation. At this late hour she knew she had to think with a clear head, to make some sense of this and decide on a course of action.

"Do you have a copy?" Jonathan asked.

"I beg your pardon?"

"Do you have a Xerox copy of the contract?"

"Why—no. We never make copies. It's a contract. We never lose contracts."

"Well, you might consider some other system in the future. I would bet this particular contract wasn't lost; it was stolen."

Ann hesitated. Talk of the contract reminded her of the man she had signed it with—Edmund Chow. She looked at the phone for a moment. "Look, I'll call you right back," she said, and she disconnected.

She stood where she was, frowning. The doll was brought to them by Edmund Chow, with Koji Sashika's help. Koji had been an integral part of Hart Toy's business for over twenty years. The man had been around long enough to see a large portion of toy manufacturing leave first Japan, then Korea, Taiwan and Hong Kong, eventually ending up in Mainland China. And this was where Chow entered the picture, quickly proving his worth with his contacts.

Ann now glanced at her watch. Hong Kong was thirteen hours ahead, which made it almost five in the afternoon, their time. And it was a city very much like New York; it seldom slackened off. Edmund was usually on call twenty four/seven. She went to get her purse, removed her BlackBerry.

Koji lived in Japan and she wanted to speak to him first. She tried his cell phone; there was no answer. She left a message and hung up. After dialing Edmund's office in Hong Kong, she waited impatiently but nothing happened. It rang and rang. Voicemail did not pick up. Thinking she had dialed wrong, she disconnected and tried again. No luck. She retrieved Edmund's cell number and dialed it. Eight rings. Nine rings. Ten...

Her skin began to crawl. Something was wrong. Very, very wrong. She called Jonathan back and explained the situation.

"And why is this unusual?" he asked.

"Because it's never happened before. You would have to know the mentality in Hong Kong, the work ethic. In all the years I've known him, Edmund Chow has never been unavailable, even for a minute."

"Then why don't you send him an e-mail," Jonathan suggested. "And we'll see what happens in the next twelve hours."

She held back from expressing her frustration. The e-mail would go out but something told her it would do them no good. "I'm going to book a flight to Hong Kong," she said and paused, waiting for his response, knowing it suddenly mattered.

"Then count me in," Jonathan said, not disappointing her.

CHAPTER 33

Patrick stepped into the court room, his mind churning. Ann was there, with Jonathan beside her. No sign of Irene, he thought with relief. For the most part, the gallery was full of strangers, people there for different cases, not his alone. And in that crowd only one sane face, one comforting presence—Frank Ketch, at the defense table.

The prison guards delivered Patrick into the lawyer's care. Patrick was sure that Ketch believed him. They'd talked relentlessly that morning, going over the evidence and the fact that the D.A. didn't have much of a case. Ketch pulled out the other chair at the table for him. "Sit down."

Patrick did, clumsily. The guards left.

"You're squared away here?" Ketch asked him. "You know what to say?"

"I want to go home," Patrick said.

"In due course."

"I *need* to go home."

Ketch ignored the comment, then stood suddenly and identified himself to the court.

A ferret-faced woman at the next table, skinny, in a dark blue suit, did the same, declaring she was the Deputy District Attorney representing the people of the State of New York. Patrick's skin started to feel clammy.

He was finding it difficult to concentrate. Last night in his cell, he'd gone through the DT's. It had been inevitable and he'd anticipated them. He couldn't recollect a single day in the last year and a half that he hadn't had a drink. Maybe longer. Maybe three years, or five. By now, today, his craving for cognac had grown teeth.

"What?" he jolted when Ketch elbowed him. Then he remembered what he was supposed to do. Patrick stood. "Not guilty, your Honor."

Of course, I'm not fucking guilty.

He started to sit again. Ketch kept him upright. "That was the DUI charge," the lawyer said in an undertone. "Keep going."

Pat recited the words two more times as the other charges were read.

Ketch offered no argument on the DUI matter. He was giving the prosecution a bone, he'd said, mostly because a 2.2 was indefensible anyway. The not-guilty plea was standard, and for appearances' sake. It would give them the option of plea-bargaining with the issue somewhere down the line.

The judge moved on to the cocaine charge. Ketch asserted that the substance had not been Patrick's. The prosecution chewed on that for awhile; they had the edge there, too. It had been in Patrick's possession, plain and simple.

They finally got around to the fraud charge. Ketch stood and went into gear.

"Your Honor, I'll be filing a motion this morning to dismiss that charge. It has no merit. My client is an executive at a reputable firm in the toy industry. He has no prior criminal record and has lived an exemplary life. This particular charge involves a new product that has not yet been released on the market. It was acquired through legitimate means. We contend, and will prove in court, that there is a conspiracy against my client, and that it involves a plot to discredit him as well as his company, thereby rending this new product worthless. A product, I might add, that was purchased for an advance of one point five million dollars."

The judge looked only mildly interested. He shuffled through papers as though to remind himself of something. "The State has concrete evidence, correct?"

"Incorrect," Ketch argued. "They do not have anything but a sworn affidavit accusing my client of conspiracy to commit fraud. This is based on a groundless subpoena issued in Hong Kong, by Lord knows what authority."

The Deputy D.A. stood. "Your Honor, it's our position that the subpoena is legitimate. We will prove in court the merit of its validity."

"Then let the court return to these charges when this proof is provided," Ketch insisted. "Until then, I'd suggest my client deserves to be released on his own recognizance."

The Deputy D.A. stood her ground. "We have three separate charges here, Judge!"

"No, in fact, we do not," Ketch said. "This so-called fraud was not even committed on American soil. In all honesty, I fail to see how the State of New York has any jurisdiction in the matter at all."

"We're not only permitted to hold the defendant for extradition," the judge said, "but we're bound to do so by international law." He took off his glasses and rubbed the bridge of his nose, looking both thoughtful and frustrated. "I can't let the defendant walk out of here, giving us nothing but his word that he'll return for the preliminary and extradition hearings. The drug charge alone makes that an impossibility. And, if I remember correctly, he attempted to run from the arresting officers in the first place. I'd say he's something of a flight risk. I'll set bail at two hundred and fifty thousand dollars, but I will hear your motion to dismiss, Mr.

Ketch, as soon as you file it." He reached for his gavel and seemed to relish clunking it down.

Patrick stood and grabbed Ketch's arm. "I'm not a flight risk!" *Where the hell was he going to come up with that kind of money?* "You said you could get me out today!"

"I said there was an excellent chance of that. You'll be free to go once bail is posted. They'll take you back to the holding cell until that happens."

"Let me say something to the judge. I was drunk. I didn't understand what was going on when I tried to run."

"I don't think so. You'd only make matters worse."

Patrick felt dread move into his veins like cold sludge. There were many kinds of hell, and he was well-acquainted with a number of them. There was his wife's blistering tongue and his brother's arrogant perfection. There was his mother's chiding eyes, always judging him and finding him lacking, especially when compared to Jonathan. But this hell, the very personal hell he found himself in now, was completely unfamiliar to him.

Then he saw his brother—and Ann—standing behind the attorney. "Jon." Patrick wanted to hug him. Jonathan had saved him before; he'd get him out of this now. "Do something about this. Please."

Jonathan planted a hand on Patrick's chest and kept him back. "Hold yourself together."

Patrick blinked as a sense of misgiving moved inside of him. He looked at Ann. Something bad was happening and Ann was behind it. She was always behind everything.

She held out a paper, legal-sized and crowded with too much small print. "Sign here, Pat."

"What's this?" He had the sudden conviction that if he took it from her hand, he'd be damned.

"Six weeks of nice, cushy living. In a rehab clinic."

"I'm not—"

"Fine," Jonathan said, turning away. "Then sit in jail until this is resolved."

"Wait!"

But Jonathan didn't stop.

What the hell was wrong with him? Why was he acting like this? Patrick grabbed the paper from Ann's hand and hurled it to the floor. He went for his brother, grabbing him from behind.

The guards caught him. Ketch was apoplectic. "We'll finish this back at the jail."

"No," Ann said. "Now."

"That's not wise," Ketch said. "We need privacy. We don't want to play this out in front of the prosecution."

Jonathan bent and picked up the paper. "Pat, you need help."

Patrick's heart was slugging his rib cage. He felt sick.

"We don't know where Irene is at the moment, but by law she can claim half of everything you own," Jonathan went on. "We can't get to your assets without her. You can't even come close to making bail on your own. Mom will give you the money provided you stop drinking. Those are her terms. It's called tough love, pal."

Patrick felt his own eyes shift as he struggled with the situation. His mother wasn't with him twenty-four hours a day. There was always a way out. He grabbed the paper out of his brother's hand.

"Sign at the bottom," Jonathan said.

Patrick stared at it. "Mom's making me commit myself?"

"She doesn't trust you to do it otherwise."

"I didn't *do* anything! This is all some fucking mistake! You heard Ketch." He waved a hand at the lawyer. "They don't even have probable cause!"

"You blew a 2.2," Ann snapped. "You were inebriated enough to allow someone to set you up for the rest. Damn it, for once in your life, Patrick, take some responsibility!"

He tried to kill her with his eyes. Then he signed the paper, slashing his name across the bottom. Patrick thought about making Ann eat it. Then, with utmost control, he handed it back to his brother instead.

"I'll show you where to go to post bail," Ketch said to them.

Jonathan nodded. "My mother has requested that you or one of your associates transfer Patrick to the clinic personally. We need to know that he gets there."

Ketch paused. "How can I reach you?"

"My cell phone." Ann rattled off the number. "We might be in Hong Kong, trying to sort some of this mess out. But my phone will work there."

Patrick watched his brother walk away, hip to hip with the woman who had single-handedly taken everything that was his birthright, everything he should have been able to call his own. He looked at Ketch. The son-of-a-bitch had known all along what Jonathan and Ann were up to.

Anger rushed through him, making him shake. He hated them all.

CHAPTER 34

"How many does that make?" Jonathan demanded. He stood behind Ann, leaning forward to stare at the computer monitor.

She clicked the *send* button on the screen. "Five e-mails. I've also sent two faxes."

Jonathan swore softly and moved away.

They were still trying to reach Edmund Chow. Koji had called them back twice, once to ask how he could help, the second time to let them know that he, too, had been unable to reach Edmund. "Do you want me to fly to Hong Kong?" he had asked them. But Ann didn't see the point. The job was hers to do. She had to resolve the mystery of Edmund Chow's disappearance and get to the bottom of whatever dirty tricks they had fallen prey to.

It all boiled down to keeping their doll on track, finding a way to keep her viable. Ann could practically feel the competition nipping at her heels. The way that Sidney Greenspan had questioned her when they saw each other in Spain was just one small indication of the circling that would begin. She could not lose the doll now.

Ann came to her feet. She did a few shoulder shrugs to try to work out some of the stiffness. "What time's our flight?" she asked.

"Ten o'clock. That means we have to be ready to go at 7:30. We have one hour."

"I need to go home and pack. I'll check my BlackBerry on the way to the airport to see if Chow's responded."

"He's pissing me off," Jonathan snapped. "He's supposed to work for us, right?"

"Presumably." She was wracking her brain to come up with an explanation.

"Damn it, will you stop that?" Jonathan said with emphasis. "You're making *me* hurt."

"What?" She looked at him blankly.

"This." He imitated the way she had been rolling her shoulders. "Turn around."

Ann obeyed without thinking. His hands came down on her shoulders. She jumped forward and pivoted. "Don't."

"You prefer pain?"

"Actually, I'm numb." Something in his eyes made her understand this went beyond a simple shoulder massage.

"Let's go," she said. She grabbed her briefcase and started out of the office. "Do you want to call your mother on the way?" They'd given Felicia no details of the mess they were in, hoping for an easy fix. But the woman was too astute, she'd realize they were holding something back. For the time being, she was completely preoccupied with Patrick's problems. Sooner or later she would turn her considerable mental resources to the issue of the doll.

Jonathan hesitated, then shook his head. "Not quite yet."

When they got outside, the sky was starting to brighten, with the rising sun and the light actually hurting Ann's eyes. They got into separate cabs and sped off, agreeing to meet an hour later. Their game plan for Hong Kong was to find Chow, as well as Charles Ling of Mae Sing Creations, the inventor of Baby Talk N Glow. His was the only name—other than Chow's—that Ann could remember from the contract she had signed. Her desperate hope was that, if nothing else, Ling would be able to confirm that he was in the loop when it came to the negotiations that had taken place.

As for Jonathan, his cab ride home found him thinking about Koji Sashika. He could not find it in his heart to doubt a man whom he had known since he was a boy—one who had spent countless hours with him, bringing him treats and gifts from Japan. This was another piece of the complicated puzzle which was driving Jonathan to get some answers. Regardless of what they ultimately discovered, he could guarantee that Koji was blameless.

By seven o'clock Jonathan was through packing and knew he could no longer delay. He had to call his mother. When Cal Everham answered the phone, he was so spinelessly glad, he was ashamed of himself.

"How is she?" he asked the doctor.

"Sleeping. Holding up. This whole situation with Patrick has galvanized her. But personally, I've known her too long and too well. I understand that she hides her weaknesses by pushing herself beyond endurance."

Jonathan frowned when he heard Cal's words. Ann was exactly like his mother. Two peas in a pod. "Well … at least you convinced her to rest."

"I slipped a little something into her wine."

He laughed. "You'll see her as often as possible until we return?"

"Of course. Jonathan, try to make quick work of this. She's being inundated with calls. I'm trying to intercept them, and Sidney Greenspan is going to come by tomorrow to do phone duty while I go to my office. He's just back from China himself, as I understand it."

For all his foibles, Greenspan was a good friend, Jonathan thought. "He ought to keep Felicia on her toes."

He disconnected and made one more call, this one to Frank Ketch's home number. "How is Patrick doing?" he asked when the man came on the line.

"All tucked away. And very unhappy about it, I must say. Let's hope this helps our case."

Jonathan hung up the phone and checked on the time; he was cutting it close. In the cab on the way to Ann's apartment, he faced the fact that they were off on another trip. The stakes were higher and the outcome even more unknown. He should only be focusing on the challenge ahead. Yet he found himself picturing Ann, the two of them in a heated embrace that would lead to bed.

He and Ann had a rocky history. It defied logic that he should be contemplating such a scene with her. Although he finally had to admit that he wanted her. No, *more* than wanted her. It was a craving that had squirmed its way into his psyche and taken hold. He was sure he had seen desire in Ann's eyes, too. But Jonathan was also aware of how conflicted she felt. Even if he could assuage her fears, where would that lead them? They would both have to know where they were headed before they began that journey.

When the taxi arrived at her building, she was lingering under the entrance awning with her suitcase. For the second or third time, seeing her there, waiting for him, took his breath away. It was with great anticipation, and some apprehension, that he realized they would be confined again. Another plane, another hotel. The two of them. Together.

CHAPTER 35

The Cathay Pacific flight was practically full in Business Class. Ann expected a fairly comfortable ride on this new Airbus. It was equipped with seats that fully reclined and there were to be no stops in either Los Angeles or Anchorage to delay their arrival. Despite the usual head winds, they would be sixteen hours in the air instead of twenty-one. Finally, a technological improvement in flying that she could appreciate.

Not that this fact lowered her anxiety level. She swallowed a few antacid pills and lowered her window shade. She would not be at ease until they arrived in Hong Kong.

"Hey," Jonathan complained. "I can't see."

"Better that way," she retorted.

The staff of Cathay was more accommodating than most and there was no shortage of food or alcohol. Sleep, however, was difficult for them both, even with the newly configured seats. A quarter of the way through the flight, Jonathan picked up the conversation by asking how many times she had flown to Asia.

Ann had to think for a moment. "This is number twenty, I think." She started counting on her fingers. "Yes, twenty."

"So you like going there?"

"Me? I hate it."

"Then why go so many times?"

She sighed, remembering that she was dealing with a novice. "There are two sides to our business, Jonathan. The domestic side, where we ship out of our own warehouse, and the F.O.B. side, where we act as the sales agent and sell goods directly from Eastern Asia—mainly China—to the retail accounts."

"I still don't see why you have to go there so often."

"Neither do I."

"What do you mean?"

"Look—let me make this as simple as possible. Ever since television advertising began, margin has taken on more importance for our industry. Sales increased dramatically while profits diminished to dangerous levels. The North American toy buyer, especially, began to search for creative ways to guide him back to a healthier bottom line. Barbie, for instance, might cost nine dollars, yet retail for nine ninety-nine. Not a positive trend. Not if the buyer wants to keep his job. So what we end up with is the constant search for *mix*, that magical combination of advertised toys that are sold close to cost, with basic goods, many classified as parallel developed products, which is a fancier name for knock-offs. These *copies* retail for close to the original toys but bring in profit margins of fifty percent or better. *Capisce*?"

"No." Jonathan's frustration began to show. "You're still not telling me why you have to be there."

She shrugged. "Simply stated, our competitors go, so we have to do the same. Years ago, when market conditions were different, buyers were able to search out unique product that was exclusive only to them. Today, for the most part, what one buyer finds, the others find as well. There is no longer a practical need for anyone to go to Hong Kong. Having the goods manufactured in China should not necessitate visits to Chinese showrooms. Samples can be flown to the States and shown to buyers there."

"I get your drift. One retailer goes so the others follow. And we at the supplier end must cater to their needs. But isn't it expensive?"

"Very. Millions upon millions of dollars spent. And most of it wasted. A vast sum of money that shows up in the cost of goods sold, ultimately paid for by the consumer."

Jonathan sighed and shook his head.

They were both silent after that. Ann closed her eyes and tried to sleep. Jonathan turned to a novel he was reading.

Three-quarters of the way through the flight, Ann became restless again. This was the worst part. So near and yet so far. The air was thick. She stood in the aisle and stretched. She went to the bathroom. It was inhumane, she decided, to ask anyone to take a flight this long. Inhumane and stupid.

When she got back to her seat, Jonathan opened his eyes and she talked him into a few games of Rummy. Another meal was offered, but they both declined. Ann slept and Jonathan fiddled with the personal video system. Then they reversed roles.

Finally, their landing approach was announced. It was nearing three o'clock in the afternoon, Hong Kong time. Two o'clock in the morning back in New York.

Ann raised her window shade and peered outside. She smiled at the memory of her first time arriving here, almost fourteen years ago. Nothing could beat the sight of the old airport and its surrounding environs. They had flown across Victoria Harbour, then the Tsimshatsui district at the tip of Kowloon Peninsula, with rows of modern hotels spreading inland from there to the oldest part of the city, and still further into Mainland China. It had been an impossible corridor for any aircraft to traverse—skimming rooftops, it seemed. So close, Ann could see laundry hanging from apartment balconies, people leaning out of windows, as the plane narrowly wended its way between buildings.

Remembering that first visit now as they landed at Chek Lap Kok, all Ann could see was open space. The thrill of landing at the old airport was gone. Another example of the city itself, how it had been transformed from something magical into just another port of call.

"A penny for your thoughts," Jonathan said as they both stood when the seatbelt sign went out.

She shrugged, a wave of vertigo hitting her. It was always the same after this miserable flight. She could hardly wait to get her feet on solid ground.

They cleared customs, then Ann led the way to the transportation desk where a representative of their hotel was waiting. Fifteen minutes later they were relaxing in the back seat of a stretch Mercedes, hand towels provided by the driver, followed by bottles of water.

"Nice way to live," Jonathan commented.

Ann smiled. "It's a service provided by most hotels here. Of course, we pay for the transportation, but the towels and water are free."

"Aren't we being a little extravagant?"

"This is one place where extravagance rules. Besides, our only other options would be a cab driver who might not understand English, or the train with its irregular schedule and a stop far away from our hotel. Which would you prefer?"

He sighed. "I get your point."

"Thank you," Ann said. "Now—look outside."

They were passing the high-rise apartment buildings of Lantau Island and more open space than Jonathan expected, including the distinctive area of Discovery Bay, and the road leading to Hong Kong's Disneyland.

Once through the Cheung Tsing Tunnel, they passed one of the world's largest container ports. "Almost one hundred thousand containers shipped daily," Ann pointed out.

Then, fifteen minutes later, they entered the tourist area of Hong Kong known as Tsimshatsui, where space was not only at a premium, but appeared nonexistent. Row after row of mid-rise apartment buildings, alongside office towers, hotels, restaurants and shops, all crammed together in some kind of weird urban grid.

Traffic slowed to a standstill. Horns honked. Thousands of pedestrians, dressed in everything from business attire to jeans, jammed the narrow sidewalks.

Jonathan caught Ann's expression and asked why she was smiling.

"You should see your face," she told him. "Isn't it what you expected?"

He shrugged. "I didn't know what to expect. But it sure is crowded."

"And it keeps getting worse, especially since 1997, when Hong Kong reverted from a British Colony to being controlled by the People's Republic of China. For the first time, the border has opened up to many Mainland Chinese, and they are flocking here in droves, monopolizing the tourist trade and sending prices, which were always high, skyrocketing."

The Mercedes finally eased to a stop in front of the Grand Palace Hotel, one of the newest and most popular in Kowloon, a glass and steel monolith, rising thirty-five stories. They went inside and came face-to-face with an ultra-modern lobby—marble walls and ceiling with an almost infinite variety of sculptures and paintings—so crowded with visitors that Ann felt disoriented.

After they registered at the front desk, Jonathan asked is she'd like to jump in and start looking for Chow or if she'd prefer to rest for a while.

Ann shook her head. "No."

"To which?"

"Both. I'd like to take a walk first, if you don't mind. Just tip the bellboy. He'll take our bags upstairs."

CHAPTER 36

Their hotel was located on one of the intricate side streets that populated this part of Hong Kong. Traveling through what felt to Jonathan like a maze—many of the streets intersected at the weirdest of angles—it took them a few minutes to reach Nathan Road.

They started north, squeezing their way through knots of people on the sidewalk. Ann's ears buzzed with conversations in Mandarin and Cantonese, French, German and Italian. She wasn't sure, but she thought she recognized Hindi and Arabic as well. Traffic snarled around them, belching fumes.

Jonathan nearly stepped in front of a car, when Ann tugged hard on his sleeve and pulled him back safely to the sidewalk "You must look in the opposite direction to back home," she warned. "Always remember, cars have the right of way here, unless there is a traffic light, and even then you have to be careful."

"Yeah." He coughed. "And I bet they never heard of unleaded fuel, either. Man, I'm choking on their exhaust."

"Get used to it," Ann said. "Hong Kong's pollution keeps on getting worse."

Jonathan paused. "Remind me again why we're not in our rooms relaxing?"

Because I'm afraid I'll end up in bed with you. "Because you're generous and kind, and you're humoring me."

"I don't humor my own mother."

Suddenly, a diminutive East Indian fellow accosted Jonathan. "Make nice suit for you, sir," he said, pulling on Jonathan's jacket. "How about tailored shirts? Can be ready in twenty-four hours. No problem, sir. We have the finest materials."

Jonathan came to a full stop and began to apologize to the man, to explain that he really wasn't interested, when Ann more or less told the fellow to get lost.

When they were alone, Jonathan muttered that she shouldn't do that, treat people in such a rude manner.

"Okay," she said, rather too easily.

Less than a minute later a twenty-something-year-old Chinese man was blocking their way, holding his wrist out. "Copy watch?" he asked. "Rolex? Cartier?"

Jonathan looked around for Ann but she had walked ahead. "Er ... sorry," he tried to say, but the man was being persistent. "Very cheap price. Okay? Also have Louis Vuitton purse. Gucci. Valentino..."

"Uh, no. I'm really not interested." Jonathan tried to escape but the man wouldn't leave his side. Jonathan started a slow jog. The man finally gave up when he crossed onto the next block. But six or seven more offers came his way. Suits, shirts, purses and watches. The spiels were endless.

When he reached her side, Ann began to laugh. "Still want me to be polite?" she asked.

Jonathan just looked at her.

"These are professional shills," she informed him, "paid by their bosses to snare tourist suckers like you. Everyone wants to make a fast buck in Hong Kong."

Something in a storefront window caught Jonathan's eye and he turned towards it, came face to face with a smorgasbord of opulence unlike anything he'd seen before: from row upon row of twenty-four-karat gold jewelry, to a display of brilliant diamond broaches, rings, and necklaces, to the most exclusive watches, resplendent in their showcases.

Every few steps produced a variety of the same, jewelry stores that intermingled with shops that featured designer eye glasses and the latest in electronics.

Finally, Ann had to tap Jonathan on the shoulder. "I didn't know you were a shopper."

"Huh?" He came back to her as if fleeing a stupor. "I'm not."

"Then why are you stopping at every shop window we pass?"

"I don't know. There's so much to see."

"Well, you have a choice," she said. "You can either enter one of these fine boutiques and buy me a little trinket, or we can continue our walk."

He did not require further motivation.

Turning east, they left the modern part of Tsimshatsui behind. The streets narrowed and the congestion on the sidewalk clotted even more. The odors of raw fish, chicken, and meat saturated the air. Shops and food stalls were jammed together elbow-to-elbow.

"We should be scenting down Chow," Jonathan complained, "not Moo Goo Gai Pan."

"Can't we please just enjoy this?" The words rang false to her ears.

"I can't enjoy it. I've got too much on my mind."

Me too, she wanted to say, realizing she was wasting precious time. But she'd been on edge more and more lately. Something was combusting internally and it was dangerously close to the surface.

Crossing another street, they happened upon a small park, isolated and on its own. It seemed so out of place, it drew their attention. A handful of elderly women were going through the movements of Tai Chi. Ann paused to watch, fascinated by their slow and deliberate steps, the women shifting their weight from one leg to the other, almost as if they were defying gravity.

One individual caught her eye, somewhere between seventy and seventy-five, wrinkled but still elegant, a Chinese version of Felicia. She was about to point this out to Jonathan when he abruptly joined the group of women. Soon, he began to mimic their movements, except it was no imitation, it was the real thing. And he was good. Ann caught the delicate turn of his artist's hands gently caressing the air. For a moment, time stopped. Yet again, Jonathan transformed before her eyes, and not for the first time in recent weeks, she felt something stir inside.

When he returned a few minutes later, she had an urge to take his hand, to touch him. Instead, she quickly led the way back to Nathan Road. A slight breeze had picked up and her hair blew across her face. It was hot and humid for November. "Now I'm ready to look for Chow," she announced. "His office is in the Tung Ying Building."

Much of the Tsimshatsui district was within walking distance, and they quickly reached their destination. They entered the lobby and rode the elevator to the fifth floor.

Edmund's office seemed unoccupied. There were no lights on inside. Jonathan rapped a closed fist hard against the opaque glass.

Ann grabbed his wrist. "You're going to break something."

His fingers caught hers and Ann tugged away. "Will you stop?"

"Where the hell is he?" He looked at his watch. "It's barely four-thirty in the afternoon. There should be a secretary here, *someone*."

He had a point. This time Ann did the knocking. Some movement caught her eye. She rattled the doorknob. Finally, a lock was unlatched. Her blood pressure seemed to spike. Until that moment, faced with seeing him, Ann hadn't realized how insanely angry she was at Chow. But when the door opened, an elderly Chinese woman with a large beauty mark on her cheek peered back at her.

"Yes," Ann started to explain in a slow and deliberate manner. "We ... are ... looking for Mr. Chow. Mr. Edmund Chow?"

The woman muttered something in Chinese. It was so rapid-fire, Ann felt as though she had done something wrong. Then the woman was gesticulating, words flying from her in a fury.

"Edmund Chow?" Ann repeated, taking a step back.

The barrage became worse. Ann tried to look past the woman, to see if anyone else might be in the office. There was no way she was going to leave without some answers.

Jonathan was about to push through the door when a man suddenly appeared. He was younger-looking than the woman, tall, with thinning black hair.

"There is no Chow here," he said in perfect English.

Ann turned to Jonathan.

"Where is he?" he asked.

"I do not know anyone by that name."

"This is his office," Jonathan said.

"Sorry. No. You are mistaken."

Ann stepped back, wondering if she had indeed made a mistake. 508. No, this was right. She'd been here on business many times before.

"You can see for yourself," the man said, surprising her by stepping aside and ushering them into the office.

He flicked on the lights. Ann crossed the threshold, feeling vaguely spooked. The woman remained by the door, her angry stare poking at Ann's back.

Nothing was the same. The walls wore paper instead of paint. The furniture was new, sleek and expensive. Chow had kept the place littered with cheap folding chairs.

"What the hell!" Ann murmured aloud.

"We have been here for over ten years," the man volunteered. "And I do not know any Edmund Chow."

Ann dug the heels of her hands into her eyes. But when she looked again, nothing had changed. She took another step, then two, looking around for some piece of stationery, some toy sample … something that was as it should be.

"You might have the wrong place," Jonathan said from behind her.

"The heck I do."

Before either could resist, the woman took both their arms and propelled them out of the office and into the corridor. The door slammed shut behind them.

"Where are you going?" Ann demanded when Jonathan hurried ahead and buzzed for the elevator.

"To check for his office number in the lobby."

That would make utter sense, Ann thought, if she had been mistaken.

They rode the elevator to the lobby. Chow wasn't listed on the marquee. Ann pressed a hand to her forehead. "They're lying."

"Come on, Ann, why would they do that?"

"I don't know. Why would someone plant cocaine in Patrick's briefcase? You tell me."

She was rewarded when something dark settled in his eyes. Then he looked up as though he could see through five floors to Chow's office above. "That was too easy," he said. "Too neat."

Ann thought about it. The guy had just ushered them inside to prove his point … almost as though he'd expected them.

"When you called Chow yesterday," Jonathan said, "was it the same number as always?"

"Yes."

"I guess he could have moved and taken the phone number with him."

Something hit her. "There were two separate phones on that desk upstairs."

"When was the last time you were here at his office?"

"I don't know. Six months ago or thereabouts. Why?"

"Chow didn't disappear ten years ago, Ann. That guy said they'd been in the office for ten years. He offered it right up. We didn't even have to ask." He paused. "The son of a bitch is lying. And I bet you I know why. How much money did you give Chow?"

Ann jerked, though on some level she'd known it all along. "The full million-five he asked for. He took our money for the doll. He took it and—and—"

Jonathan finished when she couldn't bring herself to spit it out. "Rabbited."

"All those negotiations I went through with him. Second and third year percentages. He knew all the while that it was just bullshit. He'd have my million-five and be long gone."

"He paid those people upstairs to cover for him."

They turned together, ramming shoulders. Ann slapped at the elevator button. They rode in silence back up to the fifth floor. This time Jonathan shouted when he punched his fist against the door of number 508. "Open up, damn it. *Now!*"

The man did, but he kept the door on a chain. "Go away."

Jonathan drove his weight against the door. There was a cracking, splintering sound as the metal tore free from the wood. The man leaped back, stumbling, hollering. Then Jonathan was on the man. He grabbed him by the lapels of his suit and lifted him just enough to drive him back against the wall.

"How much?" he demanded.

The man started shouting in Cantonese. Telling the woman to call the police, Ann was sure. She was nowhere to be seen now.

"Hurry." She barely recognized her own voice.

Jonathan thumped the man against the wall again. "He pays you to tell anyone who asks that you've been here for years, doesn't he? He pays you to let him leave his phone hooked up here! Tell me and I won't hurt you."

"He'll kill me." This came out in wretched English.

Ann grabbed Jonathan's arm and pulled. "That's answer enough." She listened for police sirens. "*Please.* Let's get out of here."

"I want to know where the bastard is." He shook the man. "Where's Chow?"

"I don't know!"

"How do you get the money?"

"He wires it into my account!"

Jonathan abruptly let the man drop. He grabbed Ann's hand and they fled the office.

They were on Nathan Road when the first police vehicle careened onto the street, lights flashing a sickly blue. Ann instinctively tried to duck lower.

"They don't know who we are," Jonathan said. "We're not the only Americans visiting Hong Kong."

Her brain was chugging, trying to work. "We should change hotels," she said. "We need to tangle our trail in case they make inquiries."

He surprised her with a bark of laughter. "You've got a criminal mind." Then he caught her chin, turned her face toward him, and kissed her.

She didn't see it coming. Something exploded behind her eyes and stars rained in her head. She brought a fist up to hit him and heard herself moan instead.

She was mortified by her reaction. But she didn't stop him.

The first lick of his tongue was fast, forbidden. Then his hands were in her hair and he held her steady for an assault. Again. Deeper. He tasted dark and dangerous, like everything she feared, but Ann still wanted more. From him, this man she'd hated, wanted, through almost half her lifetime. He broke away first.

Ann stared at him, feeling drained and electric, dazed and alive. "If you ever do that again, I'll kill you."

He smiled slightly, then moved in for another kiss.

"I mean it!" She pushed him away.

This time, he laughed.

CHAPTER 37

When they finally got back to their hotel and she reached her room, Ann swiftly entered and locked the door behind her. She moved tentatively to the foot of the bed and dropped there, looking around vacantly.

There was a courtesy bar. The cabinet faced the room, a dark glass front threaded with pretty decorative wire. And just inside was a neat little bottle of Dewar's. The sight of it made Ann jump to her feet. Just what she needed.

When she tried the glass door, it rattled in its frame but didn't give. She slid her palms over the counter beneath it. It couldn't be locked—Hong Kong hotels *never* locked their mini-bars. Then again, this was a new hotel, with perhaps new rules. So where was the key to the damned thing?

Ann pressed her hands to her cheeks and fell gently to her knees. She could feel herself coming undone.

The contract for their doll was missing and Edmund had hit the highway with the company's money. Her vice president of finance was up on conspiracy and drug peddling charges. Her dearest friend in the world was dying. And Jonathan Morhardt had just kissed her like he wanted more.

A crazed laugh worked its way up in her throat. Ann dropped

her hands and let it take her. She would handle all of it, she thought, but she wanted a drink first.

"One step at a time," she whispered aloud, pushing to her feet. She'd learned a long time ago that when things got amazingly out of hand, the only thing to do was prioritize.

The problem with Baby Talk N Glow was that it was going to take days, perhaps weeks—along with the collective minds of many people—to unravel. She'd done what she could this afternoon.

Patrick was in Frank Ketch's hands now—there wasn't much she could accomplish on that score, either.

Only God could save Felicia.

That left Jonathan for immediate consideration, and the Dewar's. She went to the phone and called his room.

"Do we have keys for these contraptions?" she demanded when he answered.

"What contraptions might you be speaking of?"

"Some sadist locked up the Scotch."

"Ah. That key. I have it."

"You have mine?"

"I guess I forgot to hand it over."

"Thanks. Very thoughtful of you."

"I'll be there in fifteen minutes and we'll have that drink together. I just want to jump in the shower first. I ordered room service. It's coming to your door. I got you a steak. Sign for it."

Fury at the way he spoke to her, the way he took over, hit her first. Then a wave of helplessness, something she hadn't felt in a very long time. She understood instantly that there was nothing she could do to stop him. So she decided to get cranky. "I don't want to eat in. I want to go out."

"Too late. The food's already on its way. Besides, I've had enough of the great polluted outdoors for one day."

"I don't eat red meat."

He paused for a moment. "On principle, or is it a health thing?"

"Principle."

"Oh. Then either call down and change the order, or live dangerously for one night."

"Why would you do something like this?" she demanded.

"Something like what?"

"Order dinner for me!"

"Must be these Lancelot tendencies of mine."

"I don't need anyone to…to—"

He waited.

"I don't need anybody," she finished, hating the hitch in her voice.

"Ann, I really don't feel like discussing your amazing strength right now. I want to take a shower. I stink."

"Well, I want my key."

His sigh gusted into the line. "Fine. Meet me in the hallway. I'll toss it to you."

They had not been given adjoining rooms. Or a suite. Ann tried to be grateful for that. She hung up and went to the door. He was already in the corridor. Shirtless and barefoot, in jeans, looking amused. Something poked at her insides. He lofted the key in her direction and she caught it across some twelve feet of space.

She turned without saying anything and went back to her room. She freed the Dewar's from the cabinet. With drink in hand, she hit the bathroom, turning the shower on hot, then she stared at her reflection in the mirror. He'd had her doing the same thing in Chicago, she remembered, just staring at herself in the bathroom glass. But this time she didn't feel brittle and empty. She felt … achy.

She wanted very much to break her own rules; it was a yearning that almost folded her in two. She wanted to be normal and weightless, and just give in to what he was suggesting. To touch and shiver and explore without walls. She didn't want to be scared.

Ann began ripping off her clothes—the khakis and shirt felt like they'd begun to adhere to her skin. She balled them up and heaved them to the floor, then grabbed her glass and took another deep guzzle of Scotch. She wasn't just angry at him, she realized. She was upset with herself.

In every other way—in *every* other area of her life—she had triumphed. No matter what Jonathan had said at the precinct, she'd taken nothing free from anyone. Yes, Felicia had given her a job, a series of jobs, but she'd made the company money. Yes, Felicia had gotten her a private tutor, but she had paid back every dime. No one would look at her now and think she was the daughter of a wayward, drugged-out mother. No one would look at her and correctly surmise that she was the loneliest person on earth.

No one ever had to know, Ann thought. What she did personally was really no different from what she did professionally. Lovers and associates got from her exactly what she chose to give. She could offer up to Jonathan the woman he thought she was and never let him be any wiser. But, oh, God, how she wanted just one person, one man, to really know her.

Ann began to shower. A sudden knocking on the outside door jolted her out of herself. She remembered that Jonathan had ordered room service.

She shut the water, dragged herself into the bathrobe that had been left hanging next to the shower, and dashed to the corridor door. She jerked it open ... and there he was. He still wore jeans, but now he had topped them with an obnoxious Hawaiian-print shirt.

"Where's the food?" She craned her neck to look behind him.

"Ann, you really need to put on some clothes."

Heat streaked through her, followed by cold. She stared at him, her mouth forming words that wouldn't come.

"I meant that in a wholly hygienic sense." He stepped past her into the room, holding a beer and his laptop. "But it got you thinking, didn't it?"

"No." She turned to follow him with her eyes, then finally thought to slam the door shut.

"Liar. By the way, while we eat we can see if we have any e-mails from home." He indicated the laptop.

"I'm not going to go to bed with you," she blurted.

He laughed.

She wanted to jump on him. Wanted to just fling herself across the room and pummel him. Or drag the clothes off his body. She wanted to drive her fingers into his still-wet hair. She wanted to hate him and she wanted to give herself over to him completely.

In the end, Ann went back to the bathroom. It wasn't until she finished with her shower and stood dripping on the tile that she asked herself what she really, truly wanted. She towel-dried her hair. The pin-striped shirt was long, hitting her at mid-thigh. She put that on, along with panties, then sailed into the room, still rubbing her head with the towel. She wondered if she *was* playing games with him, trying to get his attention with what she was wearing.

Room service had arrived. There was a small oval table in one corner and it was laden with food. Jonathan sat there, working at the cap of a fresh bottle of beer. Ann smelled fish. Good fish. Something like … Dover sole.

Her stomach rolled. It had been entirely too long since she had last eaten. She went to the table and plucked the silver dome off her plate.

It *was* sole. With lemon and a cream sauce she was sure contained wine. "How did you do this?"

He looked up at her. "I learned to use a phone when I was three."

"You changed my order?"

He sliced off a bite-sized portion of his steak, forked it into his mouth, and chewed. "That's the general progression of things when one commits such a social gaffe," he said finally, swallowing.

She had to get her equilibrium back. "That wasn't a gaffe. You just didn't know."

"Watch it there, Ann. You're starting to sound magnanimous."

"Stop eating and listen to me a minute."

Jonathan put his fork down too exaggeratedly. "Go ahead."

Ann sat. Carefully. "Thank you. For dinner."

"You are very welcome."

"But I'm still not going to bed with you."

CHAPTER 38

Jonathan let her fall asleep in the chair. He closed his laptop and went to the door. He paused and looked back at her. She was tucked sideways, her knees drawn up protectively, offering a nice, long angle of leg. *What was she afraid of?* Sure, there'd been bad times between them, some jousting and nipping, but nothing to warrant the kind of unease he'd sensed in her today.

He had never liked complicated sex. Her reaction to him should have turned him off, turned him away. But Jonathan found himself intrigued, picking at it. Theirs would be a temporary liaison anyway, he reasoned. They scraped off each other just a little too much for anything long term.

He went back to his room. Worn out from the time change and too many hours without rest, Jonathan slept like the dead and was roused in the morning by an insistent rat-tat-tat on his door. He opened one eye. The bedside clock read just past seven.

Feeling bleary-eyed and sluggish, he got up, narrowly remembering to pull on a pair of sweat pants before he opened the door.

Ann was wearing a crisp white suit. She was rubbing her neck as though it was stiff, but she was all business. "Get dressed," she said. "I talked to the police sergeant who issued the subpoena for Patrick's arrest. He's agreed to meet us at nine o'clock."

"Do I get to eat first?"

"Is that all you ever think about?"

He let his gaze climb her legs deliberately. "No."

"Damn it, stop that!"

"Then take your clothes off and assuage my curiosity."

Ann felt it like a punch—an electric, immediate arousal all tied together with something that hurt. She turned away, heading for the door. "I'll meet you downstairs."

"You'll have a long wait. I'm going to order up breakfast first."

That stopped her. "We can grab something on the way."

"That makes no sense, Ann. They can be frying my eggs while I'm in the shower."

She rubbed her forehead, then came back into the room. "I'll order. What do you want?"

"Two eggs over easy, toast, potatoes, bacon. And I don't want to hear a word about my cholesterol."

"Hey, they're your arteries." She watched him head for the bathroom, finally breathing again when he disappeared inside and closed the door.

She'd had another night of dreams. Mad Dog woven in with Jonathan, the two metamorphosing back and forth. She remembered thinking vaguely—as she had nodded off—that it was okay to let herself drift into sleep because Jonathan was with her. As though Mad Dog couldn't come around if he was there. She'd just doze for a little while until he left, she'd thought. Then she'd woken, whimpering at two o'clock in the morning.

She'd been awake ever since, trying to decide what to do about these recent developments between them.

Give in to him, something inside her whispered. *Give it up.* She already knew that sex with him would be wild and exciting. And then it would be over. No harm done and she would move on. And if it was horrible, if he somehow sensed everything inside her that was lacking? So what? They'd never been close until now. They'd just go back to what they had been before all this had started—antagonistic, vaguely familial strangers.

That was when she realized she had started caring about his opinion of her. Because she didn't want him to know she was lacking. Broken. Used. Cold.

She was still standing there, staring at the bathroom door, when it opened. Jonathan came out and looked around. "No food yet?"

"Oh, shit," she muttered, and went for the phone.

She called room service, then she phoned New York. She tried to ignore his presence as he wandered in and out of the bathroom. At one point, she heard the buzz of a blow dryer. Then her call went through and she had her secretary on the line. She had briefed Dora on the Baby Talk N Glow situation before Patrick's bail hearing.

"How's everything going?" Ann realized she was almost afraid to ask.

"About what you'd expect," Dora replied. "The wire service has picked up the story of Patrick's arrest and we've been all over the news, except the truth has been exaggerated, making everything sound worse. Rumor has it that we won't be able to continue with the doll. We've had calls from no less than eight competitors, all offering to take her off our hands."

"The damn sharks! What else?"

"All the major buyers are howling."

Ann felt her anger rise. "Call them back and tell them nothing's changed. We're still going ahead with Baby Talk N Glow as planned."

"Okay, then." Dora sounded pleased. "I'll do my best to convince them."

"Tell them all that I'll be in touch personally as soon as I get back to the States."

Ann hung up just as room service arrived. Jonathan sat at the table and dug in. She nibbled toast and drank coffee, and kept on her feet. At some point he'd changed into navy blue slacks and a white Polo shirt. She was glad he'd lost the Hawaiian print.

"I want to go now," Ann said, putting her half-eaten toast back on the plate.

"Then by all means, let me jump to my feet and race out of here." But he pushed his plate aside anyway.

Ann went to the door and waited for him while he collected his wallet and key card.

Outside of their hotel Jonathan was surprised to see how few pedestrians there were compared to yesterday afternoon. But it was early and Ann had mentioned that people no longer worked long hours, even if most owners and executives were on call day or night. Vehicular traffic was still congested, however. Jonathan had never seen so many Mercedes in one place at any one time. Walking a few blocks, he soon got caught up in the magic of the street names—Hanoi and Mody, Peking and Canton—all spelled out in Chinese as well as English.

A few minutes later Ann had guided them to the entrance to the Star Ferry. It was far busier here. Men, women, and children, mostly locals mixed with a few foreigners, all lining up at the turnstiles, the majority willing to pay approximately the value of thirty American cents to travel first class on the upper deck, while a surprising number, bent on saving close to half that amount, were entering the lower deck.

Hong Kong was comprised of two parts; Hong Kong Island itself, home of the stock market, banking, and head offices servicing the business community, and Kowloon, which catered more to tourists and whose territory led directly into mainland China. In the city guide in his hotel room, Jonathan had read that the Star Ferry, or Ferries, included twelve boats that traveled between Kowloon and Hong Kong Island on a regular basis, every day, seven days a week. Up until 1972 when a tunnel was built, and then the subway, or MTR, in 1979, this had been the only means of transportation between the two parts.

Standing beside Ann now, waiting in line to board the ferry, Jonathan looked at her, grinned, and said, "1841."

She waited.

"That was the year the British got the Chinese to sign a treaty ceding the barren island of Hong Kong to them."

"Wonderful." She frowned, giving him a look that said she was really not interested.

"This agreement was soon extended to include Kowloon."

"This is better than Paris, Jonathan. You seem to know everything."

"1898," he said.

Ann purposely kept her comments to herself.

His grin extended. "That was the year the mighty British Empire had China sign a ninety-nine year lease giving them control of the New Territories, thereby lessening the chance of attack from the mainland." He paused. "A little shortsighted, wouldn't you say?"

Despite herself, Ann asked, "And why is that?"

"Because," he said, "the first treaty left them with the rights to Hong Kong Island and the Kowloon peninsula in perpetuity, but the second was a lease that would expire in ninety-nine years. We arrive at 1997 and the British are caught looking ridiculous. It would have been impractical, if not foolhardy, for them to have tried to hold on to one part of the colony without the most important part, the New Territories, the parcel of land that bordered the mainland. Bye-bye British protectorate, and so much for perpetuity. It's a shame, really. But what else could they have done?"

Silence followed his little speech. Then Ann asked, "Are you through now?"

Her disinterest didn't bruise him, but he kept quiet after that. They entered the ferry through the gangway and took a seat on one of the wood benches. There was nothing glamorous about this ride. It was all a throwback to another era, with elderly coxswains, many of whom had missing or rotting teeth, riding alongside them. Yet the short journey across Victoria Harbour, all of eight minutes or so, was eye-catching if nothing else, despite the refuse in the water which included everything from pop and beer bottles to toilet paper, and too many other varieties of waste to count. The view was what made it worthwhile, however. In the near distance, high-rise office towers with neon signs gave off a multi-colored display. Closer, the odd sampan, oil tanker or cruise ship passed by.

They arrived at Central District and Ann led the way off the ferry. A short walk brought them to Harcourt Road, where they turned east. Jonathan found this area to be more sterile and less cluttered.

"What time did you call this guy, anyway?" he asked Ann, meaning the police captain.

She shrugged. "I don't know. Six-thirty, maybe?"

"And he was there already, working?"

"I got lucky." Ann felt jagged, irritable. She wanted to sleep. She wanted to continue to tease Jonathan. She wanted to run and hide from everything.

They arrived at the police station with twenty minutes to spare and were put in another dingy room with stone walls and a yellow linoleum floor to wait. Cop shops were the same the world over, she thought.

Someone went to find Bruce Tang.

The door opened within minutes and the man came into the room. "Sorry I kept you waiting," he said with hardly the trace of an accent.

Ann towered over him by a good four inches, but he was twice as round. Not fat, exactly, but stocky. He wore a white, short-sleeved dress shirt with an aquamarine tie that was slightly askew. His black hair was razor-cut and his face oval. He had eager eyes.

Ann moved to shake his hand. "You didn't," she said. "We're early."

He pulled out a chair at the single table in the room and sat. "We've contacted your authorities in New York," he said, looking only at Jonathan. "We certainly want Mr. Morhardt for questioning, but we are not charging him with a crime at this moment."

"Oh?" Jonathan said. "Then what's this all about?"

"Does the name Edmund Chow mean anything to you?"

"Of course," Ann said. "He has looked after our company's manufacturing and product development here and in mainland China for the past ten years."

"He gave me the impression he hardly knew you. The story he told was one of duplicity. Patrick Morhardt attempted to steal one of his products from under his nose." Papers on the desk were shuffled aside. "Yes, here it is." He turned a sheet over. "Baby Talk N Glow. A doll that he says he was negotiating to sell to Hasbro that Patrick apparently took without authority for your company or himself, it was unclear which. Mr. Chow was quite adamant that this doll belonged to him and him alone. I was going to—"

"Did he mention the inventor of this doll?" Ann interrupted. "Or the fact that our company signed a contract for worldwide rights, and that we paid him an advance of one point five million American dollars?"

Captain Tang rose to his feet. Directing himself to Jonathan once more, he said, "My dear sir, if what this lady is saying is true then we had best get Mr. Chow in here for a round of serious questions." He made to walk out of the room. "I'll get one of my men on it right away…"

"Don't bother," Jonathan stopped him. "The man's absconded. We've been trying to reach him without success."

"Is that so?" the policeman said, returning to the room and reclaiming his seat. "We will see about that. Please—let me have the contact numbers you have for Mr. Chow."

Ann rattled them off. "But we have a more pressing issue," she explained. "We must locate Charles Ling, the inventor of the doll. His company is called Mae Sing Creations. If anyone can shed some light on the situation, it should be him."

The policeman raised his pen and, without looking at Ann, asked Jonathan for Mr. Ling's phone number.

"We don't have a number for Mr. Ling," Ann answered, placing a firm hand on Jonathan, who seemed ready to protest against the policeman's obvious sexist attitude toward her.

"Address?"

She shrugged. "Sorry."

Captain Tang leaned back in his chair. "Then may I see a copy of the contract you have signed?"

Ann took her time, began to explain the precise details of how they had acquired the rights to the doll, then how the contract had gone missing. "We could really use your help, Captain," she said, "starting with finding Charles Ling."

"I will find Mr. Ling," the policeman said with some determination. "And Mr. Chow as well. What hotel are you staying at? I will call you with some news before the day is out."

Ann gave him the information, then stood. Captain Tang gave a slight bow in her direction but shook Jonathan's hand.

The minute they were out on the street, Jonathan pounced on her. "Sonofabitch! Why didn't you tell him how rude he was being towards you!"

"It wouldn't have done any good!" Ann flung back at him. "Do you think he'd be helping us if I had?"

"Fuck him! We don't need his help." He left her standing and started to walk away.

"Hey—" She came after him. "I'm touched, Jonathan. I really am. But the fact is we *do* need him."

"Oh, yeah? Well, screw it! I want out of this rat hole!"

"Why? Because of his rudeness? Come on, Jonathan. The stakes are too high for this. Besides, this is China. I've gotten used to it."

He hesitated. Yes, it did bother him that someone treated her with such obvious disrespect. And it bothered him even more that he cared so much, and that he was powerless to do anything about it.

But Ann was right. He had to keep his personal feelings out of it. Finally, he took hold of her hand, noticing with pleasure that she did not try to pull it away.

CHAPTER 39

They disembarked the Star Ferry on Kowloon side and began the walk back to their hotel. The muffled sound of her ringing cell phone sent Ann into a panic. Where was it? In her briefcase? Her purse? A second later she held the phone to her ear and heard the voice of Emeril Lacey. "I've got good news and bad," he said.

Too much good always made her nervous. "I'll hear the bad."

"In all likelihood, you're out the million five you laid down for this baby doll in the first place."

As bad went, it was digestible. "I knew that."

"If the authorities ever find Edmund Chow you might get it back, but my guess is he's gone for good, and our time would be better spent moving forward."

At least they were thinking along the same lines, Ann thought. Finding the inventor of the doll, Charles Ling, was what mattered, but she didn't want to get into that now. "What's the good news?" she asked.

"I've spoken to Felicia. She wants you to know that the loss will be covered by her reserves. She asked me to tell you not to worry."

Ann shrugged. "Tell her I'll try."

"Call me if there is anything else I can do."

"Will do," Ann said. She thumbed the off button.

"And you're agreeing to what?" Jonathan asked.

"Huh?" She looked at him as if she'd forgotten he was there. "Oh—nothing. Emeril Lacey just wants us to know that your mother is not concerned."

They walked another block and a half before Jonathan said, "Ann, what happens to you personally if Hart Toy folds?"

"I'll have let down the one person who matters most to me."

She said it without hesitation or guile. And Jonathan found himself believing her. But that wasn't the point he was making. "Could you get another job?" he asked.

"I don't know. Probably. But it wouldn't be the same."

He cocked his head quizzically, listening for more.

"Felicia taught me this business. I wouldn't be comfortable anywhere else."

"What I'm trying to get at here is that you're not likely to go personally bankrupt any time in the near future. Nor is my mother. You'll both survive if there's a crash."

"Financially, maybe. But emotionally?"

He ignored that. "Charles Ling has a lot more to lose—or gain, as the case might be. Think what you know about the working class of China."

Ann had a sudden, vivid flash of one of her first trips to Hong Kong with Felicia. Edmund Chow had taken them to one of his factories. She remembered traveling a dirt road that led to a cramped alleyway. The air had smelled of desperation. Too many people jammed helplessly and hopelessly into tiny dwellings. The 'factory' had been housed in one of those, with wooden, unpainted support beams, and gaping windows void of glass. At least a dozen people—men, women, crying children—bellied up to a table like thirsty drunks in a bar, fingers plucking, snapping, flashing, as pieces of plastic came together. The image of a stoic, arthritic old woman forcing her hands to cooperate, soundless tears streaming down her cheeks, flashed through her mind. The sweltering heat in the room had been unbearable.

Ann doubted that Charles Ling was in those dire straits—and she realized that working conditions had vastly improved since then—but she got Jonathan's point. If they were desperate to find him, he must be just as desperate to find them. But would he even know where to look?

"I'm not going to claw him out of one cent," she said quietly, "not because of our own misfortune, not because we're already down a million-five."

"No," Jonathan said. "I don't want that either. If we find him, then we pay him what we were willing to pay Chow."

All this talk was making Ann anxious to talk to Felicia. She looked at her watch. Thirteen hours difference meant it was 9:30 the night before in New York. She punched numbers into the cell phone and Felicia answered herself, sounding groggy. "Okay, get rid of the male strippers," Ann said lightly, wondering if Cal was still feeding her medication. "We need to talk business."

"Ann?" A confused pause. "Are you back home, dear?"

"No, I'm still in Hong Kong."

"Is Jonathan there?"

Ann frowned. Felicia knew they were making this trip together. "Yes. Would you like to talk to him?"

"I've been so worried," she fretted. "I've been trying to reach him."

Ann's heart cramped. "He's fine, Felicia. We're working to straighten this mess out, remember?"

"Sidney's here," she said by way of response.

"Who? Oh—" Greenspan, Ann remembered. Jonathan had said something about him dropping by for phone duty.

"He says to tell you—wait." Felicia seemed to move her mouth away from the phone for a moment. "He says he told you so. And he called our doll a nasty name. Oh, Sidney, really," she chided.

She was absolutely vacant, Ann thought. The Felicia she knew would never wander through aimless conversation when important business was at hand. "Can I speak to him?" Ann asked suddenly.

"To Sidney? Of course."

After a moment, Greenspan's voice ricocheted into the line, a roar that pinged and echoed. Ann held the phone slightly away from her ear.

"She doesn't sound good," she said to him. She felt Jonathan shift his weight quickly, suddenly, beside her.

"Old girl's got some miles in her yet," Greenspan boomed.

"Does Cal have her sedated?"

"The doc? Been here, gone. He should be back in a couple of hours. Want me to have him call you?"

That probably meant yes, Ann thought—but Felicia hadn't caught on to it yet. "Please. In the meantime, do me a favor. If you get a somewhat lucid moment with her, tell her that the Hong Kong authorities are not proceeding with the charges against Patrick at this time. They just want him for questioning."

There was a pause. "I'll tell her," Greenspan said. "Is there anything else?"

"No. Thank you, Sidney." She disconnected.

"Felicia sounded horrible," Ann told Jonathan. "Cal must still be slipping things into her drinks. She forgot you were here, then she didn't remember she wanted to talk to you."

"Maybe she knows I'm in good hands."

Ann was about to comment when she felt Jonathan's fingers at the nape of her neck, kneading out tension there. In spite of all the reasons not to, she leaned back with a soft groan and let herself enjoy it. "Stop it," she said in a small voice.

"Here's what we're going to do," he said, ignoring her protest. "We're going to grab a bottle of champagne from the bar and celebrate."

"It's mid-morning. And there's nothing to celebrate."

"Not yet there isn't. But my intuition tells me there soon will be. We can hit the pool at the hotel," he went on. "They'll probably have a Jacuzzi or whirlpool, or something good like that."

"You want to blow off the rest of the day?" Ann straightened away from his hand reluctantly.

"We'll have the phone with us. Captain Tang said he'd call us before the day is out."

"I don't have a swimsuit."

"We could use the tub in my room."

It rolled over her in a slow ache. Needing. Wanting. Wishing. "Try again."

"All right. I'll buy you one."

"A tub?" she asked, purposefully dense.

"A swimsuit."

"Where?"

"I don't know. Why would you need one anyway?" His face was deadpan.

They arrived at their hotel and Jonathan led the way inside.

I'm going to do this, Ann realized. *I really am.* She was going to drink champagne in the middle of the day and probably end up in bed with him. But she'd never been swept away in her life. Mad Dog had seen to that when he had taken what she had never intended to give. So sex had always been a difficult decision for her. And it was the same now, but the decision was somehow accompanied by an unfamiliar sense of elation.

Jonathan guided her to the gift shop, pausing at the rack of swimsuits. "What's your favorite color?" he asked.

Ann focused on him. He was standing at a skinny rack of bikinis. "White."

"Won't work. You're too pale." He paused. "I know. Blue." He pulled a suit off the rack.

Ann grabbed it out of his hand. "I'm paying for it," she said.

"You're not going to try it on first?" he asked.

"If it's a size six, it'll fly." She wasn't going to be in it long anyway, she thought giddily. And her pulse quickened. She paid and headed towards the lobby, clutching the bag as Jonathan made for the elevators.

"Last chance to weasel out," he said, grinning back at her over his shoulder.

"If I did, would you leave me standing here like an idiot?"

"Yeah," he said. "But I'd come back for you."

CHAPTER 40

Jonathan watched her push through the door to her room. A flash of common sense intruded on his thoughts and erased the image of Ann in the blue bikini. If there was any chance of stopping it, now was the time. Was this a mistake?

It would—beyond a doubt—be utterly complicated. And there would, most certainly, be some kind of fall-out. From Pat, from his mother. They would know. His chemistry with Ann would inevitably change, their mark on each other lingering long after their goodbyes.

Then there was the issue of Matt, he thought. Flames, death, bitterness and broken promises. All that should matter, too. But it didn't. Why? He would leave the answer to that question until tomorrow … or the day after.

Jonathan went on to his own room. He found gym shorts—good enough—and he changed. Then he called down to room service for a bottle of Taittinger.

After the champagne was delivered, he stepped into the hall at the precise moment Ann came through her own doorway. He expected to see that blue bikini and nothing else, but she wore white cotton drawstring pants and a short red top over it. Her blond hair was loose now. Her eyes seemed clearer.

"Ready?" he asked, his voice remarkably mild.

In response, she headed for the elevator and pushed the down button.

They exited at the bubble-domed pool area, looking for the hot tub room. The first door they opened revealed two men with Buddha bellies in a sauna, sweat pouring off them. Jonathan muttered something apologetic and backed out.

The second door led to the steam room, air thick with eucalyptus. Inside there was a brunette in a black thong bottom and a top that wouldn't quite hold her. Ann closed that door faster than Jonathan had closed the first.

Third door. Nowhere left to go. She eased it open.

The hot tub was empty. For the moment, anyway. Ann sat down and put her feet in the water.

Jonathan couldn't keep his eyes off her. Those long, long legs. Yellow-blond hair spilling forward, hiding part of her face. Hands clasped together in her lap. The tiny swatch of blue bathing suit barely covering her breasts. The suit fit. Well.

He closed the door behind him and—eureka—it had a lock. Privacy, he thought. He turned the knob and waited for the audible click.

She looked up, her eyes the color of a cloudless sky. "You forgot glasses," she said.

He looked down at the bottle of champagne in his hand. "Ah. Right. So sorry."

One corner of her mouth curled.

It hit him with almost debilitating force. He had never wanted a woman more than he wanted Ann right now. Maybe it was the month of teasing that had created such a rush of anticipation. Or maybe the sense of taboo. Or was it the memory—a tall, pretty girl walking away from him on the beach, her long skirt gathered in her hands, making him feel randy and grateful that she would not exchange vows with his brother.

Somehow, Jonathan managed to maintain his dignity and took his place beside her. He put the bottle between them and dropped his legs into the scalding water, wincing at the shock of it.

Ann picked up the bottle and poked a fingernail into the wire mesh holding the cork.

"I'll take that," he said, and snagged the bottle from her hands. Her eyes went pale and wide.

She was in an evident state of panic, he realized. The best thing would be to give her no time to think. He adeptly popped the cork, tipped the bottle and slugged from it. Then he poured a splash straight down her cleavage.

Ann gasped at the cold. Her eyes skirted to his, slid away, came back. It was all the time he needed to put the bottle down and lean into her.

She thought he was going to aim for her mouth. She was ready for that. In some murky inner place, she knew this had pended for far, far too long.

That was why there would be no finesse, she thought. No gentle playing. Just something finally breaking free. And she could handle that.

His mouth slid over her collar bone, diving to her breasts. Ann knew one moment, one nearly shattering moment, of terror. Then it was gone. Her fingers were in his hair, holding his head against her, and she thought no more at all.

His tongue found her skin, sliding where the champagne had flowed. Then it traced over the edge of the bikini top, hot, rough, licking, teasing. Ann felt herself sliding off the edge of the tub, into the steaming water. He went with her, then he brought his head up.

She saw his eyes through the fog rising off the surface. She told herself not to look. She had to close her own eyes and go with this in some deep internal place. That way it would be safe. But he never did anything the way he was supposed to. Nothing in the kind of order she could categorize. And he wouldn't let her hide.

"Ann," he said. "Look at me."

She moaned and opened her eyes. Then his mouth finally took hers. His kiss was nothing like before. This was hard and devastating, pushing her lips apart so she'd meet his tongue. Just when she thought they would play at that for a while, she felt his thumb at her hip. He dragged at the scrap of blue bikini bottom. Down, strangling her thighs.

Ann told herself to get this back onto ground she was used to, where she was in control. But she felt herself kicking the bottoms off frenziedly, her own hands moving all the while, plucking and tugging at the shorts he wore. Suddenly frantic. Hurrying. Now, now, now, she thought.

Now, right now, need screamed inside her. For an immediate sense of fullness. To have him there, where he belonged. They floated together until her back was against the edge of the tub. She lifted her legs and wrapped them around him. She felt him probing, almost gentle at first. Then with a sound like his soul was being torn apart, he drove into her.

They sank beneath the surface.

Breathing was the furthest thing from Jonathan's mind. He moved inside her, because that was pure instinct. He wrapped his arms around her and pulled her closer still. Too soon, too suddenly, she arched backwards and came. And he thought that if he lived another fifty years, he'd forever see the bubbles rise from her mouth, forever hear her soundless cry, as her eyes flew open then closed, as she floated back to him, connecting one more time.

CHAPTER 41

Rage was alive inside Vincent when he rapped his knuckles against the apartment door. Frustration was an animal that moved just under his skin, with painful scales and vicious claws.

Ann Lesage wasn't giving up. She was in Hong Kong, wheeling, dealing, trying. The stubborn, kiss-my-ass bitch refused to understand that she was up against a brick wall and could go no farther.

She had been on the hunt for Chow. Vincent knew that she hadn't found him. He'd gotten a call from the whimpering, whining fool whom Chow had put in the office there. Perhaps she had found Ling. Vincent was waiting for further word to ascertain if that had happened.

A call to the New York district attorney's office—he had posed as a reporter—had informed him that Patrick Morhardt was temporarily off his legal hook. He would be tucked away, drying out, for another five and a half weeks or so, thanks to Felicia. Vincent intended to wrap this up before Patrick got out of the clinic and could cause problems.

From all reports, Felicia would not survive much longer. But no matter. If she didn't go quietly, he would find a way to help her along.

227

Jonathan Morhardt might still only have a limited knowledge of Hart Toy, but he was proving to be the biggest nuisance of all. Vincent knew the time would come where he would have to be dealt with as well.

As for Ann, he would have his release. The years of waiting would soon pay off. But first there were other loose ends to attend to.

Verna's door opened a crack and she peered out at him.

"I have to see you," he said. "Let me in."

She went to close the door, but his foot was wedged behind it.

"I just came for the contract," he explained quietly. "Were you able to get it for me?"

Despite the promise of safety the chain on the door provided, Verna began to break out in a sweat. "Not yet," she said. "I'm sorry. I'll take care of it tomorrow."

Without commenting, Vincent threw his weight against the door and crashed his way into her apartment. In a matter of seconds, he had her pinned against the wall.

He hit her before she could recover, hard, in the jaw, hearing the crack of bone. He pushed the apartment door closed behind him and locked it.

Verna lay spread-eagled on the floor. She was so dizzy she thought she would pass out. Her mouth was on fire.

"Verna?" he called her name.

She hoped if she ignored him he'd disappear, like a ghost.

He bent over her, reached down and forced her to her feet. She was wobbly and could not support herself. He guided her to the closest kitchen chair. "I will ask you one more time," he said.

"Please…" she whimpered.

His fist came up and caught her on the other side of her jaw. Her bare toes caught in the chair support. It jerked her weight towards him and threw her off balance.

This time there was no crack of bone, but her eyes rolled back in her head and she started going down.

On the floor, she collapsed in the fetal position.

He saw an opening and kicked her in the ribs. Then he leaned over her. "For the last time, where did you put the contract?"

When his question was met with silence, his foot found the back of her neck, and he stomped down, putting his full weight behind it. She went flat suddenly and was still.

Vincent reached for a fistful of her hair and used his grip to roll her over. Then he cracked her head, again and again on the floor. He caught her arm and twisted it back, feeling bone give. He kicked her in the hip, got down on his knees and pummeled her with his fists. Now there was blood. Everywhere.

When he finally stood, his hands were stained. He went into the bathroom, washed up, and began his methodical search of the apartment. He had instructed the bitch to steal the contract, and he suspected it was here … somewhere.

He began with the hall closet, checking the few shelves, going through her sweater and coat pockets. From this closet to the one in the bedroom. Then drawers in the kitchen were opened, and the ones in the bureau in the bedroom.

Nothing. He couldn't find a thing.

Losing patience, he was just turning away when the bed caught his eye. He reached under the mattress. Nothing there. He strolled to the other side and raised the pillow … and there it was.

Satisfied, he pocketed the contract, and with a final glance at Verna's broken body, headed out the door.

CHAPTER 42

This was bullshit. *Bullshit.* Four days now without a drink, Patrick thought. Four days.

He looked around at his prison-like room, breathing hard. White walls. A narrow single bed, with a mattress about as deep as a postage stamp. One pillow, hard as his mother's heart. With the intention of slamming it against the wall, he went to pick up the lamp from the bedside table but it was clamped down. Just as well. If he threw anything, nurses and various personnel would come running. They'd give him another needle. The last time he'd caused a fuss, he'd slept for thirteen straight hours.

It was almost suppertime and he'd just gotten a call from Frank Ketch. The lawyer had told him the Chinese were sending someone to the States to talk to him. Big deal. No hardship. He was going to lose his driver's license for a while. Nothing anyone could do about that. Ketch was working on convincing the D.A. that the cocaine was part and parcel of the attempt to frame him. In the end, in all likelihood, he'd get off with the DUI charge and its ramifications—the lost license, the auto insurance jab—and maybe probation on the cocaine. So he was stuck here for five and a half more weeks. For *nothing*.

He had to get out. There was no reason for him to be here anymore. He had signed himself in, but he wasn't permitted to sign himself out. This was insane.

Patrick went to the door and opened it. At least they didn't lock him in. The long hall outside his room was empty and led to a common area with an elevator. The elevator went down to the lobby, and there was always a security guard there. To get to the common area, he had to pass by the nurse's station. There were—to his knowledge, and Patrick had looked—no other exits off the floor. Fucking fire hazard, he thought. A death pit.

They fed him breakfast in the morning, then threw him outside for exercise, like a dog. When they brought him back in, he spent an hour with a shrink, then another hour in group therapy. Lunch, then the infirmary for a physical check-up, going over all his vital signs, drawing blood, probably to make sure he hadn't sneaked anything into his room. Finally, there was 'common' time—he hated the expression—with a group of drooling low-life drunks and addicts in the big room down the hall, playing board games, watching the tube.

He wasn't an alcoholic. There had never been a time in Patrick's life when he had been unable to function just because he'd been drinking. He wouldn't even have run from that bloody cop if the guy had just talked to him. If he'd had the opportunity he might still have gotten the DUI, but his briefcase would not have been searched, and he would have charmed his way out of this whole ridiculous mistake.

Patrick stood in the doorway of his room and let out a loud groan. Then he saw the night nurse leave her station. She stepped down the hall, into the rest room, and his pulse raced.

He never gave any thought to what he would do if he actually managed to get out of this place. They had taken his wallet, all his money and his keys. Currently, Patrick had nothing to call his own except the trousers and T-shirt he wore—clinic-issue. But he walked past the nurse's station anyway, right into the common area and into the elevator. It was then that he realized he was barefoot. Screw it. He'd never get past the guard in the lobby.

But a ray of hope lit his imagination, tantalizing him. Once he was back in his life, he would fight them—holier-than-thou Jonathan and vindictive Ann. And his mother, if he had to. He still couldn't believe that she had turned on him.

The elevator doors opened to the lobby. The guard at the desk was on the phone. Patrick punched the third floor button fast. The doors slid shut.

So he'd ride up and down all night, he thought. Until someone noticed the elevator's movement. What the hell. It beat watching TV.

Then Patrick paused to study the button panel. There were three patient floors, then L for lobby and B for basement. He hit B. It peaked on the third floor and started on its way.

This time when the doors opened, he looked out into a furnace room. Feeling another skitter of excitement, Patrick stepped off the car onto cold concrete. He headed past an incinerator, six separate hot water heaters and the furnace itself. On the far wall, behind all that, he found an exit. He had every expectation that if he opened that door, an alarm would sound. But they wouldn't have dogs out there, or armed guards. This was a rehab clinic, not a jail. What would they do if they caught him? Shoot him?

Patrick pushed on the door and stepped out into the night. Nothing happened. He waited, every muscle tensed, every nerve tingling, but there was nothing.

His legs started moving. The cold bit into his skin. Within five minutes, his feet went numb. He reached a parking lot, then a long driveway.

Patrick started running. Not down the drive, no, because he believed he'd be too exposed. Instead, he crashed into the woods that lined the asphalt. More than once he swore aloud when his bare feet came down on something painful. He finally sat on a fallen log to pull his feet up and try to see the bottoms. The trees blotted out any moonlight, so he ran a hand over one sole. It came back wet. Probably blood, he figured.

But he was free. He was actually out of that horrible place. He was his own man again. In fact, a highly intelligent man who could certainly think his way out of this dilemma. No vehicle, no keys to his own home, no money. Still...

He was pretty sure he was somewhere in Jersey. He seemed to remember crossing a bridge when Ketch's man had brought him here, and he thought they'd come west, not east.

He needed to find some kind of town. He'd have to bum change from someone—God, that rankled, to be reduced to such a thing—but then he could go to a pay phone and call Verna. She'd come get him.

She was the only person left on his side in the whole fucking world.

CHAPTER 43

Ann's fingers found the edge of the hot tub and she pulled herself up. A little. Halfway. Enough to lay her upper body on the cool tile. Then she collapsed there with a small groan.

Someone was knocking on the door.

"We need to open that," she murmured.

Nothing. No answer.

"Jonathan?"

Ann pushed up off the tile. He was floating on his back. Incredibly, impossibly, at the sight of him, need speared through her. Just a moment ago she'd thought she'd never feel a hint of life in her limbs again.

The knocking was getting insistent.

"Jonathan. Someone is trying to get in here." She splashed water at him.

"Yeah, yeah. Later. Possession is nine-tenths of the law."

"Even in Hong Kong?"

"I hope so."

The rapping intensified. Ann thought she heard voices.

"How could I have known you for seventeen years and not have known this about you?" Jonathan asked suddenly.

Everything inside her stopped. "Known what?"

"That you could make me so crazy. And I still haven't shown you my really cool moves."

A laugh scratched Ann's throat as her heart started again. "Pressure's on now. I won't believe it until I see them."

Jonathan finally opened one eye. "All right. Get back in here and I'll see what I can do."

"Later." She pulled herself out of the tub.

"There *is* going to be a later, Ann. Another time. You know that, right?"

Did she? All she knew at that moment was that she had never given herself over to anyone like she had to him. And she realized with a start that she'd never let herself *feel* before. It had been more than good; it had somehow made her complete in its fierceness and devastating complexity.

Ann finally nodded because she didn't entirely trust her own voice to answer.

"Open up in there!" a man shouted. "Are you all right?"

"Are you all right, Jonathan?" Ann asked.

"I'm great. You?"

"Feeling good. Fish my bottoms out of there, will you?" She was feeling on top of the world, frisky even. He swiped his hands through the water, retrieving pieces of their clothing. He tossed her the bikini bottom and she had to wiggle it over her wet skin. Then she heard a key in the lock of the door.

"Oh, God, Jonathan, hurry."

He splashed out and managed to dress with half the effort it had taken her. When the door opened and the lifeguard burst in, they were standing on the tile. A middle-aged Asian couple—the woman wore a flamboyant muumuu—stood just behind him, peering over his shoulder.

"Sorry, folks, you're not supposed to lock this," the guard said.

Jonathan grabbed a towel and dried his face. "Then why's it there?"

"What?"

"The lock." He lowered the towel and grinned.

"Ah, well." The guard smiled back, looking between them. "Who knows?" He pointed at the champagne bottle. "No alcohol in here, either, sir."

"We'll take it straight back to our room," Jonathan promised.

Ann gathered their things along with an extra towel and they pushed past the muumuu lady and her skinny, mystified companion. Back in the pool area, she dropped everything on a chaise lounge and fished out her pants.

"You won't need them where we're going," Jonathan said.

She tugged them on anyway. "Where are we going?"

"Your room, my room, take your pick. There's still the issue of my cool moves."

"So you say."

He caught her wet hair in his hand and pulled her back to him. He kissed her.

This time it was only a quick lick over her upper lip, followed by a solemn press of mouth to mouth.

"You're good," she breathed. Then her cell phone rang.

Ann dug past their damp towels and her top to find it at the bottom of the pile. "Local number," she said, checking the ID window. She put it to her ear. "Hello?"

"Ann Lesage?" said Captain Tang's voice. "Is Mr. Morhardt with you?"

"Yes. Hold on." She passed the phone quickly to Jonathan. "Tang," she mouthed.

He took the phone in hand and said hello.

"Mr. Morhardt," the policeman said with some satisfaction, "I promised to have news for you today and I do. Are you able to take notes?"

"Um—not quite at the moment. Is it possible for you to hold on for a few minutes?"

"Yes, of course."

"Thank you." Jonathan motioned to Ann for her to follow.

Quickly, she gathered everything off the lounge and headed after him, into the elevator and disembarking on the lobby floor, where Jonathan proceeded to the front desk. "Do you have something I can write on?" he hurriedly asked the young female clerk. "And may I borrow a pen?"

"Are you still there?" he said into the phone once he was equipped.

"Yes, yes," the Captain said, now sounding impatient. "Look— perhaps it would be best if I fax this to you. I could not find any trace of that company—Mae Sing—listed anywhere. But I do have a list of 21 Charles Lings. That's just those who reside on Kowloon side. There are another 30 on my side. I apologize but I do not have the manpower to investigate them all on my own. My thinking was that I could interview those on Hong Kong Island if you and your lady would do the same in Kowloon."

My lady, Jonathan thought. He liked the sound of that, especially after what had just transpired between them. "Fine," Jonathan said, then he turned to the clerk at the front desk and asked for the hotel fax number, which he repeated into the phone.

"Good enough," Captain Tang advised him. "Our fax machine is usually busy so this might take an hour, perhaps a little more. Watch for it then."

"I will," Jonathan said, already having forgotten that it was just a few hours ago that he was ready to ream the guy out. "I'm certain we can keep busy until it arrives." He disconnected, then winked at Ann and turned back to the clerk. "I'll have a fax coming through in about an hour," he said. "I'm in room 1014."

"I'll send someone straight up with it, sir," the clerk promised.

"No, don't do that. Just ring the room and let me know it's here. I'll pick it up on my way out." Jonathan leaned close to Ann's ear.

"Cool moves," he said in an undertone. Then his hands found her back and he turned her away from the desk.

Inside the elevator, the door no sooner closed then he was on her, pressing her against the wall of the car with his body. His hands cupped her head and this kiss was like the one in the hot tub, hard and insistent, demanding. Then one hand left her hair and his palm streaked up her midriff and closed over her breast, pulling the bathing suit top away.

Ann gasped and came off the wall, leaning into him as the car stopped on their floor. The doors slid open. "Oh, God," she whispered. "Oh, God." She tried to find her top.

Jonathan flashed the bikini bra he was holding in his hand and stepped off the elevator. "Don't worry. No one's in the hall."

"I'm a corporate executive," she gasped, grabbing for the top.

"There's not a single person in this hotel who knows that."

She scooted out and jogged to his door, holding one of the towels against her chest. He poked the key card into the lock and they went inside, laughing.

Jonathan pressed his palms against her shoulders, his fingers splayed, and gave her a little nudge until she dropped backward onto the bed. Ann threw her arms out in surprise and everything spilled to the mattress. Except the champagne. Somehow, she still held that. Then he was kneeling over her, straddling her. And he kissed her, hard and quickly.

"That wasn't a cool move," she managed.

"Hold on. I'm getting to that part."

He took the champagne from her hand. Then he snagged her bottoms down.

Ann giggled like a school girl.

Jonathan upended the bottle of champagne, splashing the last of the bubbles onto her breasts, her tummy, her crotch.

"Tasted pretty good the first time around," he said.

He lowered his mouth to her skin … and she was lost.

CHAPTER 44

Ann was lying flat on the bed, face down, when the phone rang. She rolled over to see Jonathan pull himself up against the headboard to answer the call. He spoke briefly and hung up.

"Tang came through for us." He sounded almost—but not quite—as hollowed-out as she felt.

"Better late than never," Ann murmured, looking at her watch. "It's ten after five."

"Do you want to try to do something about this list now?"

"Not if it involves standing or walking."

He hesitated only a heartbeat. "I agree. First thing in the morning, then?"

"Okay." She let her breath out as though they had just reached a momentous decision. Then she realized she was hungry. *Famished*, actually. For the first time in a long time, her stomach didn't burn. Ann sat up. "Are you hungry, Jon?"

"You betcha, ma'am."

"Pasta." She stood off the bed and stretched. "Could I have pasta?" She paused. "But first I'm going to take a shower."

Jonathan watched her make her way to the bathroom. He wondered how he could possibly have any want left. But there it was, pushing at him.

Food first.

He spoke to room service, then called the desk to have them make two copies of the fax and send it up with their meal.

Ann returned from the shower and put on one of his T-shirts. Their food came and she studied her copy of the list while she ate. "Okay, here's what I think we should do," she said finally, putting it down beside her plate.

"Go back to bed?"

She gave him just a glimmer of a smile. "You're insatiable."

"You say that like it's a bad thing."

Ann finally grinned fully. She picked up the list and waved it at him. "Charles Ling?" she reminded him.

Jonathan reached for his burger. "Yeah. Him. You were saying?"

"There are twenty-one names here. I think we should divide the list in half. You take some, I'll take some. Calling them won't work for obvious reasons. It'll be difficult enough to make ourselves understood in person. By splitting up, we'll be able to see all of these people in half the time it would take us to do it together."

Jonathan picked up his beer and thought about her suggestion. "The idea of you running around this city by yourself makes me nervous."

She gave him a level look. "I've run around this city by myself for quite a few years."

Maybe that was one of the first things that intrigued him about her, Jonathan thought. She definitely didn't cling. She wasn't needy. "I'll bet this city has some nasty areas."

"And I know where they are. But Hong Kong is safer than most other places in the world."

"Says you. Look—I need you to humor me on this."

She crossed her arms over her chest. "No."

"Are we fighting again, Ann? After such a swell afternoon?"

"We're not fighting. I just hate the idea of wasting time." She hesitated. "Jonathan, I want to finish up here and go home."

Felicia. He saw it in her eyes, a certain fear moving there. "Did she sound that bad?"

"Yes."

"I should have talked to her."

"I'm not sure I could have kept her on the phone any longer."

"Damn it." He threw his napkin down and stood.

Ann watched him restlessly move around the room. He'd pulled on a pair of boxers but that was as dressed as he'd gotten. He had an incredible body, and she'd managed to discover a great deal of it over the last several hours. She wanted more. How could she possibly want more? A moment ago, she had felt completely drained.

Jonathan stopped moving and looked back at her. "If we can find Ling we could be on a plane by tomorrow night."

"That's what I was thinking." Ann wondered if this new part of their relationship would continue at home. There would have to be some kind of shift, she decided. Things would change by necessity when they were back in the real world.

He returned to the table and plucked a French fry from his plate. "Okay, here's the only way I'll go for your idea." He picked up his copy of the list and studied it. "We'll figure out which half of these are closest to our hotel and you'll take those. I'll do the rest."

She could have argued with him—but she knew by the set of his jaw that she wouldn't win.

"And no matter what," he continued, "we'll set a pre-appointed hour to meet back here in the hot tub room."

"The hot tub room?" Ann laughed.

"Or the location of your choice."

"I'm fine with that. We'll do the hot tub again." The thought almost made her feverish.

He grinned fast. "Good. Anyway, as I was saying, we'll set a pre-appointed time to meet back here. Whether we're done by then or not, we'll come back and check in with each other. Got it?"

"And if we're not done with our respective lists?"

"Then we'll go back out together and finish it off."

It was the best she could hope for. Ann twisted her fork into more fettuccini. "Sounds like a plan."

"But for now, let's finish eating and go back to bed. What do you say?"

She blushed despite herself. "Okay."

Ann managed three-quarters of her meal before yawning. Jonathan stood and held a hand out to her. She got to her feet and reached for him, permitting him to twine his fingers with hers.

He tugged her back toward the bed. When they landed there, he only tucked her head against his shoulder and reached for the TV remote. "Let's rest a little while," he said.

Taking over, Ann thought. Again. Deciding for her. This would have to stop. It made her nervous. But she also liked it.

She had every intention of going back to her own room tonight. She could not—would not—sleep with him. Sleep was different from sex. It was ... taboo. It was too close. It was something she just didn't do.

It was the last thought she had before dropping off into a deep, dark sleep. And for once, she didn't dream...

CHAPTER 45

Patrick walked his way through small lifetimes before he came upon a town that had pretty much rolled its sidewalks up for the night. His feet were in agony. The cold had gripped his bones with a unique pain all its own.

Then he saw a bar. For a moment, he thought he was hallucinating. The neon beer sign in the window winked at him like a dear old friend. He made a hoarse sound in his throat and stumbled forward, down a winter-dead street so silent he wondered again if he was dreaming. But when he came up against the planked door, it was real. He closed his hand over the knob; found it to be ice cold.

He twisted open the door and stepped into blessed warmth. The place was a dive, with black vinyl stools and a chipped green linoleum floor. He practically staggered to the bar.

Two men and a woman sat there. They all had the kind of bleary, dull eyes that said they had nothing to go home to. Not one of them seemed to notice that his feet were bare.

"Get you something?" the bartender asked. He was a small, skinny guy with greasy brown hair. A crop of acne dotted his chin.

Patrick thirsted for a taste of cognac. But first things first. "I need a phone."

The guy stuck a thumb over his shoulder. "Back by the toilets."

Pay phones, Patrick thought. "No, I—" He broke off. He would have to come up with a good lie to explain his predicament. The last thing he needed was for the bartender to become suspicious.

"I just … I had a fight." Patrick said. "With my wife."

The bartender chuckled. "She toss you out, buddy?"

"She … threw some of my clothes onto the lawn. But nothing else. I don't have any change on me for a phone call."

The guy shrugged. "So reverse the charges."

Patrick hadn't thought of that. He had not used a pay phone in years. He wondered if Verna would accept the call.

He went to the back of the bar, wincing with each step. He found the phone and dialed. Verna's line rang and rang. Voice mail did not pick up. Where was she in the middle of the night, Patrick wondered. He briefly entertained the thought that she might be seeing someone other than him.

He slammed the phone down and went back to the bar, trying to look pathetic. "No answer," he said to the bartender. "What the hell am I supposed to do now?" He sat and put his head in his hands. Then he looked up, feigning a brilliant new idea. "How would you like to earn an easy hundred dollars?"

The guy backed off and gave him a suspicious look. "You just said you don't have any money."

"I don't. Not on me. But if you take me to where I need to go, I'll give you a hundred when we get there."

"Where?"

"Queens."

"You've got to be fucking kidding." The kid shook his head. "You want me to drive you to the other side of *New York*?"

Well, Pat thought, he was definitely in Jersey. "Two hundred?"

"To drive you to Queens?" he wanted clarified.

"And for a shot of cognac while I wait for you to finish up here."

"Now you're pushing your luck."

"What's the cognac going to cost you?"

"Not much. We don't got any."

"Brandy, then," Pat said.

The kid paused to think about it. "Two hundred dollars?" He went for the brandy bottle and poured him a shot. Patrick almost wept with gratitude.

He'd meant to savor it, the sweet thickness of it on his tongue. Instead, he knocked it back and shuddered. Oh, God, he thought, oh, yes, that was good.

"What time do you get off?" he asked the bartender.

"Half an hour. But then I got to clean up."

"Two hundred fifty for one more shot."

"You're crazy, man."

"You don't know the half of it."

By the time the guy finished, Patrick was into him for three hundred dollars and he had a decent buzz on. He felt the tension in him—all that gnarly, nasty fear that had gripped him for days—melting away. He could finally think again.

If his house was locked, if Irene really was gone—and he'd called her three times from the clinic without getting an answer—then there was always the extra key in the potting shed out back. If she'd taken that, too, then he'd break through one of the rear windows. He kept a little cash taped to the lid of the toilet tank in his bathroom for just such an emergency. He thought there was probably about five hundred dollars there.

By the time they got into the kid's car—an ancient Ford with a muffler problem—Patrick spotted the time on the dashboard clock—twenty past four in the morning. How long had he wandered through those woods? Now that they were warm again, his feet were giving in to a stinging burst of pain that was beginning to radiate up his ankles.

"So where exactly are we going anyway?"

"My … brother's home," he lied. *The bastard who was fucking Ann Lesage.* Pat was sure of that now. They'd been too chummy at the court house. Comrades-in-arms. Bowling him over, punishing him, tucking him away like a common criminal.

The sky was going gray by the time they reached Patrick's home. He went to the front door and tried the knob. Locked. He rang the bell. Nothing. He pounded his fist on the door.

No response. Irene—the ungrateful bitch—was really gone.

He returned to the car. "Hold on a second," he said to the guy. "I'm going to go around out back."

"Oh, man, if you got me all the way out here with nothing to show for it, I've got a fist for you."

"That won't be necessary," Patrick said. There was still a drop of brandy in his blood, and the prospect of more right behind those den windows. He'd get into the house somehow. "Just sit tight."

He went to the rear of the property, limping. He let himself into the potting shed and ran his hand over the upper shelf just inside the door. His fingers closed over the small piece of metal. Relief hit him with a jolt.

He went to the back door, turned the key in the lock and let himself in. The house smelled empty and stale. She'd probably been gone since the night he'd run from the cops, Pat thought. Irene had abandoned him in his worst hour of need.

He went upstairs to his bathroom and found the money. He hurried back to the front door and minced his way to the driveway on tender feet, screaming with pain. "Here you go," he said to the guy. "Three hundred dollars."

The bartender reached out and grabbed it. "No shit," he said. "I thought you'd stiff me for sure."

"You saved my life," Patrick told him, and meant it.

The guy half-saluted, got into his dented Ford, and was off.

Patrick went back inside his house. To the den. To his Courvoisier—only to find that Irene had poured every last drop of it down the drain. Four empty bottles stood sentinel in the bar cupboard. Spite, Patrick thought, nothing but spite. Why hadn't he seen how nasty she was before he married her?

He was angry enough to want to throw one of the empty bottles against the wall. The sound of smashing, tinkling glass would be satisfying. But Patrick had no time for recriminations. He had to get a grip on himself. Come up with a plan. The bar was still stocked with vodka, Scotch, rum, and wine. Any one of those would do as well.

He made himself a strong rum and Coke and went upstairs to his bathroom, getting into the shower to wash the stink of the clinic off his skin. He had two more drinks while he dressed, then he took a straight shot, undiluted and right to his gullet, to get him through the pain of easing his battered feet into shoes.

The sun was up by the time he let himself out of the house to greet the waiting cab. He had business to see to. He had to get to the bank and get some money—if Irene hadn't cleaned their account out, too. He needed money to wheedle back into Verna's good graces. He was going to need her help, her support, in the days to come. He hoped it wasn't too late, He prayed she'd give him a chance, now that Irene was out of the picture.

The cab took him to the train station and Patrick rode into the city. It was after seven by the time he arrived at Verna's apartment. The door was ajar, which immediately struck him as odd.

"Verna? It's Patrick. Hello?"

Silence. Some … twitching thing, deep beneath the liquor, told him this was not good.

Patrick leaned on the door a little. It gave way. And there she was, her body twisted on the wood floor in the entrance to the apartment. Blood everywhere. Even fortified by the booze, it was too much for Patrick to handle. He began to scream. Screamed until he grew hoarse. Screamed again and again, without being able to stop.

CHAPTER 46

They made love in the morning, slowly, methodically, without the crazed rush of the day before. Ann found it sweet, something to savor. After they showered and dressed, and with breakfast completed, they prepared to go their separate ways in search of Charles Ling.

Jonathan turned to Ann and took a moment to study her. "Take it down," he said.

She paused and looked at him, confused. "What?"

"Your hair. Why do you always put it up like that?"

"I don't know. I look … it's more … professional."

"I like it down. Pushed up like that it's too severe. Not feminine."

"Well, when I'm doing business, I don't want to be feminine."

He reached behind her head and pulled out the clip, just as her cell phone rang.

Ann quickly reached for it.

Frank Ketch uttered a single word to her hello. "Trouble." Felicia, she thought. *Oh, dear God, not Felicia.* But if something had happened to her, then Cal or Lacey would have called them, not Ketch.

Patrick, then. It had to be Patrick.

"What did he do now?" Her voice ended in a squeak of despair.

"He strolled out of the rehab clinic last night."

"*Strolled?*" Her voice rose another notch as she looked to Jonathan. "Your brother," she mouthed.

First there was confusion on his face. Then anger. Then tired acceptance. "He checked himself out?" Jonathan asked.

"He checked himself out?" Ann repeated to Ketch. "That wasn't supposed to be possible!"

"It's not. He just walked out the door. No one is sure how."

"Where is he now?"

"Back in jail."

Ann thought distractedly that by now she ought to be accustomed to this sensation in her legs—the emptying of emotion from her heels. The noodle effect. "Why?" she asked, not really wanting to know.

"His secretary is in the hospital, beaten to a pulp. She's in critical condition, currently comatose, hanging on by a thread."

"His *secretary?*"

"Patrick turned up at her apartment first thing this morning and says he found her like that, then he called 9-1-1. The paramedics arrived with her half-dead and Mr. Morhardt sitting beside her in a puddle of various body fluids, intoxicated. Yesterday I was in front of the judge going through the motions of dismissing the cocaine charge. Now this."

"Are you telling me you're quitting?"

"No, no. But I'll need more of a retainer."

She laughed a little crazily. Ann removed the phone from her ear and shoved it at Jonathan. "Here. You talk to him."

She turned away and took a seat on the unmade bed, afraid she might throw up everything she had just eaten. She closed her eyes and breathed deeply, willing her stomach to settle. Mind over matter, she told herself. When she could take air in again without everything rolling inside her, she straightened and looked back at Jonathan. He was off the phone. He stood in the middle of the room, looking empty.

Ann approached him on unsteady legs. "I'm sorry." She gripped his arm. His muscles were tense, hard as a rock beneath her fingertips.

"How the hell did he come to this?"

"I don't know."

"What a legacy. And … Matt … Mattie was … such a good kid."

"Mattie had wings." He'd been an angel, Ann thought. In her darkest moments, she'd been sure that God had only loaned him to the Morthardts. She let go of Jonathan's arm. "I loved him. But he really was too good for me, Jon. I knew that from the start."

He turned to her, took her chin in his hand to make sure she couldn't look away. "What about me?"

Where was her voice? "You're tough as beef jerky."

"Not always. This takes the wind out of me."

Was he talking about Patrick's latest mess? Or what was happening between them? "I think … I hope … you're strong enough … for the likes of me."

"So far, the likes of you are just fine."

He dropped his hand. She already missed his touch. "About Patrick…"

"If he hurt that woman, there's no saving him, Ann."

"Your mother—"

"We have to get home to her."

Yes, she thought, they did. "What about Charles Ling? We can't forget about him."

He pushed fingers into his hair. "You're right. If we don't find him, then our chance of putting out the doll will be lost. Our only other option would be to go home and fly back here in a couple of days."

"That would be a waste." She looked at her watch. "Nine-thirty. We can probably wrap this up by mid-afternoon."

He went over to the desk by the window and picked up the hotel phone. "Let me see when we can get a flight out of here."

It took him a while, but he finally connected to the airline and got the information. "There's an available flight at 6:30," he said.

"Get us on it," Ann urged.

He made the arrangements and turned to her, handing her back her cell phone. "Where are our lists?"

Ann got them out of her briefcase as she dropped the cell phone inside. "What time do you want to meet back here?"

"I think we can safely give ourselves until one o'clock." He paused. "Ann, it's with the utmost regret that I say this, but I think under the circumstances, we need to skip the hot tub this afternoon."

Her gaze jumped to his. "A woman does what a woman has to do."

One corner of his mouth tried to smile. "You're incredible."

"Tell me that after I dismember your brother."

He looked away. Then his eyes came back to her. "Maybe you were right about him."

She could see how difficult it was for Jonathan to admit this to himself, let alone her. She didn't want him to hurt. Yes, she had grown to actually despise Patrick—really *hate* him for his weak, conniving ways. "He's got Morhardt genes," she said finally. "There has to be something redeemable in him, somewhere."

"Maybe." Jonathan kissed her once, quickly, then they headed out of the room.

"One o'clock," he said before setting off on his own. "No matter where you are or what you're doing, you cease and desist and come back to home base."

"Right on, Captain." Ann half saluted, trying to appear playful. But when she was sure he was gone, she paused and admitted to herself that maybe it was time to give up. Yes, Felicia wanted this doll project to proceed, and more than anything she wanted it for her. But at what cost? More money would be needed for Patrick's lawyer. Another million five would have to go to Ling, if they ever found him. At what point would it be too much?

A lot was working against them. Her mind spiraled back to what she had thought was the worst point in this odyssey, her previous version of rock bottom—the meeting at Kmart with Tom Carlisle. She couldn't do this anymore.

She took a deep breath. No. She would continue, she thought. She would see it through. She would find a way to do it. For Felicia, and—by association—for Jonathan. Prioritize, she told herself. Find Ling. That came first.

The cab ride took her west on a few side streets, then north on Nathan Road. In all her trips to Hong Kong, Ann had never ventured much past Mong Kok which, she now reminded herself, was actually a misnomer. The true name in Cantonese was Wong Kok but the sign painter many years ago was rumored to be dyslexic and replaced the 'W' with an 'M' in error. Despite herself, Ann smiled. Only in Hong Kong would this sort of thing be allowed to stand.

The cab turned east on Prince Edward Road and drove past Yuen Po Street, home of the Bird Market where, despite fears of virulent strains of flu running rampant among fowl, people still gathered in droves to admire the hundreds of songbirds. Ann remembered coming here once, but that had been many years before, when the flu was something you caught from a person, not a bird.

Just approaching Kowloon City, she became cognizant of a noticeable change. The touristy things she was familiar with—the jewelry and electronic shops, the fast food joints and pastry stores—now gave way to apartment building after apartment building, some in disrepair, stacked one next to the other.

The cab turned on a small side-street and came to a halt a hundred feet or so from the corner. Ann gave the driver seventy Hong Kong, the equivalent of nine American dollars, which reminded her that taxis were one of the few bargains left in the city.

She stood for a moment on the sidewalk, experiencing a strange sense that she was indeed a *gwilo*, a foreigner in unfamiliar terrain, and that she was being noticed.

She unfolded the piece of paper she held in her hand, meaning to verify the address, when suddenly, something impossibly hard hit her in the back of the skull. She cried out and pitched forward, losing her grip on her briefcase. It hit the sidewalk and skidded. As she went down, she felt her knees scrape the concrete. Then her chin connected with enough force to make her see stars.

She rolled out of pure instinct. Every day of her life since she'd been fourteen years old she considered all of the things she could have done, *should* have done, to fight off Mad Dog. Now, all those well-rehearsed alternatives came to her in a flash. She slid onto her back, brought her legs up close to her chest, and kicked out hard. Blindly.

He was Chinese. He stood above her in some kind of fighter's stance. Without thinking, she repeated the gesture, gathering her knees close, shooting her feet at him with more power than before, aiming straight for his groin.

He screamed out in Cantonese, doubled over, staggered back. But there was another man standing by. *Another? No, no, no, she couldn't fight two of them!*

She felt part of her mind sinking down. Going wild, feral. And she roared a sound of pure rage. Her legs pumped and her fists flew as the second man leaned over, trying to grab her. She caught a glimpse of a gun at his belt. She wouldn't—couldn't—let him get a grip on it. She kept screaming and kicking. Somebody, please see this, hear this, she thought.

The first man had now recovered and hit her in the face. Something red then white mushroomed in her vision before Ann's teeth found the flesh of his hand. She bit down with everything she had.

She continued flailing her arms and legs, until she realized she was just swiping at air. The men were gone. An arm in a short blue sleeve reached to help her up. She bit hard on that hand, too, and heard the sound of pain and surprise. Ann scrambled away, crouching at a safe distance.

She was sobbing, shaking. The stranger was saying something she didn't understand.

"I don't speak Chinese," she choked.

The man moved toward her, holding his hands out to show he only wanted to help. Ann mewled low in her throat. She noticed her briefcase on the pavement where it had fallen. She shot to her feet, swayed, then lunged and grabbed for it, almost losing her balance. "I'm okay," she said to the man. "I'm okay." Then she turned and ran.

CHAPTER 47

S he limped to a stop at the first corner she came to, her breath still coming in jagged gasps. She'd lost a shoe and thought about going back for it. No. She needed to keep moving ahead. Away from them. She hurried off, no destination in mind.

Who were they? She wondered.

She removed her other shoe and tossed it into the street. By the time she reached a small Chinese restaurant her stockings had shredded. Her steps finally faltered and she veered inside, past the tables to a restroom in the back.

Closing the door, she leaned her weight against it, her cheek pressed to the cool wood. When she stopped shaking, she straightened and looked around. She was alone. She locked herself in, let her legs give out, and sank to the floor. She fumbled with the latches on her briefcase. She needed her cell phone—had to call Jonathan.

Ann shoved the briefcase abruptly to the floor. *No.* She couldn't—wouldn't run to him like a kicked puppy. She'd been through worse before. Alone. She'd always saved herself.

She had to figure out what to do. *Why* had it happened? A random mugging? No, they'd had a gun. So what? *Muggers use guns, you idiot.* Ann shook her head in disgust and her brain throbbed with pain. She rested her forehead on her drawn-up knees, willing the hurt away.

Still, it could not have been a random attack. They had not taken her briefcase. Their plan had been to drag her off somewhere. And somehow she knew, if they had succeeded, she would not have survived.

Why? Was this part of Chow's bizarre plot to ruin Hart Toy and the Morhardts—to *kill* her?

None of this made sense. *None* of it. Why would Chow destroy the company that had been the source of his livelihood for so long? Did a million and a half dollars warrant the risk? Yes, she supposed it did, especially here in Hong Kong, where money was worshiped like a religion.

But why would Chow choose to disappear now? Why not allow things to move along and collect as much money from Hart Toy as possible, including the additional percentages? Why settle for the first million-five?

Unless … Patrick *was* somehow involved? The accusations against him were serious. Could he actually have beaten up an innocent woman, battering her nearly to death? Where was the connection? What, if anything, did Patrick have to do with any of this?

Ann was stymied; she couldn't get an angle on it.

They would have to locate Chow, she thought. Once the authorities get their hands on him, the pieces of the puzzle would come together.

Someone knocked.

Ann groaned as she stood unsteadily and pressed her palms against the door. "Just a minute," she called. Her throat was raw.

She limped to the mirror. Her hair was wild. A bruise was growing under her left eye. She pressed her fingers to the back of her head where she'd first been hit. There was a noticeable lump.

Of course, it was impossible for her to go on to the people on her list. She was a mess. It was a miracle she'd gotten through the restaurant without being stopped.

She cleaned up at the sink as best she could, stuffing the paper towels into the trash bin. When she opened the door to exit, there was no one on the other side.

Ann made her way out, keeping her head down to hide her battered face. She had to get back to the hotel and do whatever damage control she could: change her clothes and apply sufficient makeup.

Thinking ahead grounded her, gave her something on which to focus.

She began to walk, unsure of the correct direction. At the first corner she came to, she looked around, then crossed the street. There was no sign of the men who had accosted her.

Finally, a taxi appeared. She slid into the back seat and gave the driver the name of her hotel. Fifteen minutes later, she was just entering her room when her cell phone went off.

"Mr. Morhardt, please," Captain Tang said.

"Hello, Captain," she greeted him, having recognized his voice. "Mr. Morhardt is busy right now. May I help you?"

"Yes, Ms. Lesage. I have wonderful news. I found Charles Ling. He is with me now. He can be at your hotel within the hour."

Her mind sizzled. Could she have heard right? This was too good to be true. "Did you say you—uh—found him? *The* Charles Ling we are looking for? The inventor of our baby doll?"

"Yes, yes, the very same."

Quickly, she looked at her watch. The crystal was broken, but it seemed to be keeping time. Not wanting to take a chance, she said, "Let's see, it is now 11:48. Correct?"

"That is correct, Ms. Lesage."

"Okay, then. One hour from now should be fine."

She no sooner disconnected then a well of emotion burst inside of her. This was good news. No—*great* news! *Move, move, move.*

The spray of the shower hurt and she had to force herself to withstand the pain. She clenched her fingers into fists and extended her arms upwards. Her curses were camouflaged by the roar of the water.

By the time she stepped out of the shower, her sole objective was to find a way to conceal the damage, especially the bruises on her face.

Pancake, rouge, lipstick; she tried it all, going so far as to apply an extra layer of each. She was careful with her choice of dress, finally picking a simple Yves St. Laurent number in lime green that suited the color of her hair.

When she heard an abrupt rap on the door, she sighed. This would be Jonathan, she was sure. She turned her face away as he strolled past her into the room.

"And how was your—" he started to ask. He broke off and stared at her. "Jesus. What happened to you?"

So much for makeup, Ann thought.

He came at her fast, reached a tender hand to her swollen cheek. "Who did this to you, Ann?" His voice was pained.

She let him hold her, but something shattered in her head. Whatever it was that had kept her moving after the attack, now broke into a million small pieces and rained down inside her. It happened with a sound like a pop behind her eyes, within her ears—something only she could hear. And she felt herself coming apart.

He finally peeled back, held her at arms length. "What happened? Please tell me."

Despite her resolve, she began to cry.

He'd only seen her cry once before, when she'd gotten misty-eyed during their trip to the American retailers. But this was gulping, shuddering. She couldn't seem to get her breath. He wrapped his arms tightly around her. "Come on now. Easy does it."

Even while she buried her face in his neck, her hands started pummeling his shoulders. "I needed you!"

The knot in his gut twisted. "I'm sorry. God, I'm so sorry."

"No! I *needed* you!" But her fists slowed in their pace.

"I should have been there."

"No, you should *not* have been there!" She yanked away from him. "And I shouldn't have run for you!"

"You couldn't have run for me, Ann. We were far apart."

"Would you stop being so reasonable and just *get* this?"

"Ann, darling—I'm not sure what it is I'm supposed to be getting."

"I was going to call you!" she shouted. "The first thing I thought to do was *call* you!"

Ah, he thought. The independence thing again. It wasn't just sex that made her panicky, he realized. It was more a matter of this … needing.

"I'm here now," he said.

She couldn't tell him how happy she was to see him. At least, not yet. But she did allow herself to soften a bit. She began to give him the details of the attack. She kept it as simple and as abbreviated as possible, purposely leaving out the part about the gun. Before she could finish, however, the hotel phone rang.

"Ms. Lesage?" a stranger's voice asked.

"Yes?"

"My name is Ling." Broken accent. "Charles Ling."

"Yes. We were expecting you. Is Captain Tang with you?"

"No. He no come. So sorry."

In a way, Ann was relieved. "Well, could you join us in my room, please?" She gave him the room number.

By the time she disconnected, Jonathan was curious. "Who was that?"

She shrugged. "Sorry. I should have told you. Captain Tang found Charles Ling. He's on his way up to see us now."

"He is? That's fabulous, Ann."

As if on cue, there was a knock on the door and Jonathan went to answer it. A moment later, Charles Ling shyly stepped into Ann's room. Like many tall men, he seemed to hunch a little, as though trying to minimize the impact he had on his environment. He was gangly and nervous. Around forty-five, Ann would guess. In spite of his height—or maybe because of it—everything else about him seemed small: his features, his hands, his feet. Only his brown eyes loomed unnaturally large, the effect of black-framed glasses.

Ann and Jonathan took seats on the small sofa, allowing their guest to have the only chair in the room, a hardback model that was positioned next to the desk.

"Do you know Edmund Chow?" Ann asked without preamble.

"Yes, he is one of three people I showed my latest invention to," Ling said. But Ann realized these were not quite the words he was using. His English was fractured. As he spoke she automatically adjusted the grammar in her head, knowing if she didn't she would lose the meaning of whatever it was he was trying to tell them.

"But other people showed no interest," he continued. "Only Mr. Chow. I asked him to sign the agreement. He told me it wasn't necessary." The man's voice broke, genuine grief causing his face to spasm. "He took my one-of-a-kind sample. And I haven't heard from him since."

Ann could see how upset the man was. "Who is Mae Sing Creations?" she asked.

Ling made an odd gargling sound, then blanched.

"What is it?" Ann said.

"That is my wife."

"Mae Sing Creations?" A headache swelled inside her skull as she tried to assimilate it.

"It is my wife's name. We have no creations, other than our children." He gave a weak smile.

Ann looked from the man to Jonathan, and back again. "How do we know you are the creator of Baby Talk N Glow? I mean, what proof do you have?"

Ling frowned. "Baby what?"

"I'm sorry," Ann said. "I should explain. That is the name we have chosen for the doll."

The man's smile didn't exactly expand but his countenance transformed. Where there had been anxiety and hesitation was now resolve. From his jacket pocket he removed a four-page legal document, written in Chinese and stamped by some Hong Kong authority.

"This is proof of the copyright," Ling said. "You are welcome to show it to your lawyer."

Ann passed the document to Jonathan who gave it a perfunctory glance. It could have been Greek, for all he knew. Looking for more familiar ground, he turned to Ling and asked the man to tell them about himself.

Ling's look revealed his bewilderment.

"Where were you born?" Jonathan began again. "Where did you go to school? How did you become, of all things, a doll inventor?"

Ling finally understood the line of questioning and began to talk about being schooled in Quangzhou. "I studied creative arts but was always able to draw, ever since a child," he said. "My cousin opened a toy factory in Shenzhen and I joined him as chief designer. I worked many years for low pay. Even after I got married, had two children. Still, my cousin did not increase my salary. But it was my creations that were being sold to countries around the world, even America. My wife begged me to leave, to go out and open my own business. She got her family to loan us money. Eight months ago we moved to Hong Kong and set up an office in an apartment that was also to be our home. It's been very difficult. Creating something from nothing takes time. Finally, I came up with my baby doll. Everyone told me she was unique. Weekends, evenings, every moment I could, I spent to make her perfect. The electronics make a difference, but I concentrated on the styling, the balance…"

"And you did well," Ann interrupted. His words were so stilted she had to concentrate to understand him. "Mr Ling—if we can verify the authenticity of your copyright, would you be willing to sell us the rights to your doll?"

A strange sound came from the man's throat. It could have been one of grave discomfort, an expression of disbelief, or a combination of both. "Yes, of course," he gushed, or something to that effect.

Ann realized that they could probably get away with offering him quite a bit less then they had intended. The businesswoman in her wanted to try. But over the years she had learned her lesson from Felicia well: it was never right to take advantage of another person, especially when they were at your mercy. It had become the root of her philosophy and she wasn't about to change.

Jonathan's imperceptible nod helped her gain confidence in her decision. Taking a deep breath, she said: "Mr. Ling—we are willing to offer you what we actually paid Edmond Chow—an advance of one million five hundred thousand American dollars based on a royalty of ten percent."

His face paled and Ann thought the man might faint. "One … million … five," he repeated very slowly.

"Yes," Ann confirmed. "We feel that is a fair and equitable offer. Our hope is that the authorities will find Mr. Chow and return the money he unlawfully took from us, thereby negating our doubled risk. Either way, we are ready to proceed."

Ling was instantly on his feet, bowing to Ann and Jonathan, lower, and lower still. When he came up for air, his face was streaked with tears. "Th..thank you," he said, and he pumped both their hands. "I am … happy…"

Jonathan turned to Ann and winked.

For the first time in hours, her insides stopped hurting. Hallelujah, she was thinking. The stars might be aligning themselves, after all.

CHAPTER 48

When Ann and Jonathan returned to New York, they went straight from the airport to Felicia's apartment. They had made arrangements for everyone to meet there for a brainstorming session.

As she stood before Felicia's door, Ann remembered the excitement of Baby Talk N Glow's coming-out party, and she had the impulse to grab Jonathan's hand and walk in together—a united front. The dread of this meeting hung heavy. Jonathan lifted the brass knocker and let it fall. Patrick opened the door and stood before them. Ann's head swam. She'd thought he was still in jail.

"You look like hell," Jonathan said to his brother, shoving past him. Ann had to agree. Patrick's complexion was pasty. His eyes were bloodshot and his hair looked like it hadn't been combed in days.

Without thinking about it, she removed her coat and handed it to him. Patrick allowed the coat to drop to the floor as he turned away, and Ann chided herself for teasing him.

As she picked up her coat, she took notice of the faces present—Cal Everham and Frank Ketch, Emeril Lacey—then her gaze went to Felicia. She was relaxing on the divan with a blue afghan tucked under her chin. Her complexion and the look in her eyes told Ann she was back to her old self.

Ann went up to her and asked how she was feeling.

A spidery hand sneaked out from beneath the afghan to stroke the bruise on Ann's cheek. "I am fine, dear. But what in God's name happened to you?"

"It's nothing," she told her. "I had a little incident in Hong Kong"

"A *little* incident?" Felicia questioned.

"This is touching, Mother," Patrick interrupted, "but we need to talk."

Felicia sighed. "Yes, we do. Mr. Ketch, please bring Jonathan and Ann up to date."

Jonathan was standing near the window, ramrod straight, his hands deep in his pockets. Without thinking about it, Ann took the chair closest to him.

"Ms. Sallinger regained consciousness last night," Ketch said. "Briefly. Long enough to tell the police investigator that Patrick was not her assailant."

It explained why he wasn't in jail, Ann thought.

Jonathan's voice came sharply from behind Ann. "Who was it, then?"

"She knew him only by the name Vincent."

Ann cleared her throat. "Is she going to die?"

"By all accounts she should be dead, so with every passing hour the doctors become more optimistic," Lacey broke in. "She's got five broken ribs, a ruptured spleen, a broken jaw, a broken arm, and a skull fracture. There's been some brain swelling, a severe concussion. But she's no longer comatose. She comes in and out. Mr. Morhardt has instructed us to pay her medical bills."

Ann glanced at Patrick. At least he had the foresight to do something right.

"Yes," Felicia broke in. "The company will not leave Ms. Sallinger stranded. But as for you, Patrick, your bail was the last money you'll see from me. When you walked out of that clinic, I'm afraid you lost my benevolence. And, as of tomorrow, you are officially fired."

Patrick's face went flame red. "Fired?" He shook his head as if to clear it. "Mother, you can't mean this." He approached the divan. "Ever since you started up with *her*—" He broke off and waved an erratic hand at Ann.

"Control yourself, Patrick," Felicia chided. "This is neither the time nor the place for your petty jealousy."

Patrick moved off, taking steps like a toddler who had just figured out how to walk.

"Well," Cal said, breaking the mood, "there's never anything quite like a Morhardt family meeting."

"Yes, well—where were we?" Felicia asked.

"You were doing everything but cutting me out of your will," Patrick muttered.

"Not yet, dear," Felicia said. "That's next week. So I suggest you hurry back to that clinic before I die and leave you without a cent." Her gaze fell upon Jonathan and Ann. "Please tell me about Edmund Chow."

Ann filled her in on the incident at Chow's office, then went into the details about their meeting with Charles Ling. "It'll cost us another million five," she said. "I'm so sorry, Felicia."

Felicia closed her eyes. "Ann, this is not your fault."

Patrick made a snorting sound. Everyone ignored him.

"But we *do* have the rights to the doll, correct?" Felicia asked finally. "We have the doll now?"

"We will, as soon as we can verify the authenticity of the copyright," Ann replied.

"Well, then, let's wrap it up as quickly as possible. Emeril, what are you doing about Mr. Salsberg?"

"He's hiding behind counsel and the Bar Association. There's a gray area of illegality here, at least where he's concerned.

It's difficult to prove that he was involved. It's his word against Patrick's."

"Don't let up," Felicia said. "I want that man brought to justice."

"I won't. Of course."

"Does that cover everything?" Felicia asked.

Ann looked at Jonathan. "Yes, at least on our end."

Ketch and Lacey began moving in the direction of the door. Patrick hesitated. For a moment Ann thought he would enter into another argument with his mother. Then he left as well, looking back at them, his expression as angry as she'd ever seen it.

Ann stood and went to kiss Felicia's cheek. "You're a tough old broad," she said quietly.

She expected a good comeback. She *needed* a good comeback from her. But she only felt Felicia shiver. "Oh, Ann, he breaks my heart."

Patrick. "Do you really want me to fire him?"

"No, but don't let him know that. Go through the motions, please. Give him a few unpaid weeks off. Maybe this ... finally this ... will straighten him out."

And if it didn't, Ann thought, she was determined that Felicia would at least think it had.

"Stop trying to shield me, Ann," Felicia said suddenly. "I'm too smart for that."

Ann felt grief rock through her. *How would she survive losing this woman?* She stood abruptly and Jonathan's hand caught the small of her back. Then he helped her on with her coat.

"Well," Felicia said to Cal after everyone had left. "It's certainly about time."

The doctor came around the other side of the divan and moved her feet aside so he could sit with her. "For what?"

"They're sleeping together, Ann and my Jonathan."

"Felicia…" He chastened her with his eyes. "Stay out of it."

"She's going to need him when I'm gone, Cal."

"As I remember it, you were only going to keep her for a week or two, all those years ago."

She smiled complacently. "You'll help me?"

"Meddle?"

"I'm very happy about this. Ann was never meant for my Matthew, bless his soul. But those two … there was always something between them. I always thought they'd be good together, if they gave each other a chance."

Cal turned on the divan to gather her hands in his. "They're grown adults. It's none of your business, Felicia."

She didn't acknowledge that. "I don't believe I ever told you, but Ann did finally confide in me. About where she'd come from and how she ended up on the streets. Though I never breathed a word of it to the boys."

"And how long did it take you to get it out of her?"

"Four years. She's stubborn when she wants to be."

Cal laughed. "And you're not? Never let it be said that Felicia Morhardt ever gave up on something she set her mind to do."

"Yes, well." Felicia sighed and rested her head back against the cushions. "I'm not quite done yet."

CHAPTER 49

A nn and Jonathan collected their luggage in the lobby of Felicia's building and, as they left, Jonathan discreetly tipped the doorman.

"What now?" Ann asked as they hit the street.

He knew what she was asking. "My place," he said after a moment. "I have furniture." Why did it feel like a commitment, like the very thing he'd fought tooth and nail against all his unattached, muse-driven life?

"I have all the furniture that counts," Ann pointed out.

He stepped into the street to hail a cab. "Ah, but you don't have beer."

"You don't have Scotch," she countered.

"Sure I do."

Her eyes widened. "You do?"

He'd bought an expensive bottle of Macallan in a crazy moment several years ago and had never opened it. "Live dangerously and find out."

Settled in the cab, Jonathan felt the full effects of jet lag taking hold. He looked at his watch—a little past 9:00 P.M. It was ten o'clock the following morning in Hong Kong. He should feel as if he had just woken up. Instead, his eyelids were heavy and he felt like hell.

"So what's it going to be, Ann?" he asked when they turned the first corner. "Your place or mine?"

"I don't need you," she said. "But ... your cool moves are really something."

He half smiled. "That'll do."

They rode the rest of the way in silence. Ann nodded off and then he did the same. When they arrived at his loft, the cab driver had to wake them both.

Upstairs they barely had the strength to undress and go to bed. Jonathan slept so solidly he did not hear Ann get up and leave in the morning. He came out of a deep sleep and was surprised and disappointed to find her gone. He made himself breakfast, showered and shaved. The cobwebs wouldn't leave him. Traveling all that distance was not something he wanted to do again, anytime soon.

Despite how discombobulated he felt, a certain sense of urgency crept up and spurred him to action. Two phone calls later he was on his way to the Metropolitan Hospital to pay Verna Sallinger a visit.

Jonathan asked himself what he hoped to accomplish. It wasn't like him to act in haste. Was it clarification he was seeking? Edification? He didn't think Verna was in cahoots with Edmund Chow. But he had a hunch she could shed some light on their situation and at this point that was all that mattered.

Cal had arranged for Dr. Phil Steinberg to take Jonathan into the intensive care unit. Verna's condition had improved but he would only be allowed a few minutes with her.

The blinds were drawn and it was dark in her room. The beeps and blips of various machinery jumped out of the shadows like an arcade game with a nervous kid at the controls. They were mostly green, but one screen showed red numbers. Jonathan moved to the bed, looked down, and flinched a little.

He had always found Verna Sallinger to be an attractive woman; seeing her this way brought bile to his throat. She was hardly recognizable. What had been done to her face was beyond comprehension. He would give anything to get his hands on the SOB responsible.

He pulled up a chair and sat down. "Are you awake?" he whispered softly.

Verna's eyelids fluttered.

"It's Jonathan Morhardt. I want to ask you a few questions."

The woman's eyes opened briefly, found him, and closed again.

"I know you want to save Pat from his problems," he said.

Verna finally spoke, her eyes still closed. "I … told them," she said. "He didn't … do anything."

"We know that. I want you to help me understand what happened, help me catch whoever did this to you."

Verna's entire body started to spasm. Jonathan looked around for the emergency cord. Before he could pull it, however, she calmed down. Then, still with eyes closed, she began to speak. It was barely above a whisper.

"I didn't want to cooperate with him but Vincent threatened my mother." Tears began to leak from her eyes. "Everything is my fault," she continued in the same, barely audible tone. "I would never do anything to hurt Patrick, yet not only did I get him to keep drinking, it was me who called the cops. I knew he would get caught with what I had planted in his briefcase. And then I stole the contract for Baby Talk N Glow. I brought it home with me. I lied about it and wouldn't hand it over, but Vincent barged into my apartment … and that's the last I remember. When I woke up, I was here, in the hospital."

Jonathan could not imagine her making up this story. And more than anything he wanted to find this Vincent fellow.

Suddenly, as if reading his mind, Verna opened her eyes and looked at him. "Don't even think of going after this guy," she said. "He's … the devil!" She shut her eyes tight.

Jonathan felt the impact of her words. He rose to his feet and thanked her, told her he would return when she was feeling better. "We'll see you through this," he promised.

Outside the hospital, Jonathan found his anger returning. Despite the fact that it was snowing, he broke out in a sweat. He ducked into a Starbucks on First Avenue, purchased a cup of Columbia Narino Supremo and took a seat at the back, away from the few other customers.

He sipped slowly, then pushed the coffee aside. From his jacket pocket he removed a small notepad and pen.

At the top of the page he wrote the name, Baby Talk N Glow. Then he drew a line straight down from just beneath the center of those words to the bottom. On the left side he made his list of bad guys, from Edmund Chow, to Richard Salsberg, to Mr. Vincent. In the center he wrote the names of those he wanted to trust but was still uncertain about: Koji Sashika, Charles Ling, Patrick, and Verna Sallinger. The list he completed on the right only included Felicia and Ann, the good guys.

Without thinking about it he started to sketch their faces. Although he wasn't a portraitist by nature, his drawing of Ann showed a real likeness.

Jonathan now thrust his pen in mid-air as if he suddenly realized what he was doing. He looked down at his list of names. When he came to Verna's, he paused. Had she been a means to an end, he wondered, or the prime target?

Edmund had disappeared with their money. The contract for the doll was most definitely in the hands of Mr. Vincent. Neither action had proven fatal because they had found the inventor of Baby Talk N Glow and he was willing to grant them the rights.

This left the attack on Ann in Hong Kong. And that was the part that disturbed Jonathan the most. Stealing the doll away from Hart Toy was one thing; hurting Ann was quite another.

Ann wanted this doll to succeed because she knew it would please Felicia. But what if the doll's introduction was only a side issue? What if someone out there was using Baby Talk N Glow to mask his true motive? What if Ann was the real target?

Goosebumps attacked Jonathan's skin as he jumped to his feet. Intuition was telling him he was on to something. If he did nothing else, he would have to protect her, at least until this mystery was solved.

Forgetting his favorite Columbian blend, he hustled through the coffee shop and out the door. The snow had picked up. He walked a few blocks before finding a taxi. He took out his cell phone to call Ann, to tell her to wait for him, to not move from her office until he got there ...

CHAPTER 50

I t wasn't that many weeks later when Ann found herself standing on 11th Avenue, halfway between 34th and 39th. Toy Fair was still important. The excitement and nervous tension Ann felt inside was the same as always.

Charles Ling had his money. Hart Toy had Baby Talk N Glow. Somehow, incredibly, they had come this far. Ann knew that this New York Toy Fair would not be her last stop, that she still had many months ahead of hard work, but at least she was finally aimed into the home stretch.

For a moment she just stood in front of the Javits Convention Center, letting the frigid February wind beat against her.

Years ago, Hart Toy and many others still had permanent offices and showrooms in the original Toy building, located at 200 5th Avenue, a building that dated back to the early nineteen hundreds, once a hotel and host to Mark Twain, the Prince of Wales and various presidents.

Today, the massive Javits Center stood as an impersonal reminder of how the toy industry had changed, forsaking valuable tradition along with it.

Ann looked around. Where was Jonathan? He had said he'd meet her here.

They'd fought—one of their good, old fashioned, teeth-baring spats—over the issue of how overprotective he was being, and how she needed her space.

Ann heard the sound of a car stopping behind her. She pivoted on a heel. Jonathan, finally. Stepping out of a cab.

"You're late," she said.

"The muse flew in from Bangladesh this morning."

This was good. To the best of her knowledge, he hadn't lifted a paintbrush since their trip to Canada to film the TV commercial. But when she'd left his place this morning to swing by her apartment and pick up some things, he'd been in a strange, pensive mood.

He leaned in to kiss her hello. "Sorry. I lost track of time."

Since they'd returned from Hong Kong, they'd settled into what Ann thought of as their New York Relationship. It was marginally different from their Traveling Relationship, and it was comfortable … to a point. More and more lately Jonathan had become obsessed with her safety. He attributed it to what had happened to her in Hong Kong, but she suspected there was more to it then that. The attack on Verna had shaken everyone. Maybe he assumed she would be next.

Now, they began jostling their way through the crowds, aiming for the nearest entrance they could find. See and be seen, Ann thought. She hadn't missed a Toy Fair since the first one Felicia had brought her to. And while there was far less importance placed on Toy Fair, this year, more than ever, she wanted to make an impact.

A clown shoved a balloon in her face. She hitched back a step, but Jonathan reached out and palmed it. "I'm a kid at heart," he said, seeing her expression. Then he took her hand.

They dodged Disney and Sesame Street characters handing out buttons and brochures. An actor on stilts was plugging a new children's game. A shivering model in a red mini-skirt was trying to lure buyers to a company showroom.

"There's a thought," Jonathan said, eyeing her. "Maybe we need to get you out here in that blue bikini. Might drum up a little business."

Ann slid a jaundiced look at him.

They finally made it inside and were practically crushed by the crowd. Jonathan tried to stay connected to her, but she was being pulled in a half-dozen directions by various buyers and executives greeting her as she entered their midst.

Her energy began to surge.

"So many people..." Jonathan commented as they left one group and moved on.

"Not as many as a few years ago." She elbowed past someone trying to get to the main hall.

"You're kidding." He felt someone's arm collide with his back, heard a quick apology before the voice resumed hyping some toy product to a clutch of Asian men.

"Not kidding. Adding a show in October was bad enough. Then being forced out of the Toy Building and moving to Javits. The whole situation has discouraged not only buyers but some major manufacturers from attending. Pretty soon, there won't be a Toy Fair at all."

They finally arrived at their destination. Javits allowed those companies willing to spend the money to put up temporary showrooms with a guarantee of privacy. The cost was alarming but Ann considered it a necessity.

She tossed her briefcase on the desk in her closet-sized office. "C'mon," she said looking at her watch. "Let's go see how things are going."

Inside their showroom, in the children's bedroom they'd constructed, Baby Talk N Glow was everywhere. On the bed, on the dresser, on the desk.

Ann assigned one of their salesmen to handle the flow of traffic. Only one major buyer would be permitted in at a time. At the moment, it was Alison Steinfeld from Toys 'R' Us.

Lisette Smile, the girl from the commercial, was hosting the presentation. The child was completely calm and at ease. No wonder, Ann thought, her mother was nowhere to be seen. Lisette was inviting people to have a seat in her "bedroom." The lights dimmed. A spotlight came on, and Lisette began demonstrating Baby Talk N Glow. She was rewarded with scattered applause.

Then the seductive and attention-getting voice of the WNBC announcer they'd hired cut in, explaining the miniature nickel cadmium battery and its five-year shelf life.

Lisette carried the doll to Alison Steinfeld.

Ann held her breath. The child caught the buyer's hand and put it to the doll's lips.

"Hello, Alison," Baby Talk N Glow said. "Thank you for visiting us today. Would you please touch my heart?"

Steinfeld smiled and followed the instructions asked of her.

"Can you feel it beating?" the doll asked.

Steinfeld jolted a little. "Yes," she said—as though the doll could understand her.

"I hope you'll carry me at Toys 'R' Us, Alison," Baby Talk N Glow said. "I love you."

Steinfeld laughed out loud. "I love you, too."

"Hey, that's pretty good," Jonathan whispered.

Ann nodded absently. And there, she thought, went thousands of dollars. Other companies might have used a similar concept in the past, but never in such an elaborate manner. She'd had recordings personalized for each of the top twenty buyers. The secret was in the voice, pumped in through the doll by wireless transmitter, monitored by a technician.

Soon afterwards, Steinfeld talked about possibly upping her commitment ... a little. Maybe to seventy-five thousand pieces from fifty. Ann told herself it was still nowhere near what it should be, but at least it was something.

The day wore on. Byron Young of Walmart was a no-show and Ann wondered if he was still bothered by the things she'd said to him when they met in Arkansas. Then Tom Carlisle of Kmart arrived.

He'd been the first buyer to come through for her. Ann hoped her greeting wasn't fawning. Maybe it was, she thought five minutes later, because something was definitely off with the man. Carlisle went through the motions of his own presentation, but he showed none of his earlier delight in the doll.

Gerry McGuire from Brown's showed up at the same time, apparently to schmooze with Ann and Jonathan as if they had become his best friends. Ann was trying to ease away from him when Carlisle quietly slipped out the showroom door.

"Oh, no, you don't," Ann muttered to herself.

She left Jonathan and Gerry abruptly to follow Carlisle into the hall. Where had he gone? She looked right, left, then saw him approaching a competitor's showroom. Ann sprinted to catch up. "Tom! Wait!"

He looked back at her. She reached him just as he was pushing the door open.

"What is it?" she demanded. "Is something wrong? You can't hold up your end of the commitment? What?"

"It's nothing, Ann. You're fine. Calm down."

She had known him too long, had been doing business with him for too many years, to believe that. He was acting odd. "Something's up," she said.

He hesitated. "It shouldn't affect you in the least."

"*What* shouldn't?"

Carlisle let out a breath. "Kmart's asking me to take early retirement. I'll bring the new guy around to see you tomorrow."

"Is my commitment safe?" she asked. And Ann immediately had a mental image of herself shriveling down to something the size of a worm. "Tom, I'm sorry."

"Don't be. Business is business. As I said, you're okay, as far as I know."

As far as I know. Something else to tie her in knots. "What about you? What are you going to do? Are you going to be okay?" All the questions she should have asked before talking about his commitment, Ann thought.

He lifted his hands in supplication, maybe in resignation.

"This is ridiculous," Ann said. "You're far too young to retire."

"I'm also too damned honorable," Carlisle added.

"What does that mean?" Ann watched a play of contradictions cross his face. She thought at first that he was going to turn away, but there was nowhere for him to go.

"Tom, talk to me, please. There's something more to this, isn't there?"

He looked over her shoulder. Ann actually pivoted to see who he was staring at. No one in the hall seemed to warrant undue attention. "Rumor had it that you were going under with the doll," he said.

"Rumor is wrong," she snapped. "Patrick Morhardt was arrested but it was all a misunderstanding. You know the press— quick to accuse, much slower to recant."

"Still, I heard someone else was going to get Baby Talk N Glow."

"Not true. " She shook her head.

"You had ownership problems." It was a statement, not a question.

"*Had*, Tom. Past tense. It's all straightened out. Sure, everyone in the industry tried to take her off our hands for a while. But they've backed off."

He looked away again. What was he afraid of? What—who— was he looking for?

"Someone did more than try," he said. "He pretty much promised us that he had her. He was offering huge bonuses if we'd hold off, wait and commit to him instead of you."

A moment of dizziness swept over Ann as she tried to put together what he was saying.

Carlisle leaned closer to her. His breath smelled of salsa and onions. "Ann, didn't you wonder why I turned you down at first?"

Of course, she had. That whole trip to the American retailers had been absurdly abysmal. "I thought you were out of your mind."

"How did it go with the other buyers on that trip?"

"Like crap."

He turned to move away. Ann grabbed his arm. "Please..."

He shook her grip off. "I don't have much left to lose, Ann. I'm going to be out of this business within a few weeks. But I've got my family, damn it, and I'm not going to go out on a limb. *Think* about it. That's all I can say."

Out on a limb? For *her*? "Someone twisted your arm into turning me down? Tried to *bribe* you?" Her thoughts leaped. "And now they're forcing you out of the company because you went ahead and gave me an order anyway? *Who?*"

Chow, she answered herself, as she sagged one shoulder against the nearest wall.

"Good luck," Carlisle said as he opened the door to her competitor's showroom. "That doll is the best thing I've seen in a long time. Under normal circumstances, I would have given you twice the commitment I did. But we all thought it was risky with this other guy involved."

"Tom, please. You've got to give me more." Ann knew she was begging, but she didn't care. Edmund Chow hadn't just sold her a bogus deal. He hadn't just tried to frame Patrick. He hadn't just tried to kill her. He'd been one move ahead all the way.

Carlisle stepped halfway inside.

For a moment, Ann thought of pulling him back. "Just tell me one thing," she said. "He's Chinese, right?"

The buyer's face slackened briefly with surprise.

"No."

"No?"

"Hardly. He's from New York. Now, Ann, that's all I'm going to say." He headed inside the showroom and closed the door behind him.

Ann jerked back. Chow didn't have a New York accent, she thought, not even close. Someone else, then. Someone *else* had sabotaged her buyers?

She should have known all along that there was a great deal more at play. Chow's behavior alone just didn't make sense. But *what*? What did this mean?

CHAPTER 51

Jonathan was stuck. After Ann left the showroom, Gerry McGuire went through the presentation and asked questions he didn't know the answers to. Then Byron Young of Walmart turned up with his merchandising manager in tow.

Where was Ann? He started to get that pressured feeling in his chest again, the one he first felt after visiting Verna in the hospital. There were too many people around here. Any one of them could grab her, hurt her.

When she finally burst through the door of the showroom, he knew immediately that something was wrong. Her face was near white, with too much pink just under the surface. She had that smile on that could cut glass. He watched her press a hand to her stomach.

Jonathan tried to push his way through the crowd to reach her, but by the time he got to her side she had hooked up with Byron Young. *Later*, her eyes told him.

"Sorry about missing my appointment," Young was saying. "I should have called with our change of plans."

"It's fine," Ann replied. "We can squeeze you in now."

Lisette launched herself into the demonstration. As Ann stepped back to observe, Jonathan caught her arm and pulled her a little closer to his side. "What's going on?" he asked in an undertone.

She shook her head fretfully, then pushed her hair back from her cheek. "I'll fill you in afterwards. But I'll bet you dollars to donuts that Byron Young ends up giving us a firm commitment today."

That surprised him. From the looks of her, he'd thought something bad had happened, that something else had come undone. "How do you know that?"

"He brought that other guy with him," she said. "The merchandise manager of Walmart only turns up if a company has something unique to offer."

When the presentation was over, Young and the other man approached them. Ann rocked back on her heels a little as she waited, then she caught sight of Linda Figgures from Target out in the hallway. She wasn't scheduled until later in the week, but she was trying to get Ann's attention now.

Whoever their competitor was, Ann thought, whatever he had promised the buyers, the doll was hers. And the buyers from the major retailers were anxious to meet with her. She'd won a huge battle without even understanding the terms and conditions.

But who the hell was he, if not Chow? Her thoughts moved to Patrick. He grew up in New York. Had he crawled into bed with Chow, somehow? Had he tried to wiggle out of a deal they'd made—or had he become too much of a liability—so Chow tried to get him out of the picture?

She had to put it out of her mind for now, Ann thought. The Walmart merchandise manager was talking to her, telling her that he and his buyer felt her doll was revolutionary. "Are your legal problems are all cleared up?" he asked.

"Absolutely," Ann said. "We were able to purchase the rights to the doll directly from the inventor."

"If you can provide a notarized letter to that effect, then we're prepared to commit."

"I will," Ann replied.

"We want to feature her on the cover of our December Tab," Byron Young added quickly.

Ann felt herself fighting for balance. "How many pieces?"

"You suggested what? Two hundred and fifty thousand?"

Ann merely nodded, not wanting to rock the boat.

"We'll up that by another fifty thousand," the merchandise manager said.

Ann held out her hand to shake on it. "Great. This is fabulous. Welcome on board." She was fluttering inside.

"Ann, excuse me, can I have a word with you?"

She looked around quickly. It was Linda Figgures, pressing in from her right.

Ann held up one finger to urge her to wait and promised Young she would be in touch.

The Target buyer approached her with great energy and enthusiasm. Instead of threatening to narrow Target's vendor base and cut Hart Toy out, she wanted to run the doll in more than one ad during the upcoming fall season.

Ann didn't have to force her smile. She thanked the buyer and watched her leave, then she motioned to Jonathan and headed back to her office.

"What's happening?" he demanded as soon as the door closed.

Ann groaned a little and dropped into her chair. Her shoes came off. "Remember our trip to the American retailers?"

"Arkansas, Chicago, all that? Yeah." He began to nervously shift his legs, as if he were uncomfortable.

"I couldn't understand why it went so badly," she said.

He nodded. "I remember."

"Jonathan, things went so badly because someone was after us."

He stopped fidgeting. "What?"

"Someone else had already been in touch with the buyers, had told them we wouldn't be able to hold on to the doll. He offered them a better deal—with God knows what incentives—if they committed directly to him."

"At that point we didn't know what Chow was up to, so we never suspected."

"It wasn't Chow."

Jonathan made a low sound of disbelief in his throat. "Not Chow? Who else could have known that we were going to have problems?"

"I don't know. But he isn't Chinese. Tom Carlisle told me he was a native New Yorker. Tom's reliable and I trust him." Her neck began to hurt and she started to rub it. "They pushed Carlisle out," she said. "Upper management. He was the first of the buyers to come around and give us a commitment. Do you remember? I would guess that he told our anonymous competitor to get lost. Now he's being forced into early retirement."

"Management there still thinks they can get our doll on better terms from the other guy?" Jonathan asked.

"Maybe. I don't know. Maybe somebody just pulled a few strings to punish Carlisle. We'll find out when Tom brings the new buyer around tomorrow."

"Kmart—they're Kmart, right?—can't afford to be the only chain that's not carrying the doll."

He'd learned a lot these last months, Ann realized.

Abruptly, Jonathan said, "Turn around."

He had read her mind. His hands came down on her neck and gently massaged. Vibrations of pleasure sizzled inside. "Don't stop, please don't stop."

He leaned forward to talk into her ear. "I could do even better without that sweater you're wearing."

She was tempted. "Later," she breathed.

"How long do we have to hang around here?"

"A while yet." She eased away from his touch reluctantly. "I have to call Felicia."

"You're going to tell her about this other guy trying to shoot in beneath us?"

Ann dropped into the chair. "God, no. Just about Target and Walmart. I want her to sleep well tonight."

"Ann?"

She looked up at him questioningly. He seemed to want to say something, but then he changed his mind.

Jonathan wasn't sure what he wanted to say. How much he appreciated her genuine love for his mother? That her grit and strength and determination got to him in a place he wasn't sure he could identify? That the image of himself on the hunt for some unknown villain from New York, in a city as large as New York, overwhelmed him?

Instead of speaking, he kept his thoughts to himself.

CHAPTER 52

The crowds were beginning to thin at the Javits Center and Vincent knew it was time for him to leave. The fact that he had nailed down a spot with a bird's eye view into Hart Toy's showroom might raise a brow or two, especially since he had taken up the post more than thirty minutes ago and had barely budged since.

Watching Ann say goodbye to a couple of men, how she tossed back that mane of blond hair and laughed at something one of them said. Then she frowned in Vincent's direction as though sensing him standing there. He turned away and pretended to speak to a stranger behind him.

Yes, he thought, it was time to go.

But he was reluctant. Observing her made him feel powerful. Like God. Briefly, a sweet thought insinuated itself into his head. Could he take her out here? Right now? Simply walk up and plunge a knife into her spine? What a stir that would create: Ann Lesage found dead during Toy Fair. He could see the headlines, hear the newscasts. A lovely fantasy, but one that would have to remain so, he was afraid. He hadn't prepared for such a plan and had no weapon with him. Besides, ending her life that quickly would not give him the satisfaction he was seeking. Not anywhere close.

But he was running out of patience. He'd lost most of the buyers back to Hart Toy's corner when Ann had succeeded in grabbing the doll from Ling in time for Toy Fair. Not that it mattered all that much. The doll was only a diversionary tactic.

Vincent was keeping an eye on all the players in this little drama, including Patrick Morhardt. Patrick had left the rehab clinic and was wandering around somewhere like a loose cannon. Vincent was certain he would either self-destruct or be helped towards that goal.

For now, too many people remained standing. It was bad enough that Verna Sallinger was still alive. Just thinking about it made him cringe. He'd dropped the ball there, too. He'd enjoyed it too much, hurting her. He'd left her apartment on a fierce, hungry high. Exhilarated. Stupidly, he'd never checked her pulse. He wouldn't make that mistake again.

Verna was recovering in the hospital. There were too many doctors and nurses around for him to make his move now, but he would have to act eventually, before she had the opportunity to identify him. And then he'd get it right. Verna Sallinger first, then Ann Lesage. There would be a certain balance in killing them. And Felicia and Jonathan Morhardt, too, if necessary. But Ann was the real prize. He would save the best for last and relish every moment of it.

CHAPTER 53

I t was ten after four in the afternoon when Patrick decided that he needed to go to the bank. Unfortunately, this was going to involve getting up from his chair.

He heaved himself to his feet, putting too much effort into it. He staggered across the den before he cracked his knee against the coffee table. He swore and tried to kick it. But he missed, lost his equilibrium and went down hard.

The bottle of Courvoisier wobbled on the table, yet remained upright. "Good, that's good," Patrick muttered. He was almost out of cognac. This might be his last bottle. He had to buy more.

"Gotta take a shower," he decided.

He crawled back to the chair, leaned against it and pulled himself up. Then he took hold of the cognac bottle, wheeled his way out of the den, stopping halfway to take a swig. The liquor hit the back of his throat and went down warm and comforting. *Life is good*, he thought. Then he frowned.

No, it wasn't.

After a moment and a bit more Courvoisier, he remembered that life really wasn't … good. Irene was gone, which was a plus, because their marriage from early on had never worked. But he missed his kids terribly.

Irene had left him with only a few hundred dollars in their joint checking account, and that was spent. He'd also plowed through most of his severance pay. Patrick wasn't actually sure where the money went. He couldn't fathom having drunk it away. But perhaps that was possible.

He shook his head, which made him woozy. He approached the stairs and tried to focus on how he was going to make it to the second floor. The stairs climbed forever, like Jack's beanstalk. Articles of clothing were strewn over them. The whole house was a pigsty.

Screw the shower, he decided. Navigating those stairs would be more trouble than it was worth.

Patrick pushed himself away, got his legs under him, and moved for the front door. He remembered to leave the bottle on the entry table. Walking around in public with it would not be a good idea, he thought.

He was in perfect control. He staggered outside, hit the street, turned left, and started moving. By the time he got to the bank, it was closed.

"Son-bitch." Patrick rattled the door before stumbling backward.

"Somethin' can go wrong, it sure as hell will," he said aloud.

He wobbled around in a circle until he spotted the ATM machine. *There* was his answer.

He stuck his bank card in and waited an interminable time for something to happen. Finally, he leaned forward to peer closely at the screen. He closed one eye to read the message.

Rejected.

But shouldn't his severance pay be in there—what was left of it?

No matter. Patrick took the card back. He had good, trusty American Express on his side. No credit limit. He fished in his wallet for the platinum card and poked that into the slot instead. Still, nothing happened.

"Come on, you bitch, cough it up."

He hit the machine before he figured out what was wrong. It came to him like the sun spearing through the clouds, a perfect moment of lucidity. The American Express was a company card. Bloody Ann had canceled it.

Blackness rolled in on him. It touched the edges of his vision, then swarmed inward like a horde of buzzing flies, gnawing away, feasting on the life he'd known. Gone. All of it, gone. No kids. No job. No car. No money. No more Courvoisier.

"No fucking nothing," he said aloud, almost awed by it.

Ann had turned his mother and brother against him. She'd plotted and connived until she finally got her way, forcing him out of the company. She'd won. She'd taken it all.

Patrick sat down on the cold, hard concrete in front of the ATM machine. Verna came to mind. Poor, broken Verna. It was all too much. Life was too much for him.

Tears began to cascade down his cheeks.

CHAPTER 54

When they arrived at Jonathan's place, Ann stopped just inside his front door to remove her coat and kick off her shoes, and Jonathan pressed in close behind her. "I think I had an agenda ... something about getting you out of that sweater, didn't I?"

Ann allowed herself a smile. "You made mention of that."

"Want a drink first?"

She nodded and forced her tired legs to move forward. "I'll get it."

It had taken her some time to get used to his home, to feel comfortable here. Too much space had always unnerved her. She liked small rooms where nothing could sneak up behind her.

The night beyond the incredible expanse of his windows was bright tonight, helped by a full moon. She went to the dark oak liquor cabinet that blended in so well with all the brass and bronzed glass and warm furniture. She took hold of the bottle of Macallan and headed back to the kitchen. Halfway there, she paused and smiled to herself. She put the bottle down on the floor to yank her sweater over her head.

She didn't want to make the man work too hard.

When she strolled into the kitchen, he was headfirst in the refrigerator. All those long, delicious lines of him, bent over. His voice resonated a little as the refrigerator took it in and threw it back at her.

"I'm almost out of beer. Remind me to stop tomorrow on our way—" He stood and broke off when he saw her. "Yeah, well, who needs beer?"

"You might get parched. Bring it." Ann nodded at the bottle he held in his hand, then crooked her finger at him as she began backing up.

She managed one step.

He shot the refrigerator door closed with his foot and put the beer bottle down on the counter. Then he came toward her and caught her in mid-stride, lifting her. She gave a little hop and wrapped her legs around his waist. His hand slid up her thigh, pushing her skirt up. "Get naked," he said against her mouth.

Ann tilted her head back. "I can't. I'm wrapped around you."

He set her down.

Ann lowered her legs, shimmied out of her skirt, then her pantyhose. She gasped a little when he scooped her up again and carried her around the divider. She remembered to reach out and slap at the button that brought the blinds down over the windows.

They spilled together onto the sofa. Neither one of them had the time nor the inclination to pull it out into a bed. She wrestled with his trousers, while he unbuttoned his shirt. Clothes flew, fell. Sometimes, she thought, it was still like this. Sometimes it was the same as it had been in that hot tub, as urgent and necessary as breath.

Now, right now, need clawed through her. Now, right now, she was on a high. Whenever she got like this, Jonathan seemed to match her mood, forgetting niceties, grabbing and taking and rolling with it. He stripped her panties away and drove into her.

Then everything changed.

She felt it just under his skin, in the way he moved. He slowed down and his mouth went to her neck. His tongue, tracing, finding new spots just when she thought he knew them all.

He turned tender, but she wanted him to keep the pace up.

He pulled out of her to run his mouth down her body. Down lower.

Ann groaned with the next touch of his tongue, arched up and tried to push him away. He caught her wrists. He'd already decided, she realized helplessly. And she knew she was going to let him do anything he wanted.

Passion swept inside her like a raw wind. Nothing she could do to stop it. There was never anything she could do to stop *him*. He rose over her and found his way back inside.

"God, Ann. What you do to me." His mouth was back at her neck.

She managed to lift her arm to cover his mouth with her hand. "Shh. Don't talk."

They both came together, urgently; erupting without end, it seemed.

Ann could feel his racing heartbeat, matching her own.

They held on to each other afterwards, and both started to nod off, when the telephone rang.

Jonathan got to his feet, crossing the room to find it. He spoke into it in undertones, in half-syllables, with his back to her.

"Now what?" she asked when he hung up.

"Pat. He's in jail again. He wants me to come get him."

A crazed laugh escaped her, then stopped. "What did he do now?"

"He's in the drunk tank. The cops scraped him off the sidewalk in front of a bank in Queens."

"Are you going to go?"

Was he? He'd told Patrick that he would try to make it. But it had been an answer born out of old habit, Jonathan realized. He looked at Ann, naked on his sofa. Her skin was flushed, her body relaxed, her defenses down.

No. This time he wouldn't go. He returned to the sofa.

Ann held a hand out to draw him close. "He'll call you twenty-five times until you show up," she said.

"Let him. I took the phone off the hook. Let's pull this old sofa out now," he said.

"We could go upstairs, you know."

"Nah. I'm too lazy."

Ann decided this was a good time for a quick trip to the bathroom, then a chance to get that Scotch and water she'd intended to make before she'd gotten sidetracked.

By the time she returned from the kitchen, he was asleep. She worried briefly about the phone being off the hook. What if something happened to Felicia? But she knew Cal would call her on her cell if he got a busy signal here.

So, she thought, she would just lie down beside Jonathan and go to sleep as well.

Instead, she stood staring at him, sipping the Scotch. There was no question about it. He'd become her anchor. He was the only one who could make her laugh, make her forget that she was tied in knots about any variety of things. And more than anything, he helped her keep Mad Dog at bay. How had this happened? she wondered. How had he done this to her?

It was simply too much to ponder for a single Macallan and water. A moment later she put her glass down and snuggled into the sofa bed beside him.

CHAPTER 55

Five days in the drunk tank.

The cops had arrested Patrick in front of the ATM machine. He ended up being dumped in a solitary cell about the size of a cubby hole.

At the beginning, his craving for alcohol was only overshadowed by his anger. It began with that first phone call to his brother, begging him to bail him out. Three phone calls and a day later, it became obvious that there would be no savior this time, and he would be left to rot on his own.

He wallowed in self pity. He wanted to punish everyone he could think of, beginning with Ann, of course, then proceeding to his mother and Jonathan, even his soon to be ex-wife, Irene.

It took two days for his colossal thirst to take over, and thoughts of seeking revenge no longer mattered. Despite the various liquids that were fed him, be it water, soup or juice, nothing could assuage his need for alcohol. He started to believe that if he didn't get a drink soon he would die.

At night he lay on his cot and stared up at the ceiling, images of his life flashing through his mind, an endless spool of film teasing and tormenting him.

By the fourth day he was numb, resigned to his fate and without hope. The pain of withdrawal overshadowed everything else. It seemed as if there were giant maggots in his stomach, eating their way to his heart.

On Day Five, he awoke with an actual glimmer of hope. A future without booze no longer seemed impossible. It would take some sacrifice, obviously, but returning to the rehab center was something he now realized he would have to consider.

When they came to tell him that his brother was here and had made bail, he remained prone on his cot. It was only when the door to his cell opened and he was told he could leave, that he started to take the news seriously.

The walk seemed endless. He simply could not gain the proper balance, his feet operating as if they belonged to someone else. He hardly nodded at Jonathan when he first saw him. There was a release form that he was asked to sign, but his hands shook so badly he had trouble scribbling his name.

Finally in the car and on their way, his brother asked him where he'd like to go.

Patrick turned in the seat and faced him, waited for the dizziness to pass. "To the nearest bar," he said.

"Are you crazy?" Jonathan started to yell at him. "What the hell's the matter with you?"

"You asked me where I wanted to go."

"Yeah. But that's not the answer I expected."

Patrick held his silence. He let a few minutes pass, then in an embarrassed whisper, told Jonathan to take him back to the rehab center.

"Why? So you can walk out again?"

"I'm not walking anywhere," Patrick said heatedly. "I've asked you to take me there. I need help, I admit it. What more do you want from me?"

Jonathan paused and looked at his brother. "That's more like it," he said. "For a minute there, I thought you had lost your spunk."

They rode in silence. When they pulled up in front of the Metropolitan Hospital, a sense of fear snuck up on Patrick. "Wh… what are you doing?" he asked.

"Verna wanted to see you. I promised I would bring you over."

He shook his head frantically. "I don't think that's a good idea."

"Why not?"

"Because, it just isn't."

"Patrick—"

"Look," he tried to explain, "I just can't see her this way."

"Which way is that? You mean, sober?"

"That's not what I meant. I don't feel good—okay?" His temper flared. "I'm sick, Jonathan, maybe in more ways than one. I'll come see her afterwards, when I'm better."

"No. Not a good idea. You walk away now, there may not be an afterwards. I've spoken to her. This is your one chance to show her who you really are, the person you can be."

"That's just it—I can't do that right now."

"Patrick—"

"I can't, Jonathan."

"You have to."

They sat in silence. Finally, Jonathan opened the driver's door, came around to his side and coaxed him out of the car. "Go on," he said with a push. "Get in there. She's in a private room now. Number seven-three-five."

On his way, Patrick thought about copping out. He could hang out in the lobby for a while, then head on back. Jonathan would never know. But he would be sure to find out. And what could he gained by avoiding Verna? What would that accomplish? Hadn't he spent the last week thinking about her, worrying about her, wanting to see her? Now that his brother had forced his hand, why not do the right thing?

Still, he hesitated outside her room.

"May I help you?" a young intern asked.

"Uh—Ms. Sallinger?" he could hardly speak.

"You're at the right room, buddy. Just go on in."

Tentatively, he crossed the threshold.

She was sitting up in bed. When she saw him, she tried to smile, but sutures had locked part of her mouth in place. Bruises were visible on her upper cheeks and around her eyes. What struck Patrick most was the color of her skin, as pale as porcelain.

Suddenly, his heart went out to her. "I'm sorry," he said, needing to apologize.

"What for?" she said in a whisper. "If you hadn't shown up when you did, I'd be dead. Besides, you should be hating me, for all the trouble I've caused you."

"I don't hate you. I … just wanted to come by and tell you to get better. I've asked my brother to take me back to the clinic."

She sighed. "Do you believe in yourself, Patrick?"

"Not really," he admitted.

"But you know you can beat this, don't you?"

"I don't know, Verna. I don't know that at all. But I'm hoping to find out."

"Well, that's a start."

"Is it?"

"Don't you think so?" she asked.

He didn't know what to say. Instead, he turned. "I'd better go. I'd—uh—like to see you afterwards, if that would be okay."

Her eyes closed and she seemed to doze off.

He was headed for the door when he heard her voice behind him. "I would like that, too," she said.

CHAPTER 56

For Ann, the months directly after Toy Fair were often filled with anxiety, and certainly this year was no exception.

On this particular Wednesday afternoon in late April, she was seated at her desk in her office, going over the numbers and events of February for probably the hundredth time. Kmart had ended up bailing on them. If not for their other successes, she might have felt devastated. Instead, she was confident that even Kmart would come around. This, despite the fact that the new buyer was a disaster and couldn't hold a candle to Tom Carlisle. Ann flushed at the recollection of meeting the young, inexperienced replacement.

Flipping through the order sheets, she calculated that with Toys 'R' Us and Target now holding steady, her total of one million pieces for the United States was in line. Their break-even point had necessarily inched up, but they would still show a profit.

Her first delivery of two hundred thousand pieces of Baby Talk N Glow was set to arrive at the beginning of June. She'd spread the rest of her inventory commitment out into the early fall, ending in October.

Dora's voice piped through the intercom. "Michael Scott at American Freight Forwarders is on line three."

Ann reached for the phone. "Michael, hi. What can I do for you?"

His hesitation immediately alarmed her.

"We've got a problem here, Ann," he said. "I've been trying to bring these dolls in for you, but I'm hitting a wall."

"What kind of a wall?" She was amazed at how level her voice sounded.

"A collusion kind of wall."

"Which means?"

"Remember some twelve, thirteen years ago, when all the major shipping companies had locked hands? The economy was depressed. Ships traveling to America with full containers were returning home empty. Schedules were reduced and many ships taken out of service."

Ann remembered it all too well. Containers had been diverted to Europe instead of America, and the cost of freight had risen dramatically. "And?" she said.

"It's happening again. Not on account of the economy this time, but for the opposite reason. Things are going so well, the containers that *are* coming to the States are filling up with TV's and stereos. After all, the freight rate for these products is higher than it is for toys, so why not take advantage?"

No, she thought, *no, this isn't possible.* This sort of news usually traveled fast, yet she had heard no rumors of any kind. Ann rested her forehead against the heel of her hand. One last snag. Everything else had worked out, and now she couldn't get her hands on the damned dolls. Air freight? she wondered. No, that would be prohibitive. Her stomach started to twist into a knot.

"If you don't believe me, come on down here," Scott said. "I can show you online what's available to us—a big goose egg. There just aren't any free containers."

Ann's head reeled. There was something missing here, but she couldn't quite put her finger on it. "That won't be necessary," she said. "Look, Michael, I'll have to get back to you." She disconnected and leaned forward in her chair, started to stare out the window. Then her intercom buzzed again.

"Now it's Jonathan," Dora said.

Ann picked up. "Hi. What's going on?"

"Are you planning to leave the office at about the same time today?"

"As far as I know."

"Okay. I'm going to settle in and do some work. I just wanted to know how many hours I had left."

Displeasure and an old fear crowded Ann's heart. "Jonathan, you really don't have to babysit me like this."

"Humor me."

She always did, Ann thought. Somehow, lately, she always ended up doing just that. "All right."

"Are you okay? You sound funny."

Ann hesitated. There would be time enough at home to fill him in on this latest snafu. "Everything's fine."

She hung up, her thoughts veering off him as soon as she did. Was this real, she wondered, this shipping problem? Or was someone trying to knock her back a step again? There had been a time, before Baby Talk N Glow, when she would have accepted Michael Scott's word as gospel. But that had been before Edmund Chow had deceived her, and her life had been threatened on the streets of Hong Kong, before Tom Carlisle had told her someone else was positioning himself as the doll's distributor.

And, Ann thought suddenly, it was almost as though Michael Scott had expected just this reaction from her—that she *wouldn't* accept what he was telling her as gospel. Why else would he invite her to look for herself at the freight bookings? What was that all about?

Ann picked up the phone to dial Sidney Greenspan's office and was told he was out. She tried Alvin Pelletier next, who greeted her in his usual boisterous manner. No, he hadn't heard of any shipping problem. As a matter of fact, he had two forty-foot containers filled with his goods on the water as they spoke. This bit of news did not help Ann's anxiety. By the time she was through speaking with Hasbro, Mattel, and half a dozen others, she was reaching for her antacid tablets.

"One last-ditch effort, you assholes?" she muttered aloud, to faces she couldn't see and couldn't even begin to imagine. She chewed hard and swallowed. What Michael Scott had told her was a lie. There was no shortage of containers. No one else was having a shipping problem.

Ann surged to her feet. Her heart began to race. She would not take this lying down. No way. She got to her office door before she remembered her shoes and went back for them.

"What's going on?" Dora asked, clearly surprised when Ann hopped past her desk, trying to get her heels back on.

"Got to go out for a bit."

"Where?"

But Ann was already halfway up the hall.

She took the elevator down and jogged onto the street to find a cab. It was warm and breezy out, the wind flipping her hair into her eyes. She was in such a state that she had forgotten her purse. She should return to the office and get it. She should also stop and take a deep breath before rushing off to prove someone wrong. But the adrenaline was pumping through her veins. And she was furious. She couldn't turn back. She had to see for herself what was happening. She had to question Michael Scott and make him tell her everything he knew. A cab stopped. She realized that her cell phone and wallet were also in her purse upstairs. She checked the pocket of her slacks. She had some cash—that was good enough.

She gave the driver the location of her freight forwarder's office. Yes, she'd take Michael Scott up on his offer to look at his bookings online. She'd get to the bottom of this face-to-face.

She settled into the cab and slowed down her breathing. She told herself she wasn't crazy; she wasn't rushing off like a madwoman. There was just no more room for error.

When the taxi dropped her off near the docks, Ann was momentarily confused by the offices and warehouses around her. She'd been here before, but it was too many years ago. She thought she remembered that Michael Scott's location was in the farthest building to the south, so she headed in that direction.

He was at his desk when she found him—a tall, skinny guy, who in some ways reminded her of Charles Ling. But where Ling's eyes were sincere—a transparent window to his feelings—there had always been a certain shiftiness to Scott. Through all the time that Hart Toy had done business with him, whenever something went wrong, it was never his fault. He always had someone or something to blame.

"Ann." Scott looked up, surprised.

"I changed my mind," she said. "Show me exactly why you can't get me any containers."

"Uh, actually, I might be able to get ten released by the time you need them."

It occurred to her that he didn't seem all that keen on showing her his computer screen, after all. Ann leaned forward. Her temper was pumping little shots of pain into her temples. "You're lying, Michael."

"Oh, come on…"

"I talked to almost a dozen people between the time I got off the phone with you and now. They're getting containers, as many as they need."

"That's not possible."

"What are you trying to pull on me here? No … wait … I have a better question. Who put you up to this?"

Scott avoided her eyes. Abruptly, he stood, told her he'd be right back, and fled his office.

Ann was about to go after him, when a familiar voice caused her to freeze in mid-step.

"Hello, Ann," the man said with the utmost calm.

"Wh…what are you doing here? she asked. Then, suddenly, she noticed his New York accent, and it all became clear.

CHAPTER 57

Jonathan began cleaning up the studio corner of his loft at half past four, dipping brushes, snapping up drop cloths. He changed the angle of the painting he was working on so he could see it as he moved around the room.

It was time to head out to meet Ann. He waited for the twinge of resentment that usually came when he was forced to stop work, the grim itch that began under his skin and ended with the tightening of his jaw. But nothing happened.

He found himself curious about how it would feel if Ann intruded on one of his truly feverish spells, when his art was erupting from him, passing from his mind to the canvas so furiously that his forearm cramped and his senses stopped working. Those were the times he didn't hear the phone ring or smell a pot burning in the kitchen. Would he resent her then, if she pulled him away from that?

He punched his arms into his jacket and realized he couldn't imagine any scenario where Ann would make an unwelcome claim on his time. In fact, she never made demands on him, and frequently bucked if he made any on her. She seemed to accept as fact that he would show up each day before she left the office, but did so in a way that let him know that she understood it was useless to try to dissuade him.

He stepped outside, locked the door and started walking, his hands shoved into his pockets, humming to himself.

He was at Ann's office within twenty minutes. When he reached her floor he strolled into the reception area and waved to her secretary, who happened to be on the phone. Without stopping or waiting for Dora to return his greeting, he casually walked into Ann's office, expecting to find her there.

Not only was she absent, her desk was a mess, with reams of paper spread out in no particular order. This wasn't like Ann, he thought, as he noted that her computer was on, her briefcase open on the floor with files spilling from it.

Jonathan pivoted and headed back out to speak with Dora. "Hey," he said once she was off the phone. "Where's your fearless leader?"

"I thought she was with you."

"And why would you think that?"

"Well, she rushed out of here around two-thirty, just after she spoke with you."

Jonathan felt a swish of unease. "Okay. I'll try her cell phone." He pulled his iPhone out of his pocket, stepped back into Ann's office and dialed.

His thoughts fractured when he realized that Ann's purse was ringing at his feet. He bent over and reached for the purse, shoving his hand into each compartment until his fingers closed over her cell phone. His unease mushroomed. She never went anywhere without her phone.

Jonathan rocketed into motion. He approached Dora one more time and asked what Ann's exact words were when she left.

She blinked at him. "That she had to go out."

"What else?"

"Nothing. I asked where, but she didn't answer. So I thought—"

"Yes, I know. That she was going to meet me." Jonathan took a step back. What the hell was going on here? They had agreed

that he would pick her up at the normal time, so something had obviously come up. Okay, he thought. Where—and when—had it become carved in stone that she had to report her every move to him?

Well, she did. Under the circumstances, she damned well better. Jonathan realized he was angry. Extremely angry. Angry enough to want to holler at her, pick her up off her feet and give her a good shake, until she got it into her thick head that he loved her...

Whoa.

He pulled his thoughts up short. That was something he was going to have to consider later, after he found her. He headed for the elevator, took it down and grabbed a cab. He went to the Savannah.

He told the driver to wait and he jogged into the lobby. The concierge recognized him.

"Hey, do me a favor and save me a trip upstairs," Jonathan said. "Could you call and see if Ms. Lesage is in?"

"Of course. Shall I tell her to come down?"

"No. If she's there, I'll go up."

The guy stood with the phone pressed to his ear for thirty seconds, a minute; not speaking, waiting. "Nothing, sir," he finally said, hanging up. "No answer."

"Damn it." Jonathan looked at the man and all but shouted, "Have you seen her today at all?"

"No, sir."

"What time did you come on duty?"

"Eight this morning."

She'd left his place around the same time, Jonathan thought. That covered this base, then. He returned to the cab.

Now where? She didn't regularly go to a gym—sporadically, she used the one in her building. She hadn't had an appointment, or Dora would have known about it. Had something especially

exciting happened with the doll? If it had, she would have called Felicia.

"Where to?" the driver asked him.

"Hold on." He yanked his cell phone free and called his mother.

Cal answered. Jonathan realized he was diving ahead with no particular plan. Damn it, Felicia didn't need another worry.

"Cal, a quick question," he said. "Just answer with a yes or a no."

"Yes, she is right here, on the divan."

Smart man, Jonathan thought. "Have you seen Ann today? Have you heard from her?"

"No and no."

Damn! "Have you been there all day?"

"I was gone from noon until three. I stopped in at my office to see a few patients." Cal was nearly retired, but he wouldn't take the last step.

Jonathan felt his emotions spiraling out of control. He had to stay calm. He had to think, figure out what was going on and where Ann could be. Dora had said that she had taken off at about 2:30, so it was conceivable that Cal might have missed her. "Can you ask Francesca?" The housekeeper never went anywhere these days, had barely left the apartment since his mother became ill.

"Why don't you give me your number and I'll get back to you," Cal said.

"My cell."

Jonathan disconnected. He had one last thought. He gave the driver his own address. Maybe she'd rushed off somewhere, then figured it was easiest to just head home rather than return to the office for her briefcase and purse.

Sure. He was grasping for straws.

Fifteen minutes later, Jonathan stood in his own doorway. The place was silent as a tomb, looking just as he had left it, except now the quiet bothered him.

"Ann!" he shouted anyway. He could have sworn he heard his voice echo. She wasn't here.

Something like fear caused his lips to shudder. His cell phone went off. He still held it in his hand but had forgotten about it.

It rang again.

Please let it be her, he was thinking

"She hasn't been here," Cal said. "Is there trouble?"

He didn't know how much to divulge.

"Listen," he said. "I'm heading back to her office. If she shows up at mom's or if you hear from her, tell her to call me."

"I will," Cal said.

He didn't remember hanging up or putting his phone away. His sense of foreboding was now so strong it seemed to crush his ability to reason. Heading outside he had only one purpose in mind, and that was to find her, as quickly as possible.

CHAPTER 58

Sidney Greenspan.

Ann couldn't believe it. Sidney was one colleague Felicia considered a friend, someone the entire Morhardt family had trusted for well over the seventeen years that Ann had known them.

This revelation caused her to question her own ability to judge people. She had always considered Sidney a blowhard, someone greedy and selfish. But not a person who would go to such unfathomable lengths to get what didn't rightfully belong to him.

Sidney Greenspan. One minute she was standing in Michael Scott's office, watching Michael walk out, Sidney walk in. The next thing she knew, someone else approached her from behind and slipped a thick hood over her head. She screamed, struggling to free herself.

A man's voice, filled with menace, silenced her. Still, she tried kicking out, until a slap caught her across the cheek and stunned her.

She half-walked, was half-carried down a flight of stairs. Everything was darkness. A door opened and closed. She felt a whiff of fresh air. A side entrance to the building, she figured.

The stranger's voice again, instructing her to get into a waiting vehicle. When she hesitated, he pushed her rudely, forcing her inside and onto the floor of what seemed to be a truck or SUV.

Over the course of the ride in stop-and-go traffic, Sidney only spoke to give directions.

A trickle of fear raced inside Ann's belly. She couldn't see. Not even a glimmer of light passed through the fabric that was covering her face and head.

Michael Scott, she thought in disbelief, had set her up. For what? Money? A lucrative new account? And who was the third person in this triangle?

She couldn't even guess.

When they came to a stop, Ann heard Sidney's voice moving away, then the squeal of a door being opened. A set of hands grabbed her. She thought of kicking out, but her feet had gone numb.

She swore she would not make a sound. She would not give them the satisfaction of knowing she was afraid. Despite her silence, strong fingers clamped across her mouth, causing some of the fabric of the hood to scratch her teeth.

Then the man took hold of Ann's arm. She tried to shake herself free, but the hold tightened, to the point where it became too painful to struggle.

She was being led inside a building that had a stale smell about it. Was it a warehouse? she wondered. Where was she?

The man beside her paused.

Ann purposely slid to the cement floor. He tried to get her up again, but she willed herself to remain limp. All she could do was try to make this as difficult for him as possible.

He finally gave up the effort but not before shoving her hard. She flew backwards and hit something solid. Her shoulder started to throb where it had made contact. "Who the hell are you?" she asked.

Suddenly, the hood was yanked off her head and she was face to face with her assailant. It took a few moments for her eyes to adjust to the light. Gradually, she could make out her surroundings.

She had been right—it was a warehouse. She could see hundreds and hundreds of boxes.

She turned to the man. He was in his mid-to-late fifties. A stocky build with full head of brownish-gray hair. There was something intimidating about him. And something vaguely familiar. He had a gruesome looking scar that ran down the left side of his face. But what struck her most were his dead eyes.

The man seemed to smile, a creepy smile that wasn't really a smile at all. Her stomach went into spasms.

"Hello, Ann," he said, looking at her intently. "I've waited a long time for this."

She shook her head from side to side, averting his gaze.

The man's hand abruptly reached out, cupped her mouth hard and squeezed. "Look at me when I'm talking to you, goddamnit!"

She bit her tongue, felt blood. *Please, prove me wrong,* she prayed.

But the man's voice, his scar.

Sweet God in Heaven …

"My friends call me Vincent," he said. "But your mother named me Mad Dog."

CHAPTER 59

Pacing back and forth in the same police precinct they had brought Patrick to, Jonathan's impatience made him want to punch holes in the walls. But all he could do was wait. Detective Rondgrun was tied up. No one could say exactly how long he would be.

Jonathan had rushed back to Ann's office, arriving just past five o'clock in the afternoon. He'd taken a seat at her desk, tried to make himself believe that she had simply gotten antsy and had decided to cut him loose. This rationalization was his last-ditch effort to avoid the inevitable—the knowledge that something terrible must have happened—and it was up to him to find out what.

Someone most likely had her. But who? He cursed himself for not having figured out well before now what had been going on. Once they had signed the contract with the inventor he had become complacent, wrongly assuming that the menace in Hong Kong would not follow them here. Instead of watching over Ann twenty-four/seven, he had believed that picking her up each day after work and escorting her home would adequately safeguard her.

And now she was gone.

He glanced at his watch for what felt like the hundredth time in the last half hour, and went to talk to Dora, still at her desk. "Are you certain nothing out of the ordinary happened this afternoon?" he asked a little too sharply.

The look on her face told him to calm down. "Sorry," he apologized. "I know we've already gone over this. But I need you to humor me. Tell me again about the sequence of phone calls."

Ann had always praised Dora's efficiency. Jonathan hoped desperately that she would now come through with the one missing detail that would help him solve the mystery of Ann's disappearance.

"Michael Scott," she said as if by rote. "Followed by your call. Then she must have made nine or ten calls on her own, one after the other, without asking me to put them through for her."

"Yeah. And who is this Michael Scott again?"

"American Freight Forwarders. They handle our shipping needs from China."

Jonathan took out his pen and scratchpad and noted Michael Scott's name and phone number. Standing, he thanked Dora and exited the office.

Think, he told himself. *Manage it one step at a time.*

Jonthan had taken the information to the police precinct with him, and here he paced, willing the detective to first enter the room, then to see some connection he could not, and finally to come up with the answer that would help him find Ann.

Forty minutes passed. When Detective Rondgrun finally appeared, he shook hands with Jonathan and asked him the reason for his visit. "Your brother again?" he said.

Jonathan started into his explanation, going back to the mystery of Edmund Chow's disappearance, the discovery at Toy Fair that someone else believed they would obtain the rights to market Baby Talk N Glow, to the phone call Ann received this afternoon that preceded her leaving her office in a hurry.

The detective wore a look of skepticism. "So she's missing what—all of four hours?" he asked. "My God, all you'd need is one major traffic jam in this city to delay you that long."

"Four hours?" Jonathan shrugged. "I don't think so. Besides, it isn't like Ann to rush out of her office without her purse or her cell phone."

Detective Rondgrun smiled. "It's not only men that can be forgetful," he said.

Jonathan hesitated, fighting for control. "Ann doesn't go anywhere without her personal stuff," he said forcefully. "This isn't like her. Something has happened to her."

"Oh? So what is it that you're not telling me?"

He racked his brain for whatever else he could say. Then he remembered. "There was an incident in Hong Kong, Two men tried to grab Ann off the street. Somehow, she was able to fight them off. But they hurt her."

"And how is this related to her going missing today?"

His patience teetered on the brink. He wanted to get out of there. If the detective wasn't going to help, he wanted to start looking for Ann himself. "Look," he said. "Call it instinct if nothing else, but I know I'm not wrong. Ann's in trouble."

Detective Rondgrun sighed. "We don't have a whole hell of a lot to go on. Give me the number of this Michael Scott. It was his phone call that seems to have precipitated her dashing out in a hurry. I'll have a little chat with him, see if he knows something."

"And?" Jonathan said.

"And we'll see what he says."

"But what if he doesn't have anything new to offer? Then what do we do?"

"Then we sit and wait."

Jonathan headed for the door. "Please call me after you've talked to him." He looked at his watch. "I guess that won't be until tomorrow morning?"

"That's correct. I'll try to get at it first thing."

Frustration now fueled Jonathan's anxiety as he fled the precinct. He could not afford to wait for the detective. He would deal with this on his own.

CHAPTER 60

Memory took Ann back to when she was fourteen years old.

Home was the housing project in the worst part of town, nothing more than a two-room flophouse, with plaster-pealing walls and a linoleum floor that stank of mildew and decay.

At night, although she longed for the safety that sweet dreams offered, reality always intruded. Invariably, her eyes would close for a few minutes, then she would wake in a cold sweat. She'd listen to the sounds of her mother and the men who visited her, and she'd pray with all her might that it wouldn't be him—Mad Dog—coming back for more.

The butcher knife hidden in her mattress offered her some comfort, and she promised herself that she would not hesitate to use it. But when the moment came, when she felt the heat of Mad Dog's body upon her, she became paralyzed. Again.

Then a powerful sense of loathing swept over her, and when she heard the sound of his pants being unzipped, the knife was already in her hand. As he bent towards her, she plunged it into the closest part of him she could reach, his face.

He let out a petrifying scream.

What happened next was a blur. There was so much blood, a river of it, she had to move away or drown. So she slipped off the bed, onto the floor, snatching up the knapsack that contained her few earthly possessions. And she ran, through the door and outside, looking back to see if she was being followed, not stopping until she was blocks away.

Recalling all of this now as she lay on the bare warehouse floor, Ann realized that while the streets of New York had protected her anonymity for a while, there was still no place she could ultimately hide.

Mad Dog had found her. And this realization sparked a terrible fear in her. She was sure now that Sidney was nothing more than a pawn in Mad Dog's crazed plan to exact his revenge.

CHAPTER 61

On the street near the police precinct, cell phone to ear, Jonathan dialed his mother's number.

Cal answered.

Jonathan was reasonably sure that the doctor was all but living at Felicia's these days. "I'm coming over," he said. "Brace Mom."

"Oh, God." Cal's voice was almost a groan of despair.

Jonathan realized how his words must have sounded. "No, Ann's not—" He broke off. What—dead? Who the hell knew? His stomach seized. "I still haven't found her," he said instead. "We need to do something."

"What do you suggest?" Cal asked.

He hesitated. "I don't know. My mother and I will have to put our heads together."

"All right. I'll tell her."

Jonathan disconnected then hailed the first empty cab to go by. He had called Felicia earlier in the day to give her a heads up without divulging any serious details. Later, he had called back with an innocuous progress report that still revealed nothing. But now he knew he would have to come clean. If anyone could think of a plan of attack it would be his mother.

When he arrived she greeted him herself, explaining that the good doctor was out for a walk. He understood at once that she wanted to afford them some privacy.

Once they were seated on the couch, she took his hands in hers. "I want you to tell me everything," she said, her voice determined. "*Everything,* without holding back."

When he spoke it was as if by rote, reciting the events of the past number of months: the full scope of the initial disaster with the American retailers, Edmund Chow's duplicity, the attack on Ann in Hong Kong, and the New Yorker who was working against then.

"Tom Carlisle admitted this?" Felicia asked when he finished. She didn't wait for an answer but immediately nodded to herself. "Yes, he was always a decent man."

"Yeah, he is," Jonathan agreed. Then he told her about his afternoon, concluding with his disappointing visit to Detective Rondgrun. Felicia dropped the hold on his hands. "So what do you plan to do about it?" she asked.

He didn't know what to say.

"And what else are you not telling me," she continued.

"Huh?" Jonathan looked up in surprise.

"You're in love with Ann, aren't you? And have been for as many years as I can remember."

"Mother—"

"So why don't you tell me the full story, including the part you've been holding back. The part that includes your brothers."

He was genuinely surprised. It was obvious what Felicia was referring to. How she knew, or thought she knew, was another story. "I don't see how any of this can help Ann," he started to say, trying to bide his time.

"I'm not referring to her," Felicia jumped in. "We need closure, Jonathan. Lord knows, this can't stay hidden forever."

Jonathan stared at the wall, anywhere but at her face. Then he mustered the strength to deal directly with her questions. "You'd lost Matthew," he said. "That was enough."

"When have you ever known me to be weak?"

She was right, of course. Even now, it was only her body that was wasted. "It sincerely was an accident," he said.

He tried to gather his thoughts, to remember again what had happened that night. *She's using you, Matt!* Patrick had said. *Ann took a one-week sickbay stay and rolled it into years. Now she's running out of options! She struck out with me and Jon!* Shouting it into the wind, Jonathan thought. Shouting the lie about them both having been with Ann. They had all been straining to be heard over the engine and the noise of a fierce wind. Pat had taken a hand off the wheel of the boat to take another swig of beer.

Felicia already knew the details of Matt's death—that he had been thrown free at impact, right into the piling, that his neck had snapped. But what she did not know—what no one knew—was that Pat had been swilling beer all night, that Jonathan had sought to protect him, and that after the impact he had heaved Pat into the back of the boat, then taken the wheel himself, waiting as the flames licked over the water, until the authorities arrived.

"Matt had asked Ann to marry him earlier that same week," he said to his mother now. "She … couldn't bring herself to hurt him. Had to figure out a way to tell him no, to let him down gently. So a couple of days passed and Matt … I think he took her silence to mean she was going to say yes. I guess we *all* thought that. So Pat … Patrick lied. Trying to jolt Mattie off her, I think, to make him change his mind. Pat's heart was in the right place, but his methods left a lot to be desired."

"There is never a good reason for a lie, or for that kind of interference," his mother interjected.

Jonathan nodded stiffly. "Mattie went nuts, went after him. Pat was at the wheel of the boat. We were at full throttle. When Pat left the wheel to get to Matt, we hit the piling."

Everything about Felicia sagged. "And for fifteen years, you have let everyone believe that it was you behind the wheel?"

Because it hadn't all been Pat's fault, Jonathan thought. "He was saturated drunk, Mom. I shouldn't have let him get behind the wheel in the first place."

"Jonathan, you are not responsible for the whole world."

That startled him. "It was Matt, mom. Matthew was the one always trying to save people."

One corner of her mouth tucked up. "No, my dearest, it is you."

"He brought home broken birds…"

"And you collect and protect souls."

He couldn't help it. He gave a harsh bark of laughter.

"Jonathan, once someone makes it into your inner circle, you'd die for them. You were the role model for Matthew. Where do you think he learned it? You've kept this secret for fifteen years in order to protect your brother, to protect Ann, to protect me."

It rocked him back. To protect *Ann*? Yeah, he thought, because he'd known—he'd always known—that the truth would be too hard for her to take. She'd blame herself for not speaking soon enough. She'd take it all on her own shoulders. In truth, her peace of mind had been the most important single thing that had influenced his decision to say nothing.

Jonathan let out his breath and rubbed his face with his hands.

For a long while, Felicia was so quiet he thought their conversation was over. Then she gently cleared her throat. "If not for these extraordinary circumstances, I might have gone to my grave with this secret. But there are some things you need to know about Ann, Jonathan, to get you through this night or however long it takes until you find her. You need to understand why Ann tries to push you—to push everyone—away. You can't let her do that once I'm gone."

Jonathan suddenly felt short of breath, as if something had constricted in his chest.

"Whoever has her," she said, "whatever has happened to Ann, you must understand that she is a survivor, that she will not allow herself to be destroyed." Felicia paused and looked Jonathan in the eye. "Do you know how it was that I found her on the street? Has she explained any of that?"

Jonathan shook his head. Of course she had told him nothing about her past, it resided beyond one of the many walls she constructed to keep him at a distance.

Felicia gave him a half-hearted smile. "Well, I suppose if she wanted you to know she would have told you by now, but circumstances are such that…" Then she seemed to cave in on herself. "I'll surely be cursed for betraying her confidence. But I'm willing to live with that for your sake, and hers."

"You're meddling."

"Yes, of course, I am. Ann's mother was a heroin addict who prostituted herself to support her habit. Ann never knew her father."

Jonathan winced.

"While Ann was still living with her—she was barely fourteen years old—one of her mother's clients raped Ann. The second time he tried it, she fought him off and ran. This is why she was living on the street when I met her."

"She was raped?" Jonathan said, barely getting the words out.

Felicia nodded. "Yes. Once Ann confided in me, I hired a private detective to find the man responsible, but he was long gone and presumed dead. It was all a matter of Ann being in the wrong place at the wrong time. The poor child. She was pretty and young and this man … this man simply took her on the basis of that alone. I'm sure she somehow believes that she invited it."

The sex, he thought. Of course, it now all made sense. She'd been terrified of the sex. But in the end, she'd come to him, had allowed herself to open up.

The thought of her as that fourteen year-old made him hurt inside. *He had to find her.* Jonathan rose from the couch unsteadily.

"I tell you this because I want you to know what Ann is made of," Felicia said. "That is, if you haven't already figured it out for yourself. She fled Newark and came to New York. She hid in the church at night instead of going to any of the usual homeless places. She couldn't take the risk of being somewhere where someone else might find her pretty."

I was too pretty for him, she had said. For Matthew. By being pretty as a child, Ann had thought she had provoked a stranger to attack her. She'd consider herself soiled, unworthy of Matthew.

"Handle this gently, Jonathan."

"I will." His voice was hoarse.

Felicia sat forward. "I know that. That's why I told you. Now—I want you to visit your brother. He's just been released from the rehab clinic. Despite your differences, he is still family. Patrick, more than anyone else, might have some ideas for you."

Jonathan hesitated.

"Consult with him," his mother insisted. "You have nothing to lose."

CHAPTER 62

Without hesitating, and despite the late hour, Jonathan took his car out of the parking garage he rented on a yearly basis and raced to his brother's house. He thought he was wasting his time. Having a discussion with Patrick was not uppermost on his mind. But his mother had better instincts for this sort of thing and he was not one to second guess her.

They stood inside the vestibule, not saying anything for a moment or two, sizing each other up. Jonathan was surprised at how good Patrick looked. His eyes were clearer; a lot of the tension was gone from his face. "Welcome back," he said, meaning it.

Patrick almost smiled. "Thanks. What the heck brings you out here this time of night?"

Jonathan paused. How much to divulge was the real question facing him. His brother may have survived the rehab clinic, but how trustworthy was he?

He began cautiously, taking Patrick through the events of the past twenty-four hours. The old Patrick would have turned a deaf ear, Jonathan knew, especially where Ann was concerned. Now, his brother absorbed the news of Ann's disappearance with what appeared to be genuine sympathy.

They sat down in the den—Jonathan on the couch, Patrick on one of the high-back upholstered chairs. And they weighed every possible motive. In the end, however, they both concluded that it was highly unlikely that someone in the toy industry would want to do Ann harm.

"It just doesn't make sense," Patrick said.

Jonathan agreed with him; it made no sense at all. But not finding a toy industry connection only made matters worse. He didn't know where else he could look.

He was about to leave when Verna stepped into view. "Hello, Jonathan," she said. A little shyly, he thought.

Seeing her here surprised him. "Glad to see you back on your feet," he told her. Then he turned for the door, was about to say good night, when he paused.

Verna had contact with a man they knew was behind her beating as well as Patrick being arrested. If he could get her to describe Vincent, he could get the man's likeness down on paper. Then maybe, just *maybe*, someone might recognize him.

Jonathan asked Verna to take a seat beside him in the den. A pen and a pad of paper were provided by Patrick and he began to draw. At first he had the nose wrong, then the eyes. It took several drafts until finally, some two hours later, the sketch was apparently life-like enough to cause Verna to shrink back in alarm.

"That's him," she muttered breathlessly. "He's the one ... he's the bastard who hurt me!"

Jonathan sensed he was on to something. Vincent had an agenda involving both Verna and Patrick. He aimed to find out why.

On his way out, Patrick handed him a list of of Hart Toy's key competitors and contacts. "This would be a good place to start," his brother told him.

He got into his car, pulled out of the driveway and headed back to Manhattan. He knew he had to keep his wits about him. There were certain things that had to get done. Nothing could be left to chance.

He hit the city limits almost thirty minutes before he had any right to do so and went right to his loft. Sleep was out of the question. After making a pot of coffee he sat down in the kitchen and tried to think. Ann didn't bring much of her work home from the office but maybe there was something he could find in a closet or one of the bedroom drawers.

He climbed the stairs and started going through her things. There was nothing there. It was clothing, for the most part. He began to pace the loft. By the time dawn broke, his patience was wearing thin. He had a likeness of Vincent on paper and he wanted to show it to as many people as possible, as quickly as possible.

Now, getting into his car, Jonathan was grateful for the convenience of having many of Hart Toy's competitors relocated in one office tower close to the Javits Center.

He arrived just before nine o'clock. Taking out the list that Patrick had prepared for him, he rode the elevator to the top floor and began with Alvin Pelletier, the owner of Single-Brite, Inc. He handed Alvin the sketch and asked if he recognized the man. Alvin handed the sketch back and told him he'd never seen him before in his life.

His second stop was at a preschool company. His third, fourth and fifth included a plush manufacturer, a die-cast maker and a manufacturer of radio control cars. No one recognized the artist's rendition of Vincent.

At Sidney Greenspan's office, Jonathan was told Sidney was out, so he showed the picture to Sidney's secretary, Andrea, a brunette of average looks, with striking green eyes. At first she wore a blank expression, but this soon changed. "A few months ago," she said, pulling the picture closer. "Yes. I saw Mr. Greenspan talking to this guy outside our building. I never found out who he was, however."

Blood began to pound in Jonathan's temples. He now had confirmation that Sidney knew Vincent, a man who had nearly killed Verna. "When will Sidney be back?" he asked.

The girl shrugged. "He called me from his car two days ago to say he was on his way to our warehouse. I haven't heard from him since. I was going to contact his wife this afternoon."

Jonathan paused. Something told him this was not a coincidence: both Ann and Sidney had disappeared around the same time. He asked for the exact warehouse address, thanked the girl and left.

Sidney wouldn't disappear on his own. There had to be a connection here. And his warehouse would be a logical place to start. At the very least, someone on the warehouse staff might have overheard something.

As soon as he was out of the building, he contacted Detective Rondgrun and filled him in on what he'd learned.

The man was skeptical. "There are too many variables," he said.

"Oh, yeah? Like what?" Jonathan asked.

"You're flying by the seat of your pants. This is strictly a hunch."

"So? A hunch can pay off."

"Not in this case."

"Why not?"

"Look—Mr. Morhardt. If you've been around as long as I have, you get a feeling for these things."

"Oh? Like the feeling you had that Ann was stuck in a traffic jam?"

The pause was deafening.

Jonathan quickly realized he better drop the attitude. "Please," he said. "I'm asking you for a favor. I know it's unusual, but it's not like Ann to go off on her own like this."

The detective hesitated, then agreed to call in the New Jersey police and meet him at the warehouse in Newark at 11:00 o'clock.

Jonathan couldn't remember how he got to his mother's condo, or parking in the underground garage. When he told Felicia that he wanted his father's old gun, she looked at him as if he might have two heads, warning him that he wouldn't be much help to Ann dead or incarcerated.

It took him less than five minutes to locate the ammunition and the gun, in a strongbox on the top shelf of his mother's bedroom closet. He could only guess at how old it was. His father had died twenty-some-odd years ago.

Jonathan loaded the .38 revolver, recalling enough of his father's instructions to make sure the safety was on. He shoved it into his jacket pocket and left to meet Rondgrun at the warehouse.

When he arrived, the detective was already there, along with five policemen from the New Jersey force. Rondgrun quietly informed him that their custom's broker, Michael Scott, was also missing. Coincidence or an omen? No one knew.

The cops were getting into position. There was nothing special about the building, each warehouse in this neighborhood looking like all the others: one storey, red-bricked, stretching for twenty-five or thirty thousand square feet.

Detective Rondgrun warned Jonathan to stay in his car, to let the men do their job. "You don't make a move until I come and get you," the Detective said. "Understood?"

Jonathan nodded his head.

Half the team had circled around to the back of the building. Detective Rondgrun and two of the other men entered by the only door at the front.

Fifteen minutes passed, then twenty.

Jonathan felt he'd waited long enough. He got out of his car, approached the door, opened it and stepped inside.

The police had rounded up the employees, three women and six men. Everyone was wearing a perplexed expression.

"I thought I told you to wait," Detective Rondgrun barked at him.

"Is Ann—"

"We found nothing," the detective told him angrily, escorting him back out the way he came. "No one knows a thing."

A feeling of dread crept up on Jonathan. He had been convinced he would find her, that she would be here, that this nightmare would be over. But he was no further ahead now than he was before.

CHAPTER 63

S weat was pouring off Ann as she worked at the screen in the bathroom, trying to pry it loose from the window with her fingernails. She paused every minute or so to wipe her brow.

She was astonished to find her strength so depleted. She hurt in places she didn't know could hurt. Her right arm felt broken as did one of her ribs. The burn marks and bruises on her stomach and back ached. Her face throbbed, especially the swelling around her nose and mouth where she had been punched. She had trouble breathing.

The dampness in the warehouse didn't help. At least twenty thousand square feet, she guessed, with row upon row of pallets. It wasn't overtly dirty, but a fine layer of dust permeated the air and stuck in her nostrils.

In her weakened state, Ann found little relief in having learned the truth. That the attack on her in Hong Kong was meant to scare her off her search for the inventor of Baby Talk N Glow, Charles Ling. That Sidney Greenspan's involvement was as she suspected: the rights to the doll were to be his if he cooperated. Now he was being held against his will, able to move about the warehouse as he pleased, but not permitted to leave. Sidney found a way to get a message to her saying he would try to help, but she couldn't see how this would be possible. The last time she'd seen him—she didn't remember if it was yesterday or the day before—the man's blood pressure appeared out of control and near the danger zone.

Ann went back at the window, trying to speed up her progress. It was not easy. Her nails had splintered and her fingertips were rubbed raw. She was so weak she could not fully concentrate.

Soon, she heard Mad Dog approach. When he asked what was taking so long, she told him she wasn't feeling well, that this could take a while.

"Well, hurry it up," he said.

Just the sound of his voice made her cringe and filled her with revulsion.

It took a few more minutes before she finally pulled a portion of the screen apart. With another tug, mercifully, it came free.

She tried to push the window open.

It wouldn't budge.

She pounded with the palm of her hand, fearful of the noise she was making, but feeling powerless to prevent it.

Again, with what little strength she possessed, she banged the window frame.

Finally, it gave. She raised the window and felt the outside air brush against her face. She stood for a moment, breathing it in.

Slowly, carefully, she propped herself on top of the closed toilet seat, prepared to maneuver herself through the window. It appeared to be a daunting task. Her loss of stamina was causing her to sway from side to side.

Suddenly, the bathroom door caved in and Mad Dog confronted her.

She told herself to reach up, to make at least one effort to escape. But before she could act, he was upon her, his hands taking hold of her waist. Pulling hard.

"No!" she hollered. Tears of frustration burst from her eyes as she began to lose her balance.

Mad Dog yanked, knocking her off the toilet. She hit the tiled floor with a thud and blacked out.

When she regained her senses she was back in the warehouse, chained and immobile. She was hot, almost feverish. She looked up, noticed Mad Dog hovering above her. Her heart started to hammer in her chest.

He took a cell phone out of his pocket and tried handing it to her. "I want you to call Jonathan and instruct him to meet you here. He is to bring Verna Sallinger with him."

Just the mention of Jonathan's name filled her with regret. She doubted whether she'd see him again. Or Felicia.

"Call him," Mad Dog said, pushing the phone towards her.

Ann refused to take the phone in hand.

He came at her, aiming a punch at her mouth. She turned at the last possible moment and it caught her cheek, opening a cut. Blood trickled down her chin.

Ann remembered the advice she had given to that girl they had hired to do their television commercial—Lisette Smile. To go inside herself, where no one could do her harm. And she tried following her own advice now, forcing her thoughts inward, as she squeezed her eyes shut.

CHAPTER 64

O nce he returned to Manhattan, Jonathan didn't know what he should do. He wanted to keep active, to continue to look for Ann. But where?

Finally, he ended up back in Ann's office. Taking a seat at her desk, he started to rummage through the drawers.

The photo caught his eye and stopped him cold. In it, he was posed in front of his easel. Ann must have taken it when he was unaware, engrossed as he was in his work. He looked content, serene.

Jonathan went to lift the photo when it dawned on him that it was a typical Ann move, to want to preserve an image of him but not display her affection publicly.

Goddamnit, Ann, where are you? Give me a clue. Any clue. Please...

In the file cabinet next to her desk, he came across a report on the trip they had both taken to introduce Baby Talk N Glow to the major retailers across the United States. Did the answer lie there, he wondered. With one of the retailers?

He didn't know what to think. He had to go with what was familiar, he guessed. Removing files from the cabinet was like following a paper trail of everything he and Ann had been involved with, from the time she had first committed to Baby Talk N Glow.

Jonathan's search took him to the proposed shipping schedule of the doll out of China, showing how the million pieces would be broken down month by month, and how the inventory would be split between the company's warehouse and an outside facility to handle the excess quantity.

Everything seemed straight forward. Jonathan was about to go on, when something stirred in his subconscious, bringing him up short.

Excess quantity. Outside facility …

Wait a minute!

His move for the door was so abrupt, vertigo took over and he almost lost his balance. Slowing down, he made his way out of Ann's office, through the reception area and out into the corridor.

The office for SG Dolls was located a short distance away and Jonathan made a beeline for it. Breathlessly he asked for Sidney's secretary, then started to pace the entranceway until the girl showed up.

"Andrea," he began without wasting time on preamble, "did you hear from Sidney?"

"No. I spoke to his wife. She's thinking of calling the police."

"Then tell me this, do you ever use an outside warehouse when your own warehouse is full?"

The girl looked at him strangely, as if his question was odd. "No," she said, sending disappointment shooting through his veins.

"Huh?"

"We have no need to. We have our own storage facility that we use for slower moving goods. It's located a few blocks from our warehouse. There are no employees. Whenever product is required we send our warehouse people over to get it.

An imaginary light bulb went off in Jonathan's head. "No employees," he said as if talking to himself. "Your warehouse staff just get what they need, when they need it?"

"Yes. Exactly."

"How often would that be?"

"Maybe once a month. If that."

"Once a month ..." Jonathan's mind was churning. "Andrea," he said, "do you happen to have a key I could borrow? I'll bring it back to you before the day is out."

"A key? I don't know, Mr. Morhardt."

"I'll take full responsibility."

"I'm not sure I have the authority."

"Sidney's been a friend of our family for years," Jonathan argued. "You know that, don't you? And I wouldn't ask if this wasn't important. It could be tied in to his disappearance."

To Jonathan's relief, the girl's hesitation dissolved. When she returned with the key, he took it in hand but couldn't remember thanking her. Out of the building on the run, he hurried towards the parking lot.

He did not relish what he had to do next, so he started to drive, delaying the inevitable for as long as possible. When he finally got Detective Rondgrun on the line, the pause was prolonged.

Jonathan explained how much more sense this made—a seldom used storage facility versus Sidney's active warehouse.

Still, the detective held his silence.

"I'm not wrong," Jonathan persisted. "I need you to trust me this one last time."

No reply.

"Look—I'm going there anyway. With or without you."

"That wouldn't be wise."

Relief at finally hearing Detective Rondgrun's voice spurred him on. "Then, will you meet me there?" he asked.

Another pause.

"Detective?"

"Five o'clock. But I'm agreeing to this against my better judgment."

"Five o'clock? Fine. You won't regret it."

"I better not. And do not do anything until I arrive. Do I make myself clear?"

"Perfectly clear," Jonathan said. He shut his cell phone and looked down for an instant. The horn of a nearby car brought him up short. He had pulled into the passing lane without looking.

Get a grip, he told himself.

He drove mechanically, trying not to think. But his hands were sweating and his face felt flushed.

It was a little after three o'clock when he arrived at a low, flat building in New Jersey. The building looked deserted. Detective Rondgrun said he couldn't make it until five. A wait of practically two hours loomed ahead. Jonathan began weighing the consequences of going in on his own. His gut told him he hadn't a choice. What if Ann was incapacitated? What if she was being assaulted this very minute? He had promised the detective he would wait, but it was not a promise he could keep. He got out of his car.

Pins and needles was no longer a corny euphemism. Every nerve fiber in his body had come alive.

He approached the main door, put the key in the lock.

The minute he had the door open he made a beeline for the light switch. His hand was about to turn it on when a little voice inside his head warned him to stop. It would not be wise to announce his arrival. Instead, he opened the inner door and entered an area that was pitch dark. He palmed his father's revolver. Then he stepped a little further inside and waited for his eyes to adjust. Slowly, he began to make his way around the room's periphery, clinging to the wall.

He turned the first corner and thought he spotted someone lying on the cement floor. He crept a little closer, then jolted, involuntarily letting out a cry.

Ann's face was so battered, he barely recognized her. There was blood everywhere; too much blood.

Jonathan pocketed the gun and bent over her, letting himself down on his haunches. Gently, he cradled her in his arms, whispering to her, talking to her as if she could hear his every word, begging her to fight, to please not give up.

"I love you," he said. And he began to prattle on, telling Ann that she had changed his life, that he didn't want to—that he *could not*—live without her.

Jesus, he was babbling. But he couldn't help himself.

"Ann?" he said.

Her eyes were still closed.

Just as he went to wipe away the caked blood on her face, a sudden movement caught his eye. As he turned, something hard collided with the back of his head.

CHAPTER 65

At first there was darkness, then a fuzzy pounding in his brain. He tried to open his eyes; they began to water. He wiped them with the back of his hand. When he tried to look again, all he could see were vague shadows.

This was all his fault. He had blown everything. Instead of waiting for Detective Rongrun, he had taken action on his own.

Jonathan brought his wrist closer and tried to look at his watch. He couldn't say for certain but he believed it was nearly four o'clock. That meant at least one hour until the police arrived, which would be too late.

It hurt to keep his eyes open, but he managed to do so. His assailant—Vincent—was holding his father's gun in his hands. Jonathan could see by the way he was standing that there'd be no arguing with him, no pleading for mercy.

Resignation filled his heart, yet he knew he must try. "Let her go," he said, regretting the tremor in his voice. "I'll give you whatever you want. You can hold me instead of her. She needs a doctor …"

"Doctor?" Vincent's eyes narrowed. "What on earth for," he said, and he casually raised the gun and pointed it at Ann.

Jonathan shuddered.

"I've waited a long time for this," Vincent said.

Jonathan looked around, trying to gather his strength and wondering what, if anything, he could use for a weapon.

"Call it judgment day," Vincent prattled on. "We all must atone for our sins. You're not exempt, and neither is she. Especially not her…"

"How much money will it take?" Jonathan quickly asked.

Instead of a reply, Vincent frowned a little, pointing the gun first at Ann then at Jonathan, and back again, as if weighing the decision who to shoot first.

Jonathan's head was pounding. He wished he could think more clearly. There would be only one chance, if that. He would have to time his move perfectly.

As if reading his mind, Vincent leveled the gun towards Ann and pulled the trigger.

The gun clicked harmlessly. Once, twice, a third time. Vincent swore, then released the safety and re-aimed.

Jonathan somehow managed to leap upwards, keeping his eyes focused on the gun, while attempting to shield Ann with his own body.

The bullet caught him in the thigh. The force of it was enough to flip him over in midair. No pain, he thought in wonder as he hit the cement floor. Then it flared.

Vincent took aim again.

For a moment, Jonathan thought he might be hallucinating. A man was slowly coming towards them. He had crept out of the shadows and was rapidly approaching.

Vincent was too zoned out to notice.

Closer the man came.

Jonathan realized he must try a diversion. "The police are on the way," he said, speaking the only truth to come to mind.

"Shut up!" Vincent hissed.

The man was almost upon them.

Jonathan recognized Sidney Greenspan, his skin coloring pasty, his breathing labored ... which was ultimately what gave him away.

At the last possible moment, Vincent turned and calmly shot him in the chest.

Sidney's body seemed to pirouette, then convulse.

Jonathan attempted to lunge at Vincent. But the wound to his leg had diminished his strength.

Vincent stepped aside. "You're making this easy for me," he boasted as he raised the gun and fired.

CHAPTER 66

Felicia could not get comfortable as she sat in the small waiting room in the hospital. From time to time a doctor or nurse would appear and she would look up expectantly, only to be disappointed. This pattern continued for the rest of the afternoon and into the early evening.

Cal went down to the cafeteria and picked up sandwiches. Felicia ate half of hers and put the rest away.

Finally, just before eight o'clock, the doctor she'd been waiting for came out to speak with her.

He was a handsome man, Felicia realized, and young, but strain was etched into his narrow face. "I'm afraid Ms. Lesage is still not out of the woods," he said. "She's lost an awful lot of blood. The next few hours should tell us quite a bit more."

Questions popped into Felicia's head but she knew they would have to wait. Once the doctor was gone she told Cal she'd be back in a few minutes and she slowly headed for the bank of elevators down the hall.

Hospitals did not appeal to her. She guessed she was like most people in that regard. The correlation to illness and her own mortality was not something she could ignore.

The head nurse greeted her in the orthopedics reception area and told her that Jonathan was asleep. Still, she moved towards his room. There was always the off-chance that he would awaken, and she wanted to be there if he did.

She took a seat by his bed. It was a small private room, as drab and nondescript as most. Jonathan's leg was elevated. The bullet had caused damage to his femoral artery. It would take time to heal, the doctor said, but with physical therapy there should not be lingering side effects.

Watching her son sleep reminded Felicia of a time when Jonathan was in his early teens. He had slipped on the recently waxed kitchen floor, had banged his head and was knocked unconscious. The look on his face then was similar to what she saw tonight, troubled and drawn and sporting a peculiar expression.

She watched over him for another few minutes.

Returning to the waiting room, Cal told her there was no update on Ann's condition.

Felicia settled into a chair, but her mind was far too restless to permit her to relax. There was much to be thankful for, she guessed. Detective Rondgrun had filled her on what he knew so far. He had arrived at the storage facility almost an hour before he told Jonathan that he would, suspecting that Jonathan's impetuosity would get the better of him. The detective and the team from the New Jersey police force had no sooner forced the door when they found Vincent lying dead.

The gun he was using—now identified as the one once belonging to Felicia's husband—was so old, it had apparently imploded, killing Vincent instantly. The secret of the man's motive and identity was yet to be solved. They were hoping that either Jonathan or Ann—perhaps both—would be able to shed some light on the subject.

Detective Rondgrun told Felicia that Sidney Greenspan had also died. They had found a note from him. Apparently, Sidney's intention had been to snare Baby Talk N Glow away from her, only to find himself trapped in something far beyond his expertise or control.

Once he discovered the truth, he apparently made plans to interfere. His note included an apology that seemed pathetic yet heartfelt.

Felicia, reflecting now on what she had learned, wanted to hate Sidney Greenspan for his deception, yet found herself pitying him instead. Despite his greed, he had apparently sacrificed himself for Ann's sake. Or, so the detective led her to believe.

The thought of losing Ann was more than Felicia could bear. She closed her eyes for a moment, a sigh escaping her lips.

CHAPTER 67

Ann felt both euphoric and peaceful as a soft light seemed to surround her, lift her up and bathe her in its glow, extinguishing the pain.

She tried to open her eyes and orient herself. The source of the light shifted, emanating from above. She wanted to turn her head to look but found that her neck would not allow it. Where was she? What was happening? Was she paralyzed or was this death?

She had a memory of being hurt, badly hurt.

Ann kept her eyes closed, cozying up under the softness … until she felt hands on her, pulling her away. She opened her eyes and caught sight of a nurse's uniform, and a face filled with concern looking down at her.

"Hello…"

Ann heard the voice and tried to respond. No words would come.

The nurse fiddled with the IV line. "I'm going to try to guess what you want to know first," she said. "You had a ruptured spleen—Dr. Keogh removed that nicely, so in that respect, you're fine. Eight separate fractured or broken bones, including ribs. That's why you can't move, honey. Don't panic. You don't have a lot of parts that aren't in a cast. But they're going to mend, and you're going to be okay." She moved closer. "You're either incredibly lucky, or you have an amazing will to live."

Ann scraped her throat for her voice. "Jon…" He'd been there, she knew, somewhere in the fog.

"Mr. Morhardt is a few floors up, in room 318. He's had some damage done to his thigh, but he'll be out of here by tomorrow. He's been to visit you every day, like clockwork. As a matter of fact—" The nurse looked at her watch. "—I expect him at any minute."

But why had he been in the dark with her? Why had he been in there with all that pain? Ann couldn't remember.

"Felicia?" she said suddenly.

The nurse smiled. "That poor woman. Why, she's been looking in on you even more often than Mr. Morhardt. Are you related to her?"

Ann didn't have to think about it. "In a manner of speaking," she said.

She closed her eyes and went back underneath the light.

When memory returned—it might have been days, but maybe it was only hours—it happened all at once. She remembered trying to scream. Being shoved around in darkness.

Ann's eyes shot open.

Jonathan, on crutches, was standing beside her bed. "You're looking a lot better," he said. "How are you feeling?"

Her mind tried to focus, but words wouldn't come.

"Well, if you don't mind, I think I'm going to sit down." He moved the crutches and hopped backward to land in the chair next to her bed. Then he used his weight to hitch the chair forward, closer to her.

"He's dead," he said.

Ann felt a tremor work through her, waking up some aches.

"It's a long story—I'll fill you in on the details when your eyes aren't so glassy. Short version—my father's gun misfired in

Vincent's hands. He died instantly, which was probably too good for the bastard."

"Vincent?" she managed to say.

"Yeah."

It started to come back. Vincent was Mad Dog.

"I guess there are a few things we're never going to understand," Jonathan continued. "Like where Edmund Chow got to, and how he was involved."

Ann felt one corner of her mouth lift a little. "Did you honestly think ... I would die without ... knowing?"

Jonathan looked startled. Then he laughed. "Stupid assumption."

"Tell ... the police that Mad ... that Vincent killed him. He bragged to me that he left him ... underwater. In Hong Kong's Victoria Harbour."

He could tell she was struggling to stay with him. And Jonathan knew he should let her sleep. But there had been whole hours that were still fresh in his mind, hours when he would have given his own life just to hear her voice, and now he found he couldn't get enough. Did she remember his saying he loved her? Did she even hear it? She gave no indication.

Jonathan got his crutches together and heaved himself to his feet. "Patrick got you those containers. The shipping things."

Her eyes opened wide, all pupils. They had her drugged up. "Pat did?"

"Mom gave him his job back. He's seeing a shrink and attending AA."

"Hmmm." She was drifting off again.

"Ann—please heal and come home."

She nodded vaguely, tucked her chin, and he knew she was asleep. Jonathan hitched his way slowly out of the room.

CHAPTER 68

She was undergoing excruciating physical therapy. It was over a month ago—late May to be exact—that she was released from the hospital. With time, she was told, her bones would heal, and she had no choice but to trust this prognostication.

It was not until mid-June that she was able to make her first appearance at the office. Until then she had worked from home, driving everyone crazy with her phone calls and e-mails. Ann threw herself into the business at hand, with half-days at first but expanding her time as the weeks moved along.

A new Customs Broker was lined up and shipping schedules for Baby Talk N Glow were organized. Contact was made with each of the major buyers in the United States, then with Hart Toy's distributors around the world, some once, others two or three times. Canada held a soft spot for her, being Felicia's and Jonathan's birthplace, so she was especially pleased to see that support in that country was solid, from Walmart, Target, and Toys 'R' Us, to Sears and Canadian Tire.

Meanwhile, Ann and Jonathan avoided discussing details of their terrible ordeal, each figuring it was best not to traumatize the other. Most conversations began with, "What happened when?" only to be left unanswered.

But Jonathan was haunted by those final few moments: Vincent pointing the gun at him, the split-second realization that his life was surely over. And Ann herself, not able to come to grips with a perpetual nightmare that wouldn't die, the mental anguish she so desperately wanted to avoid hanging over her like a shroud.

Jonathan was able to walk with a cane; Ann still required the use of crutches. It drove her mad with frustration.

Meanwhile, she awoke each morning with the unspoken desire that Jonathan would rediscover his muse. She discussed his possible attendance at art exhibits that were frequently opening in the Manhattan area, dropped other hints that were aimed at stirring his creative juices. All to no avail.

It made her feel guilty, the fact that she could fully occupy her time with her doll project while Jonathan sat around the loft, moping. But her deadline was approaching and she knew she could ill afford to miss a beat.

The first shipment of Baby Talk N Glow to leave Hong Kong numbered almost two hundred thousand pieces. The dolls were packed in thirty-eight forty-foot containers on the S.S. Seahawk and arrived in the port of New York on a Friday evening in early July.

Alison Steinfeld of Toys 'R' Us approved an order of a double ship-pack for her five hundred and eighty-one stores, which was just over sixty-nine hundred pieces. WalMart's thirty-four hundred stores received a total of twenty thousand, four hundred. Linda Figgures of Target was shipped ninety-six hundred and forty-two pieces, or a ship pack of six to each of their sixteen hundred and seven stores.

For a while, nothing significant happened—whatever sales were reported were marginal. Ann realized this was not out of the ordinary, but her nerves still felt jangled by the pressure. There was no denying the truth: if these first shipments of Baby Talk N Glow did not move, the balance of orders from the retailers would be canceled and Hart Toy would be left holding the inventory. Now she was at the mercy of the consumer. No matter how many focus groups had approved of Baby Talk N Glow, no matter how much money they spent to promote her, if kids were turned off, all would be lost.

CHAPTER 69

In early October, major cities across America were introduced to jumbo posters in bus shelters and subways. Each contained a blowup photo of the doll and the words: *Baby Talk N Glow— the doll of tomorrow—available at toy stores today.*

Sales picked up, Ann noticed, but not significantly. Meanwhile, the remaining goods had to leave China now or they would arrive too late for the Christmas selling season. Ann discussed it with their distributors, with her salespeople. If she cut back, they would have no chance of earning a profit. She gave the go-ahead. Another eight hundred thousand pieces in all, fulfilling her original forecast of a million.

Towards the end of October, the thirty-second spots began to run on network and cable television. Ann waited until the middle of November before barricading herself in her office. For twelve hours straight, she did nothing but stay on the phone, polling each salesperson across the States, every distributor in South America, Europe, Asia, Canada, New Zealand and Australia.

Most were optimistic; few could report noticeable sales increases. Ann went home in a state of anxiety, and sleep was as elusive as her sales.

Then Felicia called and said she had to see her.

The moment Cal opened the door her worst fears were realized. "The cancer has spread to her liver," he told her quietly as he led the way inside.

It was what she had dreaded most. Now, approaching Felicia's bedroom, Ann had to hold her emotions in check.

Felicia was hooked up to an intravenous feed as well as an oxygen mask. Ann had seen her less than three weeks ago. In that relative short period of time, Felicia's features had withered and her weight must have dropped fifteen pounds, at least.

Ann knelt by the bed.

Felicia removed the oxygen mask and placed her hand on top of Ann's. "I have something to tell you that couldn't wait."

"Something you couldn't tell me over the phone?"

"Yes, dear. It's about Mathew and Jonathan, and something you won't want to think about."

Ann felt confused. Why would this be so important?

"Jonathan wasn't piloting the boat the night Matt died. He is not to be blamed for what happened."

Ann's head began to throb. "Why are you telling me this?"

"Because I want the truth to come out. Patrick and Matthew fought about you that night. I must—I *will*—put this to rest before I go. Poor Matt would never have intended for his ghost to tear his loved ones apart. There should be truth now, after nearly two decades. That's my last wish."

Suddenly, Felicia began to cough. It was raspy and loud and wouldn't stop. Cal quickly entered the bedroom, poured a glass of water from the pitcher on the bureau, then fed it slowly to Felicia's lips, holding the glass for her.

"Why don't I come back another time," Ann suggested.

"No," Felicia stopped her. "Please. You must hear me out."

It was so obvious what the disease was doing and it hurt Ann to the core. She didn't want this woman to suffer.

"They fought over you," Felicia said. "Matthew thought you would marry him, and Patrick made up a story about you to try to dissuade him."

"I wasn't … going to. Marry him."

"Patrick didn't know that."

"I told Jonathan … I wouldn't."

"And I do think he believed you, dear, even then, because he has protected you from the truth all this time."

Protected her? Through all the trips they'd taken together and all the times they'd made love? He hadn't protected her, she thought, her heart starting to slam.

He had lied to her.

Something squeezed in her chest. She realized distantly that she was shaking. "Was it Patrick steering the boat, then? When they crashed? Jonathan said … he always said—"

"I know," Felicia said. "He stands up for those he loves, Ann. Sometimes to a fault. I care about him dearly. In many ways, he's my best and my brightest. But he's not perfect."

No, Ann thought. He manipulates people and he lies to them. No wonder he had hated her for so long, all these years. It was a defense mechanism, to provoke her, rather than coming clean.

Oh, Matthew, oh, Matt, I'm so sorry.

Felicia let go of her hand. "I must rest now," she said, her voice becoming a whisper. "But thank you for coming. This was something I needed to do. You understand why?"

Ann paused. "No, I don't understand."

"Of course, you do. I wanted to make sure you understood my son before I gave him to you. You can trust that man with anything, anything at all. He holds secrets well, and he handles them with care. He's true."

No, Ann thought as she prepared to leave, not nearly true enough.

But she left this thought unspoken.

CHAPTER 70

She went directly to her condo. Many of her things had been moved into Jonathan's loft but there was enough left over to see her through the weeks ahead. For the moment, she knew that she could not face him, didn't know when or if she would be able to again.

Ann went to work the following morning and tried to concentrate.

It was not easy. Jonathan called constantly, at her office and at home. This went on for days. She refused to speak with him, until he finally showed up at her condo. She no sooner stepped out of a cab when he confronted her. They faced each other in the foyer of her building, with her refusing to invite him upstairs.

In a muted voice, he expressed his disappointment that she could doubt him after all they'd been through, that she could harbor such resentment over something that had happened so many years ago.

"You lied to me," she reminded him. But it sounded trivial.

"It was for your own good," he insisted.

"Bull!"

"Ann—you're proving my point. I knew you'd be consumed by guilt, yet it wasn't your fault. You played far less a role in Matthew's death than I did."

"You lied ..." Her anger got the better of her and her eyes began to tear.

He tried to reach for her hand; she pulled away.

"I ... expected more from you, Jon—" She couldn't finish. The tears were threatening to explode. Abruptly, she turned on her heels and rushed into the elevator.

"When can I see you again?" he called after her.

Mercifully, the door closed.

Seeing him in the flesh did something to her, filled her with regret and a deep-seated longing.

In some ways, she wished Felicia had never told her the truth. She wished she could have gone through the rest of her life blind and ignorant. There was some small consolation in finally understanding Jonathan's behavior in those early years. Patrick despised her in large measure because he couldn't take responsibility for his own role in Matt's death. But Jonathan...

He had taken her trust and met it with a perpetual lie. Remorse and the terrible realization of what she had done brought a dark emptiness. It had been her fault all along. If only she could have made it plain from the beginning, told Matthew that marriage was out of the question.

Ann allowed work to monopolize her time. Her doll was all that mattered now. She analyzed sales from every angle, stayed up late second guessing her own analysis. Then, at the beginning of the third week of November, she received a phone call from the new buyer at Kmart—Bruce Fleisher. Effusive in his apology, he admitted his mistake in not committing and asked if she could please—*please!*—round up a hundred thousand pieces of Baby Talk N Glow and ship them out at once.

Ann promised him half that amount and disconnected. Leaning back in her chair, she started to wonder: *Could this be it?*

Before the week was out, Walmart's Retail Link showed twelve thousand pieces had passed through their cash registers in the last three days. Sales at Toys 'R' Us reached five thousand, five hundred and thirteen pieces in the same time period.

The first story broke in *USA Today*. Mattel's lead doll, as well as the one from Hasbro, had become non-issues. Baby Talk N Glow was all the rage. When *Time* ran an article on what was hot this Christmas featuring the doll, most newspapers across the country picked up the story and ran with it.

The phone lines at Hart Toy lit up. Ann hired temps to handle the overload. For the first time since becoming involved with Baby Talk N Glow, she started to believe they were blessed with a phenomenon that rarely touched more than a handful in the toy industry.

Still, Ann remained cautious. Too many disappointments in her past had hardened her to the harsh reality of her business. She insisted on going out to get a feel for what was happening at retail herself.

At one Toys 'R' Us location on Long Island, she found a sign that read: *DUE TO THE UNPRECEDENTED DEMAND FOR BABY TALK N GLOW, OUR STOCK HAS BEEN DEPLETED.*

At Walmart, a fifteen-minute ride away, she heard the announcement: *"Attention, shoppers—we apologize for the inconvenience, but we are sold out of Baby Talk N Glow."*

Ann returned to her car, a white Audi A6, placed her crutches on the back seat, and slid behind the wheel. Without realizing what she was doing, she began to tap an imaginary tune on the dashboard.

Then she looked up at the sky, noticed the snow beginning to fall, and she finally smiled. It wasn't snow but feathers from heaven, she decided. And she wanted to shout to the toy gods. It was all true. Despite one disaster after the other, despite the personal hell she had been through, Hart Toy had taken the chance and won.

She removed her cell phone from her briefcase and impatiently dialed the number. Cal answered and asked her to hold on the line while he went to see if Felicia could talk to her.

Ann waited, thrilled when she finally heard the voice of the one person she cared so much about. "We did it," she told her. "Baby Talk N Glow is an unqualified—an *unmitigated*—success!"

Felicia's voice was barely audible.

"I'm sorry," Ann said. "I can't hear you."

Again the words came, only slightly more clear. "You did it, dear."

Her heart seized. "It was your idea. You were the one to see Baby Talk N Glow's potential. It was your vision, while everyone else was doubting you."

Felicia coughed horribly. Ann could hear Cal in the background. She winced with guilt. "Are you okay?" she asked

"I'm so very proud of you," Felicia said. And the line went dead.

Tears welled in Ann's eyes and she couldn't blink them away. "Damn it," she swore aloud.

CHAPTER 71

Felicia was buried the third week of December, in the biting winter chill of Kitchener, in southwestern Ontario.

Ann picked her way across the cemetery alone, her left leg a vicious, knotted ache from the cold. The crutches were making her progress slow and awkward.

The ground was frozen, hard as stone, so her boots—the first she had worn in months—didn't sink into the lawn. She stopped several yards from the crowd gathered beneath a green awning that glowed in the light of the sun.

There should not be sun, Ann thought desperately, and her throat closed. She swallowed hard.

She needed to join the others. She knew that. Even from this distance, she could hear the pastor beginning to speak, and she wanted to hear every word. But she did not step forward. Instead, her gaze slid over the mourners, moving from one face to another, hitching, stopping, absorbing, and moving on to the next. She lingered on Cal Everham. He was surprisingly steady. The wind had knocked some color into his cheeks.

Ann was fully aware of the tremendous efforts Cal and Felicia's other doctors had made to keep her alive, for far longer than she'd had any right to hope. Felicia had defied medical science, Ann thought, as she had defied so much else in her life, hanging in, hanging on, until all her meddling was finished.

Ann felt her face twist with grief. She drew in cold air deeply, prolonging her agony, forestalling her need to cry.

Patrick's eyes looked clear, she thought. She'd been somehow sure that losing his mother would push him once again over the edge. Maybe it would yet. There would be many cold, empty days ahead without her. But, Ann realized, he seemed sober now. To her knowledge, he hadn't had a drink in some time. Verna, by his side, was obviously a positive influence. Perhaps she'd be able to keep him on the straight and narrow.

His children were there, as well as Irene, but she did not stand beside Patrick. Their divorce had become final a month ago, and it had been a nasty one. They were still caught up in post-judgment litigation. Irene seemed intent on punishing Patrick for every disappointment he'd inflicted on her, through all the years of their marriage.

There were so many other faces, business associates and friends. Felicia's younger brother and sister, her nieces and nephews. Koji Sashika, along with Alvin Pelletier and his wife. Charles Ling, who had never even met Felicia, stood with a diminutive Mae Sing and their two children. Ann's gaze moved on. Emeril Lacey. Dora Keller, her own secretary, as well as at least fifteen other Hart Toy employees, past and present.

At last, there was nowhere for her to look except at Jonathan. Ann swallowed a small keening sound that tried to escape her throat. She had not been in his company since he'd come to her condo to talk to her, which was over five weeks ago.

Another sound clogged her throat—strangled laughter. She'd lived through hours of Mad Dog battering her. And there probably wasn't a person gathered at this graveside who wasn't surprised by her strength and will to live. But she knew there was a limit to how strong she could be. Especially when it came to loving someone.

When it came to knowing that her weakness had cost one of those people his life.

Ann wondered if she'd ever draw another breath without something breaking inside her. She had been too weak to tell Mattie no. If she had acted sooner, he would be alive now, married to someone who suited him.

She stole another look at Jonathan. Suddenly, Felicia's voice snaked in on her, as clear and as close as though the woman had materialized out of the blue. *You can trust that man with anything, Ann. Anything at all.*

"No," she whispered aloud.

He has protected you from the truth all this time.

"That's not why he did it. Go away."

The frigid wind whipped at her. She almost—*almost*—smiled. "Stop that." It hit her harder, dragging at her coat, catching the hem, flapping it open, trying to snag her hair down from its clip. "You're not done yet, are you, Felicia? Not until you have your own way."

Where do you think Jonathan got it?

Ann laughed aloud at the thought, a hoarse, short sound. Well, that made sense, she decided.

He wasn't just protecting you.

Okay, Ann thought, she'd had enough of these mind games. That was all they were—a physical yearning for Felicia so strong, so deep, that she was hearing her voice in her head. Ann finally moved toward the crowd of people at the tent.

Jonathan looked up and stared at her.

She didn't mean to, but she stopped walking. The impact of his gaze almost knocked her legs out from under her. This, she realized, was why she hadn't been able to face him. Because of what she knew she'd find on his face, what she'd see in his eyes. Regret. Torment. The knowledge that she was lost to him because of lies he had told trying to save them all.

Ann pressed her hand to her mouth. She forced herself to move again and finally stepped beneath the green awning. Somehow, she found herself beside him.

Her neck hurt. Her stomach burned. Just to the right of the pastor was Matthew's plot, and that of Jonathan's father. Ann dragged her gaze away from both.

The service was coming to an end. The pastor quoted the Bible, repeating words Felicia had mentioned so many times. "If you're not ready to die, then you're not ready to live."

Ann felt her breath stall. She had refused to die at Mad Dog's hands, and yet had walked away after Felicia's revelation, afraid to live.

She rubbed the back of her neck and felt Jonathan take over. His familiar fingers found the tight spot. She let his touch linger while people shook hands, hugged, then finally moved on.

She turned to him. "Thanks for that."

He didn't respond. The quiet between them forced her to look up and find his eyes.

"How are you?" he asked.

Too many things came to mind. Broken, she thought. Lost. Alone. "I'm kicking."

"Ann, with you that's never been an answer."

He was right. She often kicked when she had no business even standing. So she told him the truth. "I don't know how to do this," she said helplessly.

"You don't know how to talk to me?"

"I don't know how to live without her."

Grief creased his expression. Maybe that was why she let him pull her close and hold her. She told herself she was providing comfort to him.

"I know," he said.

"She was so meddlesome."

"Circumstances always had a habit of saluting her."

Ann sighed. "Nobody ever could tell her that something wasn't possible, or none of her business." She pulled away from him. "I have to go."

"Where?"

"Back to the airport."

"You're not staying overnight?" Jonathan began walking and Ann fell into step beside him. "No possible good could come from the truth," he said finally. "It only hurt everyone."

She almost stumbled. How many times had she had that same thought? That she wished Felicia had never told her? And then held it against this man that he hadn't?

"Ann, a big part of me wishes, just this once, that my mother had kept her mouth shut," he said. "But another part of me says there can't be a future until people know how they got to the present."

"You're an artist. Not a philosopher."

"I'm just saying that I won't hold it against her memory, even if she was responsible for my losing you."

Her bad leg cramped up. Ann stopped trying to make it move and covered her face with her hands.

Okay, she thought, the truth. It was all Felicia had wanted. She'd put it out there, to make sure everyone knew how—as Jonathan had said—they'd gotten to the present. It was her parting legacy.

She could honor that.

"You didn't lose me because of Felicia, Jonathan, because of Matt. I don't know if it would have worked out long-term, anyway."

He shrugged. "Because you're too pretty?"

She literally felt something seize inside. She stared at him. *He knew.* How could he know? Then she answered herself. *Felicia.*

"She told me about that, too," he said.

Ann waited for anger to fill her, for the ultimate sense of betrayal. Nothing happened. She only felt dazed. "Why? When? How long have you known?"

"She wanted me to know that you'd survive Vincent. It was while he had you. She wanted me to understand what you're made of. I couldn't have gotten through it otherwise, Ann."

She opened her mouth, closed it again. Things were spinning inside her head.

"Years ago, Pat and I hounded her about where you came from for the longest time—but she never told us anything because she didn't want you undermined in our eyes," Jonathan went on. "She said if you wanted us to know, you'd tell us yourself."

Yes, Ann thought, that was Felicia. She shuddered. "That's that, then. No more secrets."

He took her hand like he had some kind of right to and started out of the cemetery. "Wait and fly home with me tomorrow."

Ann hesitated. Even after what he knew, he wanted to be with her? "Why?"

"I want to go back to the beginning and start over again."

She let go of his hand. "I'm not going to end up in Toronto with you, just to humor one of your whims."

"I meant further back, to the beach. Fifteen years ago."

The air went out of her. She remembered that night so well. She remembered the hem of her dress getting soaked, and the way he had looked at her. Suddenly, she felt tired.

Felicia's voice popped back into her ears, encouraging her, warning that there might not be another chance. *Tell him*, she said.

Ann cleared her throat. "I haven't told you, but … it wasn't just the thought of Felicia that kept me alive through the pain of that beating I took … it was you, too, the fact that I knew you were out there somewhere, trying to find me."

Her words seemed to catch him by surprise. He hesitated, but only for a moment. "I love you, Ann. I have for a very long time. I even told you that, while you were lying half-dead in Greenspan's storage facility. I was hoping my words would get through somehow."

Something clicked in her subconscious. His expression of love was there. She had sensed it, felt it, but pushed it aside as a fantasy not to be explored. And now it was out in the open. She did not need Felicia to tell her what to say or do next. She took his hand back in hers, squeezed it. "C'mon," she said. "I'm not making any promises. But, for now, I just want you to take me home …"

EPILOGUE

Ann looked at her watch at twenty past four and shot up from her desk. She reached for the mouse and turned off the computer. It was Christmas Eve and there wasn't an employee left on the floor. She'd let them go at noon.

She put on her coat and was halfway to the door when her telephone rang. She went back to her desk to answer it. Her breath was a little short. She was impatient.

It was Charles Ling. "Am I catching you at a bad time?" he asked. "This is your holiday."

"It's okay." She wasn't supposed to meet Jonathan for another ten minutes. "Are you in New York?"

"No. We stayed in Ontario after Mrs. Morhardt's funeral. I wanted to show my wife and children Niagara Falls."

"Oh? How was it?"

"Lovely. Better than we expected."

His English was still fractured so once more Ann had to concentrate on what he was actually trying to say.

"Look—" he told her now, "—I have something new for you."

Her heart clubbed a little. "It's legitimately yours to sell?"

He laughed. "Yes, of course. This doll can carry on an intelligent conversation, can acknowledge whomever she's speaking to."

Ann sat down at her desk again. "You've got to be kidding."

"Lip synchronization makes her very lifelike," he went on. "Electronics and a memory chip give her an encyclopedic mind. And I think I know a way to keep this project in the popular price range."

Ann tucked the phone against her shoulder. Could she do it all again? she wondered.

Sure, she thought. Why not?

"I can't get to Hong Kong until the week after New Years," she said. "Will that be too late?"

"No, of course not. I won't approach anyone else. I owe you my life."

Ann winced at his comment. She didn't want anyone beholden to her. "You don't owe me anything," she said. "Look—I'll call you with my reservations and let you know what time we can meet."

"Have a good holiday, Ms. Lesage."

"Thank you very much. Have a safe trip home."

This was a crazy, crazy business she was in, she thought. Full of backstabbing, lying and cheating. But not killings. What had happened to her had been an aberration and would never be repeated.

She hoped.

Despite it all, the toy industry was in her blood. Yes, kids were forsaking traditional playthings at an earlier and earlier age, choosing cell phones, iPods, and electronic video games instead. But she was in it for the long haul, and no matter what other bastard got in her way, she would never go down without a fight.

Ann finally left her office and headed up the hall. She rapped her knuckles on Patrick's door. "Let's go," she shouted through the wood. "Time to close up shop."

He opened the door, scowling. He would never like her, she thought. There would always be bad blood between them. And she knew she would never trust him. She drew in air through her nose, checking for a whiff of cognac.

Nothing. So far, so good. For today, at least, they could still be civil enemies.

They rode down in the elevator and went out the front door. Jonathan was waiting on the sidewalk.

He turned to his brother. "So where are you going tonight?"

"Home," he said shortly. "Verna's out of town visiting her mother and an aunt from Scotland whom she hasn't seen in years."

"Don't do that," Ann said.

"I won't drink." He sounded surly.

"Why put yourself to the test?" Jonathan countered. "Don't be stubborn. Come by and have some virgin eggnog with us."

Patrick started walking toward Sixth Avenue. "I'll think about it," he said over his shoulder.

They watched until he blended into the crowd. "He won't do it," Ann said as they rode a cab toward Jonathan's place.

Jonathan took her hand. "Maybe, maybe not. You still expect the worst from him."

The taxi dropped them off and he unlocked the door. "Let's have a toast now," he said, "in case he does stop by. We'll do our imbibing by ourselves."

"A Christmas toast," Ann said, taking her coat to the closet. I'll get the Glenlivet."

"I bought champagne."

She paused in the process of reaching for a hanger. "Well, then, by all means. We'll celebrate Baby Talk N Glow."

He came toward her. "With all due respect, Ann, I've had enough of that doll to last me a lifetime."

Now was obviously not the time to tell him about Ling's new creation. "All right. We'll celebrate Christmas, then. And Felicia's memory."

"I've got a better idea." He purposely prolonged his stroll to the fridge. Then he made a show of removing the champagne, popping the cork and pouring it. "Now," he said very seriously as he handed her one of the flutes, "I have an important question for you." He paused.

"I'm listening."

He clinked glasses with her, then went down on one knee. "Ann Lesage…"

She stared at him for a number of seconds.

"…will you marry me?"

"Marry you?"

"Uh-huh."

The question hung in the air.

Suddenly, a fist hammered on the door.

Ann hesitated, trying to decide if she should answer Jonathan's question now or keep it for later.

Another fist on the door made her mind up for her.

She turned on a heel to open it.

It was Patrick, after all.

"Merry Christmas," she said when he pushed past her. "Can I take your coat?"

Patrick paused, stunned.

Somewhere in her heart, Ann was sure she felt Felicia smile.

If you enjoyed *The Doll Brokers*, you will be thrilled to read Hal Ross' novel *The Deadliest Game*, a harrowing tale of a terrorist plot against U.S. consumers using a toy company and its owner. Blair Mulligan—a thirty-five-year old divorced executive in the toy industry aims to achieve success with a brand new electronic gaming system that has the potential to revolutionize his business. However, a sinister force is at play, one that threatens to wreak havoc across the United States. Blair's six-year-old daughter becomes the pawn in the scheme, and Blair must make the deadliest decision—to save his own daughter or the lives of thousands of other children.

CPSIA information can be obtained at www.ICGtesting.com
Printed in the USA
LVOW12s2047220614

390920LV00003B/1/P